The Winter of the World

The Winter of the World

World

A Novel

CAROL ANN LEE

HARPER PERENNIAL

NEW YORK • LONDON • TORONTO • SYDNEY

HARPER ● PERENNIAL

THE WINTER OF THE WORLD. Copyright © 2007 by Carol Ann Lee. All rights reserved. Printed in the United States of America. No part of this book may be used or reproduced in any manner whatsoever without written permission except in the case of brief quotations embodied in critical articles and reviews. For information address HarperCollins Publishers, 10 East 53rd Street, New York, NY 10022.

HarperCollins books may be purchased for educational, business, or sales promotional use. For information please write: Special Markets Department, Harper-Collins Publishers, 10 East 53rd Street, New York, NY 10022.

FIRST EDITION

Designed by Philip Mazzone

Library of Congress Cataloging-in-Publication Data is available upon request.

ISBN: 978-0-06-123881-9
ISBN-10: 0-06-123881-3

07 08 09 10 11   ID/RRD   10 9 8 7 6 5 4 3 2 1

This book is dedicated to Austin Pickersgill, a coalminer from Wakefield, who fought in the Great War.
He was my great-grandfather.

And to Lily Lee, my grandmother, who worked in a munitions factory as a girl of fourteen while bringing up her younger sisters and brothers unaided.

I came back from the line at dusk. We had just laid to rest the mortal remains of a comrade. I went to a billet in front of Erkingham, near Armentières. At the back of the billet was a small garden, and in the garden only six paces from the house, there was a grave. At the head of the grave there stood a rough cross of white wood. On the cross was written in deep black-pencilled letters "An Unknown British Soldier" and in brackets beneath, "of the Black Watch." It was dusk and no one was near, except some officers in the billet playing cards. I remember how still it was. Even the guns seemed to be resting . . .

Rev. David Railton, MC, letter, 1920

No story is ever told just once. Whether a memory or a funny, hideous scandal, we will return to it an hour later and retell the story with additions and this time with a few judgments thrown in. In this way, history is organized.

Michael Ondaatje, <u>Running in the Family</u>, 1983

Contents

The Winter of the World

I

HOMECOMING

London, November 10, 1920

THE GREAT TRAIN THUNDERS THROUGH ENGLAND'S SOUTHEAST FIELDS, its titanic lamps blazing in the wet, almost moonless night.

The Kent countryside, all soft, rolling hills and wooded valleys, tucked-away vineyards and apple orchards—reminiscent, some might say, of the landscape of the Somme five years before—stretches ahead as the train and its precious consignment travels north from the port of Dover. It calls fleetingly at the cathedral city of Canterbury, leaving the dingy iron canopy of the station shrouded in a thick pall of steam as it pulls away, heading through fields dense with shadow, where a thin moon rides the clouds and glistens on the wet leaves of trees and the uneven roofs of farm buildings.

The uniformed guards on board the train stare out into the darkness, occasionally able to distinguish between field and sky, and to glimpse the odd row of houses by the lights that wink in distant windows.

At irregular intervals the train slows to pass through other stations that should be deserted, where no trains will stop that evening. But when the guards look out, they see to their surprise and unease that the dark, windswept platforms are not empty at all, but occupied by immobile figures who stand together, en masse and silent, like ghosts.

The officer in charge of the military escort turns to his companions, and in a voice low with amazement, tells them, "My God, they're all *women*." And they *are* women: mothers, wives, sisters, cousins, friends, and neighbors. All clad in deep mourning, and standing shoulder to shoulder, like an army.

The train plunges deeper into the dark countryside.

In the old market town of Faversham, a group of Boy Scouts waiting on the station platform take up their bugles and play "The Last Post" as the train hurtles by. Theirs is the first of countless impromptu gestures; every bridge and every crossing is lined with reverent, unmoving figures, and at more than one station a guard of honor stands on the platform, heads bowed upon reversed rifles.

The train is scheduled to stop at Chatham, and upon its arrival a crowd of women tear back the barriers determinedly and flood toward the locomotive with their hands outstretched. Even the heavy, slanting rain does not deter them, and as the train edges away from the station, hundreds swarm down to the end of the platform and run alongside the tracks until only a thinning ribbon of steam is visible.

Two hours after leaving Dover, the first gardens and backyards of London's sooty suburbs appear. Pools of light spill from open doors and upstairs windows where the curtains have been pulled aside for the first sighting of the train. In those drab, elongated gardens and yards stand yet more figures, not only women, but men and children too, and they wave flags, salute, bow their heads to weep, or simply gaze in their hundreds as the train rushes past, its headlamps glowing in the rain-filled darkness.

In the city itself, motorcars and omnibuses come to a standstill as people linger to watch the train steaming across viaducts and embankments, its pistons pounding and gasping in the stale, wet air. The news filters through the city that the train is approaching, and the agitated crowds waiting inside the colossal bulk of Victoria Station begin to push at the barricades that were erected the previous afternoon. Policemen and military officials assigned to receive the train try valiantly to keep everything under control, but the tension about the building with its carved, stone archway where men once went off to war is too strong to be contained.

And then the train itself curves into view, slowing, emitting a high whistle as it passes under the vaulted ceiling. It draws to a stop at platform eight in a billow of cooling steam, smoke curling about the huge arc lights of the station.

The multitude fall silent at last. The hush is broken only by weeping and praying, and the hiss and shunting of other trains.

The coffin remains inside the train until sunrise, guarded and screened. It rests upon a bier in the passenger luggage van with its distinctive white-painted roof, surrounded by wreaths so huge that each one requires four men to carry it. The wooden casket has been carved from an oak tree that once stood in the gardens of Hampton Court Palace; inside its wrought iron bands lies a sword selected by the king from the Tower of London collection.

In the pallor of early morning, the wreaths are removed from the luggage van and taken to Westminster Abbey's Jerusalem Chamber while the crowds convene outside the station in their thousands, enduring the persistent drizzle and November chill. In other parts of London, politicians and generals stir from their sleep, breakfast earlier than usual, and make their way to Victoria. The royal family is escorted to the newly built cenotaph, where Union flags enclose the stark white column. Government officials, the armed services, and war widows start to fill the long avenue of Whitehall; barricades close the area off from the general public until a quarter past eight, when a select number of mourners are admitted. Motor transport in the city center has been banned for this day and the next four, leaving the roads empty of the usual omnibuses and automobiles. London lies silent, as if under a deep fall of snow.

By nine o'clock, hundreds of troops and ex-servicemen are arriving at Victoria Station. Eight guardsmen step up into the train and enter the compartment where the coffin stands in darkness upon its bier. Carefully, they wrap the casket in a Union flag whose bright blues and scarlets have dulled during its long service as an altar cloth in France. A steel helmet, belt, and bayonet of the British Army are placed on top of the battle flag before the guardsmen gently maneuver the coffin along the corridor and into the open air.

On the platform, six immaculately groomed black stallions stand restlessly within the shafts of a gun carriage, where the guardsmen lower and secure the coffin. As the guardsmen fall into position behind the carriage, a nineteen-gun salute shakes the leaden skies over London. The children among the waiting crowds are subdued, the men and women themselves silent, and throughout the city the thirty-five thousand soldiers and policemen on duty find that they have little to do, other than listen to the muted sobbing that rises intermittently from the gathered mourners.

At half past nine, as the station clock tolls, the twelve pallbearers—Britain's highest-ranking officers—salute and join the guardsmen behind the gun carriage, waiting for the signal to walk forward. The firing party present arms and march to the front of the massed bands, preparing to lead the procession.

Not far away, at Hyde Park Corner, where a vast, restrained crowd has gathered beneath the seeping trees to listen to pipers playing "The Flowers of the Forest," one of the duty policemen feels a tug on his sleeve. Glancing down, he sees a tiny woman clutching a spray of withered flowers. Her face is lined with anxiety and sorrow. When she speaks, it is with a faint Scottish burr.

"I've come down alone," she tells him in a whisper, "I brought these to lay at the grave." Her eyes brim with unshed tears. "They're from my boy's garden—he planted it himself when he was six years old."

The policeman puts a hand on her black-clad arm to comfort and steady her, hoping to calm the emotions so near the surface of the woman's dignity.

"He was my only boy," she weeps. "They never found his body. That's why I had to come . . . it could be him, couldn't it?"

The heavy clouds over the city slacken and a flake of light drifts down. Bass drums, muffled with black cloth, begin to pound to Chopin's "Funeral March." As if taking the shard of sunlight as their prompt, the black horses outside Victoria Station walk forward, the fall of their hooves upon the stones resounding in the strange, charged air. Four mounted policemen and the massed bands precede them, and the twelve distinguished pallbearers walk alongside. Behind the gun carriage four hundred ex-servicemen march four abreast, followed in turn by the silent mass of men, women, and children.

Hundreds of soldiers line the roads, and as the funeral cortege rolls by they lower their heads and reverse arms while the civilian men in the crowd remove their hats and bow their heads. The procession advances slowly, turning toward Constitution Hill, which has disappeared behind the damp, morning fog, and then vanishes itself into the white mist that cloaks the Mall between Buckingham Palace and Trafalgar Square.

A whisper spreads among the overwrought masses lining the route to Westminster Abbey: "He's coming . . . He's coming . . ."

A young woman in a claret-colored coat stares straight ahead as she walks toward Trafalgar Square. Her finely boned face, in contrast to those who wait agitatedly in London's crowded streets that morning, is almost expressionless. Only someone who knows her intimately would recognize the tension in her unusual, pale gray eyes and the tilt of her chin.

She nears the end of the street. The wide, open square with its soaring column and gargantuan quartet of bronze lions lies ahead. A crowd of many thousands swarms in the center, along the roads, and on the steps and balustrades of every public building. Scores of them have climbed onto the backs of the lions for a better view of the cortege. The sight makes her falter for a moment before she edges through the gathering and walks quickly to Whitehall.

A bearded policeman approaches her by the barrier that shuts off the avenue. He speaks quietly, "Good morning, Madam. Do you have an invitation? Only authorized access here today, I'm afraid."

She extracts one of the coveted tickets from her bag and hands it to him. He examines it and returns it to her with a nod, then pulls open the barrier to let her pass. But as she enters the cordoned-off street, something causes her to stop suddenly and hold herself very still.

She has seen him, just as she feared she would. Despite the number of people in Whitehall, he is taller than anyone else present and her gray eyes follow every step he takes as he walks down the avenue toward Westminster Abbey. She recognizes his profile: the angular face, the slightly hooked nose, which he always used to say was good for poking into other people's business, and the slanted, hazel eyes. His unruly dark hair is untidier than ever, but with the same vivid auburn shades in the weak sunlight.

She holds her breath until it becomes painful. Her gloved hands tighten into fists as she watches and waits. Only when she is quite sure that they will not meet does she begin walking again.

From underneath the great sweep of Admiralty Arch the gun carriage emerges, the coffin high upon it, the steel helmet glinting in the faint sunlight upon the torn and faded battle flag.

In Trafalgar Square, the crowd hears the measured sound of the horses' hooves and then, at last, sees their black forms surfacing through the mist. And now men weep openly, unashamed, while the anguished cries of women pierce the air as the uncontrollable glut of grief begins to spread out, from the heaving capital to its suburbs, toward the villages, the towns, and the other cities, on to the country and the coast.

But nowhere is it felt more than at the heart of England, in London, among those who line the streets to watch the cortege go by. For they have come from near and far, from every corner of the kingdom, to witness the laying to rest of the man who belongs to all of them and none of them—the soldier without a name who has been lifted from the battlefield to be buried among kings: the Unknown Warrior.

II

THE LAPIDARIUM

Ypres, July 16, 1920,
Four Months Earlier

2

*T*HE HEAT OF A FLEMISH TOWN IN RUINS, AFTER THE WAR: *BLOEDHEET* the locals call it, "as hot as blood." The stippled streets are brown with brick dust, the color of an old photograph. There is hardly anything left of the old town; just a few houses here and there, the post office (miraculously intact), and half a terrace of homes on a single narrow, cobbled street. Women in black weeds move silently among the remains of Ypres, seeming to glide over the stones.

The tall man standing in the cool darkness of the monastery gate thinks of the paintings of the fin de siècle, of a vast Gustav Klimt canvas come to life: exotic women decked in black and gold, emanating a slow threat toward the male. He closes his eyes in sorrow; virtually all the men of his generation are dead or disfigured. Only the women they loved are left, a sinister cult of sisterhood weaving their grief from country to country, like flax on a loom.

He rests his head against the damaged pillar. Gilded fragments of a church gleam within the charred timbers at his feet and through the market square the military vans rumble just as they did when he was last in the city, in 1917. But the ruins are even more terrible than he remembers. The old cloister of St. Martin's is a graveyard of broken statues, wingless cherubs, and jagged columns of stone, while the shell cases that shine in the sunlight are collected now and sold as souvenirs. There once was a time when he knew the place well; it is imprinted on his memory, impossible to efface.

He turns and walks down the empty street in the shadow of the crooked remnants of buildings. It is possible, almost, to see straight across to the other side of town, to the ravaged fields, and as he slides into the burning seat of his car, he wonders if he will be able to get his bearings once he leaves the town, where familiar surroundings have been destroyed.

On the dashboard lie a leather-bound notebook and pen. He picks up the pen, shaking it to encourage the ink to flow more freely, then removes the lid. He opens the notebook and in boyish handwriting scrawls:

Flanders is one vast necropolis. My sole reason for being here is *The Times* commission: a chronicle of the horticultural work being done in the new cemeteries forged from the old battlefields. In addition to this, they have asked me to select one aspect of the act of remembrance that interests me. None of it does. I am a man who wants only to forget.

He casts the pen and notebook onto the passenger seat, wiping the perspiration from his forehead. The engine grinds into life and he reverses the car until he reaches the rough turning at the end of the street.

He drives slowly through the town, a dull ache in the pit of his stomach. Ypres is soon left behind; scarred ground and shattered masonry, bits of brick and stone . . . nothing else remains. On the outskirts of town, flies skim across the oily waters of a canal and concrete bunkers bulge on every despoiled horizon. In a field, men clear debris, stripped to the waists, broiling in the sun, their thick trousers dark with sweat and their braces dangling to their thighs. The flatness of the land is exactly as he remembers, those barren plains to the east and south especially, stretching into the umber distance, endless and featureless.

The same and yet . . . different.

There are blackened chasms where villages whose paths he once walked have been swept away forever, a stink of ammonia secreting near the surface of the cracked ground, and line after line of trees shorn of all vegetation. There are thickets of barbed wire, craters filled with water deep enough to drown in, and little eddies of dust swirling across the unfilled trenches he last saw in a hail of exploding stars. Here at last is the truth he suspected during his years in exile: the calamity of yesterday is unending, and places that were just places before the war will be stained forevermore by what has happened there.

The long, straight road unravels ahead of him, cutting through nothing and disappearing in the liquid shimmer of the heat haze. The aridity of Flanders during July is one of the things he has successfully forgotten, but the countryside is bone-dry and lifeless. He grips the blistering steering wheel with both hands and locks his gaze on the far distance, where a single hill pushes its snout against the sky: Mont Cassel. It was there, four years ago, in a small hotel room illuminated by remote gunfire, that he passed through the looking glass of war into another world, one that haunts him still. In his dreams, he often returns to it, and awakes in bewilderment, uncertain of what is real and what is mere recollection.

The road opens out, and where it branches to the left, a tall wooden crucifix rises from gleaming mounds of shrapnel. A crown of poppies rests on the head of the figure on the cross; the crimson petals have begun to flutter down, mottling the burnished metal with bloodred brilliance.

Cassel, he knows, lies along the road to the left. The sun flares on the bonnet of the car as he turns it resolutely away, in the direction of St. Omer to Longuenesse, and the château where the Imperial War Graves Commission has its offices.

The war is over, but the land is still being fought for as the car travels away from Ypres, the great dead heart of northern Flanders. In the course of his work, Alex has come to know all the arguments by rote: the British government wants to preserve the center of Ypres, since, according to the chairman of the Imperial War Graves Commission, Winston Churchill, "a more sacred place for the British race does not exist in the whole world." The Belgians, on the other hand, hope to tear down what is left and rebuild the medieval and renaissance structures in their entirety with a zone of silence in the center of town or to allow the British to build a magnificent memorial to their dead. The zone of silence idea is favored by local architect Eugène Dhuicque, an unsentimental man who advocates leaving the ruins of the Cloth Hall, St. Martin's Church, and the belfry as a symbol of the irreversibility of history. But, Dhuicque tells local officials and foreign journalists like Alex visiting the city, "what is lost is lost; the recent past should no more be commemorated than the middle ages."

Among the few indifferent to Ypres's fate are the gardeners whom Alex joins before sunrise on Monday morning, as they set off from Longuenesse château in a truck piled high with well-worn paraphernalia.

"Bricks and mortar," shrugs Daniel Lombardi, a thirty-three-year-old albino whom Alex has heard addressed as "Lombardi the Light" by the other gardeners. "Let them rebuild, if that's what they want. The cemeteries we're creating will be testament enough—great cities of the dead whose silent beauty and timeless architecture have no precedent."

Lombardi spreads his large hands palm-open in a gesture of regret. "We went to war to help the Belgians win back their land from the Germans. It's unreasonable to insist now that it belongs to us."

The other gardeners, less outspoken than Lombardi, murmur their agreement. There are six of them riding in the back of the truck, crouched on the low seats with tents, bedding, cooking equipment, food and water rations, plants, tools, and a tan-and-white terrier named Kemmel at their feet. Four of the men will remain together, working on one of the larger cemeteries under construction, while the other two have been assigned their own areas to prepare.

Alex is drawn to Daniel Lombardi. He is almost skeletal, like one of the trees from the poplar avenues near the shattered ground of Ploegsteert, where the four men working in a group unload their supplies and depart. Lombardi answers Alex's questions carefully in an unusual, lilting accent and has a few questions of his own for Alex, when the other gardener departs at St. Julien, leaving only the two of them sitting in the back of the truck under the green tarpaulin.

"What's your name? I'm sorry, but you spoke into my bad ear." Lombardi points at his left ear. "I can't hear on this side—a shell exploded next to me at Vampire Farm in 1917. That's why I shake a little too, my hands and head."

"Alex Dyer."

"And you're a writer?"

"I'm a journalist."

"Doesn't a journalist write?"

Alex smiles. "Yes, although mostly I type, apart from when I record things in my notebook."

"Are you planning to stay with me for the whole week?"

"I had hoped to. If it's all right with you."

Lombardi nods, looking pleased. "I can't offer you much in the way of home comforts, I'm afraid. I have a nice little shed with a corrugated iron roof that leaks in one corner when it rains, but fortunately, it isn't raining today." He frowns, the white eyebrows meeting across the bridge of his nose, like a pale caterpillar edging along a branch. "Actually, it hasn't rained for a month now. My area is very close to Boesinghe—did they tell you?"

Alex turns away in shock, the blood racing through his veins. He stares at the landscape, fighting a nauseous surge of fear, and when Lombardi hunches forward in the jolting, soil-smelling truck, he draws back from him.

"You seem troubled by something."

Alex avoids the milky irises searching his face, focusing instead on the grimy floor of the truck, where the prints of the gardeners' hobnailed boots can be seen, like afterthoughts, in the dirt. "No," he answers quietly. "I'm not."

Lombardi sits back and nudges at a clod of earth with his boots, clicking his fingers encouragingly at Kemmel. The terrier leaves its cushion of rolled blankets and presses itself against Lombardi's knees.

Lombardi strokes the dog's smooth brown head. "You'll tell me, when you're ready."

Alex does not respond; he looks back at the road along which they have driven. With every turn of the wheels it grows more uneven, deteriorating until it is no longer a road and can scarcely be called a dirt track. It disappears altogether on the outskirts of a prairie, where the truck deposits them amid clusters of tangled yellow calendula and scores of tilting white crosses that form a constellation in the long grass. Alex shades his eyes: a few splintered trees, Lombardi's hut, and the remains of an old trench system three hundred yards to the right are the only immediate landmarks he can see. The sun has risen over a ragged, blackened village on the horizon; it looks artificial, a misplaced piece of theatrical scenery. When the truck swerves away from them, spitting stones, they are completely alone.

Lombardi walks across to his hut and taps at a hand-painted sign next to the door: WELCOME TO THE VILLA VIA SACRA. Reading the question in Alex's hazel eyes, he explains, "The road from Calais to St. Omer has become a pilgrim's way. The war widows, the bereaved parents, the brothers, and the sisters—anyone, it seems, who comes to Flanders—feel as if they're walking in the footsteps of the sacred dead. Most visitors have nothing, and depend upon religious organizations to bring them here and guide them around the cemeteries." He smiles gently. "That's why I gave my little shed its lofty name."

There is a heavy padlock on the door, which Lombardi finally manages to unfasten after pushing down on the tiny key. He pulls the door open and secures it against the wooden wall.

"This is my home, three days a week."

Alex enters, ducking his head to avoid the low doorway, and looks around with interest. It reminds him of a hermit's lair, albeit one that is both orderly and welcoming. The few bits of decoration are bright, as if to compensate for the austerity of the hut: there is a green rag rug on the floor, which Kemmel snuffles happily, a sunken crimson sofa resting against one wall, and a vase of the yellow weeds standing on the table below the window. Alex notices that the legs have been sawn off the table to bring it down to a suitable height for the only chair.

Next to the vase of calendula is a thick pile of paperback books. Alex picks up a much-thumbed copy of *Ivanhoe*. "You like to read," he says.

Lombardi nods. "Yes, and thank God I like to walk too, otherwise life here would be unbearable. But look, there's something else that might interest you."

He strolls across to the corner of the little hut, where a pile of blankets are folded neatly on the floor. He lifts the blankets into his arms, revealing an almost new gramophone player; its brass, fluted horn gleams. Beside it is a stack of records in brown paper covers. Lombardi holds one up, grinning. "The greatest men on earth come from America— Shelton Brooks and James Reese Europe. I'm a jazz fanatic."

Alex sets *Ivanhoe* back down on the table. "So was I, once." He frowns and looks over at Lombardi. "By the way, where are you from? I can't seem to place your accent."

His host's grin widens. "No one can. My father was Italian and my mother was Welsh. I grew up in Wales, but my father was a huge influence on me. You would think, wouldn't you, that with that sort of background I'd be the most wonderful tenor?" He shakes his head in mock sorrow. "The truth is, I can't carry a tune in a bucket."

Wheels thump on the dirt track close by; a lorry rumbles past, having difficulty keeping to the flattest part of the field, and beeps a greeting as it disappears in a flurry of dust.

Lombardi waves enthusiastically from the door of the hut. "The Chinese labor corps," he explains, and points at the chair, indicating for Alex to sit down. "They work in the villages around Ypres, clearing the rubble, searching for unexploded shells. If I ever find something here—and, of course, I often do—then I send Kemmel over to them with a message attached to his collar. They come and detonate the old bombs safely for me. At night, they do it to pass the time." He takes down a jar of water from a crowded shelf. "Let me get you something to drink before I begin work. Tea?"

"Please."

Alex reaches his hand out to the dog. It drops its wet muzzle into his open palm and gazes up at him with earnest eyes. Alex turns back to Lombardi.

"Don't you get lonely," he asks, "out here all on your own?"

"Well, I'm not alone," Lombardi smiles at him as he draws water from the jar and empties it into a battered saucepan. He has very white, straight teeth. "Apart from Kemmel, I have whole battalions on their last parade to keep me company."

Alex stares at him, perplexed. "Dead men are your companions?"

Lombardi places the saucepan carefully on the tiny stove. He applies a match to the ring and then moves over to the sofa, sinking onto it with a sigh. "In a sense. They keep me awake at night sometimes; their silence can be deafening."

Kemmel patters across the floor to join his master on the sagging sofa. He curls up contently next to Lombardi and rests his head in the crook of Lombardi's elbow.

Alex watches them both, thinking over what Lombardi has said. A gust of wind coils in from the doorway and he hears the sound of crickets among the corn-colored grass, their abrasive song drifting on the warm airstream. He looks out at the rough wooden crosses, each one bearing a small metal plaque no wider than a woman's slim bracelet. The stillness is tangible; it has a depth to it, an eloquence that cannot be marred.

Suddenly, he understands. Lombardi is not mad or trying to give him the jitters. The presence of the dead is everywhere in this wilderness of dry earth and yellow weeds. It is the dead who provide the living with a reason for being here.

He turns his attention back to Lombardi, infinitely curious. "Have you worked here long?"

Lombardi puts his head to one side, considering. "It must be eight months now. Last autumn, in any case—a terrible time to begin. The rains came, flooding the fields, making the ground impassable. Just as it was during the war." He scratches Kemmel under the chin, earning a look of gratitude from the dog. "I've been working here, in this area, for a month."

"Isn't there anyone else nearby?"

Lombardi laughs gently. "Not unless you count the ruins of Elverdinghe on the horizon. There are four hundred of us British ex-servicemen employed as gardeners, scattered through Belgium and France like poppy seeds, to prepare seven hundred cemeteries. But we get help from the locals, and small teams of German prisoners, as well as Africans, Egyptians, Indians, and Chinese, prepare the ground first. It's a huge task, but not insurmountable."

"Perilous though."

Lombardi shrugs. "Yes, but worthwhile." He sighs again, resting his white head on the red back of the sofa. "You get used to that—the unexploded shells are something you learn to look out for and avoid. The *real* danger comes from the deserters, desperate men who've spent months, even years, hiding in the abandoned dugouts and bunkers. Sometimes they roam around in gangs, preying on men like me and visitors to the more isolated battlefields. I can't imagine how they survive, two years on, but perhaps it's better not to know."

Alex nods slowly. "Some secrets should be taken to the grave."

Lombardi's white eyebrows lift. "Fortunately, I have only Kemmel depending on me." He keeps his voice deliberately light. "No one else. I am alone in this world, apart from my ghostly companions, that is. And you?"

And him?

Alex Dyer's memory slips back three years, to an airless room with a view of tumbling Parisian rooftops and sweltering summer streets decked with flags to celebrate Bastille Day.

The woman's thin white body unbent gracefully from the bed. He stamped the vision of her beauty on his mind, to be marveled over later, when she had gone.

She dressed swiftly, not speaking until she was finished:"What were you thinking just then, while you were watching me?"

He answered with raw honesty. "That your leaving will destroy me."

"Will it?" she asked softly, standing by the bed and leaning over him until her damp hair touched his exposed stomach.

"You know it will. It's not as if . . ." He let the words tail off and threw his arm over his face defensively.

"What? What were you going to say?"

He lifted his arm so that it was resting on his forehead. "It's not as if I didn't expect this, but I didn't know how bloody *impossible* it would be to deal with."

She straightened up, pushing her hair away from her face. There was something behind the wide gray eyes that he couldn't fathom. "We agreed, didn't we," she said, tensely, "that it was what we both wanted, what we felt was best?"

"Agreeing to something doesn't always necessarily mean that I like it."

"There's no other choice."

"You *know* there is."

"And then what, Alex?"

He sat up and grasped her wrists tightly, pressing down fiercely on the fragile bones. "I want you. I want *you*. I can't live my life as it was before. Everything has changed."

She pulled her hands from his maddened grip. The loveliness of her face was almost lost under the acute suffering she felt.

"Nothing has changed," she said.

Outside Lombardi's little hut the crickets in the bleached grass have begun a new song. The water boils noisily on the stove, sending out beads of effervescence that dissolve in an instant.

The memory fills the room. In the silence, Alex finds it difficult to speak.

"No," he says at last. "There is no one, no."

3

At the end of the afternoon, ALEX LEANS AGAINST THE HUT, LIS-tening to echoes of the past unfolding. A mine has exploded on the other side of the desecrated village, sealing the sky in jewel-bright reds and oranges. Lombardi shakes his head at the interruption, then drives the pick deep once more into the ground, unbothered. He is singing, more melodiously than he has led Alex to expect, and his rich, pure baritone surges across the old trenches where so much waste lies above and below.

Alex looks at the burning sky. The smoke formations twist and weave, spiraling away from the fire. He watches them, shaping them resolutely into an outline, and in the threads of ash and ember he imagines a woman's profile. She sits alone at a table in a restaurant, her head turned, gazing at a wide river. She is very still. He sees himself enter the sun-drenched room where the heady scent of tiger lilies hangs like incense about the walls. When he says her name, she does not rise in response. She looks at him. At the edge of the white muslin dress, where the flat abacus of bones is visible above the small breasts, a roseate stain spreads across her skin.

The illusion fades in a dark swirl of smoke. He walks slowly back into the hut and brings out the chair and his notebook and pen. Then he positions himself with his back to the door, facing the trench where Lombardi labors, and begins to write.

The notebook, with its soft, walnut-shaded bindings and stiff pages stitched in thick segments into the spine, has taken on a life of its own. In the beginning, he wrote about places he intended to visit, details of the Imperial War Graves Commission, pages of stupefying statistics, and addresses and names. Sometimes he was quick to record what he saw around him for the purpose of the article he is writing, or to fix on an idea; more often, he was seized by an impulse to sketch details of a particular place that had changed—or a memory that unsettled him. Recently, his own thoughts have begun to interrupt the bald narrative. Occasionally he writes in the third person, projecting himself onto the page as if his real self does not exist. Those particular passages fulfill a febrile desire in him to work through what happened, a desperate attempt to make sense of how his life came undone and, eventually, to confront the demon that sits on his shoulder day and night.

He has to press down on the leather-bound book as he holds it on his knee; if he forgets for a moment, and lifts his hand, the thick pages spring, feathering, to close. The pen trails a line of thin green ink, its path followed by the shadow of his hand. He is alone; Lombardi has disappeared into the maze of old trenches where they run parallel with the sparse gathering of trees. Sunlight glances through gaps in the bramble thickets, the tall nettles and the loftier thistles. The warm breeze that makes the foxgloves sway smells deleterious. Earlier Lombardi told him that the stench comes from corpses lying near the surface of the soil, and the slow release of poison gas.

He bends his head.

Post-war Flanders has a savage splendor. In "Letters from Italy," Dickens writes of seeing Rome's arena for the first time, "Its solitude, its awful beauty, and the utter desolation, strike upon the stranger, the next moment, like a softened sorrow; and never in his life, perhaps, will he be so moved and overcome by any sight not immediately connected with his own affections and afflictions." He might be describing Ypres and the land around it, although few strangers visit this place without some wretched bond—primarily the loss of a loved one—to the area.

Thirty years before Dickens toured Italy, John Clare arrived at Pickworth in Leicestershire, a village pillaged during the Wars of the Roses. The ruins of Pickworth had been quarried. All that remained was an ivy-clad stone arch in the fields, the old gateway to the parish church. It was here that he wrote "Elegy on the Ruins of Pickworth," which runs: "There's not a foot of ground we daily tread . . . but holds some fragment of the human dead."

Close to the Villa Via Sacre, in the obliterated village of Elverdinghe, the church has been flattened to a ridge of red rubble. Laborers searching among the broken plaster and wood find altar cloths embroidered in scarlet and gold. The colors still shine. While peasants scythe and burn thistles, sending plumes of indigo smoke down the road to France, headless angels and saints are unearthed from the wreckage of God's house.

He reads over what he has written. The familiar swell of dread floods his mind, and feverishly he scribbles across the page his other thoughts, the ones he tries to push away while studying the landscape:

If the past is more tangible to a man than the present, is it still the past? When the present means nothing? And his own history is something that lives and breathes, which sustains him when all hope is gone?

If he cannot forget what is past, how will he live?

Lombardi is finished for the day. As he rolls his tools in a wad of tarpaulin and pushes the tube against the back of the shed, where ladybirds crawl in profusion over the flowering weeds, he thinks about his guest.

To Lombardi, Alex's despair seems even more profound than that of many of the ex-soldiers and bereaved relatives he meets during the course of his work. There is something deeper than grief in his despondency. Lombardi himself is a man content within his own skin; the trauma of Vampire Farm has settled more on his flesh than in his mind. If someone were to question him about his beliefs, he would tell them that he is a fatalist who asks for nothing more now out of life than a roof over his head—even one that leaks—and sustenance. If he can also listen to James Reese Europe's 369th U.S. Infantry "Hellfighters" Band occasionally, then his satisfaction is complete, unassailable.

A long time ago, in Turin, Lombardi's grandmother told him that unhappy people can see nothing outside their own misery, while those at peace with themselves act as a conduit to the most delicate of emotions, absorbing the vibrations like breeze on a wire. She was right: when the writer appeared at Longuenesse château, passing through the corridors of the building like a sleepwalker, Lombardi saw the sorrow etched deep in the hollows of his face and asked his supervisor to let the man join him. He hopes to be able to heal him, as his grandmother did in the past, in Turin, for those whose spirits were broken by circumstance and the lives they led.

Like her, Lombardi's methods are subtle, even skillful. He begins by saying nothing at all about his guest's troubled state of mind. As Lombardi enters the hut, he asks casually, "How's the tea coming along?" and sits down at the table with Kemmel panting at his feet. The dog's pink tongue lolls, idiotically, and he rolls over onto his back, grimy paws aloft.

While Alex pours the hot liquid into two chipped blue mugs, Lombardi's gaze flits across to the notebook lying beside the vase of calendula. He wants to ask about its contents, yet holds back, knowing it is too soon. But as he reaches out for his mug, the stiff, unbuttoned cuff of his shirt brushes accidentally against the notebook and knocks it to the floor, scattering a handful of loose sheets hoarded inside the back cover.

He bends to retrieve the book and the pages, pushing the inquisitive Kemmel aside and apologizing to Alex, who is standing beside the stove replacing the empty pan on the ring.

"Your notebook, Alex . . . I'm so sorry—some papers have slipped out." Lombardi guiltily gathers together the loose sheets. He has no opportunity to see what the notebook contains, or what the papers are that have fallen from it; Alex seizes the bundle swiftly from him, thumbing through the pages as if searching for something.

Lombardi is about to return to his seat when he notices a sheet that he missed. He crouches under the table to rescue it, stretching out his long fingers. He lifts it into the light and sees at once that it isn't notepaper at all, but a faded photograph of a young man dressed in immaculate cricket whites, standing below the spreading branches of a cedar tree. Under the pale aureole of his fair hair, the young man's face has a dreamy, pensive expression, perfectly captured in time by the camera eye.

Lombardi flinches as Alex leans in and grasps the photograph. He watches his guest conceal it within the pages of the notebook again, wrapping the narrow bands around it possessively.

Lombardi sits down. "Who is it?" he asks, still watching Alex, who holds the notebook awkwardly in his hands, unmoving, staring down at it as though disorientated by it, or by what it contains.

"No one."

The reply is brusque and uncompromising. Lombardi is nobody's fool; he can see there is no point in pursuing the matter. His guest sits down at the table, pushing the notebook away from him, and wears a shuttered, harsh look that closes out everything but his own torment.

In the evening, Alex stands outside, absorbed by the lavender and silver light falling across the fields. There is no breeze now, nothing to carry sound from miles around. Just the insects jarring in the bleached grass and the faint noise, in the little hut behind him, of Lombardi cutting bread and cheese at the table. He returns to the hut with the chair when his host calls to him, then sits down at the table while Lombardi perches on the arm of the sofa and hands him a glass of amber Belgian beer. Kemmel stretches out blissfully on the rag rug, his stomach distended with freshly killed rabbit.

Alex lets Lombardi talk about his work while he listens, watching his host's unusual eyes and drinking the beer more quickly than he realizes.

"When I first came out here we were still gathering the dead. It was terrible—we searched the Somme six times. Of course, it was impossible by then to put a name to most of the bodies, and in the end, it was all detective work, identifying a man from initials found on a spoon, or tracing a compass back to the place it was bought. And the land itself so *ravaged*. Unbelievable. The French government wanted to turn parts of it into national forest, but then it was decided that the area around Albert and Villers-Bretonneux was uninhabitable and beyond the realms of cultivation. So they called it the Zone Rouge and left it to rot."

"And now?" asks Alex, pulling the chair closer to the table.

Lombardi shrugs. "Some villages have been wiped off the face of the earth—you've seen that for yourself. But the Picards are deeply attached to their land, and in some places people *have* come back. The government has had a change of mind, as governments do. They encourage them back by promising farmers three years' rent-free tenancy, build cheap housing for them, and draft in special labor units to clear the land and fill in the trenches." He bites into a chunk of crusty bread and swallows.

"What happens to the things that people find out here when they're clearing the ground?" Alex asks. "The shells, the old bully-beef tins, that sort of thing?"

"On the battlefields? It's simple enough: the land is divided into segments with salvage contractors allotted to each one and whatever they find belongs to them. They'll make their fortunes, if they aren't blown to pieces first." Lombardi refills their glasses from the brown bottle.

"And the dead? What happens to them exactly?"

"That's something most people don't like to discuss." Lombardi purses his lips. "There's a roaring illegal trade in corpses. In France, the government insists that those who died in battle should remain where they fell, but, not surprisingly, the relatives feel very different about it. Those who can afford it make private deals with gravediggers to exhume their sons and husbands, and the bodies are brought home in secrecy, at great cost. But there are rumors that before the year is out the French dead *will* be repatriated, perhaps even at state expense."

"Like the Americans," Alex looks down at his glass. "They insist on bringing their soldiers home. When I arrived in Calais, I saw them, loading the bodies into the holds of enormous ships: stack upon stack of wooden crates on the quayside, like a peculiar catch brought in by the local fishermen." His grip on the glass tightens. "It's better than being forgotten, isn't it? I went to the Crimea in March 1914. The huge cemetery at Sevastopol was well tended by its German gardener, but no one ever went there. I was the first visitor in six years."

"That won't happen here," Lombardi insists. "It will never happen here. Too many lives have been touched. Since the armistice, thousands of grieving relatives have made the journey across the Channel, and they will come, years from now, they will still come."

"Grieving relatives . . . and battlefield ghouls." In the fading light, Alex's face is a map of shades. "To them, the landscape of the war is a mythical one. Only the names have the power to move them: Mametz, Hill 60, Thiepval . . . *Passchendaele.*"

It comes out of nowhere, that guarded rage. The last word—*Passchendaele*—is said with such vehemence that Lombardi is startled. He watches the dark, narrow face opposite him, the fervor in the slanting brown eyes. Something is moving beneath the quiet exterior, getting closer to the surface, preparing to break through.

"Passchendaele," the writer repeats softly, looking at the sky.

Lombardi waits. He remembers the photograph, sensing that at the eye of the storm is the man whose face he has only glimpsed. But his guest says nothing more. He goes on staring at the doorway, where twilight encircles the still and silent earth.

When the first stars appear in the sky, Lombardi sets a hurricane lamp in the center of the table, lifting aside the jar of yellow calendula. The light from the candle flickers across the wooden ceiling and causes Kemmel to glance up for a moment before returning to his slumber.

Alex is talking, the words tumbling drunkenly from him.

"The Greeks set fire to their dead before the walls of Troy. After Marathon, the Athenians burned the Persians slain in battle. It was 'the law of all Greece.'" His voice is quiet, his speech softly slurred. "At Agincourt a French herald asked Henry the Fifth permission to wander the bloody field, 'to book our dead and then to bury them.'" He pauses. "That was at Agincourt."

Lombardi says nothing in reply, unable to grasp the meaning behind Alex's words.

"The true measure of society is in how we dispose of our dead after battle." Alex notices Lombardi's mystified expression and groans. "I'm sorry, I'm talking gibberish. But this place makes me think of other battles, other dead. All the ones I learned of in school. And it builds up inside, *here*."

He strikes his chest violently with his fist, then raises his glass. If he twists it between his fingers, the liquid changes color, the metamorphosis caused by the candlelight on the rag rug. The liquid glows, brilliantly green, like absinthe.

He turns to Lombardi, suddenly aware of the insects' silence. "There is no sound."

"No. But the breeze has dropped. And this is your first night here since the war ended, so, of course, everything seems strange. Soon you'll hear the small creatures that live the better part of their lives at night. Little cries, the thud of a warm body against the ground as it is captured, the movement in the grass as the prey is dragged home to a burrow or a clearing."

"But still . . . such soundlessness."

Lombardi smiles his gentle smile. "Now perhaps you understand what I meant when I said earlier that the silence of the dead is sometimes deafening."

And in the silence, passive with liquor, his thoughts return to her.

Not a particular memory, but one composed of fragments: the coolness of her gaze at their first meeting in the restaurant overlooking the Thames, the tiny blue pulse on her temple, her delicate ankles encircled by the thin green strap of her favorite shoes, the small triangular scar on her left wrist just above the vein, the fresh, cool scent of her unclothed skin. Images that cause the blood to flow around his body in warm rushes that suddenly become static, like the air in the underground stations back in London.

He feels compelled to speak of her, unable to contain himself. But his words lurch away from his lips, haphazardly: "I fell in love with a woman's neck."

Lombardi looks at him.

"I went into the restaurant. She had her back to me and her hair was piled up. It was summer, and the sun was shining on the river, but in that moment all I could see was her bare neck. Her shoulder blades jutted underneath her blouse. I had never seen anything so perfect."

Lombardi raises his white eyebrows. "What was so special about it?"

"Everything. The long line of it. The color of her skin. The fragility of it. The tendrils of hair at the nape, and the film of moisture there, underneath. They talk about necks being swanlike, don't they, but this wasn't. I've never thought of it like that. It was all *her*, nothing else." He pauses. "I sound like a complete and utter lunatic, don't I?"

"Who was she, this owner of the beautiful neck?"

For a moment, he says nothing. And then: "Clare. Her name is Clare Eden."

"And now?" Lombardi asks. "Where is she?"

"She lives in London. Or so I imagine."

"It was an affair?"

"Yes. I loved her. I am still . . . in love with her." His voice cracks with repressed longing.

The wreckage of the past falls, burning him, like the charcoal flakes of ash and ember that float out from a fire. Flecks of memory drift before his eyes, and he wonders, as he repeatedly does, how it is possible to go on living when what matters most is gone, what instinct keeps him breathing, existing without purpose. It is the last, involuntary pull of life that he is experiencing now, or so he believes—just as the heart of some animals go on twitching a while, after death.

The taillight of a comet blazes through the sky above the Flanders plains. Alex stands at the door of the Villa Via Sacra again, watching its incandescent progress. When the comet has gone, leaving only a handful of stars to glimmer in its wake, he addresses Lombardi without looking at him.

"I'll tell you how it happened, shall I? How my life fell apart. I'll tell you who this woman was, and about that man—" He breaks off and gazes blindly at the shrouded landscape. "Love is not redemption, whatever we are brought up to believe." He bends his head. "I've never talked about this to anyone, not since it all finished in 1917. I might almost say that I've withered in the last three years; Clare used that term once, when she told me about her father dying. 'I felt something inside me wither,' she said."

He turns. He looks hunted, wounded by his own arrows. His eyes are dark with despair, and fury turned inward.

"It wasn't until I lost them both that I realized what she had meant."

III

THE TIN NOSES SHOP

Richmond, July 16, 1920

4

THE HOSPITAL IS DISCREETLY SIGNPOSTED THROUGHOUT THE TOWN and hidden from view behind a high brick wall that runs the length of the main road. Occasionally someone wanders as far as the tall iron gates at the end of the entrance to the east wing, where the glass room of the orangery can be seen protruding onto the terrace like the bow of a ship, and catches a glimpse of one of the patients. The trespasser stares, and the patient vanishes from sight, unwilling to become part of the callous local folklore about the place.

Once a private house, Pinderfields Hospital is a fine example of Gothic architecture and a suitable setting for the horror stories and rumors that fly around town about those who live there. Gargoyles the children call them; gargoyles come to life but kept deliberately away from the world, too ghastly to be seen by ordinary eyes. The name of the hospital has been integrated into playground jargon; "you belong in Pinderfields" is a popular insult among the older children.

During the last months of the war, Pinderfields was bequeathed to the Royal Army Medical Corps by its absent owner, who prefers to live in Scotland. Today, despite the pernicious gossip among the local people, the north wing of the building houses the section that gives residents and their visitors hope. Its official title is the Masks for Facial

Disfigurements Department, but ex-Tommies call it "the Tin Noses Shop."

The nucleus of the department is the studio. A large, square room flooded with natural daylight coming in through the sash windows, the studio is fitted with rows of shelves upon which stand the tools of the sculptor's trade alongside dozens of plaster casts of heads and faces. The most striking feature of the room is not the steel–and–black leather dentist's chair that might dominate it otherwise or the pervasive smell of oil paints. Instead, it is the long rows of professional photographs of young men before they went off to war. The pictures, most of them taken for relatives and sweethearts left behind, bear fading inscriptions from the soldiers. *"To Jessie, wait for me, all my love, George,"* reads one typical of the rest.

Within the last week, another photograph has been added to the collection. Its subject sits in the dentist's chair in the middle of the room, but there is little discernable likeness between the red-haired, lively eyed man in the photograph and the one who holds himself stiffly, his fingers curled around the arms of the chair as the surgeon's assistant tilts it backward. Three quarters of the man's face has been shot away. His mouth is intact, if somewhat dragged out of shape, but his nose is gone, together with the entire right side of his face out to the ear, and he is left with one eye, a mere slit. The flesh on the other side of his face is crumpled and yellow, and the skin that has grown over the missing half of his face has the texture of rice paper.

Leaning over the man as if she is about to give him a barber's shave is a thin young woman whose pale gray eyes glitter with concentration as she applies liberal amounts of oil to his face using an artist's flat brush. When she has finished with the oil, she smears the man's remaining eyebrow and sparse red mustache with Vaseline.

"This will prevent the plaster of Paris from sticking to the hairs," she tells him. Her voice is low and soft. "Would you close your left eye for me?"

As the narrow slit blinks shut like the eye of an owl, she places a square of tissue on the oily lid and another on the hole where his right eye should be. She swivels the chair this way and that, wanting to be certain that the oil covers every millimeter of his ruined face, then calls to the man writing at a desk in a corner of the room: "Mr. Harman is ready for you now."

The surgeon approaches, and the man sitting prone in the chair suddenly clutches the young woman's hand.

"Stay with me, Sister, please. Would you mind?"

"Of course not," she replies, closing her fingers over his. "You mustn't talk now." She puts a finger to her mouth as the surgeon begins his task.

Two years have passed since Clare Eden began working at Pinderfields. The procedure about to take place is one she has witnessed many times, and yet it still strikes her as strange magic. The practice by which disfigured men are given back not only a face to enable them to live in society again, but just as crucially their self-respect, is a modern miracle to her. The surgeon she assists began by making a negative replica in plaster of Harman's face, then several "positive" and "negative" plasters, and one in plasticine, to remove imperfections and open the eye, which was closed when the first set of plaster was applied, so that a new eye can be matched to it. Then comes the final stage, and the one Clare finds most gripping.

In Harman's case, the eyeless socket of the mask will be filled in and fitted with an eye and an eyebrow and the cheek will be built up, the nose remolded, and the missing part of the forehead restored. The surgeon works at his bench for hour after hour, his patient's photograph propped in front of him, aiming to produce a mask that resembles the original portrait as closely as possible. Once the mask is finished, it is sent away to be silver-plated and tinted to correspond with the patient's skin tone. Finally, after weeks of painstaking work, the mask can be fitted.

Clare listens as the surgeon, a dapper little man with a thick, drooping mustache, explains the final stage to Harman as he applies the wet plaster to the man's face.

"The mask is made from electroplate, the merest fraction of an inch thick. Marvelous stuff, and very light to wear. It's the easiest thing in the world to match the color of the mask with your skin tone—it's all done with oil paints, you see. Eyes are the very devil to do. I don't use commercial glass eyes because they never give you more than a very approximate match. I prefer to paint on oval glass disks that slip into the socket of the mask."

He frowns, standing back to survey his work, then adds heavier splodges of plaster to the greasy film Clare created on Harman's face.

"The eyelashes won't be made from real hair—they don't stick to the metal well enough. I use the thinnest slivers of silver foil and paint them to match your coloring. Really, you'll find the whole thing surprisingly light to wear. The mask is like a membrane but it has the strength and firmness of metal. If you want to feel extra secure, you can always wear spectacles—quite a lot of my clients do.".

Clare listens, moved as always to hear the surgeon refer to the men who come to him as clients rather than patients. It makes them feel less feeble, less dependent.

"You might have a slight problem with discharge from the eye socket," the surgeon goes on, still daubing Harman's face. "Unfortunately your lachrymatory glands have been damaged. But there's a simple remedy for that—you just place absorbent pads in the hollows behind the mask. That should put an end to it. Otherwise, you should have no difficulties at all. Most men don't. You won't even see the join, isn't that right, Sister?"

"It is," Clare answers. She feels Harman's fingers squeeze hers, grateful for the reassurance.

When the surgeon has finished applying the plaster, Harman remains in the chair, motionless. Clare stands beside him, waiting for the plaster to grow thicker and more solid. When it is completely dry, she detaches it carefully from Harman's face. The shell of plaster steams in the cold room. She holds it for a moment, almost reverently, aware, as perhaps Harman is not, that this is the first step toward *life* again.

And again, as usual during her hours in the studio, she curses her own inability to take those steps.

In the evening, Thomas Harman has a visitor. His fiancée, whom he has not seen for two years (not since his transferral from the hospital base in France to Pinderfields) wrote the previous week to request a meeting. In her letter, which Harman showed to Clare, the girl confessed that she hadn't felt up to it before. Harman asked Clare to write back to her, telling her of the extent of his injuries, and Clare had done so, heartsick in the knowledge that no words could prepare someone in ignorance of facial disfigurement for her first visit to the hospital.

She tries to explain as much to Harman, but the girl's letter has filled him with unexpected confidence, and there seems to be no means of balancing that with caution.

Harman flaps his hands at Clare in disgust. "It will do me good, anyway," he says, "to see someone new. I haven't had any guests since Mother's last visit a month ago, and I've been here so long Matron's put me on the inventory." He sighs, his breath rattling up from his chest. "Don't worry about me, Sister. You know I don't want to be mollycoddled."

Harman's visitor arrives at six o'clock. Clare's attempts to put her off for another day, one that did not coincide with Harman's first appointment at the studio, have failed; Harman is determined not to wait a minute longer than necessary to see his fiancée. But Clare needs only to take one look at the girl, a coquettish young thing wearing an expensive suit and hat, to know that the encounter is doomed. Before guiding her into the library where Harman waits eagerly, Clare gives the girl one last pep talk.

"Whatever your feelings, fight them. Try not to show pity, or fear. And look at him directly. Remember he's going to be watching your face, to see how you react."

The girl nods, her eyes already betraying her anxiety.

As the door closes behind her, farther down the long corridor another door opens in the wainscoting and a man is led out, screaming, by two orderlies. His legs kick out helplessly, and his head snaps back as though all the tendons in his neck have been severed. Clare has seen it before, in other patients: the man has come from the hospital's dental surgery, where he has been given gas, and has awoken like so many before him, convinced that he is back on the battlefield, fighting for his life.

Clare takes a deep breath and begins to walk in the other direction, toward her office. As she reaches the end of the corridor, where a short flight of stairs lead up to the administration wing, she hears the door of the library being wrenched open.

Harman's visitor collapses against the wall and sinks to her feet, crying hysterically. The veil of the girl's hat crumples under her fists, which she holds tightly to her eyes.

Clare retraces her steps to where the girl is slumped and hauls her to her feet. She leads the wailing girl along the corridor, quickly, hissing at her to calm down, nipping the girl's arm.

When they reach her office, Clare presses the girl into a chair and takes out the half bottle of brandy she keeps in her cupboard for panic-stricken visitors. She has a great deal of experience with such people but little compassion. Her objective is always to settle them down enough to get them out of the building, then to seek out her patients, whose welfare is her only concern. A month ago, she lost a patient when he committed suicide after one such visit. His death was discreetly hushed up by the authorities, as such deaths are, and a telegram was sent out to his father: "Regret to inform you that Private Brody of the 16th Battalion, West Yorkshire Regiment died this evening after a relapse."

Clare looks at the girl sitting opposite her. The hysterical weeping has quieted to a series of erratic breaths. The girl sips at the brandy, clutching the glass with both hands. Then she puts the glass down on the table and lifts her veil, gazing at Clare with imploring eyes.

"How do you stand it?" she asks, aware that the inscrutable nurse sitting across from her is scarcely older than herself. "How can you bear to look at him? To smile at him?"

"It's my duty," Clare answers. She isn't smiling now; her face, below the white cap and tendrils of blond hair, is stonily unsympathetic.

"Oh no," says the girl. "There must be more to it than that. I don't mean to be rude, but no normal woman could spend her life with— with . . . I mean, it's as if you're *punishing* yourself or something." She begins to cry again. "What am I going to do? Oh Lord, help me, *help me*—I never want to go through that again. What am I going to do?"

Clare stares back at her. She feels a vast wave of pity for Harman wash over her and responds, "You're to go back home. Continue to write to Mr. Harman for a while, as you have always done, apologizing for your behavior this evening, but after a few weeks explain to him that you wish to break off the engagement. You do wish to break off the engagement, I assume?"

"Yes," says the girl. "Oh Lord, *yes*." She bursts into tears again.

"Then do so. But give him a chance to get used to the idea. False hope, in my experience, sometimes has its uses. It can bridge the gap between despair and realization. By the time you've told Mr. Harman that the engagement is over, he will have come to that conclusion himself, without the pain of having to hear it from you while he is at his lowest ebb."

Clare stares at the girl, feeling her body grow cold with dislike. "He was fitted for his mask today. His confidence was coming back. This will have knocked him sideways, but you would be surprised by how much self-respect the men here regain when they are able to wear the mask. The psychological wounds are very deep—some never heal, but he was doing well. These next few weeks will be hard on him. Don't add to it."

"No," says the girl, shaking her head vigorously. "Of course not. I don't want to hurt poor Thomas. I—I loved him."

Something inside Clare snaps. She stands up abruptly behind her desk. "Good evening to you, Miss Taylor. I'll have someone show you out."

Clare opens the door and glances along the hallway, where an orderly wheels a squeaking trolley laden with empty dinner trays. She calls to him, and then stands back, stiffly, to allow the girl to leave.

Harman is sitting in a chair in the library when Clare enters. His chair is turned to the long window at the terrace with its sweeping lawn and sycamore boundary. The light, the gentle rays of a distant sunset, casts faint golden-brown shadows across the grass and causes the uppermost branches of the trees to look as if they are on fire.

Harman is smoking a forbidden cigarette. Clare pulls at the window fastening and slides the lower pane up until there is a gap large enough for a person to lean out over the terrace.

"Don't do that," says Harman, hoarsely. He doesn't look at her.

"I have to," Clare answers, watching the smoke drift out across the stone balustrade. "If you're going to flout hospital rules you might at least try to cover your tracks."

"The smell, you mean? I prefer cigarette smoke to the stink of hopelessness, don't you?"

"There isn't much to choose between them."

"What would you know about it?" he replies quietly, grinding the cigarette into a teacup on the windowsill.

Clare's hands curl into fists. *More than you think,* she wants to cry out. She pulls up a chair and turns her head, breathing in the summer evening air. In the far reaches of the garden, where it is coolest, birds sing, the notes hauntingly soft.

"What did she say to you?"

Clare looks at him; he stares straight ahead. "Very little. I think she felt unprepared, despite the letter I wrote to her."

"Did she say whether she would come back?" He jerks his head up impatiently. "Don't trouble yourself to answer that, Sister. Of course she isn't coming back. Why would someone like her want to be saddled with a *gargoyle* like me?" He gives a small laugh. "It's what they call a reversal of fortunes: when we met, I had to be persuaded to take *her* out. I didn't think she was attractive enough for me. How the mighty have fallen, eh, Sister?"

Clare reaches out for his hand. He makes no attempt to return the pressure of her fingers.

"You've had an awful day," says Clare. "I think you should return to your bedroom. Try and get some sleep."

"Sleep? Yes, I wish I could sleep. Sleep forever and never wake up."

"Don't say that. The mask will be ready in a few weeks. You'll be able to go out into the world again."

"But I don't want to. I don't want a mask, I want my own face back." His voice shakes uncontrollably. "Where is it now? Lying in some plowed field near Auchonvillers. Some farmer's probably got it hanging from a tree, to ward off the birds. What a fright for them, eh? Better than any scarecrow."

"Stop this," says Clare, leaning forward and moving his chin around so that the narrow slit of his remaining eye focuses on her. "You're being self-pitying. You've every right to be, but you always said you hated that in other men."

His chin jerks up again. "Perhaps I didn't realize what humiliation did to the soul."

His attempt to be flippant fails miserably. Clare sees the tear squeezing from his eye slit, and understanding that gentleness could break him now, she tells him firmly, "Then, by all means, feel sorry for yourself. But tomorrow will come, whether you like it or not. The world doesn't wait for any of us, and I've seen far worse than you. Some of those men are living again now. I mean really *living,* enjoying their lives. Life is precious—you know that."

"I'm not sure," he says brokenly, his shoulders quivering. "I'm not sure of anything anymore."

"Then stop thinking. *Rest.* I'm going home now, and tomorrow is my day off, but I'll come in and see you during afternoon visiting hours. But only if you promise to rest, Thomas."

He nods, and then suddenly falls forward, pushing his skull into her collarbone. She lets him lie there for a moment against her, like a child.

His voice, when it comes, is muffled by her cape. "You smell like the sea. Like a walk along the Cornish coastline on a breezy day."

She feels him smiling.

The city's clocks are striking midnight as Clare arrives home at her flat in Battersea. She undresses slowly before the long mirror in her bedroom, kicking off the ugly, sensible shoes she has to wear, then unpeeling the uniform from her sticky skin. She has not troubled to switch on the lamps, preferring the shadows, and the walls are lit by the shimmer of the Thames as the moon floats above London.

She looks beyond her reflection to the dark oval of the bed, remembering.

The day at the hospital fades away. The uncluttered floor and straightened sheets dissolve. She does not see them. Instead, she recalls a man's shirt thrown over the wicker chair, her own dress cast across the floor, and the sheets . . . white folds beneath which two bodies lay tangled.

In the dimly lit room she hears their voices whispering, like a forgotten song.

IV

OPAL FIRES

Early Memories of War

5

*W*HEN WAR BROKE OUT ALEX WAS IN WHITBY, VISITING HIS FATHER. They read the announcement together. Neither of them said anything for a long while; his father was dying in the large, unlovely house of Alex's childhood, where the steps from the abbey came to an end against the low garden wall. Small white clouds issued from his father's dry mouth. Alex felt the crabbed hand searching on top of the blankets to find his; when their fingers touched, his father asked him to leave: "There's no sense in you hanging about here, lad, waiting for last words. Grey says the lights have gone out all over Europe. So find what you can, in the darkness."

Alex walked up to the cliff at dusk and stood there, watching the fishing fleet come into harbor, the lights winking like fireflies in the gentle dark where sea met sky. He didn't want to leave his father, but the pull of the tornado in Europe grew stronger by the hour. In the end, he remained in Whitby for two days before packing his father's old leather doctor's bag with his passport, writing materials, books, and a few clothes.

They said an oddly formal farewell in the bedroom where his mother had died giving birth to him twenty-eight years before. The acrid stench of this impending death filled his nostrils as he kissed his father's sunken cheek and closed the door on the nurse's stern reminders to let them know where he ended up.

He stood outside in the garden, looking up at the window of the room where his father lay. The man whom he loved, who had taught him an independence of spirit, who had cultivated his gift for words, was coming to the end of his life. He remembered, as a child, his father holding his hand in his, tracing the shapes of words on a page with their fingers, following lines, reading words to the air.

"The beauty of language," his father had told him, "can be grasped only when words are read aloud, felt on the tongue. You must always think, when writing, *How will it sound if I speak it out loud?* Words have no meaning unless they can fly."

Now there were no more words between them.

He traveled to Paris, stepping out into the August sunlight from the tumultuous noise and steam of the Gare de l'Est, as his father gave up on language across the North Sea.

In the little hut on the Flanders plains, Alex looks at Lombardi. "This part I can tell you. But the other . . . I find it difficult to speak of those things. I never have, actually, not to anyone."

"Perhaps it would be easier if you got into the habit of reading to me?" Lombardi suggests. "If it is there, in your notebook?"

Alex takes up the leather-bound book hesitantly, holding it at an angle to catch the flickering light from the hurricane lamp, and reads:

"I found an apartment on the avenue Kléber and from there watched the city mobilizing after the call to arms was slipped into the letter boxes of tenements and houses on every street and boulevard. I stood among the cheering crowds as the British Army arrived, the soldiers waving and smiling at their joyous welcome, and picked my way home later along flower-strewn cobblestones.

"From Paris I traveled north, moving from town to town in order to avoid arrest.

"I was an outlaw, ridiculous though it sounds. The secretary of state for war, Lord Kitchener, had banned all journalists from entering the war zone while the War Office in London tried to suppress unsanctioned reports from France and Belgium. I lived without papers or credentials, spending no more than two nights in the same place, walking out to the front line whenever I could, gathering information from French and Belgian refugees. I worked on my own initiative and relied on my inner judgment of strangers to know whom I could trust to carry my reports safely back to England. Sometimes I even sailed to Dover to hand in my dispatches before catching the boat back to France later that day.

"There were other men, journalists similarly occupied in that disjointed, suspended life between the west coast ports and the whereabouts of the British and French armies. We operated completely independently of the War Office and reported on the effects of battle on the soldiers, on the people who lived in the vicinity, and on the landscape itself.

"I played a dangerous game of evasion with the French and British officers, who had the right to arrest me on sight, and with the enemy, who would shoot me as a spy. The British Army moved forward to Flanders to shorten its supply and communication lines with England and I based myself in Le Havre, regularly going out to the war zone.

"In October I reached the Belgian frontier without an official pass and joined the staff of an English hospital stationed in Furnes, working as a stretcher bearer by day, writing my dispatches at night, unaware that Kitchener had put out a warrant for my arrest, as he had for other British journalists working behind the front line. I helped the medical staff move south to Poperinghe as the Germans advanced. And in that small Flemish town under British occupation I set aside my writing so that I could help find food and shelter for the ambulance columns in the neighborhood.

"In December I was arrested after an enterprising British officer recognized me. They sent me to England under armed guard.

"But that winter the War Office decided that they needed press representation abroad after all, to keep the home front happy and supportive. So they released me and in March 1915, I was among a group of British journalists invited to spend a week touring General Headquarters in St. Omer. At first the request to sample GHQ hospitality pleased my vanity and my curiosity. But I became more skeptical. While we were there, the news about the appalling high losses of life in the fighting for Neuve Chapelle reached us. I was convinced that the military authorities had brought us to St. Omer under false pretenses, deliberately wasting our time and preventing us from closing in on the scene of the fighting.

"Two months later they told me that I was among a handful of journalists chosen to act as official war correspondents. I accepted, wanting to push the boundaries of what it was permissible to report. I was not interested in toeing the governmental line; my aim was to discover the facts about the battles taking place on the Flanders plains and in France. I knew there would be censorship, but I intended to write and record what I saw, if not for immediate publication, then later, when I was beyond the reach of the War Office, as a free man. When the truth could finally be told."

A cry from outside the hut causes Alex to break off and listen.

"A small death, in the midst of many," says Lombardi, with his trademark shrug. At his feet, the dog raises its head, sniffs the empty air, and lays its nose on its paws, indifferent.

Alex returns to the notebook:

"In 1915, the year we began work as official war correspondents, there were six of us, living together in a small château in a village called Tatinghem, close to St. Omer and GHQ.

"Andrew Harris was a short, balding writer with *The Times*. I liked him, although he had an annoying tendency to sit on the fence during arguments. Jack Garland was a freelancer like me. He had wiry hair like a deranged terrier and attacked life in the same way. GHQ saw him as a troublemaker but somehow he managed to hold on to his official position. Ernest Dove regarded war as a great adventure, a polo match gone wild. After the fighting at Langemarck, he wrote in his dispatch that the British dead lay on the battlefield in valiant postures and that it was evident they had been glad to die for their country. I had as little to do with him as possible. I couldn't stand Sebastian Thorpe either. He was a vain, supercilious man with a grating, nasal voice. Unfortunately, his peers in London held him in high esteem. I will never forget how, when we collected our knighthoods, he had the gall to turn to me and say, 'You see, how well thought of we are by the establishment? We played a more spiritual role in the life of the soldier than any army chaplain.'

"I had far greater respect for Julian Quint, who had the courage to do what I had intended: he refused his knighthood. We were all awarded them, all the official war correspondents. But Julian said he wasn't going to be bribed to keep silent about the corruption and incompetence he had witnessed at GHQ during the war. I accepted my knighthood because I knew how proud my father would have been, and how upset if I declined. But there was some conceit in it too, which I tried to assuage by bringing Ted's name into the ceremony.

"I had never despised myself as much as I did that day."

Lombardi interrupts, "You are very hard on yourself."

Alex looks at his host. "Wait awhile before you judge me on that."

"Who is Ted?" asks Lombardi. "Is he the man in the photograph?"

Alex's skin burns. Ignoring the interruption, he moves swiftly on, talking now from memory: "We soon got used to the hostility of the divisional and brigade staffs of the Regulars. Either they thought that we were traitorous spies or that we were puppets of GHQ, given the job not because of our ability to write well, but because of a certain capacity for obedience."

He pauses. "There may have been some truth in this. Don't think there was any honor in our work—there wasn't. It was more a matter of getting something down on paper to keep the people at home informed without breaching GHQ guidelines. Of course, there were things that we couldn't report for fear of giving too much information to the enemy, but the rules of censorship changed from one day to the next. They were so capricious; I used to ask myself whether the people at GHQ really had enough to do with their time. Once I mentioned in a dispatch that it had rained the whole day and the censor said, 'You'll have to leave out that bit about the weather. It might alert the enemy to our position.'" Alex shakes his head impatiently, "The whole thing was ridiculous."

Lombardi looks at him. "You felt trapped?"

"Very much so. If I wanted to stay close to the front—which of course I did—then I had to obey their rules. We had to skate across suffering and tell half-truths to the people at home." Alex frowns. "Julian Quint saw it differently. I remember him saying, 'We can't report everything. Think of the distress it would cause, not only to those waiting at home, but to the men at the front. This war has got to be seen through to its end. Dwelling on horror and loss won't bring it any further along.' Julian said that he didn't want to be responsible for the mothers in England tearing their hair out with worry over their sons, especially when those sons might well return." Alex pauses. "But most of the sons never came back, did they?"

Lombardi makes no comment.

Alex, sipping his beer, goes on, "Mind you, our chief wasn't too bad, Press Officer Colonel Peter St. Aubin. He kept a paternal eye on us. He was the link between us and GHQ in St. Omer. I liked him; he never pretended to be anything other than he was: a wide-shouldered, square-jawed soldier of the old school with an unshakable belief in the British Empire."

Alex smiles and the shadows of his face seem less intense, momentarily. "Actually, he provided us with endless catchphrases. One was 'For the greater good.' Everything the British Empire did was 'for the greater good.' At heart, St. Aubin was a good man, and he didn't care for GHQ's attempts to keep us in the dark either. He once came to me in a fit of pique. When I asked him what the trouble was, he said, 'Would you believe the chief of intelligence has instructed us to waste your time? Those were Charteris's exact words. He wants us to waste your time!' I was furious too. 'To hell with that,' I said. 'This isn't a professional adventure. The whole of Britain is involved, and the nation deserves to know what it is their men are doing out here. They have a right to know.'"

He lets out a small sigh and holds his glass up to Lombardi to refill. "St. Aubin considered resigning from his position. I talked him out of it; he was our champion, to some extent. But there wasn't much any of us could do."

"And what about you?" asks Lombardi, pouring the beer carefully. "Did you ever think about giving it all up?"

Alex looks down at the green rag rug and a thin line appears across his forehead. "No," he says quietly. "At least, not seriously. If I had, of course, *everything* would have been different."

He runs a finger around the rim of his glass. "I should have done." His eyes darken. "I should have done."

6

"IT WAS ST. AUBIN WHO SUGGESTED, ONE MONTH AFTER MY ARRIVAL in Tatinghem, that I should accompany him on a visit to a brigade headquarters near Vermelles. The road to Vermelles, not far from the coal mines and pitheads of Loos, cut through the fields, a flat silver belt. On one side was the old landscape, a pastoral idyll: sheep grazing and larks wheeling in the clear skies. On the other side were the communication trenches, narrow canals through the earth, no more than four feet across, zigzagging their way toward the front line in the sunlit distance. Beyond the fields and the trenches at the end of the belt was the village of Vermelles, a red, jagged ruin.

"The two of us stood on the long, straight road, looking toward that cobalt horizon with its red scar. Or rather, St. Aubin stood; I crouched at the roadside, listening to St. Aubin cursing volubly under his breath. He stood stiffly upright despite the shrapnel that pinged against the road's surface like a volley of stones hitting a tin can.

"And then a shell exploded in the field behind us, hurling the bodies of half a dozen unsuspecting sheep into the air. They fell to the ground in a series of heavy thuds, torn apart by the blast. Blood spotted the road and clumps of wool sailed about the field.

"The colonel swiveled his head around. 'How do you fancy our chances?' he asked. The blue of his irises was intensified by the color of the sky behind his head.

"I got to my feet, shaking off the unpleasant dust that clung to my clothes, the khaki uniform of a regular British officer, with the green band of the Intelligence Services around my right arm. 'Not much, to tell the truth. I don't want to end up like those poor sods,' I said, nodding at the disemboweled animals.

"There was a sound of marching feet. I looked at the road stretching out to Vermelles, shading my eyes with one hand. A small group of suntanned, weary-eyed soldiers approached, as resigned as the livestock to the constant shellfire. The officer in charge was very young, twenty at most; his drawn face was paler than that of his companions. He saluted as they came parallel with us and waggled his thumb at the wrecked village.

"'Jerry knows we're here, sir,' he said, addressing St. Aubin. 'He's hard on our tail with his damn shells. Should I lead my men on or take cover? What's your advice, sir?'

"The young officer looked earnestly at St. Aubin, who chewed his lip awkwardly. I waited, knowing it was no more St. Aubin's place to advise than it was mine, but it was clear that the officer wanted to do the right, if not the best, thing for his troops. Another volley of shells screamed through the summer air. White smoke rose from the fields.

" 'I rather think you should get into that dry ditch there,' said St. Aubin. 'That's what I'd do in your position. Stay there until this bloody barrage is over.'

" 'Thank you, sir. Very good.'

"I watched the young officer guide the group across to the ditch. It was blisteringly hot under the midday sun. Sweat trickled down the men's faces as they scrambled down the bank and arranged themselves against the baked soil ridge. They kept their packs on, and sank lower into the ditch, tilting their heads back and not speaking. They looked exhausted; most closed their eyes and fell asleep.

" 'We can't hang about here, Dyer.' St. Aubin was suddenly impatient. 'They're expecting us at Brigade HQ. We'll just have to push on and put our faith in God.'

" 'If he hasn't been blasted out of heaven,' I muttered, following where St. Aubin led, avoiding the road and sliding down the verge into the field of dead sheep. As we progressed, I became aware that the dark mounds spread throughout the grass were not hillocks, as I had first imagined, but the carcasses of recently killed horses. I wondered at my own foolishness, and tried to quell the nausea that rose from the pit of my stomach as we edged our way through the dead horses. Blood seeped from their warm, bloated bodies and onto the soil. I swallowed, and the bitter taste of bile spread into my mouth, clogging my tongue. I averted my eyes from the steaming wet entrails and looked to the right, where the high walls and outbuildings of a château loomed through the white haze of exploding shells.

"Three figures emerged, yelling, from a furrow below the perimeter wall; they ran along the top of the furrow and sprinted through the gateway. A shell burst behind them in the courtyard, killing them instantly and causing one of the outbuildings to collapse in a cacophony of clattering tiles and splintering wood.

"Determined to quash another wave of sickness, I affected nonchalance, pulling up a long blade of grass and setting it between my lips. 'It looks as though we've chosen an inopportune moment to pay a call,' I said.

"St. Aubin regarded me quizzically. 'You're a cool customer, aren't you, Dyer?' He had no idea how I felt.

" 'If you can keep your head then there's no reason that I shouldn't keep mine—unless the enemy manages to shoot it off my shoulders.'

" 'Quite,' St. Aubin said dryly. He pointed at the château grounds: 'Look at that.'

"We stood watching another group of men pitch for cover in one of the large barns within the courtyard. A black speck soared toward the tall piles of straw bales in front of the barn, whistling. Seconds after the detonation the straw caught light, trapping the men inside. There was nothing we could do to help them; we were too far from them, and the whole place went up in flames.

" 'Poor blighters,' St. Aubin shook his head sadly.

"I walked on, discarding the blade of grass. St. Aubin's progress through the field was slower, and I had to wait for him by the entrance gates. A driveway led through a surprisingly neat lawn to the open doors of the château. As we entered the cool hall, whose ceiling formed a plaster dome of dizzying height, miraculously intact, I saw that the brigade staff was standing together under the banisters of the winding staircase. St. Aubin spoke to them while I glanced around, astonished by how untouched the interior of the château was by the ferocious shelling. I grew dimly aware of St. Aubin's explaining our presence to the brigade major, a tall, spare man with an arrogant tilt to his head.

"I approached the group under the staircase. The brigade major turned to look at me. He was ginger-haired, florid about the jowls, and unimpressed by the appearance of a war correspondent. I returned his gaze with a little aggression of my own.

" 'So. You've come to have a look at us then,' said the brigade major. 'You're braver than your reputation suggests—or did you merely have bad luck in picking this particular day for your sightseeing trip?'

"I knew his remarks were not personally meant as such, but were directed at my profession. It rankled nonetheless, more so because it mirrored my own suspicions and mounting frustrations, but I replied evenly, 'Bad luck, I'm afraid, major. Still, at least I shall have something interesting to write about in dispatches now, eh?'

"The brigade major's eyes darkened. 'I rather thought your superiors provided you with copy. Isn't that so?'

"I kept my gaze steady and allowed myself a small smile. 'All the same, I always appreciate some background to the story.'

"The brigade major turned away and made a remark that I missed to his group, who laughed maliciously. Their surliness didn't trouble me; as the shelling around the château increased, my main concern was in getting out of the building alive. And I could see that as a group they were also afraid, and that any ill feeling on their part might have been a symptom of that.

"The walls of the château trembled under a volley of fire in the courtyard, dislodging a spray of plaster from the high ceiling. I brushed white flecks from my shoulders, catching the eye of a sergeant major standing apart from the crowd. He nodded at me and I crossed the floor, glad to speak to someone less antagonistic.

" 'How long do you think this will go on, sergeant-major?'

" 'Difficult to say, sir.' The flesh around the man's brown eyes was puckered with anxiety. 'It's hard to judge whether they're actively trying to destroy the place or just marking time.'

"I was about to ask another question when the shelling suddenly stopped. An unearthly silence descended, and for the first few moments, all I could hear was the painful high ringing in my ears. Gradually the men began to move about, and I heard the unexpected, sweet song of a lark.

"St. Aubin came over and clapped me on the back. 'There you are, you see. Not as bad as all that was it?'

"He ignored my incredulous expression and strolled toward the open door. 'We'll take a peep at Vermelles—or what's left of it—now, shall we?' "

"We were on the long, flat road again, but this time it was quiet. The ditch where the men had sat with their heavy packs was empty, and the carcasses in the field were already beginning to smell in the heat of the afternoon. A young subaltern from the château had offered to accompany us to the village.

"The ruins of Vermelles rose up to meet us. Our guide had been quiet for much of the time but now he explained, 'This is where the old road ends. It's usually strictly out of bounds during daylight hours.'

" 'Why?' I asked, squinting at the rubble that lay in vast heaps on either side of the disappearing road.

" 'It's an easy target for the enemy; from their positions our troops can be clearly seen marching down it. It's shelled heavily every day.'

" 'Then why in God's name did you bring us this way?' St. Aubin stopped with his hands clasped behind his back, his brow creased in perplexity.

" 'Quickest route, sir.'

"The three of us wandered about the ruins. Every house but one— the last in the main street—had been torched. Charred remains of vegetation and piles of broken bricks littered the roadside. I caught sight of a scrap of red material, which I assumed was part of a flag, fluttering on some brambles. I picked it up, and then realized it had been ripped from the voluminous scarlet trousers worn by French soldiers.

"Abandoned trenches crisscrossed the street. I peered into them; refuse lay piled up in the bottom. I could make out a few envelopes and yellowing papers among the bayonets, water bottles and cartouches: once-precious letters that belonged to the men whose bodies were scattered about Vermelles and the surrounding fields. Our guide showed us the cemetery nearby; we had to push aside a prickling mass of undergrowth and scale crumbling walls to reach it. I knelt beside one of the crosses that had been knocked over into the grass and ran my hand over the wire frame of an immortelle. I stood up and took a step forward, then glanced down as my foot sank into something soft. I recoiled in horror; it was a man's head, the features destroyed, although the back of it still bore traces of dark hair.

"We left the subaltern with a group of gunners who had their battery nearby and walked back in silence along the road and past the château in which we had stood while the shells rained down. Our motor car and patient driver waited at a secluded spot. I made some notes on the journey back. When we reached the house in Tatinghem, St. Aubin switched to another motor car to travel the short distance to GHQ in St. Omer, and I climbed the stairs to my room under the eaves, already late for the hour we had to write up our reports.

"It was ten minutes before I could think of a starting point, and no sooner had I begun than the red-and-black ribbon unspooled from its cradle. I was racing against the clock, as usual, and the setback with the ribbon made me want to throw the unwieldy box out the window. As I opened my bedroom door, I imagined the satisfying crash that would follow its collision with the gravel drive.

"The landing was alive with the noise of typewriters clicking out deceit like ticker tape in the other four rooms along the corridor. I opened the door next to mine without knocking.

" 'Julian, the bloody ribbon's gone again. Can you give me a hand?'

"The dark-haired man sitting hunched over at the desk under the open window pushed back his chair and stood up. He had a muscular, square face and a sympathetic set to his long mouth and brown eyes.

" 'You didn't carry on trying to type, did you?' he asked with mock severity.

" 'Only for a second,' I said.

" 'Let's have a look at it then.'

"I hovered at Julian's side while he deftly reinstated the ribbon to its rightful place.

" 'You need to have a bit of patience with it,' said Julian, stepping back to allow me to sit down. He smiled. 'Treat it like the woman you love.'

"I was leaning forward to examine the temperamental ribbon, expecting it to unravel again. At his words I froze, unable to give the sort of scathing response I knew was anticipated.

"Julian, sensing that he had hit a raw nerve, retreated through the room and said quietly, 'Better get on,' before closing my door."

7

"Rain was a different entity in the trenches. In ordinary circumstances it could be dreary or romantic, depending upon one's state of mind, but on the Western front it was a cruel master, dictating the lives of the men.

"There was a trench near the village of Fricourt, some three miles east of the French town of Albert, which the enemy targeted with their mines. I visited it one afternoon in August 1915. The officer acting as my guide turned to me before we lowered ourselves into the yawning earth gully.

" 'It rained like hell yesterday,' the officer said. He had a quiet manner and gentle eyes. 'It made me think of home. I pictured the women clasping their umbrellas in town and the taxis splashing by the station. It felt so real to me that when the rain fell on my face I looked up, expecting to see the trees of Hyde Park and the moisture trickling through the green leaves. It's funny, isn't it, what all this can do to a person?'

"His words moved me. 'You've made me think of it too, now,' I replied, wishing he hadn't.

" 'Sorry.' The officer slithered down into the trench. 'This quagmire should help take your mind off it.'

"Stinking, tea-colored water poured into the tops of our boots with a sucking sound. Despite being sandbagged, the walls of the communication trench gleamed with damp. Parts of the sides had broken away and red slugs crawled toward the darkest places. Small islands of coagulated yellow muck drifted by, as if the earth had jaundice.

"Ahead of us a group of men waded through the waterlogged trench without trousers, their shirttails sticking to their bare, mud-streaked thighs.

"The officer noticed my surprise and explained: 'It's the best way, when you're working in it.'

"Our boots squelched as we paddled along the weaving length of the trench toward the mine-cratered salient on the right known as the Tambour. When we stopped, I had a clear view of the churned-up ground. The German lines were close, just a few hundred yards away.

"The officer told me, 'The sound of picks has been heard, very near to our sap head. The enemy is almost certain to explode his mine within the next few hours.'

"I could see the results of earlier explosions. The Tambour was a desert in which the decaying bodies of French soldiers lay among the chicory plants sparsely pushing through the earth. The blue of their tattered coats echoed the frail color of the flowers. Out of sight, and to the rear, enemy aircraft dropped bombs, while on both sides of the trenches snipers were at work, the shrill crack of their rifle fire piercing the air. I listened, aware of another sound, like a hammer hitting iron.

"I turned to the officer. 'How close are those machine guns?'

" 'Pretty close. Make sure you keep your head below the parapet from now on. Come on, we'll go a bit farther.'

"I waded after him, determined not to slip into the water. My legs brushed a heavy object aside below the clammy surface. I looked down: a putrefying corpse stared blindly back. I took a breath and grasped hold of the yarrow growing out of the trench walls to aid my path through the suppurating mud.

" 'Watch out, it's very deep here.' The officer climbed onto the firestep.

"We walked at a crouch for several paces on relatively dry soil. At the corner of the next traverse the ground seemed to fall away under the weight of water.

" 'I hope you can swim!'

"A burst of laughter came from a well-made dugout to our left. Two men who had probably been toiling all through the night under their platoon commanders were resting on straw beds. I nodded at them. In almost every dugout we passed, the men within were reading or writing letters. In one a soldier played the mandolin, sitting on his bunk, the sodden puttees wrapped around his legs like drenched bandages. Photographs of sweethearts and families were pinned to wooden boards, curling in the damp atmosphere. The smell of chloride of lime fought for dominance over the moist animal tang of the straw and the reeking water.

"One man sat at the entrance of his burrow, hunched up with his feet on the seat of his chair, and his arms wrapped around his knees. His eyes were blank.

"I paused to speak to him. 'How are you getting on?'

"He replied without looking at me. 'I'm not. How can anyone get on in this?'

" 'Is it possible for you to keep dry?'

"Now he turned his gaze on me. High color stained his face. 'Are you pulling my leg, mate? I've no memory of what it is to be anything other than soaked to the flamin' skin.'

"I felt in my tunic pocket for the small bar of chocolate I had bought in the village. I broke it in two and gave one half to the private.

" 'What's it like here?' I asked, resting one water-logged boot against the side of the trench.

" 'It's hell. Even without the mines it's hell.' The man put his head down on his arms. The blank look had returned to his eyes.

"We walked on to the next dugout, where a younger man beckoned to me. 'Don't mind Will, sir.' The youth spoke softly. 'He's a miserable sod, always grousing. Things aren't that bad. We're alive, aren't we? And we've got Her watching over us.'

"I followed his line of vision. During previous visits to the trenches I had seen the mascots that men hung in the doorways of their dugouts to bring them good luck: a portrait of the king, a photograph of a son or daughter, an embroidered handkerchief given by a mother or lover. But here in Fricourt was something different: an altar built into the muddy side of the trench. In the center was a roughly painted statue of the Virgin, her hands clasped to her breast and her head bowed. She stood on a wooden base, and on either side of Her were puttered-down candle ends and two small vases containing withered sprays of wildflowers.

"I leaned closer to read the tablet in French attached to the trench wall: 'This altar, dedicated to Our Lady of the Trenches, was blessed by the chaplain of the French regiment. The 9th Squadron of the 6th Company recommends its care and preservation to their successors. Please do not touch the fragile statue of trench clay.'

"The officer acting as my guide explained, 'It was left by a French battalion who once held this section. The padre says mass here every morning.'

"We walked on again, coming to the battalion headquarters, where a colonel greeted us from his table. He was playing cards alone when we arrived, but rose to welcome us as profusely as if it were a social call. I sat down in the cramped space and for a moment I thought that the opposite side of the dugout had been covered in red wallpaper. Then I saw that it was swarming with hundreds of strange beetles, waving their long horns.

" 'I see you have company,' I said, pointing to the insects.

"The colonel laughed. 'They don't bother me. For some reason they stick to that side of the quarters and I stick to this side. Did you see any frogs on your walk? No? They must have deserted then. Yesterday there were hundreds of them, swimming past my doorway as if they were part of an Olympic team.' He shook his head. 'I don't mind anything like that. What gets me are the rats. Impudent devils. There are thousands in this part of the line; I've never seen anything like it. On my first day here I went to climb into bed and thought that someone had gotten there first. The straw was writhing, you see. And then, of course, I saw them: rats.' He grimaced. 'There are mice too, but they're not so bad. Actually, I have one who joins me for dinner every night. He's a pally little chap who sits at the end of the table there, waiting for my leftovers. I'll miss him when we move on.'

"We stayed talking to the colonel for a few minutes, then returned along the path. The officer climbed out of the trench to walk with me to my motor car. The clouds were gathering in a metallic-colored mass above the village and the first drops of rain began to fall.

" 'Sorry about your trousers and boots,' said the officer.

" 'Don't give it another thought.' I was embarrassed. When we parted he would be going back into the trenches. My evening would be spent getting dry and warm in the bathroom of the château in Tatinghem.

"'They didn't blow the mine after all,' I said. 'Do you think they still will? Today?'

"The officer glanced back in the direction of the fields. 'No idea. It'll come, though. The shelling business is bad enough, but it's the mines that tear at one's nerve.' He lowered his voice. 'I feel like screaming sometimes. I'm afraid of losing my nerve. I can't sleep at night for thinking that I might.'

"I didn't know how to console him. 'Everyone feels the same,' I said.

"'Do they?' The officer gave me a penetrating look. 'One of my men was frightened of the rats. He used to take potshots at them all the time. Then one night he was sitting in his dugout and he saw two bright eyes glinting at him in the darkness. He felt for his revolver and fired at the rat but the bullet ricocheted from one wall to the other. It caused havoc—six men were wounded. He was court-martialed.' He paused. 'Anyway. There's no sense in getting maudlin about these things, is there?'"

"It was early evening when I arrived back at the little white château in Tatinghem. The raised voices of my colleagues came from the end of the dim landing as I went to my room.

"I opened the door and walked across to the window, throwing the shutters as wide as they would go. I breathed in the warm air and looked out. The garden walls had a soft glow from the descending sun. The white church, with its square tower rising to a point, stood serenely on the other side of the lane.

"I took off my boots and lay down on the bed, stretching until my feet struck the iron frame. I stared at the cream-painted ceiling with its swirling plaster reliefs. I could hear the birds singing in the woods around the village. Their clear, pure voices reminded me of England.

"I tried to think about the men I had met that day, in the water-logged trench far away at Fricourt. Their mud-streaked faces and tattered, graying shirts began to list before my eyes, becoming other faces, clean and staring straight ahead.

"I closed my eyes and was back at school: I saw the choir, row upon row of pupils standing on a terrace in the Buckinghamshire sunlight, a great house behind them. Hundreds of proud parents there to witness their sons' last day at school; my father was among them. The tutors, the headmaster, as stiff as we were, all in their official robes.

"The choir was singing. In the filter of my memory our voices had the innocence and clarity of the birds singing in the woods of France.

Lead, kindly Light, amid the encircling gloom, lead Thou me on,
The night is dark and I am far from home; lead Thou me on . . .

"I saw myself among them, standing next to a youth whose beauty set him apart from the rest of us. We were the best of friends, insepa-rable. He was in the First Eleven and won every scholarly accolade there was to be had. I could hear his voice; he sang fervently, his heart in the words.

I loved the garish day, and in spite of fears,
Pride ruled my will. Remember not past years . . .

"He could have been anything he wanted. To our tutors he spoke about a career in politics. Privately, to me, he expressed a far more prosaic wish: he wanted a wife and a family. He had grown up with a guardian, dutiful and kind but unloving. At school he was the object of every boy's blurred lust. The affairs he had with other pupils were not sexually fulfilling; it was love he went in search of.

So long Thy power hath blessed me, sure it still will lead me on.
Over moor and fen, over crag and torrent, 'til the night is gone . . .

"He had never loved a woman before his wife. After she agreed to marry him, he wrote to me. He was euphoric, telling me how uselessly his hands had been occupied in the past, holding a pen, a cricket bat, sheaves of paper, a glass of whisky or a shirt. Now they had a purpose: to hold her, to love her.

"I watched the hours moving across the ceiling of my bedroom in France and I was consumed by jealousy. My love was a terrible, twisted thing because the woman I wanted to spend my life with was denied to me.

And with the morn those angel faces smile, which I
Have loved long since, and lost awhile."

8

"At the beginning of September I noticed an escalation in traffic on the roads around Loos. Ambulance trains began to converge in the area. I thought about Clare, wondering where she was, whether she was working at the hospital in Rouen, where she was based as a nurse, or if, as often happened during the major battles, she had been posted to work on one of the hospital trains or at a field dressing station. I prayed that she was safe, wherever she was, for the delayed offensive was imminent: large quantities of shells were unloaded from the railheads and stacked in the dumps, the roads throbbed under the winding convoys of gun limbers, lorries, and motor wagons, and the skies were thick with German balloons searching the region.

"During our briefing on September twenty-first, St. Aubin told us that the preliminary bombardment had begun. When lots had been drawn to decide who should cover which parts of the sectioned-up area, I climbed into a car with St. Aubin and another officer from GHQ, Robert Farrar.

"I addressed my questions to St. Aubin; Farrar was a silent, morose-faced individual with thinning hair plastered across the pale dome of his skull.

" 'How long will the bombardment last?' I asked.

" 'Four days,' replied St. Aubin. 'That should be enough to ensure that the enemy is pulverized.'

" 'And the attack itself?'

" 'Will be eastward. The artillery bombardment is on a twenty-mile front between Arras and La Bassée, leaving a four-thousand-yard strip facing Líeven and Lens. The cavalry are to take the area of Ath and Mons.'

" 'That's . . . what . . . fifty miles north?'

" 'Correct. Subsidiary attacks will be launched north of the La Bassée canal and near Ypres. Should be a walkover.'

" 'Any idea of the numbers involved?'

" 'Seventy-five thousand British infantry in the initial attack. I can't tell you any more than that.'

" 'At Neuve Chapelle lives were lost under concentrated fire when troops attacked on a narrow front. How do you plan to avoid that?'

" 'The attack will be as wide as feasible. I told you, it's a twenty-mile front. It's impossible to anticipate the outcome —'

" 'The supporting artillery must be colossal. There have been questions raised in the past about whether we're producing the amount of shells necessary to guarantee a successful attack. Have we got it right this time?'

" 'It is never possible to guarantee a successful attack, but we're confident that this offensive will prove a major breakthrough. The so-called shell crisis was little more than the product of a warped journalist's mind, and I can assure you that the levels of artillery for the attack are more than sufficient.' St. Aubin cleared his throat. 'In addition, we'll be using heavy smoke barrages to obscure the front.' He turned away, indicating that he had no wish to be drawn further.

"Julian Quint had seen a document that mentioned an 'accessory' to be used in the coming battle, and I suspected that it referred to poison gas, a weapon so far used by the Germans alone. I didn't expect to discover the truth before the event, but I had intended to question St. Aubin on the issue. His closed expression told me it was useless to try.

"We watched the preliminary bombardment from a slag heap outside Nouex-les-Mines. Although I was familiar with the area, each time I returned to it I was struck anew by the ugliness of the place. The coal mines expelled vast pyramids of refuse on the plains below the outlying ridges of Vimy and Notre Dame de Lorette. Behind the desolate villages were the trenches stretching to Vermelles, and farther north at Hulluch, Haisnes, and La Bassée were the German strongholds. Dotted about inside this area were the slag heaps, the pitheads, the hanging coal trolleys, and the gantries, all standing silent on that black plain, their steel structures twisted and broken by gunfire.

"We stood with our boots entrenched in the dark ground of the slag heap, buffeted by the cold wind, its strength heightened by the absence of natural obstacle. There was a relentless drizzle and the smoke of gunfire. It was impossible to see beyond the dense fog that, from time to time, was lit by bright flashes as shells burst on the battlefield.

" 'It's rather dull, isn't it?' St. Aubin looked from me to the inscrutable Farrar. 'Can't see a thing. Still, it sounds ferocious—I can't imagine the enemy will survive this.'

"For once Farrar spoke. 'I think you might be wrong there,' he said. 'The Germans are like rats: they go to ground. Ten to one they're sitting in their trenches with their feet up.' He stared at the swirling fog. 'They'll come through it all right.'

"Another shell exploded, its blinding whiteness splitting the black cloud in two. The guns pounded and the ground beneath our feet quivered. My eardrums were on the point of bursting.

"Later that day we walked up to the Loos redoubt, where the thunder of the guns was even greater. It was one of a pair of redoubts built by the Germans in their front trench system, and spanned a rutted road from Vermelles across the valley to Loos. I made a few notes on the area and sketched the soaring twin pylons linked by steel girders and gantries that the British soldiers called Tower Bridge. From there we walked back to the motor car, my ears still throbbing with the scream of the shells and the retort of the guns.

"On the journey back to Tatinghem, I tried to clear the noise from my head by sticking my fingers in my ears and wriggling my fingertips, but it was impossible to alleviate the constant humming. I gave up, and rested my head against the cold glass of the window."

"Day after day I stood on the edge of the fighting and saw nothing at all. My dispatches were compiled from GHQ reports, all of them slanted in our favor.

"The most revealing moment came toward the end of the offensive, when I interviewed a group of German prisoners.

"They sat together in a thousand-strong huddle along one side of a partially flooded field in Chocques. It had rained heavily again the night before, but now a wide blue ribbon hung above the trees. I stood at the entrance to the field listening to Stephen Masefield, the officer in charge of the German escort, explaining how the prisoners had been captured.

"Masefield, a short, squat man with closely cropped black hair, admitted that the seizure of the haggard Prussians and Slavs in their thick gray coats had been surprisingly simple.

" 'There was a terrible scene during the fighting on the southern outskirts of Loos in the old cemetery there. One man said it was Armageddon. The Londoners found a number of German machine-gun nests built into the vaults. They set about bayoneting as many of the enemy as they could. While the killing went on, shells were falling about the place, blowing the corpses out of their coffins. Can you imagine it: men being massacred in a hail of old corpses? It makes you wonder, doesn't it, how much worse it can get if it has already come to this?'

"He paused for reflection, then concluded his account: 'The Londoners went down into the village where they could see nothing at first because of the smog caused by explosions. Then a crowd of civilians, mainly women and children who had been hiding in the cellars, came out screaming. Among them were a group of Germans. Well, the Londoners took the enemy along to join others who had chosen rather to surrender.' He shook his head. 'They're horribly ashamed of themselves—capitulation is tantamount to blasphemy in the German vocabulary, or so it would seem. They're also hungry. Some haven't eaten for almost five days, cut off from their supplies by our guns. They'll get their rations shortly. Speak to them by all means. I hope your German is better than mine.'

"We looked at the prisoners. They sat slumped against one another, their heads sunken into their chests, their filthy, sodden coats pulled up to their cheekbones to shield them from the cold. They slept fitfully, or stared ahead with empty, desolate eyes. A few paced up and down in the wet earth like caged animals both longing for and fearful of freedom. A German medical orderly went among those who were dying, administering shots of morphine to lessen their pain.

" 'Poor devils,' said Masefield softly. 'Most have seen their comrades die slow, brutal deaths and, on top of everything, they've lost their pensions by surrendering.'

"I felt someone clutch my hand and looked down at a man close to death. The collar of his coat crawled with lice and his beard was full of gray movement. 'I need a doctor,' he pleaded in German. 'Get me to a doctor, for God's sake.'

"I glanced at Masefield, hovering behind. 'Can we get him a doctor?'

" 'Not right now. The orderly will inject him with morphine if necessary.'

" 'He needs something. Look at his mouth—it's almost blue. This man is dying of thirst if nothing else.'

"Masefield pursed his lips doubtfully. 'There's water over there . . . '

"I approached one of the fresh-faced English guards. 'Can you give me some water? There's a man who will die if he doesn't get something down his throat soon.'

"The guard fetched a water jar and handed it to me reluctantly. I gave the man half of it, then offered the rest to the man beside him, whose head was wrapped in a bloody, frayed bandage. He lifted his dull eyes and spoke in heavily accented English.

" 'I don't want it.'

"I hesitated, assuming that the refusal was due to the difference in our nationalities. The man pointed to another comrade lying curled up in a fetal position farther down the line.

" 'He needs it more than I do,' he said quietly."

"Masefield asked another officer to let the prisoners know it was their turn for rations and water at a nearby dump. Despite their shambolic, wretched appearance, even the sickest prisoners pulled themselves to their feet at the shout of *'Achtung.'* I half-expected their dead comrades to rise from the chalky mud of the surrounding fields to join them, so ingrained was their habit of discipline.

"The prospect of easing their desperate hunger animated the majority and when a few noncommissioned officers distributed rations, they gnawed at the hunks of bread in a rage that made me ashamed to witness their condition.

"Masefield said, 'I don't hate them. Somewhere our men are suffering the same humiliation. Did we honestly once speak of the glory of war?'

"A group of German artillery officers stood together at the back of the rows of prisoners, smoking and mocking their captors. I was curious about their arrogance, and the way they antagonized the English guards, who kept their bayonets fixed.

"I asked one of the German officers if they had been the recipients of a British gas attack. The man, tall and elegant despite the state of his clothing, laughed. 'A little. It was not very effective, I'm afraid to say. But it smelled rather nice.'

"One of the other officers joined in. 'What is it about you English? You try to copy our weapons and methods, but you never quite manage it, do you?'

"The officers laughed. One offered me a cigarette, which I declined. The officer shrugged and lit the cigarette himself. I left them to their jeering observations. They shouted, *'Guten Tag'* after me, capturing perfectly my inferior attempt at a German accent.

"On my journey through the field I saw another German officer standing apart from the rest and went up to him. He told me how he had been buried alive in his dugout but had managed to claw his way back to life only to be captured by two middle-aged Highlanders who treated him with a courtesy and respect that took him by surprise.

" 'The British are stupid,' he said in a matter-of-fact way. 'Those pylons—you know them, the high, twin towers by Loos?—provided us with an excellent observation post for the entire front. We saw all your battle preparations. Then you tried using gas and what happened? You poisoned your own men. The ones who tried to reach us were gunned down like game birds at a shooting party. Do you know what we call this place? "Leichenfeld von Loos." Do you know what that means?'

· " 'Field of corpses.'

" 'Yes.' He wiped a hand across his forehead; the air was damp with the promise of more rain. 'But you have courage and ... what is the word? ... Tenacity. That is a good word for the British soldier. Tommy, huh? Tenacious Tommies. But we are also like that. And we are ready to fight another winter of campaigns if we must. Two, if necessary.'

"I looked at him in surprise. 'Do you think it will last that long? I don't. It's madness to think otherwise.'

"The German officer gave me a sympathetic smile. 'You are the mad one, my friend. Men can endure a great deal—and in the end, it is this ability to withstand so much that proves our undoing.'

" 'I don't believe that. Both sides will revolt against their leaders if the killing doesn't end soon.'

"The German officer shook his head. 'Wrong. The generals keep pushing us because they can, we keep striving to gain just a little more land at a time, and in the meantime no one has noticed that the numbers of dead keep increasing while the amount of new recruits gets smaller. It is like a river running dry, and all because we are creatures of stamina, of fortitude.' He looked at me intently. 'It is not the British and the Germans and the French who are enemies; it is ourselves.'

"We stared at each other in silence, then I shook hands with him and wished him luck."

In the Villa Via Sacre, Lombardi puts out a hand and touches Alex lightly on the shoulder, feeling the tension in him.

"What are you doing?" he asks gently. "Why are you telling me about the work you despised, instead of the woman you fell in love with?"

Alex stares down at Lombardi's long, thin fingers. "I'm sorry," he says, in a low voice. "Evasion is an art I learned to perfect during the war."

Lombardi removes his hand, frowning. He pushes Alex's glass toward him, indicating that he should drink the last of his beer. "Are you afraid I will judge you?"

Alex presses his palms against his temples, his elbows resting on the table. "No," he says. "It's not that." He turns to Lombardi with a rueful, diffident smile. "I'm afraid of diving back into the pool of remembrance. I find it easier to circle than to clamber straight in."

Lombardi smiles back at him, the candlelight making his unusual appearance seem more otherworldly than ever. "Then go in gradually. I will catch you if you fall."

V

FAITH LIKE A JACKAL

Chocques, October 10, 1915

$\mathcal{A}$T NIGHT THERE WERE NO LIGHTS ON BOARD THE HOSPITAL TRAINS. The dark locomotives would arrive at base in the morning with their windows blown in and their roofs collapsed, as if they had traveled through the eye of a hurricane. Clare had to clamber along the footboards to get from one ward carriage to the next, the train jolting and jerking beneath her, the earth showing occasionally through the gaps below.

And it was cold, "colder than a polar bear's belly" as Sister Quint phrased it, with driving winds and bucketing rains that seeped in through every gap, every door and window frame. The surrounding countryside was flat and relentlessly dismal, dominated by conical charcoal slag heaps and mines. Tiny pit locomotives and tub trains crawled through the shattered, desolate landscape of north Picardy like half-dead locusts and shrieked with ear-splitting magnitude amid the boom and echo of the bombardment.

The carriages of the hospital train were divided up into sections: medical stores, sleeping quarters, a kitchen, a laboratory, a cramped operating theater, and wards filled to capacity with casualties. The aim was to transport the mutilated men to Boulogne, where they could be loaded straight onto ships bound for England, but more often than not the soldiers were simply admitted to any hospital that could accommodate *blessés.*

During her time on the train, Clare had grown accustomed to the horror of watching men drown as the gas rose in their lungs, cutting their oxygen supply as cleanly as a knife. When gassed soldiers came onto the train their hair and clothing exuded the smell of poison, reeking of it. She undressed them, frustrated by her inability to ease their agony, and worked with painstaking care to avoid bursting the giant water blisters that covered every inch of their discolored skin. Those who could talk always wanted to know if they would remain blind. She lied and told them, *No, of course not, your sight will return as good as it was before,* while bathing their oozing, inflamed eyelids with sodium bicarbonate. Their mouths leaked blood and green slime when they tried to talk to her and their rasping for air filled her ears with a grinding whine. Their sickness was partially hers; after working on the gassed wards she found it difficult to breathe, her eyes burned and ran, and when she swallowed her throat chafed excruciatingly, as if it had been scoured with broken glass.

Sometimes she felt as if her soul had gone into the trenches with them.

The Indian troops suffered most of all. They found France's sinking temperatures intolerable, succumbed to rheumatism, and lay crippled in their beds while she moved among them. The members of a lower caste kept to the drafty corridors of the train, where they wept unceasingly and cried out in Hindustani; quiet, unintelligible mutterings that Clare found queerly hypnotic. One man had a head wound, and as the medical officer removed his turban, Clare watched in astonishment as the patient's hair unwound like a length of thick rope, beautiful and rich as a magpie's blue-black wing.

Working on the hospital trains caused her to understand at last the true purpose of the identity disks all Queen Alexandra's Imperial Military Nursing Service nurses were required to wear. They were no different from the ones worn by the soldiers and their purpose was the same: to put a name and religion to the dead body of the wearer.

Hers had only her name scratched upon it: *Clare Eden.* No religion.

"Faith, like a jackal, feeds among the tombs, and even from these dead doubts she gathers her most vital hope." Clare thought of this sometimes

when she felt the identity disk slide against her skin. To her, faith meant the negation of reason and she found reason so much easier to believe in than God. Religion was something she could never grasp; the mere thought of it enraged her in her rare moments of weakness.

Where was God when her father died during her thirteenth year?

Where was God when her father's replacement in her mother's affections had rattled her bedroom door at night with rape on his mind?

Where was God when the German aircraft cut across the starless sky emptying its fire along the length of the scurrying train?

Inside the motionless carriage the body of a young soldier of the Black Watch lay on a stretcher, inert and rigid as a corpse. Clare leaned over him, pulling gauze from his wound, millimeter by dripping millimeter. His genitals had been blown off, leaving him with a gaping hole between his narrow hips. She cleaned the suppurating cavity as gently as she was able and replaced the silver tube that acted as a catheter from the hollow flesh into his bladder. He cried silently as she worked, biting down on his knuckles and squeezing his eyes tightly shut. Her actions were deft and infinitely careful. As she filled the wound with unpolluted gauze, she wondered at his age; instinct told her he had lied to get into the army.

She stood up straight and touched his cheek. "It's done, Frankie."

The boy removed his knuckles from his mouth and opened his eyes. "I didn't swear, did I, Sister?"

She shook her head. "No, but it wouldn't have mattered to me if you had. I feel like swearing when I have to put you through this."

He looked at her, his eyes brimming pain. "Thank you, Sister."

Clare crouched down until her face was level with his. "Why do you thank me, Frankie?" she asked softly. "I see you recoil when I come into the carriage and then afterward you're grateful."

"Will I live?"

"Yes."

"That's why I'm grateful to you."

"Even . . . ?"

"Even though I never thought I would end up as a eunuch, yes."

She turned to the dressing trolley and searched for the small bottle with the yellow label. She poured some of the liquid into a cup and handed it to him.

"Drink this, Frankie. It will make you feel better." His name was Frank Stephens; he had asked her to call him Frankie, as only his mother and sister did.

He drank it and handed it back to her, pulling a face. "I've never tasted whisky before."

She smiled. "Nor rum, then." She returned the bottle to the trolley.

He was looking at her, his face glowing with the unexpected warmth of the drink. "I should have died, shouldn't I, Sister? When this happened?"

"Possibly, but I'm very glad you didn't. And your family will be too."

He gave her his sweet smile and she touched his hand where it rested on the stretcher. He closed his eyes and mumbled incoherently; he was already asleep. Clare pulled the sheet up to his chin and gazed at the sheen on his smooth forehead under the long dark fringe, the delicate whorls of his small, shell-like ears, and the tender set of his young mouth. She was thankful that the old goods vans used by the medical staff the year before, at Le Cateau, were no longer in service. He could at least get some rest while they traveled at the regulation twelve miles an hour; the old goods vans had had no suspension to speak of and an appallingly ineffective brake system.

She saw him flinch in his sleep and a knot of pity rose in her throat. She fought the impulse to lay her cool hand on his flushed cheek; instead she turned away and pulled up the window blind, releasing the stench of the pus-drenched gauze onto the open field.

Some of the walking wounded were so exhausted that they fell asleep standing or talking as they lined up outside the train in the incessant rainfall. Clare processed them as rapidly and fluently as if they were commodities on a factory floor: shearing through uniforms to expose wounds, ripping off the waterproof wrapper of the field dressing each man carried in his pocket, nipping the ampoule to release iodine over the gauze pad, then binding it to the injury until they could be seen by a medical officer. The worst cases were given morphine while they waited; the rest had to depend on their inner stoicism.

After dusk, the rain eased and the clouds dispersed, revealing an early moon that suffused the field and its inhabitants in an eerie, mercurial light. At six o'clock, Clare returned to the train to tend to her last patient for the day.

Sister Quint briefed her on his condition before she climbed into the ward carriage. "He's in too much pain to sleep—give him morphine if you think he needs it. I don't think he'll last the night, to be perfectly honest."

Sister Quint paused, running a hand across her forehead. She was smaller than Clare, but sturdy, with quick, darting eyes that seemed to mirror her hands in never remaining still. Her widow's peak of chestnut hair edged out from under her cap. "The gunshot wound to his pelvis hasn't emasculated him, not like poor Stephens, but the bullet entered through his right buttock and tore into his left on its path through his body. We've managed to stem the hemorrhaging of the lower bowel, but it'll almost certainly flare up again. The dressing will need changing." She patted Clare's arm. "Good luck."

As she entered the carriage, Clare was assailed with an overwhelming sense of foreboding. The lamp, which would soon have to be turned down, immersed the narrow space in an oily, greenish light that left the corners in pitch-blackness; it was like entering a disused tunnel. The smell of wounds hit her more strongly than ever before and for the first time she feared that she might gag from the odor. The light was enough to work by, and yet she felt as if she were groping her way forward, half-blind, like the men who caught a whiff of poison gas before pulling on their protective hoods. All the patients, including Frankie, were sleeping. She saw their hunched, huddled shapes below the regulation gray blankets; most instinctively found a position that afforded the best chance of rest.

The man who had been brought in earlier, while she worked in another ward carriage, lay on his stomach, but with his fists under his chest to keep as much of his body away from the stretcher as possible. She approached him silently, unsure if he had managed to fall asleep or not. As she came into his line of vision, he turned his head awkwardly and looked up at her from under heavy, swollen eyelids.

Clare reeled backward in shock.

She grasped one of the leather straps hanging down from the low roof and clung to it, lifting her other hand to hold the loop more firmly, and steadied the violent trembling of her body by crossing her arm over her chest and pressing it against herself.

The man spoke in short, staccato gasps. "Clare . . . I wondered . . . if I would see you . . . I think I'm dying . . . Clare . . ."

She stared in revulsion at her stepfather's corpulent face. Sweat made his florid skin glisten as it had during the nights he had forced himself upon her and his crown shone under the thin, graying strands of hair, just as she remembered it. Her grip on the leather strap tightened until her fingers felt numb.

To be confronted with him now was as if all those years between had never happened; she was thirteen again and locked in his terrible embrace.

Outside the train the shelling started up again. From the other end of the ward carriage she heard Frankie cry out in his sleep. The sound brought Clare immediately to her senses; she let go of the leather strap and turned slowly to the small space where the dressings trolley was kept. Her stepfather's disjointed words seemed suspended in the putrid, still air of the carriage. She pulled on her gloves, shaking uncontrollably from the shock, and began removing the old dressing from his right buttock. She gritted and ground her teeth as she worked, her jaw moving compulsively, and her head swung slightly from side to side in perpetual disbelief.

"Clare . . . I thought of you so many times since you left . . . you've never written us a line . . . I'm not blaming you . . ."

"What happened to you?" Clare's voice sounded shrill and harsh in her own ears.

"What . . . ?"

"How did you get the injury?" She doused a large pad of lint in Eusol and applied it to his concave buttock, waiting for it to absorb the pus, blood, and feces before throwing it away and beginning again.

He gasped. "We were in the middle of a coalfield . . . couldn't see the enemy's line . . . too much fog . . . bit of a breeze, skittish, like a young mare . . . we had our gas helmets on . . . Clare, I want to ask you—"

"Tell me about the battle," she said fiercely, pushing another pad of wet lint into his wound.

He forced himself to think. "The light . . . it was dawn . . . smoke curling along our line . . . I watched it . . . like a wall . . . couldn't see a thing through it."

He moaned as Clare pressed the lint around the edges of his wound.

"Was it gas?" Clare said.

"No." He sucked in the saliva that had gathered around his lips. "Smoke bombs and shells . . . then the smoke went all patchy and seemed to thin out . . . I saw the parapet . . . could smell violets—that was the gas . . . no one moved . . . then I heard bagpipes . . ."

Clare held a clean pad in midair. "Bagpipes?"

"Aye, bagpipes . . . I'm from Glasgow, remember? I know bagpipes when I hear them . . . it was our piper—he tore off his gas mask and played his heart out, to bring us to our senses . . . We hadn't gone over."

"Keep talking."

Clare realized that she wasn't shaking anymore; she was able to pour the Eusol on the pads without spilling it.

"I ran toward the wire," he rasped. "Looking for a way in . . . Our line was being machine-gunned . . . There were only a couple of laddies on either side of me . . . we were screaming, 'The wire hasn't been cut! The wire hasn't been cut!' . . . I fell into a hole . . . lost track of time . . . both ankles gone . . . I couldn't get out . . . someone found me and carried me back . . . I don't know who it was, but he was shot when he reached our trench . . . he fell across me, knocking me flat . . . I tried to lift him off, but I didn't have the strength . . ." He began to weep. "They were all dead, my friends were dead . . . I thought of those bagpipes, playing us out . . . I was glad they'd heard them . . . like home . . ."

"Lean forward for me," Clare said, hoarsely. *Home,* she thought, what about what you did to me in my home? The pad came away from the wound with barely any discharge. She applied another and covered it with a material that kept the bed dry and the dressing moist, then secured it with strapping.

He was quiet, his breathing ragged.

"Your wound is dressed," she said, tersely. "Are you able to sleep?"

"No . . . not now I've seen you . . . they said I could have morphine . . . I'll be dead before sunrise, won't I?"

"Perhaps."

She took out the small vial of morphine.

He began to weep again, pressing his face into the bed. "I'm sorry about . . . what I did . . . I was another person then . . . but I don't want to die with it on my conscience . . ." He lifted his head, and she saw that his eyes were bloodshot through the tears. "I want you to forgive me . . . if I can just have that . . . It would make it easier for me, when I go . . ." He held his breath as she gave him the morphine injection.

"Would it?" she asked quietly.

His eyes seemed to slip back underneath his lids until only the white pigment was visible. "Can I have more?"

"Of this?" She held up the syringe. "No. You've had exactly the amount allowed."

"But if I'm going to die . . ."

"You might not." She set everything back in its place on the trolley and removed her gloves.

"Clare, please say that you forgive me . . . I'm begging you." He wiped his mouth back and forth on the blanket. He was in agony, despite the morphine. "If you can't forgive me then . . ." He took a deep, painful breath. "Will you at least stay with me until I die . . . Sister?"

She looked at him coldly. "I think we both know that's impossible, don't you?"

Grasping the sheet, she laid it over him until it covered his shoulders, then pushed her foot against the brake of the trolley, lifting it onto its back wheels and maneuvering it into position. She turned down the lamp and began to walk away, down the darkened aisle.

As she passed him, he reached out his hand to her and she threw it off, hearing the death rattle rise from his chest and feeling her own body consumed by a powerful shudder.

At the end of the carriage, she stopped and laid her hand on the door frame, to give herself strength. Without looking around, she said in a voice as clear and final as the shells exploding across the landscape, "I don't forgive you. And I hope you go straight to hell."

She was beside Frankie's bed. She ran a hand over his soft, straight hair before opening the ward carriage door. As she stepped out into the cold blackness, she heard her name being called by a voice that grew fainter and fainter until it ebbed away to nothing. She closed the carriage door.

There was no more sound, only the wind as it tore around the rocking, creaking train.

VI

The Tarnished Mirror of the World

London, Summer 1914 and Winter 1915

10

IN THE LITTLE HUT ON THE FLANDERS PLAINS, ALEX REACHES FOR HIS notebook.

After telling Lombardi about his experiences at Loos, he had replaced it on the table. Now, in the fanning light of the hurricane lamp, he slowly unwinds the ties that bind it, and takes out the photograph that lies tucked inside the thick pages.

"The man in the photograph is Edward Eden. Ted, as I knew him. We met at prep school, when we were eight years old. We arrived on the same day and were put in the same house in the same room. From that moment on, we became inseparable."

He pauses, looking down at the floor. "Of all the memories I have of him, the most vivid—for whatever reason—is of a school trip to Westminster Abbey in 1899. How long ago that seems now. We were not quite fourteen . . ."

The Villa Via Sacra diminishes before Alex's eyes and in his mind he sees them: two adolescent boys dressed in the formal scarlet and black uniform of their school, standing side by side, gazing up at Henry V's tomb in the cool shadows of the abbey arches. Both were tall and lean, with the awkward, too-long limbs of youth.

"It doesn't seem right, does it?" said the blond-haired boy, frowning. "Sticking him up there, behind that clapped-out chair. I know it's the Coronation Chair, but you'd think they could have found him a better spot."

His friend, the taller of the two and dark-haired, shook his head in disgust. "Old Batty's had us rehearsing our parts in the play for so long that I was quite looking forward to seeing this. I expected something more than a rotten wooden block to stow his remains though." He ran a hand through his thick hair. "I suppose his surroundings make up for it a bit."

His companion nodded thoughtfully. The tomb lay at the eastern end of the Confessor's Chapel. The low, arched ceiling above the oak vault was ornate, and the chantry itself, lit softly and hushed, was decorated with intricate carvings of kings and saints. His gaze fell back to the tomb. "What does it say in the guidebook?" he asked.

Alex felt in the pocket of his coat and pulled out a small, crumpled leaflet. Quietly, he read: "'Henry the Fifth, who died of dysentery in France, was regarded as a saint in his day. After his death at Vincennes, his body was returned to England and a great procession accompanied the cortege from Dover to St. Paul's Cathedral . . .' blah-blah. 'The coffin was brought to the abbey on November 7, 1422, for burial. At his magnificent funeral four horses drew the chariot into the nave as far as the choir screen.' Gosh, imagine that—horses in the Abbey. . . . 'Henry had directed that a chantry chapel should be raised over his body in the Confessor's Chapel. His tomb was completed around 1431. Above him is the Altar of the Annunciation. His shield, helmet, and the saddle used in the 1415 battle of Agincourt are displayed on the wooden beam above the chantry.'"

Ted squinted upward. "I can't see them."

"They're up there somewhere."

"I still can't—" Ted broke off, and pointed at the beam, suddenly animated. "There they are. Look, you can even see the dent in his helmet where he took a blow to the head."

The dimpled steel helmet glinted in the muted light. A faint flush crept up Ted's neck; he closed his eyes and imagined the weary English Army following the flooded river Somme from the French coast and heading north past St. Pol to the battlefield of Agincourt. He heard hooves pounding through a clinging mist, and the cries of wounded men as they fell, barbed with arrows, to the muddied earth.

Alex watched him and grinned; he was used to Ted's flights of fancy. He cleared his throat and threw out his arms, declaiming in a surprisingly deep voice: " 'Once more unto the breach, dear friends, once more, / Or close up the wall with our English dead! / In peace there's nothing so becomes a man, / As modest stillness and humility . . .' Rats, I forget the rest."

Ted took up the gauntlet Alex had thrown down, reciting in perfect pitch: " 'But when the blast of war blows in our ears, Then imitate the action of the tiger; Stiffen the sinews, summon up the blood, disguise fair nature with hard-favored rage; Then lend the eye a terrible aspect.' "

Alex's grin widened. "Superb. I'm glad I'm only your understudy."

Ted looked again at the unadorned wooden tomb. "I wonder what it was really like at Agincourt? Batty says that the French dead lay piled higher than a man."

"A small man, or a very tall one?"

Ted ignored the remark. "What do you think he looks like now?"

"Who? Good King Henry?" Alex put his head on one side, considering. "Shouldn't think there'd be much left of him. Remember that story Batty told us, about how they once dug up a king buried here and found his face had gone chocolate brown and he was shriveled like a prune, covered in black dust? Apparently the whole place reeked of spices for months."

"Why spices?"

Alex shrugged. "I don't know. To preserve the body perhaps?" He gave a heartfelt sigh. "I've had enough of Henry. Come on, I want to see that door—the one with the skin on."

"You're disgusting, Alex." Ted shook his head. "As if being flayed wasn't enough—"

"The thief *did* try to rob the abbey, don't forget."

"Even so."

They wandered through the chill arcades of the great church, pausing often to allow Ted the opportunity to decipher the inscriptions on the marble tombs and memorials, and to inspect the baleful effigies. Alex grew restive; he appreciated the suits of armor but had no interest in the recumbent figures on the tombs, or in walking at a snail's pace down the empty cloisters and galleries that captivated Ted so thoroughly. He glanced at his friend, amused. Ted had a thing about the abbey: its chalk-dust smell, the luminaries buried within its walls, the echo of feet upon the worn flagstones, and the air of romantic decay. At the beginning of the nave, Ted stopped and stared up at the ceiling, a thousand feet above their heads.

"I love this place," he said fervently. "All England's history is here."

Alex laughed. "You're turning into old Batty."

Ted shook his head. "No, I'm not," he said defensively. "All the people buried here have died for their country, one way or another."

Alex grimaced and raised his eyes to the soaring ceiling. "Well I'd rather live, if it's all the same to you."

Ted's blue eyes were wide with sincerity. "I think it's rather fine to die for one's country, for honor."

"Rubbish," snorted Alex, scuffing his shoes against an iron grille. "My father says too many people get honor confused with pride."

"What does that mean?"

Alex frowned. "I don't know, but I have a feeling he's right."

"You can mock, but who is to say that you won't end up here, one day?"

Alex turned to Ted, incredulous. "*Me?* What on earth could I do to warrant being buried here?"

Ted answered, "You want to be a famous writer. If you make it, you might be given a spot in Poet's Corner, over there."

Alex threw his head back in laughter. "You're completely mad."

Ted allowed himself to smile. "You could end up next to Shakespeare's monument . . ." He held out his arms, tucked his chin into his chest, and in sonorous tones began: " 'Can this cockpit hold; / The vasty fields of France . . . '"

Alex gave him a gentle punch in the ribs. "Shut up, Ted."

Their form master, Mr. Battern, gesticulated to them from the main doors where he was gathering together the whole class. The troop of immaculately uniformed boys set off down the long stretch of the nave, the pillars rising on either side of them like bare, branchless trees.

Before they reached their group, Ted put his arm around Alex's shoulders. "Listen, whether you're buried among kings or not, I'll always be your friend. How does Shakespeare put it? 'Would I were with him, wheresome'er he is, either in heaven or in hell.' "

"Stop it."

Alex grabbed Ted and wrestled him to the floor, where they fought until Mr. Battern descended upon them with a swanlike hiss to warn them to remember where they were.

The two boys looked at each other, their eyes bright with suppressed laughter, before joining their irate tutor and classmates. The vast doors of the abbey's north porch were open, and the sunset flooded in where they stood, a group of eager schoolboys, at the end of the long, golden nave where the flagstones glowed, faintly red.

Lombardi holds the photograph closer to the light. Kemmel protests with a brief whine at his shift in position. Lombardi tilts the photograph; the man's fine bone structure is accentuated by the shadows of the cedar tree and an unseen breeze ruffles his blond hair.

"He's very striking," Lombardi admits, handing the photograph to Alex. "There's something almost seraphic about him."

"Not just his looks," Alex responds emphatically, slipping the photograph inside the leather notebook, "but his personality too. At school, I used to be very protective of him—he had a defenselessness to him then. The war . . . changed everything."

"For all of us," says Lombardi, pouring more beer into their glasses.

"Yes, but—" Alex breaks off and picks up the notebook, gripping it with both hands. Anguish twists his mouth and causes the muscles in his jaw to spasm. " 'And now we see through a glass darkly.' It was like that for us. We seemed to have passed through something, gone beyond the people we once were. Everything was warped and bubbled and blistered—nothing made sense. I thought I would go mad. I think perhaps I did, toward the end."

He drops the notebook onto the table, where it lands with a thud, falling open where he has held the pages back to read. "I must have done, otherwise I couldn't have acted the way I did."

Lombardi passes him the refilled glass. "Tell me," he says softly. "Tell me."

11

"LONDON IN THE SUMMER OF 1914: THE FIRST NOTES OF THE jazz age are being cranked out of box gramophones in a city suffused in the gilt light of a perfect hour.

"A woman sits alone at a table in a restaurant, tilting her head to watch the passage of a small boat on the glittering waters of the wide river. A faint, warm wind drifts in through the open window, lifting the tendrils of hair at the nape of her neck. She curves up to the breeze until her shoulder blades meet under the thin fabric of her dress.

"Her name is spoken by an unfamiliar voice.

"She turns slowly.

"The clink of fine bone china, the elongated starbursts of sunlight on crystal, the heady scent of tiger lilies: these things they will remember, but nothing more than that first locking gaze, the kindling of a fire that will consume the three caught within its robes of flame.

"The small room above the great river is submersed in undulations of light that play across the white ceiling. He sees them as she rises, and when his hand touches hers, it is as if the sun has left the waters to enter the room; his skin burns where their flesh meets.

"Fire and light, but in the end there will be only darkness."

Alex raises his eyes to Lombardi, closing the notebook and setting it back on the table. He takes a deep breath, preparing for the explanation that will follow.

"Ted wrote to me in July of that year, 1914. He had fallen in love and was getting married at the end of the month . . . "

"His letter was one of those proverbial 'bolts from the blue'—it was the last thing I had expected of him. But I was delighted; my work took me to some far-flung corners and I worried about him, wondering how he was while I was away. We remained in contact by letter, but it wasn't the same, of course. I suppose I thought of myself as his older brother, even though we were the same age and couldn't have been more different in appearance, other than our height. Anyway, he wanted me to meet his fiancée before the wedding and asked if I would have lunch with them at Lampedusa's, a new Italian restaurant on the Embankment, on July twenty-fourth.

"It was the day that the tide of peace turned: Germany issued an ultimatum to Great Britain, Russia, and France warning them not to become involved in Austro-Serbian affairs. I was late arriving at the restaurant because of these developments, which I had been frantically tracking. When I got there Ted was absent; he had returned to his flat nearby to collect the belated birthday present he and his future wife had bought me during their recent holiday in Monte Carlo.

"I entered the restaurant with my mind pounding over the ultimatum, but still eager to meet the woman Ted would marry. Lampedusa's was empty, apart from a group of elderly men in one corner and a woman sitting alone by the window. I walked across the room, the sunlight drenching everything with its brilliance.

"She had her head turned to the river.

" 'Clare?' I said.

"She turned and looked at me with eyes the color of the sea in winter. I was twenty-eight years old, but I didn't know what desire meant until that moment, when her gaze met mine, and the rest of the world failed to exist anymore for either of us.

"I wish I could explain to you exactly how I felt then. But perhaps I can: imagine yourself in a plane, flying across the ocean. Beneath you is nothing but water, the most perfect blue conceivable, something from a dream. Now imagine that the plane, with all its mechanisms and metal casings, is gone and you are soaring alone, flying unaided, just as you thought you could when you were a child, if a little magic would only come your way. What do you feel? Take the fear and exhilaration and multiply them to infinity, and then you will have some idea of how I felt that day, in the empty restaurant overlooking the river, before the lights went out in Europe.

"I took the seat opposite her. The vase of brimming lilies unfurled their petals between us, dropping their orange pollen silently onto the white damask, but neither of us thought to move it.

" 'I'm so pleased to meet you at last,' she said. Her voice was stiffly formal. 'Ted has told me so much about you.' She flushed slightly and the pale redness of her skin made me want to reach out and run my fingers along her collarbone, tracing a line down from her shoulder to the collar of her dress. 'I've read some of your articles. The recent piece on Sevastopol—I found that very moving. All those forgotten graves . . .'

"She tilted her head slightly when she spoke, as if she found nothing in the world more interesting than that small fragment of time in which our first encounter was contained. But our conversation was uneasy, and we said nothing of any import. I found myself being abrupt with her to hide the tumult within.

"Then Ted came back with the gift. He entered the room with the easy elegance I always associated with him, his face lighting up as he saw us sitting there together. It was months since I had last seen him, and he seemed taller somehow, more filled out. It suited him, and made me feel as though I were a gangling youth again.

"He came to me, a smile wider than the river illuminating his face, and I stood up. He embraced me warmly, laughing. 'The wanderer returns!' Then he turned to look at Clare, his arm still about my shoulders. 'I told you he was a handsome devil, didn't I, my darling?'

"Very sensibly, Clare said nothing. She only smiled at us, and when he left my side to sit next to her, I saw how in love with her he was, how his life was caught up in hers, spilling over into her like one vessel emptying itself into another. I sat there, rigid with confusion, forcing myself to act normally, to talk with Ted about the situation in Europe and then their holiday. Ted told me how he had met Clare a month before, at a party where she knew no one apart from the old family friend who had invited her, and how he had been too intimidated to approach her until he realized that she was leaving. Romantic, I suppose that was the word someone else might use to describe their meeting; in a week's time they would marry in seclusion in Scotland, and that would be romantic too. I drank my wine and smiled as Ted insisted that I should be there, as his best man.

"'You know that you're the most important person in my life apart from Clare,' he said seriously, putting his hand over hers where it rested next to the vase of lilies.

"I looked at Clare. She sat quietly listening to the two of us talk. 'What about your family?' I asked. 'Won't they be disappointed not to be invited?'

"A shadow passed over her lovely face. 'I don't really have family. Only my mother and my'—she faltered—'my stepfather.' She paused and rolled the silver napkin ring back and forth across the table. 'We don't get on.'

"Ted kissed her hand and smiled at her. 'What a bunch of misfits we are,' he said cheerfully. 'Alex is motherless, I am an orphan, and you don't speak to your mother and stepfather. We have all the makings of a Greek tragedy between us.'

"I watched him turn to her and tenderly take a strand of blond hair, caught on her eyelashes, between his thumb and forefinger. She lowered her gaze and went back to rolling the napkin ring across the tablecloth. It struck me as an oddly childlike gesture.

"'I promise to be there,' I said untruthfully. 'Providing my father's condition doesn't get any worse.'

"'Of course,' said Ted, nodding, his eyes sympathetic. 'We understand.'

"I made a show of opening the gift they had bought me and told them how pleased I was with it. But I knew that I wouldn't be attending their wedding. My father's ill health provided me with a useful excuse that was loathsome to exploit . . . yet exploit it I would, already anticipating how I could avoid watching Ted claim her as his when I knew that, ever since I had walked into the restaurant, she belonged to me.

"We lingered over coffee, and it was late afternoon by the time we went outside. The heat rose around us like sea spray, and across the water, the dome of St. Paul's Cathedral seemed to float above the white haze that drifted downriver.

"I was about to say good-bye when Clare turned to Ted, leaning against him. 'Do you mind if I speak to Alex alone?' she asked, tempering the request with a smile.

"Ted looked surprised and then relaxed. He grinned at me. 'Don't tell her the truth about me, will you?' he said, before giving me another fierce hug and bounding up the steps onto the bridge to wait for her.

"I was alone with her again. Close to where we stood, a plane tree rustled its leaves in the warm breeze, and a quartet of cargo boats chugged by, the smoke curling from their black chimneys. I was aware of Ted's silhouette up on the bridge, against the sun.

"In my hands I held the book of poems they had given me as a birthday gift and without saying a word, Clare took the book from me, slipped her fingers through the pages until she found what she wanted, and tore it out. Then she ripped the page in two again and threw the redundant half into the river.

"I was startled by what she had done; compared to her childish rolling of the napkin ring in the restaurant, this act was potent, incendiary. Over our heads, on the bridge, I could hear Ted whistling happily.

"She handed back the book and the jagged-edged page, then looked at me with those clear gray eyes. 'I hope I haven't misjudged the situation. I don't think I have.'

"I waited, not knowing how to respond, or even if I should.

"She bent her head. 'This is preposterous,' she said, half under her breath. Then she looked up, shading her eyes with her hand. 'But if you want to know how I feel about you it's there, in black and white, on that piece of paper you hold in your right hand.'

"I looked at her. Her eyes were pale silver, mesmerizing. 'The power of a lighthouse beam on a lost sailor,' Ted had written in his letter. Now I knew what he meant.

" 'Please don't come to Scotland.' She spoke stiffly, as though she were holding herself away from me.

" 'I have no intention of it,' I said.

"Her husband-to-be called to us from the bridge. I wondered what explanation she would give him for this brief interlude. She waved at him, then turned to me.

" 'Well. Good-bye, Alex.'

"She held out her hand. I moved the book and torn page to my left hand, letting my fingers close over hers. She had long, slim fingers and a small palm. They were quite cool, unaffected by the intense heat.

" 'Good-bye, Clare.'

"I watched her walk away and then followed their progress across the bridge together. They were easy to pick out in a crowd with their blond hair and innate grace; from a distance they looked like brother and sister. I felt something twist against my ribs, an ache that would never leave me, although I did not know it then. When they were out of sight I climbed the steps in a sickened sort of daze, elated but desolate at the same time. I couldn't quite believe what had happened that afternoon; I don't suppose I wanted to believe it.

"I didn't look at the page she had torn from my book until I reached the other side of the Embankment and Parliament Park. There, in the olive shade, with a breeze coming off the glinting river below the wall, I read it:

> *We that were friends tonight have found*
> *A sudden fear, a secret flame*
> *I am on fire with that soft sound*
> *You make, on uttering my name.*"

"I closed my eyes and let the sun dance across my lids."

12

"I DIDN'T SEE CLARE AGAIN UNTIL THE WINTER OF 1915. TED MEN-
tioned her frequently in his letters, but without giving her whereabouts. I forced myself not to think of her, and when the thoughts
inevitably came, I battened them down and tried to focus instead on
my work. For the most part, during those first few months, I succeeded.

"The Loos campaign meant long hours of observation, daily reports, and intensive discussions both with my colleagues and at GHQ.
There was one instance when I had a row with Sebastian Thorpe,
whom I had never grown to like. It was toward the end of the fighting
at Loos and came after another wretched, pointless day for St. Aubin,
Farrar, and me. The three of us had returned to the motor car in low
spirits. In Bethune we got caught up in a three-hour stream of ammunition wagons, horses, ambulance convoys, and forage carts trailing
through the town. It was raining again and water dripped from the
wheels, the horses' tails, and the tarpaulin covers of the motor vehicles.
The infantry brigades passing through the streets en route to a nearby
bivouac were soaked to the skin. As we drew to a standstill behind an
ambulance with its Burberry unsecured, I saw six pairs of brown boots
coated in thick chalk sticking out from underneath a pile of blankets.

The owners of the boots were still alive—drenched, but still alive—though for how much longer? I would never find out, but that vision of their chalk-crusted boots has stayed with me; I think it always will.

"We crawled out of Bethune and along the flat road past Vermelles, passing scores of similarly destroyed villages on the journey back to Tatinghem; I counted thirteen churches whose towers had fallen and lay in the debris of what remained of the buildings. The whole of Europe was being laid to waste, or so it seemed.

"When we arrived in Tatinghem, my colleagues (apart from Ernest Dove, who was in northern England on a lecture tour) were already there, waiting for me. At some point during our afternoon meeting, held around the low table in the shabby gentility of the sitting room, I asked them whether they felt that GHQ had dealt us a fair hand regarding our access to the Loos battleground.

"Sebastian Thorpe had to get his opinion in first. In the nasal voice that grated on my nerves like nails on a blackboard, he said, 'Not if you're looking to report on the military ins and outs of the battles, no. But I think it was made clear enough to all of us what we could expect. And although some of us might wish to dwell on endless, long-winded descriptions of the type of shells used, the methods of attack, etcetera, etcetera, I for one am sure that the home front would prefer to read about the human aspect, the personal side of things. Your average Mr. and Mrs. Smith wouldn't understand anything else. Why should they? Their sons are out there fighting, and they want to know what the experience is like.'

"He set his teacup on the low table and looked at me over the tortoiseshell rim of his glasses. His eyes had a watery film across them. 'I realize you feel shortchanged by GHQ, Dyer, but going on about it won't alter a damned thing.' His thin upper lip curled. 'Or perhaps you are hoping to provoke us into mutiny?' He shook his gray head. 'Sorry, but it's not going to happen. Some of us are content with the honor we've been given and the trust shown in us. You must realize that we can't get any closer to the actual fighting in any case? You might think that you're invincible with nothing more than a khaki uniform and riding boots upon your person, but I don't. Besides which, visibility has been poor during this offensive because of the weather and the battle conditions. Even the soldiers themselves can't see a bloody thing.'

"I was about to respond when Andrew Harris leaned forward in his chair. He never took sides or expressed a firm judgment of his own, and it came as no surprise when he offered diplomatically: 'I think you both have fair points to make.' He ran a hand over his bald head. 'I must admit I've seen nothing of the battle so far. My vantage point is close to Alex's on the slag heap by Noeux-les-Mines. It's ludicrously frustrating to stand there, hearing the artillery plugging away and yet to see no farther than a foot in front.' He clasped his hands together, resting them on his knees. 'But, as Sebastian says, that isn't entirely the fault of our "superiors." And even if it was, then the question you have to ask is whether it's been chosen less to limit our access to what's taking place than it is to ensure our safety? I think it's a safety issue rather than them trying to scupper our vision.'

Jack Garland tapped his teeth with a pen. He sat in front of a tall lamp, the light making his red wiry hair look as if it were on fire. 'Well, I'm with Alex on this one,' he said decisively. 'I think it's pretty obvious to anyone with a bit of brain who reads our articles that none of us are witnesses to the offensive as such. Every single one of us gets our information secondhand, whether from Charteris at GHQ or from one of the lads in the casualty clearing stations. What do we write about? The weather, the landscape, the fact that we can't give a thorough assessment of the day's proceedings on account of the fighting being ongoing. It's something we're all guilty of—tapping out a load of old flannel when things aren't going to plan or when we can't get near a sodding trench.'

" 'You're right about the old flannel,' I said, glad of his support. Julian hadn't spoken yet, but I knew he was with me. 'I feel as if I'm back at school. The whole business reminds me of having to write compositions for my English tutor. Back then, if I couldn't think of anything to write I'd just fill the blank pages of my exercise books with waffle.' I pressed my feet against the table legs, feeling disgust rise in my throat. 'It's the same now—the only difference is that it's forced upon me and the rubbish that pours from my pen ends up on the front pages of the national newspapers.'

" 'You may well be writing rubbish,' Thorpe said, slurping his tea loudly. 'But I, for one, don't consider my dispatches to be anything of the kind.'

" 'Really?' I said, disliking the man more thoroughly than ever.

'You wrote in glowing terms of the first day of battle, yet it actually ended in stalemate, didn't it?'

"Thorpe puffed out his cheeks and straightened his glasses. 'I felt that it had gone well, all things considered. Now, with hindsight, I am still of the same opinion. Whether you like it or not, Dyer.' He stared at me. 'Professional jealousy is an ugly thing, you know.'

"I could feel the color draining from my face, as it always does when I am about to lose my temper. 'And do you still stand by that other piece of arrogant make believe you managed to get printed right around the world?' I asked.

"Thorpe stared at me, his weaselly eyes glinting behind his spectacles. 'I haven't the foggiest idea what you're talking about, Dyer.'

"From his armchair near the fireplace, Julian said quietly, 'I think Alex is referring to the Crucified Canadian.' He turned to look at Thorpe. 'Actually, now that Alex has brought it up, I'd quite like to hear about it, too.'

"Garland gave his rumbling laugh. 'Yes, come on, Thorpe, you certainly got plenty of mileage out of that one, didn't you? It made you quite the brightest star among our humble galaxy.'

"Thorpe looked at me furiously. 'You think I made it up, don't you, Dyer? Invented the whole damn thing?'

" 'You,' I said, 'or someone who had a great deal to gain from it.'

"Andrew Harris shook his bald head nervously. 'I'm sure Sebastian can explain—'

"Thorpe pushed his spectacles farther up his nose. He was clearly rattled. 'Look,' he said. 'The story is this: I was at Versailles early last summer, at a base hospital there. A flood of wounded Canadians came in and every single one of them told the same version of events: namely, that one of their officers had been crucified by the Germans. The enemy had pinned the poor fellow to a wall by sticking bayonets through his hands and feet. They drove another bayonet through his gullet. Then they shot him, sixty times.' He cleared his throat. 'The wounded Canadians heard the whole thing from the Dublin Fusiliers, who saw it happen.'

" 'And no one tried to stop it?' asked Julian skeptically.

" 'I don't bloody know,' Thorpe snapped.

"Garland gave a short laugh. 'It's funny, though, isn't it? Because the French press who caught onto your story after it made headline news in *The Times* and the *Toronto Star* said the man was hung from a door, not a wall. And my wife wrote to me that our parish priest said in church that the man was pinned to the floorboards.'

"Thorpe shook his head in frustration. 'Door, wall, floorboards—it's all the same to the poor chap who's crucified, isn't it?'

" 'Excellent timing, though,' I said. 'I have to applaud you on that.'

" 'What the hell does that mean?'

"I shrugged and held up my hand as if reading a headline. 'Canada's Golgotha: an effective metaphor for the searing savagery of war—and the godlessness of the Hun. It was a brilliant piece of propaganda, coming just after the first use of poison gas by the enemy, and coinciding nicely with the Bryce Report and the sinking of the *Lusitania*.' I paused. 'It was certainly a very useful military counterpart to all that. No wonder GHQ were so happy to promote it.'

"Thorpe glared at me. 'I didn't invent it, Dyer.' Through clenched teeth he said, 'There were other incidents before that. What about the British officer crucified and set alight near Le Cateau a year ago? Or that story in the Ian Hay book about a British soldier crucified by Uhlans?

" 'No one paid them any attention,' I said, scornfully. 'It was obvious that they *were* invented.'

" 'Not so. They simply got lost in the sheer volume of atrocities carried out by the enemy at that time,' said Thorpe.

"I snorted. 'They didn't have the support of GHQ, you mean.'

" 'Your story *did* cause a lot of upheaval, Sebastian,' said Harris, looking troubled. 'Questions asked in the Commons, riots in London's East End, attacks on Germans and German shops.'

" 'But it got more men on to the field, didn't it?' Thorpe said, banging his fist on the low table and making the teacups tremble in their saucers. 'There was a tremendous rush of recruits from what I heard.'

"I shook my head slowly. 'And how many of those men are alive now?'

" 'And how many rumors did it spawn?' asked Julian, frowning. 'I seem to recall that the House of Commons debate was about *three* Canadian soldiers captured by the enemy. There was another version, too, wasn't there? About forty Canadians were killed in a barn by the enemy and one of them—a sergeant, I think—was hung from an actual crucifix belonging to the village. The Germans had removed the figure of Christ from it.'

" 'Chinese whispers,' said Jack Garland, lighting a cigarette. 'Rumors are like worms; try cutting them in half and all you end up with is twice the trouble.'

"Thorpe, desperate to defend himself, blurted, 'Well, then I suppose the Germans must have turned it into a practice, not a one-off.'

" 'What was the name of the "first" crucified man?' I inquired. 'I don't remember whether that was ever made public knowledge.'

" 'Harry Band,' said Thorpe angrily, fiddling with his spectacles again. 'His name was Harry Band. He was with the 48th Canadian Highlanders. I didn't let *The Times* print it out of consideration for the man's family. But he damn well *was* crucified, by the Germans, near St. Jean on April 23, 1915. GHQ has the written depositions.'

" 'Do they?' I said. 'How interesting. I wonder how big a role GHQ *did* play in this whole sorry saga?'

" 'Ask Charteris,' Thorpe spat, referring to our chief of intelligence. 'He'll tell you.' He got to his feet, shaking with anger. 'The end justifies the means, Dyer. Especially in wartime. You'd do well to remember that.'

"He pointed at me. 'Today I saw a long, long line of German guns that had been captured at Loos. British soldiers were guarding them. There was a group of French people there as well, and they were as delighted as I was to see the artillery lying in the mud.' He wagged his finger from side to side: 'Do you know what was written on the side of one of those guns? *Pro Gloria et Patria.* And now they belong to us, Dyer, to us.'

"He stalked out of the room, slamming the door behind him and leaving the rest of us sitting in bemused silence.

"I shook my head. '*Pro Gloria et Patria.* What the hell has that got to do with anything? Pompous old fool. He should be working up at GHQ, feeding the War Office ducks little scraps of optimism.'

"Julian laughed, then wagged his finger at me and said sternly, in good imitation of Sebastian's clipped vowels, 'And now they belong to us, Dyer, to us.'

"After a while we retired to our rooms in the long corridor upstairs to write our reports. I didn't join my colleagues again that evening; I stayed at my desk, sifting my uncensored notes into a leather document wallet, adding my sketches and GHQ maps to what now amounted to a substantial collection. I pushed the wallet into the deepest drawer of the desk and locked it, then lay down on the bed. I fell asleep there, fully clothed, and dreamed of my father."

"I've already mentioned Bethune; it was the capital of French 'Black Country' and had, until then, escaped severe shelling. It still had much to offer the British and French armies billeted nearby. A couple of evenings after the row with Thorpe, I went there with Julian for a night out. The locals were gathered in the streets at sunset, cheering on the battalions of Londoners and Scots off to the front. The troops waved and grinned wearily as they marched through pretty little Bethune in full fighting kit, trailed by an everlasting convoy of gun limbers, wagons, motor lorries, and ambulances.

"'We will think of you!' shouted an old woman with tears rolling down her plump red cheeks. She buried her face in her black shawl. 'Fantôms,' she wept. 'Fantôms.'

"I turned to her, disquieted. 'They aren't dead yet.'

"She looked at me as though I were insane. 'Every man who passes has the mark of death upon him.'

"My blood ran cold. Julian pulled my sleeve. 'Leave her alone,' he said. 'She'll want to read your palm next.'

"We walked through the town center, where the convoys were beginning to thin out. It was a fine evening for once, and the cafés and tea shops were open, selling hot food and cold beer to the Tommies who lingered on the terraces, practicing their pidgin French on the waitresses. Julian suggested an estaminet at the end of the main street. The doors had been thrown open and a tinny piano cast its poignant notes into the air. Toward the back of the café was a wide scarlet curtain, and whenever someone lifted it aside we could see a group of British officers sitting behind the velvet with amenable French girls on their laps.

"We chose one of the tables on the cramped, thronging terrace and sat down after placing our order with the young dark-haired waitress. The high heels of her shoes clicked on the cobblestones as she walked, drawing the lustful attention of the clientele. She brought our beers and left to chat with the young subalterns at the next table.

"Julian held up his glass and made a toast: 'To the success of the offensive. We haven't seen much of it, but I hope it went our way.'

"I clinked my glass against the one Julian held high and took a long drink. It tasted strong and clean, the smell of the hops energizing after the cloying smoke and earth-scented mist of the bombardment.

"Julian glanced about the terrace. 'I pity these poor chaps,' he said. 'Most of them have just come out of the line, but it won't be long before they're kissing their saucy *mamzelles* good-bye and heading back to the trenches again. No wonder they're all drunk.'

" 'Desperate, you mean,' I said, taking my cigarettes from my tunic pocket and offering one to Julian. He declined. I struck a match and lit the cigarette. 'Trying to remind themselves that there's another sort of life, one that doesn't have to end in sacrifice in the name of patriotism and valor.'

" 'I should have left you with that old woman in the black shawl. You could have had a nice chat about misery and death. It would have cheered the pair of you up no end,' said Julian, grinning as he lifted his glass to his mouth.

" 'Sorry,' I said, putting the cigarette to my lips. I breathed out slowly, expelling a small ring of smoke. 'But you know how it is. God, when I think of the gas victims after Ypres, last year ... There'll be hundreds more after this offensive, whether they're British, French, or German. And what do we do? We type.'

" 'Join up then,' said Julian, draining his beer. 'If you feel so guilty about it.'

" 'If we could report the truth,' I said, 'I'd feel better about it.' I tapped the cigarette against the table edge. 'You do know, don't you, that after the fighting at Langemarck, Ernest Dove had the nerve to write that the British dead lay on the battlefield with grateful smiles upon their heroic faces?'

" 'Then why are you here?' asked Julian, reasonably. 'If you despair so much, why go on?'

"I stubbed out my cigarette and said quietly, 'Because I *have* to be here, even under these circumstances. I try to get things past the censor. I do my best. And after the war I intend to tell the truth. All of it.'

" 'I think to some extent we're our own censors, anyway,' said Julian, gazing across the street, where two small boys were tussling over ownership of a tin soldier. 'GHQ should have more faith in us.'

" 'Absolutely,' I said, 'one day this war will be over and *we'll* be held accountable for not having reported matters accurately. The public isn't stupid—the returning wounded and the casualty lists tell their own story.'

"Julian put his hand in the air to attract the waitress's attention. 'Things may alter,' he said evenly. 'Look at me: this time last year I was in Hazenbrouck jail on Kitchener's orders. Now I'm an official appointee, here with you. It might get easier yet.'

" 'I hope so,' I said. 'I really do.'

"There was a burst of song from the table behind ours. The waitress, perspiring from the briskness of business and the officers' interest in her shapely form, brought us two more beers.

Julian waited until the singing had stopped, then told me, 'I must admit, I'm one of the lucky ones. I don't have any brothers or sons fighting out here. My father is too old, of course, I'm unmarried with three sisters, and don't have any close male relatives. What about you?'

"I hunched my shoulders against the cool breeze. 'Both my parents are dead and I was an only child. Somewhere I have two uncles who have sons my age, but I haven't seen them since I was five or six.' I pushed my hair back from my forehead, keeping it out of my eyes; it needed cutting again. 'But I've been friends with this chap called Ted Eden for years, and he's out here as an officer.' I paused. 'I'm hoping for a letter from him soon.'

" 'When did you last see him?'

"I looked down at the table. Scored into its wooden surface were initials and dates, crude carvings made by men passing through Bethune on their way to or from the front, who had wanted to mark their presence at the café in some way.

"I looked up. Julian's eyes were curious, but not unfriendly, waiting for me to justify my hesitation. 'I saw Ted in July last year,' I said. 'It was a special occasion.'

" 'Because?'

" 'He was getting married.' I paused again, then went on slowly, 'It was the weekend before the wedding. He and his bride-to-be had known each other for a month—it was the archetypal whirlwind romance. They decided to get married in Scotland without telling anyone except me. I was supposed to join them after visiting my father, who was dying. I never made it to Scotland.'

" 'I'm sorry. Your father died, then?'

" 'I avoided Julian's kindly eyes. 'Yes, he died, but that's not the reason I didn't go to Ted's wedding. I chose to go to Paris instead, to report on the outbreak of war.'

"Julian's brown eyebrows rose. 'You're more dedicated to your job than I realized.'

"I finished my beer and set the glass heavily back down on the table. 'Another?' I asked, squinting at Julian. The sunset was almost gone, but the last vestiges of it reflected on the café windows, almost blinding me. Julian raised his hand again and summoned the waitress, who brought us more beers without troubling to ask what we wanted.

" 'Did you like her?' Julian asked when the girl had gone.

" 'Who?'

" 'Ted's wife.'

"There was another rousing chorus from the terrace. An officer stood up and threw out his arms to sing, knocking over his chair and causing ribald hilarity among his party.

" 'I didn't really get to know her.' My voice was low and Julian had to lean in to catch what I was saying. 'We barely spoke to each other.' I dug my thumbnail into one of the carved names on the table's wooden surface, *David MacDonald*. I wondered who he was ... I stopped my thoughts from growing maudlin by finishing my beer and turning, reluctantly, back to the conversation Julian had begun.

'I don't think she liked me, particularly,' I said, lying blatantly. How could I tell Julian the truth when it was hard enough to admit it to myself? I ran my fingernails over the name again.

" 'Would it matter if she didn't?'

" 'Yes.'

" 'Why?'

" 'We both love Ted.'

"The statement gave me inner resolve. I left the carvings alone and looked at Julian. 'We're like bookends to his life. No one else really matters to him. I'm on one side keeping him upright and Clare is on the other.'

" 'You make him sound ... unstable.'

"I smiled. 'He's not at all. But he has a sort of vulnerability that most men don't possess. A fragility of spirit.'

"Julian grinned. 'Must make him terribly attractive to women.'

"I laughed at this. 'It does. They all want to mother him—you'd have to see it to believe it. And Clare is a nurse, so naturally ...'

" 'A proper nurse, or one of those useless VADs?'

" 'A proper one with Queen Alexandra's Imperial Military Nursing Service, no less.' I felt sudden pride in Clare's achievement as I said it.

"Julian's eyes widened in surprise behind his spectacles. 'Really? My younger sister, Frances, is with Queen Alexandra's. She was posted to a hospital in Rouen in September last year.'

"I felt my head swim, rocking the terrace and its drunken soldiers from side to side. This is why people shouldn't have affairs, I thought, this is what happens. Someone, somewhere, always knows those involved.

" 'In Rouen?' I asked, affecting casual interest, 'That's a coincidence: Clare is based there. Do you suppose they know each other?'

" 'There's more than one military hospital in Rouen, of course, but I'll ask Frances. She's due a letter from me anyway.' He leaned back in his chair and clasped his hands behind his head, smiling. 'How extraordinary. Perhaps I can get some news of her for you to send on to Ted when you next write to him.' A thought occurred to him and he asked, 'Or . . . are you and she in touch anyway?'

" 'No,' I said shortly. I decided to stick to the lie I had told: 'I told you, I don't think she likes me.'

"Julian grinned, 'Well, if my sister does know her, this might be your chance to find out why.' He drained his glass and nodded toward the street, where the sun had disappeared behind the irregular rooftops of Bethune. 'Shall we move on? That blasted piano is starting up again and I'm not sure my poor ears can take any more sentimental tinkling.'

"We walked to the vast square where the locals had begun to converge in front of the Hôtel de Ville to talk about the war as they did every evening. British soldiers drifted across from the terraces to listen to the guns booming around Vermelles, Noeux-les-Mines, Grenay, and beyond Notre Dame de Lorette, where the artillery of the French army kept up a deafening refrain. The impact of the roaring concussions, the white explosions and scarlet bars tearing through the darkened sky, made us subdued. The women of Bethune, whose sons and husbands were away fighting, walked to the wayside shrines and crossed themselves, murmuring prayers. Julian and I turned away respectfully as we passed them on our way back to the motor car.

"Our transportation, and its mulishly patient driver, waited at the end of a narrow street where the bellow of gunfire was amplified by the road widening onto a grassy quadrangle. There were stars overhead, but the spreading white glare of the crashing shells obscured them, illuminating the ugly landscape for miles around.

"As we climbed into the car, on an impulse I said to Julian, 'When you write to your sister, I'd appreciate it if you *would* inquire about Clare.'

" 'Oh, I will,' Julian agreed, trying to find somewhere to stretch out his legs. He settled for an ungainly sprawl, his feet wedged under the seat in front. 'By the way, just to give Frances something more to go on, what does she look like, this Clare . . . Eden, isn't it?'

"I glanced out the window and into the cavernous darkness that seemed to engorge when the lights from the explosions faded. 'She's blond,' I said. 'Clear, unusual gray eyes—lucid eyes. Small nose and mouth, long neck. A few freckles across her nose. Tall for a woman, and willowy.'

"Julian raised an eyebrow. 'She sounds attractive.'

"I went on staring out the window, where the horizon was lit by bursting shells. I thought about Clare in the restaurant the summer before, how dependent she had seemed upon Ted when they were together, but how detached from him the minute we went outside.

" 'She has a brittleness to her,' I said. 'I can't quite describe it.' The motor car veered to avoid an animal carcass lying by the roadside. 'Apart from that, I suppose she's the most exquisite creature I've ever seen.'

"Neither of us spoke again. Julian fell asleep, lulled by the motion of the motor car, drooping in unconscious stages until his head rested against my shoulder, while I remained upright, staring rigidly at the darkened villages and flat wastes that formed the geography of the battle underway."

13

"When the Loos offensive was finished, I was awarded my first leave. I agreed to give a series of eight lectures on my work as a war correspondent at the University of London and left the château in Tatinghem not expecting to return to France before January.

"London felt like a foreign city after my months away. I wore my officer's uniform on the streets to prevent women handing me white feathers and elderly men gazing at me in disgust for shirking service. When I wore it—this fraudulent jester's outfit I had never grown to believe in—people offered me cigarettes and smiled, and one daring young woman outside a theater even gave me a kiss on impulse 'to celebrate your courage.'

"The only men more popular than I was were the ones in wheel-chairs, or those with empty sleeves pinned against their chests. Everyone wanted to talk to them, to do something for them. Children presented them with flags and in the railway stations they got free tea or coffee. It was different for the ones whose faces had been destroyed. People averted their eyes quickly, the blood flooding their skin. No one wanted to make eye contact with a disfigured soldier; they were modern-day lepers.

"I still have a cutting from *The Times* of that Christmas, about old ladies being encouraged to comb their snappy little Pekinese dogs several times a day; the hair they collected was woven into light garments to cover the bodies of injured soldiers who couldn't bear any weight. I picked up nonsensical facts like this, slipping them into my lectures, which contained more truth than any reports of mine that appeared in the newspapers.

"The lectures were given in an annex on Gower Street, in a sort of wooden amphitheater that smelled strongly of ink, with a long corridor running behind it, the full length of the building. Most of the lectures took place in the afternoon, apart from two evening events to which the general public were also invited. After the last but one lecture on a December afternoon, the professor who had introduced me to the audience pressed a slip of paper into my hand.

"I read it in shock: it was from Ted. He and Clare were in town, on leave, and waiting for me at that very moment in Lampedusa's. A nauseous fusion of euphoria and dread rushed through my veins. I vacillated between going to them and sending a message to say I couldn't make it, but only for a moment. I would have hated myself had I not gone, and the desire to see Clare, and Ted, swiftly won out.

"I threw on my coat and headed into Gower Street. It was not yet six o'clock, but winter dusk shrouded the city. My pace instinctively quickened as I cut through the streets of Covent Garden, since I knew that if I hurried I would be at the restaurant within a quarter of an hour. Any fears I had began to fade as I reached Blackfriars Bridge; there, hidden in the tumbledown darkness of the old wharf-side buildings was Lampedusa's.

"Buoyed now by the prospect of seeing Ted again, I told myself that the attraction Clare and I felt for each other was something that couldn't survive this meeting—it had to be put aside, forgotten, left unpursued. I kept repeating this under my breath, lulling myself into a false sense of security, even while the thought of being with her again made my blood feel as though it were on fire. The self-admonishments worked to some extent, for when I entered the now familiar room overlooking the river—where the curtains had been drawn, shutting us in intimate seclusion—I was confident that the evening would pass without incident. That I would return home, perhaps drunk, amused and shamefaced at my obsession with Clare over the past year.

"But when I saw her, all my good intentions and my determination to behave like a decent human being vanished. She sat with Ted at the same table as before, wearing an unusual blue silk dress, the color of *bleuets*. Her collarbone was bare, and the long straps of the dress tied in ribbons around her back, which was also exposed. It was the sort of audacious gown women influenced by the Russian ballet might wear, but without any decoration at all, and it hung loosely from her frame, accentuating her small breasts and slender limbs.

"I stood for a while, unseen, watching Ted's animated face as he talked to her and she laughed with him, and I wondered how it must feel, not to have to conceal your happiness in being with the person you love above all others, all else. The freedom to love and to be loved in return—I felt the blade of a terrible envy twist inside my heart. She looked as blissful as he did, and I began to doubt whether the attraction I thought she felt for me still existed, outside my own head.

"Ted must have seen me standing there, although I wasn't aware that he had noticed me. But suddenly he was beside me, his left arm around my shoulders, turning to call to Clare with his other hand held high, brandishing a glass of red wine. Those next few minutes are a blur: we went over to the table, I shook Clare's hand with the same absurd formality as before, and then—as if time had rolled forward like an incoming tide—food and drinks were set before us and the evening was under way.

"Ted did most of the talking. Neither I nor Clare had known exactly where he had been fighting during the months the three of us had been apart. He told us that he had been involved in the Battle of Loos, where his company was detailed to hold the position of a trench south of the village of Le Trou, which I knew well. He was very open in what he said; I think perhaps because Clare was a nurse he felt he could talk about the brutality of war as other men couldn't before their wives.

"He sat back in his chair, one hand on Clare's shoulder, the other again holding a glass of red wine. I tried not to look at his fingertips resting on her skin. I had to force myself to listen to what he said. It wasn't that I had no interest in him; it was simply that the room had narrowed, sharpened, as if by a trick of the candlelight, to where she sat, her hands folded on the table and her cool gaze fixed on her husband.

" 'We fought parallel with a French attack,' he was saying. 'On the first morning, the wind was blowing from the German trenches toward us. They used smoke bombs—exactly what we had intended to do, if the weather had been on our side. I was the first in our trench to smell the gas; I shouted for the others to pull on their masks. The rocket went up at half past six for the gas to cease and for us to begin our attack, but I swear I climbed that parapet completely blind. At first, there was no answering fire from the enemy, but then their machine guns started up.'

"His fingertips were underneath her hair, on the nape of her neck. 'There were more of them than there were of us, I'm sure of it. I ran across No Man's Land, my nose bleeding with all the noise and my ears . . . well, there was some sort of liquid pouring from them. By the time I reached the German wire, only two of my men were still with me. I couldn't find a way through. As I was searching, a shell went off behind me and I was thrown forward.'

" 'It's a miracle you weren't killed,' I said, with difficulty.

"Ted nodded. His hand moved down to the middle of Clare's back, where the blue ribbons met in an intricate knot. 'I landed in a crater. The bottom of it was filled with burned scrub, and a dead man. He saved my life, gave me a soft landing. I couldn't get my left leg into the hole properly, and later a piece of iron hit me in the ankle and I felt my skin slicing off the bone, as cleanly as if a butcher had done it. It's all right now, but it hurt like hell then. One of my men—one of the two who had made it to the German wire with me—found me there and dragged me back to the trench. I don't need to tell you what that was like. The Germans were still shooting.'

" 'But you got back,' said Clare, still watching him. Her meal lay on her plate, where she had moved it around in a circle instead of eating it.

" 'Yes, I did. I made it, just as the enemy fire stopped. I pulled my mask off and scratched my head until it bled. The stench in the field was like nothing I've ever smelled before or since but at least the gas was gone. Then I looked up.' He paused. 'Hanging over our trench was a dead German, his mouth open as if he were still screaming when I shoved him away. His helmet came off and rolled into our trench. I kicked it out of sight. I was about to climb out to see if there was anyone out there who could still be saved when the other man who'd made it with me to the German wire landed next to me with a whoop of sheer triumph. Jimmy Previtt, that's his name, about nineteen. He tore off his mask and grinned at me. "I'm ready for my breakfast now, sir," he said.' Ted smiled. 'I forgot the pain in my ankle then.'

"We smiled back at him. I glanced around the room. There were about twenty tables, all filled with well-dressed people. They seemed normal enough. And yet, just across the narrow English Channel, men were still being blown to bits, experiencing the sorts of things—and far worse—as in the story Ted had related to us. I felt suddenly repulsed by all of it: by the diners and the staff who waited upon them, by myself, and by the thought of what was happening back there.

" 'Shall we get drunk?' I said rashly. I felt an urgent need to get lost in some dark corner of London with a woman. There was an ex-girlfriend of mine who lived nearby, and I thought I might call on her, later that evening. Her easy warmth would blot out Clare and her heroic husband, and the war. I wanted that, more than anything.

"Ted threw back his head and laughed. 'Why not? Eat, drink, and be merry, for tomorrow we die.'

"We pushed aside our plates and ordered more drinks. Clare kept to the wine we had enjoyed with our meal; Ted and I switched to whisky. The ice slid about our glasses, the candlelight made the liquid glow, and I was glad of the burning sensation in my throat, the hot spread of the drink as it filled my veins with calm. I tried to avoid looking directly at Clare; whenever she turned her eyes on me, I wanted to behave in a reckless, stupid manner. When I talked to Ted, I could tell that she was looking at me. Once she excused herself, and as she left the table, both Ted and I watched her walk away. I imagined tearing apart the ribbons of her dress and letting my mouth drag across her pale skin, the smattering of freckles gliding under my tongue.

"Before she came back, Ted leaned across the table and confided, 'Aristotle said that a life truly worth living is one that produces *audaimonia,* the feeling of being watched over by a good angel.' His eyes shone. He laughed. His being was lit up with pure joy. 'I have *audaimonia* in spades—I married the good angel who watches over me.'

"I smiled at him, awkward, angry, brutally jealous.

"When Clare joined us again, Ted asked proudly, 'What do you think of my wife's dress, Alex? Shocking, isn't it?'

"Clare lowered her eyes.

"Alcohol made me careless. 'That isn't a dress,' I said. 'It's a web of sorcery.'

"Ted laughed and nodded. Clare pushed her glass across the table to him and said quietly, 'Refill it, will you?'

"I looked at her. She had hardly participated in our conversation the whole evening. When she lifted her glass to her lips, her hand shook almost imperceptibly; a small band of wine spotted the damask where the glass had been. She wore the lightest of makeup, yet her skin was flushed whenever one of us spoke to her or of her.

"Ted began to talk about our schooldays, using the phrase 'the idiocy of our youth' repeatedly. He was drunk, I realized, but I was not. There was too much I wanted to commit to memory, too many small nuances of Clare's that I knew I would turn over and over again in my mind when I returned to my flat that night. I abandoned the idea of visiting my ex-girlfriend, whom I hadn't seen for months anyway. I would only close my eyes and think of Clare when I was in bed with Katherine; it wouldn't be fair to her, and I couldn't stand the disappointment that would burden me afterward. There would be too much hate, because the love I had was denied itself.

Toward the end of the evening, when most of the other diners were leaving, Clare talked at last a little, about herself and her work. It was the first time she had spoken of it in front of me, and I was fascinated by the vignettes she gave us. She was a skilled raconteur, sketching with a few well-chosen words the men she cared for, the hospital, and its convalescent camp in Rouen. Then she mentioned working on a hospital train in Chocques. I felt excitement leap in my stomach.

" 'When were you there?' I asked.

"She looked at me. 'In October.'

" 'I was there,' I said. 'I was there then, too.'

"For a second, our gaze held. It was as if she had spoken to me, silently, words that no one else could hear.

"Ted didn't know. He didn't see. He was discussing the merits of two particular whiskies with the waiter. After he had made his choice between them, he turned back to Clare. 'Tell him about Frankie,' he said.

"Clare told me. Despite her professionalism she had become attached to this boy, whose injuries had necessitated his transferral from the hospital train to Rouen, where he would remain until being sent back to England. She was glad to have him near her, she said, because of all her patients he was the one who had touched her heart the most.

"Her voice faltered. 'I have to stop,' she said, 'I don't want to make a fool of myself by crying.'

"Ted leaned his blond head against hers and kissed her forehead tenderly. 'Silly old girl,' he said. 'As if anyone would mind.'

" 'I would,' said Clare, suddenly fierce. 'I'd mind.'

"Wanting to help her, to reach her in some way where Ted had failed, I said passionately, 'I think it's a marvelous thing—that you should care so much about all your patients.' I hoped that she would look at me and see the truth of what I said.

"Instead she tightened her hands into fists and pressed them down on the damask. Her blond hair fell across her face, hiding it from us. 'Not all,' she said, swallowing. 'Not all.'

"Then she turned to Ted. 'I haven't told you about this, but I've had a lot of wine and now I shall.' She didn't look at me; her eyes were on Ted, all the time. 'They brought in my stepfather.'

"I saw Ted's face whiten.

" 'He was very badly wounded. He was dying. I didn't see him until the end of my afternoon shift. I didn't know it was him until I came face-to-face with him, in the ward carriage.' Her voice had dropped, but her eyes remained fixed on Ted. 'The others—the patients—were all sleeping. I dressed his wound. He told me what had happened to him. And he asked me to forgive him.'

" 'Did he know he was dying?' asked Ted, his skin as white as the chalk that clung to a soldier's boots.

" 'Yes.' She nodded, slowly. 'He knew.'

" 'And?'

" 'He could have morphine. I gave him exactly the amount permitted. He wanted more—'

" 'Morphine?'

"I watched them both, my breath caught fast in my throat, the alcohol dulling my senses, not understanding the significance of what Clare was telling him, nor of what was passing between the two of them.

" 'Yes. But I didn't give it to him. Anyway, it isn't allowed.' She took a gulp of air and I heard it go in through her mouth, as if it had scratched her. 'He said that he was sorry for what he had done to me. He asked me again to forgive him. And he wanted me to stay with him until he died.'

"Ted stared at her intently, but he asked no more questions, although she paused, as if to give him the opportunity. Then she said, in a voice that had lost all expression, 'I put away the dressings trolley. I pulled the blanket up to his neck, for warmth. He tried to catch my hand as I walked past him, but I shook him off. By the door of the carriage I stopped. I didn't look at him. But I knew he could hear me and so I said, "I don't forgive you. And I hope you go straight to hell." And then I left him.' She sat back in her chair, her head drooping slightly. 'He would have been dead within minutes.'

"There was a deep silence. I saw the last of the other diners paying his bill at a table some distance from ours. The woman he was with was laughing, a revolting, screeching sound like a seagull's cry. And then I looked at Ted.

"The whiteness had gone from his face. In its place was a livid red, and his jaw was set, his eyes troubled. Surprised, I recognized the signs of his anger, and wondered if Clare did too.

"Ted spoke, his voice low with rage. 'What you've just told me is appalling. I can't believe that you could be so cruel. That the wife I thought I knew has such depths of spite.'

"Clare stared at him. Now she, too, was white. She looked stunned, as though he had struck her publicly.

" 'What he did to you'—Ted lowered his voice to a whisper, and I had some idea, then, what this stepfather must have done to her—'was deplorable. But in that moment, you should have put your personal feelings aside. You were his nurse. Your job was to give him whatever comfort you could. Even if you couldn't bring yourself to forgive him, you should have stayed with him until he died. Because, at the very least, your training should have kicked in.'

" 'Ted—' I began, but he held up his hand for me to be quiet. Clare sat like a statue, still and impassive.

" 'His actions when you were younger were wicked and depraved. But he must have had another side to him, Clare.' The sinews in Ted's throat were taut with strain. 'He fought for his country, and died for it. In that sense, he was good. And brave. I don't know if your forgiving him would have pulled him through. I really *don't* know. But we have one man less to fight for us now. And in his last excruciating minutes on that train, on that godforsaken field, he heard your voice telling him to go to hell.' He swallowed. 'I never thought I'd say this, but as an officer who knows what it costs each man to put on his pack and run toward the enemy, I have to tell you that I'm ashamed of you. Ashamed and . . . disgusted.'

"He got to his feet clumsily, knocking against the table, upsetting Clare's wine. He picked up the glass and set it down again, then stumbled toward the cloakroom. I had never seen him so inept, and knew it was emotion, not alcohol, that was the cause.

"I looked at Clare. She sat very straight-backed in her chair, staring at me. Her hair, which had been partly swept up on her crown, seemed to have lost most of its pins and fell around her flushed cheekbones in soft waves. There were no tears, but her eyes were huge, the silver-gray irises glistening.

" 'And you?' she said. 'Are you going to condemn me too? Do I . . . disgust you?'

"For a while, I said nothing. Then I reached out to her, my hands closing over her small fists where they lay clenched on the table.

" 'No,' I said, quietly. 'I'm not going to condemn you at all. And there is nothing—*nothing*—you could do that would make me feel disgust for you.'

"Gently, I opened out her fingers and held them in mine. My whole body burned for her. 'If it's any comfort at all,' I said, feeling the quick pulse of desire as I looked at her, 'I would have done exactly the same as you.'

"During the silence that followed, I saw that she had fallen in love with me, although perhaps she didn't know it then. And if I hadn't loved her before—if all it had amounted to up until then was basic human desire—now I did. And I knew it."

14

"T ED AND I MET THE NEXT DAY. HE CAME TO MY FLAT IN CHALCOT Square and we had coffee before catching the omnibus to Knights-bridge. He wanted to buy a Christmas present for Clare before he went back to the front the following day and apparently she had seen a shawl she liked in Harrods. We didn't mention the quarrel between the two of them until the shop assistant wrapped the gift; while she folded it and wrapped it in fine tissue paper and ribbons, then slipped it into a green box with gold lettering on the lid, Ted turned to me with a regretful smile.

" 'I hope this will aid my campaign to get out of the doghouse,' he said. 'I was too hard on Clare last night, after she told us about her stepfather. He really was an absolute swine to her.'

"I stood with my hands in the pockets of my coat, not knowing how to respond. But I wanted to defend Clare and said, 'Was he? In that case, perhaps you should tell her that you were in the wrong.'

"Ted stared at me, frowning. 'That's not what I mean at all. I still stand by what I said. I just feel that I said it too harshly. But that was probably the drink, too,' he said, ruefully.

"He paid for the gift and we wove our way through the various bustling halls and departments and out on to the cold street. It was dry, but the prospect of rain scented the air and made the clouds sag dismally. We stood there for a minute, uncertainly.

"I pulled my scarf up to my nose and mumbled through it, 'I hope you don't think I'm speaking out of turn, but I think Clare was hoping you would be more understanding. I think your reaction came as a shock.'

"Ted frowned again, holding the gift in its bag against his chest, a poor barrier against the bitter cold. 'I didn't mean to upset Clare. But I was disappointed in her.' His frown deepened. 'I didn't think her capable of such callousness.'

"I dug my hands farther into my pockets and blew on the inside of my scarf, to warm it. 'You're going to have to forget how you feel,' I said. 'If you don't want this to come between you, then you should do what you advised her to do last night: put aside your feelings. Think of her, instead.'

"Ted grinned suddenly. 'I'd forgotten what a ladies' man you are, Alex.'

"I burst out laughing, then ducked my chin back into my scarf. 'I'm not,' I said, 'I'm utterly without morals.'

"Ted smiled. 'Hardly.'

"We had lunch together, then strolled for a while, reminiscing. We didn't talk about Clare again, for which I was grateful. I was able to enjoy Ted's company as I always had, listening to his experiences in the trenches and 'at rest,' and sharing with him some of the events that had taken place in my life during the past twelve months. I told him about the row with Thorpe as we walked under the bare trees in Parliament Park. He sympathized with me, adding, 'When you're cooped up with the same people, day in, day out, there's always going to be one person who gets on your nerves to the point where you could scream.'

"We were both walking with our heads down against the wind and our arms folded across our chests, though Ted carried Clare's gift in his arms.

" 'It's funny,' he said, his blond hair blowing back from his face, 'at first, it was the lice that I hated most. Sometimes, especially at night, it can sound like a forest fire, with the men running lit cigarettes and matches along the seams of their clothing to burn the eggs. That drove me mad for a while. But now it's the much smaller things.' He shook his head. 'If I'm trying to sleep, it isn't the lice or the bombs or the shells or even the prospect of death that makes me want to break free of the whole damn business: it's the chap gnawing dry biscuits for ten minutes on end or the one who's slurping from his water bottle.'

"He sighed heavily. 'But after twenty-four hours in the firing line, eight in the supports, and sixteen spent digging, what can you expect? It doesn't make for sanity, does it, being the Devil's infantrymen?'

"I agreed, feeling guilty because there was no hardship I had to bear that was half so unpleasant as Ted's life. It began to rain then, and Ted suggested that before we said good-bye we should visit Westminster Abbey 'for old times' sake—and to get out of this blasted weather— I've seen enough rain to last me a lifetime.'

"We crossed the street and, in a huddle of damp clothes and wet hair, entered the vast church. I looked at Ted and smiled. With his hair darkened by the rain he appeared younger and more vulnerable than ever. He still clutched Clare's gift to his chest, shivering as we walked toward the chapels on the eastern side of the empty abbey.

"We came to the tomb of Elizabeth Nightingale; I didn't recall ever having seen it before but now we stood before it, awed by the marble monument that depicted a woman cowering against her husband, who tried to fend off the skeletal figure of death as it emerged from the tomb below to claim her.

" 'That's how I imagine it,' said Ted, suddenly.

" I turned to him. 'Imagine what?'

" 'Death. A terrible, grinning skeleton who comes for you when you least expect it.'

"I laughed. 'You haven't changed a bit. You have far more imagination than I do—of the two of us, *you* should have been the writer. Anyway,' I said, adjusting my wet scarf, 'death is just death. It doesn't look like anything. It just *is.*'

"Ted made no reply. We walked on, coming to the ancient Coronation Chair and Henry V's tomb in the shadow of the arches.

"'When we came here with school,' I said, running my fingers over the worn plush of the chair, 'you said that you felt it was an honor to die for one's country.'

" 'Yes.'

" 'Do you still feel like that?' I asked curiously. 'I mean, now you're . . . well . . .'

" 'In a position where it might happen?' Ted finished the sentence for me. 'Yes, I do, as a matter of fact.' A faraway look came into his eyes. 'I still feel that way, even if the cause has lost its focus. Even if . . .' He hesitated, then shook his head quickly, as if he were trying to rid his hair of the rain. 'Never mind. Stop rubbing that chair, Alex. It's falling apart as it is.'

"We lingered another ten minutes in the abbey, then said good-bye outside, on the small patch of lawn at the front. There was quite a bit of traffic on the road; the horses' hooves and the wheels of the motor cars and omnibuses sent sprays of water onto the pavement.

"Before he left, Ted gave me a brief hug. He had always been affectionate, but now he seemed to be holding himself back, afraid to show any emotion. I sensed that he was steeling himself for our good-bye, not knowing what faced him on his return to France.

" 'Good luck with the writing,' he said with uncharacteristic awkwardness. 'And don't worry about Clare and me. Everything will be fine.'

" 'Of course it will,' I said, wanting, in that moment, to believe it as much as he did. 'And good luck to you, too. I hope this bloody war ends soon and we can all get on with our lives again.'

"He gave me a tight smile. 'Yes,' he said. 'That would be a fine thing, wouldn't it?'

"And then he walked away, crossing the road again in the downpour and heading toward Whitehall. I watched him from beneath my dripping hair until he reached the corner. When he had gone, I sat on the low wall surrounding the abbey and lit a cigarette. I didn't care about the rain anymore; in fact, I rather liked it. It was clean and fresh, and brought nature into the city. Not like the rain in Flanders, the rain in the trenches."

"I gave my last lecture before Christmas two days later.

"From where I stood, in the bowl of the amphitheater, it was impossible to see more than the first four or five rows of expectant faces. During the evening lectures, huge lamps on either side of the highest level of seats were switched on, and it was only when I had finished talking, and answering questions, that the lights were turned down and I could see if the room had been filled to capacity or not.

"On the evening of December nineteenth, as I stepped back from the podium, the lights dimmed and I looked out at the audience. It was almost midnight and people were gathering their coats, hats, scarves, and other belongings quickly, eager to return home. I turned to talk to one of the university lecturers, but lost the thread of what I intended to say: Clare was leaving the ink-scented amphitheater and disappearing into the long corridor that ran the length of the building. I can't remember what I told my hosts, but I know that I leaped down from the podium, pulling on my coat, and pushed through the small crowd who had listened so politely to me, calling my apologies over my shoulder as I left the room.

"I ran out into Gower Street, in the driving rain and the gusting winds, not knowing where she was or how she had traveled to see me. My actions were scarcely rational, but even if I didn't meet her in the street, I knew I should find myself standing on her doorstep, asking if I could come in. I rushed past theater crowds and shuttered bookshops, and down the last stretch of Charing Cross Road, where the familiar tall spire of the church of St. Martins-in-the-Fields rose in a thin line against the sky.

"She was crossing Trafalgar Square when I caught up with her. I was soaked to the skin, the rain running from my hair and around my collar, my coat plastered against my legs. London was in darkness, plunged into impenetrable night by the threat of zeppelins. The black lions stood out like sentinels in the pale square.

"I touched her shoulder.

"She wore tiny diamond earrings, a wedding gift from her husband, bursts of white fire at her delicate earlobes. Her hair, too, was sleek with rain.

" 'Do you love him?' I shouted desperately, feeling the air fill my lungs again.

"She lifted her chin.

" 'Yes.'

"Her eyes, even in the darkness, were mesmerizing. Then she held out her hands and I bent down to them, taking the slim fingers into mine, pressing my mouth against them.

She sank a fierce whisper into the wet shallows of my hair, 'But it is you who possesses me.' "

In the little hut on the Flanders plains, Alex puts his palms against his temples and presses hard. His voice, when it comes, is almost inaudible.

"In the beginning of every story lies its end, wrapped like a seed inside the skin of a pomegranate."

He turns to look at Lombardi.

"By the time we were lovers, it was already too late."

VII

GOWER STREET AT MIDNIGHT

London and France, Summer 1914 and Winter 1915

15

WHEN SHE LEFT ALEX STANDING BY BLACKFRIARS BRIDGE THAT day in the summer of 1914, she was already appalled at what she had done.

Her husband had spoken of him with profound affection many times before they met. The photographs she had seen of the two of them together showed a man as disparate in looks from her husband as it was possible to imagine. She was convinced that their first encounter would disappoint her, or set them against each other in some way. But in the glittering sunshine that poured into the empty room at Lampedusa's, she felt the vortex open between them with a roar, and watched as he succumbed to its pull, taking her with him.

All afternoon, as the three of them sat beneath that ceiling of eddying light, she had been unable to think of anything other than the decency of her husband and how little he deserved the betrayal that was already set in motion. She wanted to save him from the inexorable cruelty of her desire for another man. She loved her husband deeply, but with none of the fleet passion, the violence of emotion, that twisted between herself and the man sitting opposite her in the restaurant. She wondered at Ted's innocence, and his inability to see this, the turbulent force behind their polite smiles and dead-wood conversation.

When they left the room and went outside, she knew that something had to happen. It wasn't clear in her own mind what she intended when she asked her husband to leave them alone for a moment. All she knew was that she wanted to give expression to her desire, to let Alex know what was happening within her, but—paradoxically, perversely even—to make it clear that she was not about to break off her engagement or embark upon an affair. The words she had chosen, on paper, would fulfill that need. She thought, even then, that everything would remain, on the surface at least, undamaged.

If Alex had said something, responded in any manner other than the one he chose, she would have been lost. As it was, when she turned and climbed the steps until she was above the outspread branches of the tree that had sheltered them, she almost hated him for not claiming her as he should, for his silence.

Distraught, she put her hand out to her husband, panicking, having narrowly escaped from the abyss into which she had almost fallen.

After their wedding, she and Ted traveled to the tiny fishing village of Portmahomack, for a brief honeymoon before he joined up. On a cliff overlooking the gray expanse of the North Sea, she told him about her past, the one she had before her other, more recent and secret past where she had fallen in love with another man. She told him about her childhood, how she had closed herself off from the world when she was thirteen years old. They had already talked about their histories, but now she went further, trying to explain why she felt so different from how she imagined other people felt. She owed him that much at least.

So she told him about her father dying, and how her mother married a man who would furtively rattle the door handle to her bedroom at night, terrifying her when she should have been sleeping. She told him how she shook as her stepfather stood over her, his shadow towering on the wall opposite her bed, and how she kept her eyes on that shadow as it became the stuff of nightmares, while all the time her mother lay asleep in a room nearby.

"I talked to the shadow," she told her husband, "in my head. I thought that if I could make friends with it, then one night, when he came to my room, the shadow would unpeel from the wall and raise its arms, to kill him and save me." She gave a bitter laugh as she sat tearing the grass on the cliff with her fists. "I had read *Grimm's Fairy Tales* once too often, perhaps."

"But your mother?" asked Ted, sitting beside her with eyes smarting red from the effort of stifling his tears. "Didn't she ever find out?"

"Oh yes," said Clare, throwing a handful of green blades into the cool air. "I told her. It took me months to find the courage to do it, but I did tell her." She watched the blades fall back to earth and scatter. "She had nothing to say about it. She was cold from that day forward. She had a lock put on my door and left the key under my pillow. In that sense, I suppose, she put a stop to it." She took a deep breath and gazed at the gray, furling sea. "I realized then that love can alter its shape, shift from protective, if unexpressed, devotion to frozen disregard."

Ted shook his head in disbelief. "But, my darling, you *needed* her. If you had tried to talk to her a second time . . . I mean, my God, what if you had started a baby?"

"No." Clare frowned, pushing her hair away from her face. She wrapped her arms around her knees, pulling them into her chest. "I didn't begin my monthlies until I was fifteen. But I made a decision. At the age of thirteen, I shut up my real self as a traveler packs away his belongings in a suitcase, ready to open it again when he arrives at his destination. Do you see?"

Ted leaned toward her, smiled, and held her close to him, kissing her hair. "My clever girl," he said, "I can't tell you how glad I am that you feel able to open that metaphorical suitcase."

Clare said nothing. She leaned in against him, staring at the water pouring over the rocks below. She didn't tell him the last part of the story, her story.

How, when she pulled back the lid, she looked in and found the suitcase empty.

And yet, to some extent, he had realized and understood the truth about her.

On the night that they met, at a dinner party in one of the stuccoed houses on Grosvenor Street, she had gotten as far as the front door when he suddenly found the courage to approach her. She turned and looked at him, this handsome boy who had charmed everyone but her with his attention and laughter, and waited for him to explain why he was standing between her and the warm, quiet street.

"I'd rather you didn't go just yet," he said, his skin flushed from excitement and shyness.

"Why not?"

"Because then I won't have the opportunity of trying to save you."

"Save me from what exactly?"

"From looking so unbearably sad."

He had taken her coat and led her back into the house, where he spent the remainder of the evening dispelling her customary reticence in the company of strangers. He introduced her to everyone, and at the end of the evening, when they said good-bye on the street outside, he lifted her chin up to him and kissed her very gently.

He drew back and looked down at her. "I think I'm falling in love," he said and smiled, his face radiant.

She felt herself grow a little less cold.

Ted's suggestion, three weeks later, that they marry filled her with an extraordinary sense of calm and gratitude. The lares and penates that governed her life seemed to have reached a mutual, peaceable agreement and she felt as though, at last, she could let go of the past.

She married him for security, a sense of self. And now, with Alex, she relinquished what she treasured most, and threw it away from her like a small red ball.

16

AFTER THAT FIRST MEETING IN LAMPEDUSA'S IN JULY 1914, WHEN SHE had no further contact with Alex, she began to think that she might succeed in submerging her fixation, that the war would keep them apart long enough for her rage—the secret word she gave to her desire for him—to weaken.

She was posted to a hospital in Rouen. Spartan in its facilities, both for patients and staff, it was housed in a group of tents on one of the great crags above the town. It was unlike anywhere she had worked before, but it was the very primitiveness of the arrangements that appealed to her. There was no Sister's Room, only a few chairs arranged around a table in the middle of one of the ward tents. Sugar boxes served as medicine chests, and sterilized equipment and containers were stacked on an old farmhouse kitchen table. Linen was kept in tea chests and all "sick-bay" articles were stored in a bell tent. There was no running water; a boiler outside dispensed hot water into buckets. The canteen was in a marquee, with tables laid end to end in a long row, and at the back of the marquee were a group of wire cages, to trap rats and keep their escalating numbers down.

Her day began at six thirty, when she awoke in one of the large bell tents shared by nurses and VADs. Breakfast was at seven. Afterward she reported to Matron for uniform inspection and orders. At seven thirty she went into the ward. Each day the wards were inspected and every Wednesday the colonel, his ADC, Matron, and the MOs made a special round. Clare never suffered nerves like the other nurses; the beds in her care were always neat and everything was in its place. Her day generally ended at six o'clock, but during the major offensives her time was flexible and it was usually well after midnight when she finally reached her own bed, too exhausted to contemplate eating.

During the day she would hear the bugle wailing through the hospital compound and echoing around the crags for reveille, meals, lights out, and the rousing *"fall in"* when a convoy of wounded arrived. She became accustomed to the bugle calls punctuating the hours and only the unscheduled "fall in" caused her nerves to prickle.

But however closed off she felt herself to be from the rest of the world, the sound of "The Last Post" played at each funeral never failed to penetrate her heart. For on the open fields above the town, a cemetery had been laid. White crosses stood in the long, sun-bleached grass, spreading relentlessly, day by day. The first burial Clare witnessed was an officer's. Under a sky the color of beaten tin, twenty men followed a hand-pulled cart on which the coffin lay beneath the Union flag. The chaplain waited beside the grave and read the service in a clear voice, intoning the words with the precision of a church bell. The dead man's wife had been notified of the funeral only the day before; she stood weeping in her widow's weeds, letting earth sift through her fingers onto the coffin. The guns issued a staccato salute into the autumn sky and wreaths of lilies were laid around the dark mouth of the grave. Later that afternoon there was another burial. In the evening there were four more. At the height of the main offensives, there were sometimes thirty burials a day. The last procession was always at sunset and the gatherings around the side of the grave sometimes seemed to stand against a wall of flame.

The funerals brought her closer to loving her husband as she felt she should. His death, even the prospect of it, made her rage for the other man buckle. She thought of her father's unexpected death, and of the appalling loneliness that had followed it. Death was her greatest fear; not her own death, but that of someone whom she loved. She had told her husband this once, and he had given her Marcus Aurelius's

Meditations to read, with one passage about death indicated with a leather bookmark.

Clare read it, but she didn't agree with what the Roman emperor had written: that when we die we lose only the present moment, for the past has ceased to exist and the future has not yet come. His belief that we should comfort ourselves with the thought, "Is this present moment really worth keeping?" made Clare frown. Don't past and future meet in the present? she wondered. And isn't sudden death comparable to ending a book mid-sentence, before the story is complete? What about the readers it leaves behind? They would feel cheated by the absence of a real ending, wouldn't they?

She pushed *Meditations* away.

The funerals were part of her life at the hospital in Rouen, as were the regular evacuations from the convalescent camp. Very often, Clare and the other nurses stood at the main gate to watch the drafts going up. In September 1914, she was given her movement orders for her first duty on the hospital train, and after her shift that evening, she threw her traveling cloak on over her uniform and walked down to the gate.

It was a clear, cool autumn night. The first stars were beginning to penetrate the velvet darkness. She looked at the long road and the lights of the camp opposite. After a short time, she heard singing and gravel being ground underfoot.

The battalions swung into view at the end of the twilit road. Their voices were raised to the tune of "My Little Grey Home in the West," but the words had been changed:

> "I've a little wet home in a trench,
> Where the rainstorms continually drench,
> There's a dead cow close by,
> With her feet in the sky,
> And she gives off a horrible stench.
> Underneath, in the place of a floor,
> There's a mass of wet mud and some straw,
> But with shells dropping there,
> There's no place to compare,
> With my little wet home in the trench . . ."

They waved when they saw her standing at the gate. One young subaltern cupped his hands to his mouth and called, "Wish us luck, Sister!"

Clare raised her hand, unable to speak.

She followed their progress along the road until they turned a corner and passed from sight. The wind carried back the plaintive cry, "Are we unhappy?" and its immediate, shouted rejoinder, "No!"

And then the singing voices grew faint, and the marching feet marched on, until she could hear them no more.

That night she dreamed about Alex for the first time since their meeting in Lampedusa's. His sudden appearance in her dreams disturbed her. When she awoke, she could remember only the feel of his skin against hers, and then a lurching gap in her consciousness, after which she became aware of a great silence.

She picked up Flaubert's *The Temptation of St. Anthony*, the book she had been reading before she fell asleep: "I shall show you what you tried to glean, by the light of tapers, from the faces of the dead—or when you vagabonded beyond the Pyramids, in those great sands composed of human remains. From time to time a fragment of skull turned beneath your sandal. You grasped some dust, you let it sift through your fingers; and your mind, mixing with it, vanished into the void."

17

I N THE AUTUMN OF 1915, AFTER TEN MONTHS WORKING AT THE HOSPI-
tal base in Rouen, Clare was given her movement orders as the Battle
of Loos began. Aboard the hospital train, there were four nursing sisters, two medical officers, and numerous RAMC orderlies trying to
cope with an unprecedented number of mutilated men pouring back
from the casualty clearing stations.

And they came in droves, vast multitudes of men, most of them
Scottish, after the first wave of attacks around Loos. Those whose injuries amounted to no more than a Blighty—as they called a wound
that wasn't life-threatening but necessitated the bearer being sent
home—sat in the misty dampness of the field at Chocques, their
wounds dressed and bandaged under the flapping cotton of their
partly sheared uniforms, comparing the souvenirs they had collected
from the enemy: watches, letters, caps, belt buckles, and bullets. They
hobbled about the field in torn kilts with the help of their comrades,
crowded onto the train to search for their friends on board, and joked
about whether the village had an estaminet where they could while
away their time with a drink in one hand and a farmer's accommo-
dating daughter in the other. They had done well on the battlefield
and the fact that they were going home without serious injury was

enough to raise their spirits and warrant a song or two beneath the lowering skies.

Those were the fortunate ones. The others lay soundlessly on stretchers ranged along the wooden platform, communicating with no one. Their hands and blind, bloated faces were livid and the brass buttons on their chalk-streaked uniforms had turned green. They were covered with blankets, but their convulsive shudders knocked them aside as they struggled to breathe, clawed at their own throats in terror, and pulled their knees up to their chests in agony as their lungs struggled to break free of the rising fluid that would eventually drown most of them.

At the end of the line of gas victims was a man for whom nothing could be done; his limbs were gone and the lower half of his face left behind in molecules at the foot of a pylon that had been damaged by his own gunfire. His friends prayed for him, hoping for his death, knowing that their comrade, a former heavyweight champion from Glasgow, would sooner draw his last in a foreign country than return to Scotland as an amputee, wheeled about in a box by his mother.

On the night that Clare left her stepfather dying in the ward carriage, she made her way to the compartment she shared with the other nurses and sat down on her bed. For a moment she allowed herself to succumb to the tearing exhaustion that numbed her limbs while she was working but filled them with a rapid, painful pulse when she retired. She didn't want to think about her stepfather, only yards away. Instead she pulled off her cap and bent down to drag out the canvas basin under her bed and unfolded it, then took the pitcher of water and emptied it into the bowl. She untied her cuffs and collar and washed every inch of exposed skin with the precious cuttlefish-sliver of lavender soap she kept in a muslin cloth, then opened the window and poured the fogged water away outside. She ran a comb through her limp hair, felt for the cigarettes inside her valise, and walked to the door in the corridor, crouching slightly before jumping to the ground.

Beyond the dark mound of hedges and the dilapidated roofs of farm buildings was the main road. As Clare walked away from the wooden platform and onto the grass, she could see its straight course through the village; a long, unending line of army vehicles and marching troops whose forms disappeared when they reached the tall pylons and black pyramids on the horizon. She lit a cigarette and watched the passage of men and horses into the unknown country, wondering how many would return in the incalculable varieties of disability that followed a new offensive.

"Do you mind if I join you?" asked a pleasant voice.

Clare turned. The voice belonged to Frances Quint, the young woman with whom Clare had never spoken until they both reported for duty on the hospital train, when they were formally introduced. She had been surprised by Frances's earlier declaration that she knew her by sight, since they worked in different departments of the same hospital and had not, as far as Clare was aware, come into contact.

She shook her head and Frances stepped down from the train. Clare replaced the stub of her cigarette in the packet; she didn't offer one to Frances, knowing the cheery young woman didn't smoke.

Frances untied the short scarlet cape that all QAIMNS nurses wore and breathed in deeply. The sound of distant traffic drew her attention to the congested road through Chocques.

"Future *blessés*," she said softly, folding the cape over her arm. Her dark hair lifted back from her forehead in the evening breeze; she had dispensed with the statutory gray bonnet before leaving the train. "I'm glad my brother isn't among them."

Clare barely heard her. The terrible scene in the ward carriage, and her stepfather's voice calling to her as she left him to die, roared in the farthest recesses of her mind.

"You're married, aren't you?" Frances sat down at the open door of the train and looked up brightly.

"Yes," said Clare.

Frances put her elbows on her knees and rested her chin in her cupped hands. She was intensely curious about Clare, who never seemed to speak unless she was addressed.

"You must miss him tremendously," said Frances sympathetically. "How long have you been married?"

Clare turned away. "Not so very long," she said.

"Is he in the army?"

"Yes," Clare replied. She stood very straight, staring at the distant lights of the vehicles moving along the road through Chocques. The low-lying mist had returned to screen the ugly slag heaps and machinery of the mines; it hung down from the black sky like a thin curtain.

Sensing that Clare did not welcome any sort of intrusion, however mild, into her personal situation, Frances changed the subject. "My older brother, Julian, is a war correspondent," she said, shivering. It was growing cold. She unfolded the scarlet cape and replaced it over her shoulders.

Clare turned again, catching the hem of her dress on a thistle. She bent down and unstuck the fabric from the flower's barbs, then looked at Frances without question or comment, though her face had tensed involuntarily.

"He's based in northern France, near St. Omer," said Frances. She sighed. "I haven't seen him for almost a year. There are only six official correspondents, so our family is terribly proud of him."

Then he must know Alex, thought Clare, her head still throbbing with the relentless distress of the encounter with her stepfather. My God, he must . . . She stiffened. Don't ask, she told herself angrily, don't ask.

A sudden, inexplicable fury suffused her. "It's not the same as being in the front line though, is it?" she said. Her limbs felt like steel; cold, immovable.

Frances was unable to hide her surprise at the discourtesy. "No," she said slowly, "but it certainly isn't a bed of roses either. He goes into the trenches and risks being blown to bits by a gun or a shell or a mine just as the other men do. And it's a big responsibility to keep the public informed about what's happening over here—it isn't as straightforward as it sounds."

"Oh, I read the newspapers," said Clare, unable to stop herself. "They report the war as if it were a *Boy's Own* story, one long saga of battles where no one seems to get hurt very much. I never read *anything* about the injuries we see, or the tedium of life between the big offensives, or the deprivations endured by the men."

Frances stared at Clare, astonished. "But . . . you don't understand the difficulties—" she began.

"I'm sorry, but I know whitewash when I see it," said Clare, coldly. She bunched up the hem of her skirt to avoid getting it caught on the barbs of the plants again. "I'm going to bed. Good night."

She nodded abruptly at Frances and pulled herself up into the train. Her arms and back ached unbearably. She cursed herself for her rudeness as she made her way to the compartment where she slept, and wondered why she had done it. Tomorrow she would apologize to Frances. Now all she could think of was her own excruciating fatigue, and she felt as if she might fall asleep on her feet, just as soldiers did.

She reached the compartment and sat down on the edge of her bed, her head drooping. She went on sitting there for a while, then turned and felt under her pillow for the newspaper cutting that she had concealed there.

A shout came from outside; the bombardment was starting up.

It was too dark to read the small square of paper, but she knew it by heart anyway. It had been cut from the pages of *The Times* and one edge was torn, splitting through *lectures* to create two nonsensical words. The piece had arrived inside an envelope dated October 31, sent by her husband.

A sudden breeze buffeted the train. Gunfire rocked the distance, its low, booming dissonance seeming to linger on the wind. She stared down at the fragile scrap of newspaper and knew that she would be in England on leave when Alex was giving his lectures.

A shadow moved against the blind of the hospital train. There was an apathy in the voice of the wounded soldier that sent a chill through her: "Attrition, they call it. *Attrition.* It's fucking deadlock, boys. That's what it is."

She pushed the ragged slip of paper back under her pillow, lay down, and closed her eyes.

18

WHEN CLARE ENTERED THE LECTURE ROOM SHE FELT CONSPICUOUS, as if her motives had walked in before her, claiming their place among the audience.

She sat down, trembling, her fingers feeling for the clutch on her bag, her shoes sliding noisily over the parquet floor. Her neighbor shuffled along the bench, making room for her, and she looked down into the bowl of the auditorium.

Alex had risen to his feet after the introduction and walked across to the lectern, dressed in black, as her husband told her she would only ever see him. She shrank back against the wall as he glanced up at the audience, hoping nervously that he could not see her. When he looked away again, she was relieved to realize that she was invisible behind the searing lights and that his gaze outward was as blind as that of a theater performer.

He talked about reasons. Reasons for war, reasons for continuing with it, balancing his own objections with a careful understanding of his audience, judiciously avoiding conflict with them, and succeeding. Clare thought about her own reasons for attending the lecture, for slipping guiltily into the building on Gower Street with its bright lights in an airless room while the rest of the city was in darkness. She decided that *her* reasons were egotistical, filtering down to one: her rage, which knew no boundaries, no kindness, no logic. Her immorality, as she saw it, made her evil; the most biblical of bad women.

As the crowd stood to applaud him, she got up, stooping to avoid the glare of the lamps, and rushed out into the corridor, calling for someone to show her quickly where she might find the exit and with it, redemption. She went out into the street and saw that it was raining hard, and she was unprepared for it, with only her coat—no hat or umbrella—to shield her.

London swerved in the dark, in the falling rain. The downpour filtered thickly through the sooty leaves of the thin trees outside the West End theaters and flowed in oblique streams into gutters clogged with wastepaper. It spattered around her heels as she ran down the steps toward the black lions on the other side of Trafalgar Square.

His touch. She turned toward him, her life spilling from her eyes.

"It is you who possesses me."

They clung to each other for two days, not going out, simply remaining together in the small space of his Chalcot Square flat, like drowning people hanging helplessly to a raft they know cannot save them. They were cocooned there, and the street lamp outside the bedroom window, with its light perpetually left unlit, seemed to offer them isolation from the rest of the city and the world beyond.

After wanting her for more than a year, Alex felt amazed when he held her, blessed and cursed forevermore. "I can't believe this," he said, shaking his head slowly. "I look at you, and I think, *I can't believe I'm allowed to touch her.*"

She laughed softly at him. "It's the same for me," she said. "I dreamed about this, when I was in France. And since being in London again, I've thought of nothing else. But I never thought it would happen."

He moved lithely above her, finding areas of her freckled skin with his mouth and hands, claiming them as a cartographer maps a new continent. "A place always belongs to its discoverer," he told her, "regardless of how many other travelers might wander through it."

She smiled at him. "I'm not sure I like what you're inferring."

He laughed. "I didn't mean it like that," he said, pressing his forehead against hers and looking deep into her eyes, her soul. "I was implying—no, *stating*—that you belong to me. Not just now, but later, and always. Don't you?"

"Yes."

She made journeys of her own, running her fingertips along a thin silver scar on his left hip, like a blade, three inches down the narrow brown strip of flesh and bone.

"How did you get this?" she asked. "It isn't recent, is it?"

He shook his head, his hands glorying in the feel of her skin and her touch on him. "No. It's no heroic war wound, I'm afraid. When I was ten, I began having pains in this leg. The doctors operated, even though they didn't seem to have a clue what was actually wrong. But one doctor thought that it happened because I was growing so fast, that the bones had slipped and were rubbing against each other, wearing down the gristle or some such. Anyway, the pains stopped, but I was left with this indentation, in my hip."

"It doesn't hurt now, does it?"

"Almost never. If I'm very tired, then I have a tendency to drag this foot. But not often."

"This scar belongs to me now," she said, kissing the white, knife-shaped mark.

There were other, subtler forms of ownership.

"Put on some music."

At her request he crossed the floor and took out a record from the pile stacked haphazardly on a bookshelf next to a tower of geographical hardbacks with gold lettering on the spines. The gentle sounds of the gramophone flooded the room, washing out onto the cramped balcony where she stood in the rain, luxuriating in the freshness of the hour.

"What is this?"

" 'The Long, Long Trail.' It's rather sentimental, I'm afraid."

She listened to the singer's plaintive voice filling the room. "I like it. Come and hold me."

His arms went around her neck, drawing her back against him. He stared over her shoulder, through the wet gleam of her hair to the eggshell-tinted houses on the opposite side of the square, their tall chimneys and shuttered windows. The trees bowed their branches under the fall of moisture, gray with the secretive hour before sunrise, when the city breathed quietly in its last turnings of sleep. It seemed to him as if the world had turned color—the pale shades were not dull, as he normally thought of them, but translucent, mother-of-pearl, with a thousand subtle nuances within. He loved London more than he ever had; in that particular moment, London was a genial, surprising benefactor, it was everything he wanted it to be and more. London, he believed, had brought this exquisite girl into his life.

She whispered, "I love you. Do you know that? I love you."

"Is that why you came to the lecture?"

"Of course it is, you idiot." She twisted around in his arms and looked up at him, her eyes searching his. Her expression changed from one of joy to fear. "What are we going to do?"

"I don't know. Oh God, Clare, I just don't know." He held her tightly against him, his jaw resting on her damp, blond head.

Later, she went back into the sitting room and curled up, unclothed, on the sofa, the early sunlight dappling her skin. He handed her a glass of water and sat down beside her.

"Tell me a secret," she said impulsively.

Alex searched for something, trying to think of what might appeal, of a secret that would make him more attractive to her, not less.

He said, "When you gave me the page you'd ripped out of my book, I didn't read it until I was sure you had gone. I was afraid that if I read it when I could still see you, I might race up to the bridge and ask you not to marry him."

"Do you regret it?"

"No. In a perverse way, the fact that we are together now makes me trust your feelings for me more."

She wound her arms around his body, feeling her skin brush against the smattering of downy hair on his naked chest. "Tell me another secret."

He thought for a moment. "Actually it's not a secret. I wanted to ask you something. A colleague of mine, Julian Quint, has a sister called Frances who works at a hospital in Rouen. Do you know her?"

Clare bowed her head. How much closer they had been to each other than they realized in the time they had spent apart—little invisible strands of wire linking his existence to hers, unseen but undeniably there, as if one day, someone would gather the strands together and in so doing, decide their fate.

"Yes. She was on the hospital train with me in Loos too. But I don't really know her. Why?"

"No reason, really. I just wondered."

Clare lifted her head. "Actually, she mentioned it to me—that her brother is a war correspondent." She hesitated. "I knew then that you and he must be colleagues, but I didn't say anything about it."

"Why not?"

She hesitated again, then lay down, her head in his lap, looking up at him. "I don't know. It was the end of a particularly long day. My stepfather . . . it was that night when I saw him. I was exhausted, and in shock." She turned down the corners of her mouth. "What could I have said, anyway? That I was in love with you?"

"No, of course not. But—"

"You promised to tell me a secret, and that wasn't one. Tell me another."

"No. My secrets get harder to tell from now on. Perhaps next time." He leaned down until his lips were in the hollow of her throat, and whispered, "I'll buy you with little pieces of me."

She closed her eyes, forgetting all else.

"What was it like, falling in love with him?"

They lay, still naked but wrapped now in a heavy blanket to ward off the cold, on the floor of his sitting room, smoking the cigarettes he had found in a kitchen drawer, staring at the cracks in the ceiling.

Clare answered, "I was like lost property, waiting for someone to claim me. Ted saw something in me that no one else had ever seen. I loved him for it."

"What did he see?"

She exhaled, trying to make the smoke reach a particular fracture in the plaster above. "That I am dead inside. When my father died, I felt something inside me wither. The fear of one day being completely alone came down like a great bird and carried me off to a high mountain. I never came back from there, not properly. Ted didn't care one jot; he loved me, even though he knew that I was incapable of normal feeling."

Alex turned to look at her. "You don't really believe that."

"Yes, I do."

"But you love me. That's a normal feeling."

"I also love my husband. Is that normal? To love you both? I don't think that's normal at all. But in a strange way, because I have this sense of being always detached from life, I am better at my job. I'm a good nurse, because of it."

"How? I can't see that."

"Because I am methodical and get the job done. The bad nurses are the ones who feel too much. They're no use to the men at all. It's very ironic—the nurses who care deeply are the ones who, in my opinion, don't do their work as well as they should."

"Don't you feel pity for the men in your care?"

"Of course," she said, nipping the cigarette and throwing it with remarkably precise aim into an ashtray. "But pity is not a sign of compassion. If you were to follow pity to its natural end you would find only scorn."

"That's ridiculous. What about Frankie? That boy, the one you told us about in Lampedusa's? You care about him, don't you?"

"Yes. He's such a child, though. I don't know how old he actually is, but he can't be more than seventeen, and he looks much younger."

"Well, I don't believe you," said Alex, stubbing his cigarette out, his arm at an awkward angle. "That isn't you at all. You would *like* to be like that, you would *like* to be as tough as you claim to be, but you're not. You can't fool me."

She rolled onto her side, her cheek against his shoulder, her fingers trailing across his chest. "Can't I?" she said.

"No. I know you feel tremendous pity for the men in your care."

"Yes, I do, but . . ." She closed her eyes. "The truth is, I don't want to feel too much—not for anyone."

"And where does that leave me?"

"Here," she said, opening her eyes and smiling, sliding down under the blanket and then pushing it away to rest her head on his stomach. "With me."

"You're afraid of getting hurt, aren't you? Everyone feels like that. But you can't close yourself off to experience. That would be a half-life."

"And where will this end?" she said quietly, breathing in the warmth of his skin. "This can lead only to great hurt."

He twined a lock of her hair around his fingers. "I can't answer that. But even if it kills me, I won't ever regret being with you like this. Sometimes the pain *is* worth it, Clare."

She gave a short, bitter laugh. "If this is what they call bliss now, when it already hurts so much, what will it be like later?"

He didn't answer. His hands explored the curve of her back, her spine under his fingers. "I want to know everything about you."

"Why?"

"It's what lovers do, isn't it? When they're trying to find out if they fit each other."

"But I don't want to know everything about you, Alex. I asked for secrets, but I don't want to know everything. Just a few things—mainly, that you love me. That will be enough, for me."

The following afternoon a letter arrived for Alex. He opened it while Clare was in the bath, putting his thumbnail to the fold of the envelope, and pulled out two sheets of blue paper. It was from Ted, written during his last evening in London.

As Alex read it, he froze; it was as if Ted had anticipated the conversation that had passed between the two of them the night before, for he wrote: "Clare is reading beside me as I write this. She reads all the time. It's one of the things that I love about her, I love watching her read but she doesn't like it. When she sees me looking at her, she demands, *'What?'* All she and I do is read, drink, eat, and make love. We don't talk much, which suits me perfectly. I've lost the desperate need to know everything about her. That is what kills relationships—the need to know and be known."

Alex put the letter down, shaking.

When she got out of the bath, he told her about it, and what it contained. She stood in the narrow white hallway, binding her long wet hair in a blue towel. "Are you jealous?" she asked softly.

"Yes. But not about the sexual relationship between the two of you as such. More the fact that he may know something about you that I don't. We're all selective with the truth and different with everyone we meet." He dug his hands deep into his trouser pockets, leaning against the door, biting his lower lip.

She finished wrapping the towel about her head and looked at him. "Alex. There is nothing else you need to know about me. I am everything I am when I am with you. No dark corners, no secrets, no lies."

"But that's what I mean. When you leave me, you become someone else."

"What do you mean? Who do I become?"

"His wife."

Her lovely eyes darkened. "And you then? Who do you become?"

"Someone less important to you."

Her anger was apparent. "That's a lie."

"Is it? If I asked you to leave him, to be one person for the rest of
your life, what would you say?"

She answered swiftly, "That you don't mean it. That you are testing
me." She paused. "I think you love him as much as you love me."

He looked away and said nothing.

She stared at him for a moment, then slammed the bathroom door
and went into the bedroom to dress, hating him with every ounce of
feeling she had.

It was Clare who had to leave first, catching the boat train from Victoria for Dover, and the ship to France. Alex's unwillingness—or was it
inability? she wondered—to reply to the question she had asked after
the arrival of Ted's letter still tormented her.

She made it clear that she didn't want him to accompany her to
the station.

On the afternoon she was due to leave, the two of them stood outside her flat in Battersea, where they had gone to collect her belongings, and stared at each other. It was dark again, and beginning to sleet,
pale streaks falling into the river where crusts of ice formed about the
moored boats and jetties.

"May I write to you?" he asked quietly.

"If you wish." She stared up at him, white flakes gathering in her
hair like bridal flowers. She tried to place where it came from, that
need to create a barrier between them, to punish him for their treachery, and his silence.

"What are you thinking?" he asked.

"I'm trying to work out which one of us is the more evil: you, for
betraying the man you regard as your brother, or me, for committing
adultery."

"Is that how you see us? As *evil* people?" He was aghast.

She gritted her teeth. "Aren't we? I think we are."

He stumbled back as if she had struck him. "I thought we were simply two people in love who had met at the wrong time." He drew a deep breath. "But if you see it like that, then . . . leave. If I am so repellent to you, *leave.*"

She looked at him blindly, the gray pigment of her eyes almost transparent. Then she turned and walked away, her footsteps hushed by the falling, slanting flecks of sleet.

Alex looked up at the sky above the river, at the whirling whiteness, and felt appalled.

VIII

WINDS IN RESTLESS TREES

*France, New Year's Eve 1915
and February 1916*

19

IN THE VILLA VIA SACRA, IT HAS BEGUN TO GROW COLD. THE LIGHT across the plains has dimmed to little more than a faint sheen on the tips of the ruins of Elverdinghe, and the destroyed village resembles a row of small, jagged-peaked hills beneath the stars.

A breeze makes the flame of the candle in the hurricane lamp lurch back and forth, passing a thin veil of radiance over Lombardi's face as he leans forward to talk.

"Were those two days in London the end of the affair?"

Alex looks up, as if startled by the interruption. "No. No, that wasn't the end of it. I suppose I thought, then, that it might be. I wrote to her, but she didn't reply. Then her husband came to see me."

"Did he know about the two of you?"

"No. Not yet." The distance in his eyes is infinite as he remembers. "He was already different, but it was much later when . . . it happened." He pauses. "When he lost his mind."

"I returned to France earlier than expected; I wanted to go back. Late afternoon on New Year's Eve 1915 found me sitting in an estaminet in

Armentières with a group of artillerymen, sheltering from a howling gale and waiting for Julian Quint and Jack Garland.

"I was already familiar with the gunners' exuberant company; I had spoken to them in their billets the day before for a series I was writing about life between the battles. As the bitter winter drew in, the campaigning season on the Western front began to wind down, and the army took up a new, defensive position. The British newspapers found the routine of war too lackluster to cover in general, but *The Manchester Echo* had taken one of my experimental dispatches about work in the trenches: draining them, building the walls, boarding the ground, timbering the dugouts, and underpinning the parapets. On the back of that, I was commissioned to write six eight-hundred-word reports on the day-to-day life of the British soldier. The dispatches were still scrutinized by the censors at GHQ, but I had expected that and was satisfied that, even in their edited form, articles about an unexplored aspect of the conflict were finding their way into people's homes.

"Armentières wasn't a town destined to survive another year of war. It was too close to the front; many of its shops, houses, and lively cafés opened almost onto the trenches themselves. The insatiable German guns had killed hundreds of civilians already. The buildings were shell-pocked, the streets reduced to piles of smoldering rubble.

"But the café, at least, was alive with the soldiers' singing. After a few drinks, I scraped back my chair and went over to the door, whose glass panel rattled like dice in a coffer. Two old men shouted at each other in the crooked street, one standing crouched against the high wind, gesticulating wildly to the other, who peered out of a broken window. I could hear guns firing in the distance, beyond civilization. Farther down the street was a bookshop, and among the newspapers and novels on display in the window were locally made cards. They were eye-catching: holly leaves, angels, and seasonal good wishes in faulty English, worked in brilliant silks.

"I glanced at my watch and saw that it was almost half past five. Jack and Julian had been due at five o'clock, but I assumed their car was having problems negotiating a road through the flooded countryside. I thought they might have preferred to return to the château instead, having spent the day wading through the trenches at Neuve Chapelle to report back on the Christmas period for those still in the firing line.

"I paid for a second round of drinks for the gunners before leaving the café and crossing the road. The wind hurled the rain at my face, soaked my clothes, and trailed cold fingers around my neck. I bought a cigarette lighter and a card I had seen in the window and tucked them inside my coat. Then I braced myself before heading back out into the storm.

"I arrived back in Tatinghem an hour later than Julian and Jack, and went straight up for a bath and to change my clothes. I joined them in the sitting room for a nightcap, retiring to my room in the early hours of the morning. By then, the storm had spent itself, and I lit a cigarette and stood there staring out into the quiet night, thinking about Clare. I couldn't concentrate on anything else. She was imprinted upon me; however I tried to fight it, my body still remembered her body, my skin her skin, my mouth her mouth.

"I took the card from the pocket of my tunic, slung over the chair. The floorboards to my right creaked as Julian closed his bedroom door. I sat down at my desk, shivering in the cold breath coming in through the window frame.

"Then I opened the card and took up my pen."

Lombardi looks at his visitor, at the thin frame in black, the sharp angles of his shadowed face. It is as if his body is a husk containing the blood and bones but not the spirit. The man has been effaced, what makes him human is gone. He is very far away, in a landscape that no longer exists.

Lombardi listens, silent and thoughtful, as the writer turns the pages of the notebook again, half reading from it, half talking from memory.

"Before midday on the twenty-third of February 1916, snow began to fall in Flanders. Within hours it lay in great drifts across the plains, forming peaks on the wooden crosses that marked the graves of the fallen. It covered the red roofs and deep thatch of the villages where soldiers were billeted, in a turreted white mantle, and created fragile patterns along barbed-wire fences above trenches turned into soft, silent furrows. An infinite stillness descended on the battlefields as the mute guns of the batteries vanished under a knoll of rushing flakes.

We had been given a new home for the new year, a magenta-walled country house in the village of Tilques, a few miles northwest of St. Omer. Ted came to see me there, on the night that snow stopped the war in Flanders. It was less than two months since his wife and I had become lovers."

His voice falters over the last word, then picks up the thread and weaves it back into the story.

"Ted had been in the hospital at Boulogne, recovering from a bout of dysentery. We had written to each other; I thought he was still there, but then he appeared at the house in Tilques, skeletally thin. The pure light within his eyes seemed dimmed.

"I was shaken by his arrival. It must have shown on my face, for he asked, 'Do I seem like a ghost to you? I feel like one.'

"And then he broke into a smile. 'You've no idea how humiliating it was to come through so much on the battlefield only to face the possibility that I would die of the screaming shits.'

"I didn't know what to say to him. His smile was fragile, as though a breath of wind could shatter it. He was pale, tremulous. I wondered if he knew about Clare and me, and a welter of apprehension—even fear—gripped me by the throat so that I could barely speak without betraying myself.

"He walked into my room, touching the objects on my desk as if he had never seen such commonplace things before.

" 'I've got five days' leave,' he said. 'I wanted to see you as well as Clare. She tried to get some time off, but could arrange only one free day. When that was up, I came straight here. I have to go back tomorrow.'

" 'Where to?'

" 'Reninghelst. Rest period—thank God. It's a little village just south of Poperinghe.'

" 'And then?'

" 'We'll see. You're looking well. How are things?'

" 'Fine,' I said, swallowing hard. 'Listen, do you think you'll be able to get back to billets? Nothing's moving on the roads around here.'

" 'I've cadged a lift with an ambulance heading for Pop. They've got to get back somehow, even if it means me walking in front with a shovel.'

" 'Where are you staying tonight?'

" 'In Tilques. There's a small guesthouse whose windows positively glow with the landlady's welcome.'

· " 'It's not . . . ?'

" 'What? A den of iniquity?' The same brittle smile. 'No. I've just spent time with my beautiful wife. The last thing on my mind is climbing into bed with some bad-tempered French floozy out to empty my pockets. Shall we go downstairs? Your colleagues were just going in to dinner when I arrived.'

"He didn't know about Clare and me, about the affair; I was certain of it. Almost euphoric with relief, I showed him out onto the long dark landing, where the murmur of voices and the clink of glasses being brought together in a toast drifted up from behind closed doors below.

"He seemed cheerful enough during the meal, but in hindsight I realize that it was all on the surface and mostly for my benefit. Underneath, he was somehow diminished. But I was too absorbed by my own problems to see it then.

"After dinner we sat in the library. Julian joined us for the obligatory nightcap, sitting in one of the leather wing chairs opposite the two of us on the sofa. Ted was uncharacteristically subdued at first, but then he began to talk of his hatred for the generals in charge of the war. I listened and understood, but at the same time, I realized with a shock as cold as the snow mounting the steps to the front door, that here was a quite different man from the one whom I had seen just before Christmas, in London.

" 'They're all alike,' he said sourly, staring at the oil painting above the mantelpiece, opposite where we were sitting. 'They think alike and they look alike. Somewhere there is one woman giving birth to them all, squatting them out like a cat with a litter of runt kittens. They muddled their way through the South African war and now we're letting them muddle their way through this one. They're mired in old, fusty-smelling traditions, caste privilege, and a belief that the Empire depends upon their way of thinking. And what do they actually do all day, up there in their pleasant offices at GHQ? They write to each other, and the ones who write the most letters receive the most decorations. They think they're "getting on with things." '

"He didn't look at us while he spoke. His voice was low, warm with an anger that was foreign to him. 'I've been to St. Omer and spent a few hours in their citadel. It's like a medieval court—they have their rivalries, their intrigues, and their perjuries. Each general and staff officer has his sycophants who squabble among themselves for jobs and grovel at their senior's feet and tell him that he is invincible. They're all graded, of course, and those in the lower grades fight for a higher grade using every trick they've learned along the way and as much backstairs influence as they can muster. At night they ring one another on their internal telephones on some pretext to remain in their offices, so that they might appear conscientious and diligent.'

"He gave a bitter laugh. 'It's true that they live and breathe war at GHQ, but not the reality of it, not what we see. They have their own little world. A trench, good Lord, what's that? Oh yes, they've *heard* of them and some of them have even *seen* them, in the way that our kind of people like to go slumming on occasion to remind us of our superiority. Visiting the trenches makes them feel brave, and they think that it gives them the right to say that they know what it's like down there, on the battlefields. But they don't, you see, they don't.'

"His voice, which had risen with passion, now became flat and lifeless. 'The trenches are the slums. And we who live in them are the Great Unwashed. We are the Mudlarks.'

"The room became silent. Julian and I exchanged glances, and I put my hand out to Ted, trying to reassure him, but he flinched from the contact and went on, 'There used to be a trench in the salient called J3. You won't have heard of it, away out in advance of our lines. It wasn't connected with our own trench system but had been left to rot by us, and by the enemy. It was really just a ditch, out there in the middle of No Man's Land. But we were ordered to hold it, to save sniping. One of the battalion commanders protested to GHQ. 'There's no point in holding it,' he said. 'It's senseless, a target for German guns and a temptation to German miners.' GHQ told him it had to be held until further orders. So we went on holding it. The mines exploded and five hundred men were killed. Five hundred . . . in a place no one knows or cares about. If they ever did.'

"His voice stopped abruptly, like a dropped watch. I put my hand out to him again and this time he didn't recoil. Instead he let his head sink into his chest, as if he had fallen asleep.

"In the silence, Julian got to his feet. 'I think I'll turn in, if you don't mind,' he said quietly. 'It's been a long day.'

"I nodded at him; Ted didn't even seem to notice that he was leaving.

"The door closed quietly behind Julian, leaving us alone. The library was warm and comfortable, but the cold reek and clamminess of the trenches seemed to cling to Ted as he sat there, his head bowed. We sat without speaking, the wind gently pressing against the windowpanes and the white flecks of snow drifting in the darkness.

"Hesitantly, I said, 'I hope you don't despise me. I'm only a visitor to your sort of life too.'

"He looked at me, surprised. 'Of course not,' he said, 'I don't think like that at all. It's just *them* ... I feel as though, even though we're grown men, that we have lost our innocence.'

"There was another silence. Ted reached for the whisky decanter and poured us each a stiff drink. I noticed that his hand trembled.

" 'I feel like I'm bursting inside,' he said. 'Sometimes I hear a sort of buzzing in my head. The only thing that keeps me going is the thought of what comes after.'

" 'Is it?' I said, feeling as if his pessimism had rubbed off on me. 'How will we live again? Have you thought of that?'

" 'It won't ever be how it was, but life will go on, whatever happens. Some of my men don't even want to try. And their wives and families are the problem—they say they can't live with women who know nothing of what they've endured. At least Clare knows. She understands.' His face softened. 'I can't wait until it's over. It's what keeps me alive and sustains me despite all the horror: the thought of being with Clare again properly, and raising a family in the country somewhere.'

" 'The country?' I said in mock horrified tones, disguising the turmoil I felt inside. 'The country? You can't leave London—you'll deflate like a balloon.'

"He gave a short laugh. 'No I won't. Clare won't either. She was born and raised in Scarborough. We've discussed moving back to Yorkshire, after the war. You're a Whitby boy—why don't you come too?'

" 'To do what exactly? Write for the *Middle-of-Nowheredale Gazette*?' I shook my head, glad that the conversation had switched to another subject, even one that also caused me pain. 'I'll take my chances in London, if it's all the same to you.'

"He smiled at me. 'You always did chase after glory.'

"I felt stung by his remark and responded more sharply than I intended. 'If I did, it's only because I knew I would never succeed otherwise. You always got there first.'

"Ted finished his drink. 'Did I?' he said, placing the glass on the table. 'It was never intentional.'

"His honesty made me relent. 'I know. That's why no one ever begrudged you anything. Everything came to you so easily, and afterward you were always so surprised, so charmed by the accolades that came your way, that no one minded.'

" 'You make me sound horribly spoiled,' he said, frowning. 'I wasn't, was I?'

" 'No. You were the boy everyone wanted to befriend. Then later, you were the one most of them fell in love with.'

" 'Rot,' said Ted, pulling the decanter toward him again. 'Not having a family and being brought up by a guardian in a country pile had far more to do with it. I was like something from a Fielding novel to everyone except you. They all romanticized me, that's the truth of it.'

"Silence again. And then all at once he asked, 'If you had met Clare before I did, do you think you would have fallen in love with her?'

"The floor-to-ceiling shelves of books seemed to sway and retract. I watched a spider run along the dado rail beside the heavy wooden doors. I held my breath for a moment, then said, in as normal a voice as I could muster, 'What an extraordinary thing to ask.'

" 'But would you, do you think?'

" 'I've no idea. There's no earthly reason to assume that I would . . .'

" 'And no earthly reason to assume that you wouldn't. After all, she has the kind of ethereal blond beauty you always seem to go for. And she's clever and funny—'

" 'I don't know her,' I said, clutching my glass. 'And it's not just a matter of looks and personality. Love is more than that. It's the sum of all things; it's a set of circumstances, it's your past and theirs, it's what you want and whether they want the same thing. It's a belief system that I'm not even sure I believe in.' I stared down at the floor, counting the grains on the wooden boards until I reached twenty. Then I turned to him and asked, 'If I said yes, what would you do?'

"He smiled, 'I'd say that you have impeccable taste.'

" 'Is that all? I thought you'd tear me limb from limb.'

"He shook his head slowly. 'I wouldn't even do that if she fell in love with you too. I care about you both too much.'

"I looked at him, curiosity getting the better of me, as desire had done. 'So what would you do?'

"He turned to me, the light falling across his face, illuminating it softly.

" 'I'd die,' he said."

"That night, when he had gone, I lay in bed, unable to sleep.

"I drifted in and out of consciousness, hearing the guns starting up again in the salient; the weather had not kept them peaceful for long. But it was another sound that had awoken me, something I could not place.

"I sat up and looked out the window. On the bedside table lay the book of poetry Clare had ripped a page from, before the war, before she and I became lovers. The winter landscape and the terrible quarry concealed beneath it brought one particular verse to life:

"*Night on the blood-stained snow: the wind is chill.*
And there a thousand tomb-less warriors lie
Grasping their swords, wild-featured. All are still.
Above them the black ravens wheel and cry . . .

"I thought of the dead, lying out there, their faces pressed against the ermine mantle of the blizzard. I imagined the purity of the snow becoming stained with their blood, spilled in agony.

"Then I knew. It wasn't ravens I could hear out there in the darkness. It wasn't their cries that had disturbed me from my sleep.

"It was the dead. I could hear them.

"The dead, screeching beneath the white snow."

———————

The dog, Kemmel, gets up slowly from the floor and climbs onto the sunken red sofa, his back to them.

"It was a premonition," Lombardi says. "Wasn't it? Hearing the dead cry."

Alex doesn't look at Lombardi, but at the dark blue horizon. His fingers trace the words he has read out loud, as they did when he was first learning the power of language. "Yes," he replies finally. "I think it was."

The cold wind grows colder, sliding in through the knots and gaps of the wooden hut.

Lombardi asks, "That was the turning point in your friendship, wasn't it? That night in Tilques?"

Alex puts his hands on either side of his head, in a despairing gesture now familiar to Lombardi.

"Yes. I had spent my whole life loving him. But when he needed me most, I did something far worse than failing him. I betrayed him." His voice drops. "My affair with his wife was the only thing that mattered to me, even when we couldn't be together, even though I didn't see her again until almost a year later, in October 1916."

He raises his head. His eyes are blank, fathomless. "Because, of course, that summer the war shattered into violence unlike anything that had gone before, keeping us apart."

IX

When Heaven Was Falling

Somme, 1916

20

THE HOSPITALS WERE BEING CLEARED OUT. IN ADVANCE OF THE "BIG Push," those patients well enough to travel to England were sent on and the ones whose convalescent periods were nearing an end returned to the front. Spring in Rouen had passed quietly while the French army struggled in the battle for Verdun; most of the casualties were sent on to Lyons or Paris. Toward the end of May, Clare learned that the hospital in Rouen was planning to increase its number of beds by several hundred more.

In mid-June, she was given her movement orders.

Frank, the emasculated boy from the Black Watch, was still in her care and when Clare went on duty that afternoon he asked her if it was true.

"Yes," said Clare. "I'm being sent up the line."

For a moment he looked at her speechlessly. In the months that had passed, she had often visited him during her breaks, and they would sit and talk companionably. At night, when he couldn't sleep despite the medicine he was given, if Clare was not on duty she would sit with him, telling him stories. One was a cherished childhood story told to her by her own father, about a cat who had used up his nine lives but went on having adventures just the same. She felt foolish at first, telling him such childish tales, but they seemed to calm him.

"Are you afraid?" he asked her now.

"No," she said. "I'm not afraid for myself."

"You would have made a good soldier."

"I don't think so."

He looked at her hands, folded neatly over each other on her flat abdomen as she stood at his bedside. He wished he could summon the courage to reach out to her.

"You'll be well looked after here when I've left," she said, breaking into his thoughts. "And in less than a month you'll be going home."

"You won't be back before then, Sister?"

"I shouldn't think so." She stuck out her chin and said firmly, "I must go. Take care of yourself, Frankie, and be the same brave, strong boy for your family that you've been for me." She leaned down, and her lips touched his forehead briefly before she left the ward.

Frank lay his head back against the flat pillow, staring upward at nothing. Since arriving at Rouen he hadn't shed a single tear, glad beyond all reason that he had ended up in the hospital that was base to the young nurse who had cared for him on the train. Her calm beauty engendered in him a tranquillity he had never thought to possess, and although he still dreamed of tearing flesh and impending death, he was able to accept what had happened to him because he wanted to show her that he could. But as Clare's footsteps faded on the wooden boards set into the grass and soil outside the ward tent, he let the tears slide down into his hair and ears. Even then, the warm moisture on his skin reminded him that he was alive.

Clare packed her kit methodically, immune to the feverish anticipation of the coming offensive that had spread throughout the hospital affecting both staff and patients. She put in her husband's letters and a small envelope postmarked "Armentières," then turned as a movement by the open tent flap alerted her.

She lay the kit bag down on the bed and went across to the entrance. One of the middle-aged orderlies stood there uncertainly, holding out a parcel wrapped in brown paper.

"Yes?" said Clare, surprised by his sudden appearance.

"I was asked to give you this, Sister." He held out the parcel.

Clare took it, turning it over curiously in her hands. Her name was on it, but nothing else, no postage stamps of any kind. She looked up to inquire about the sender, but the orderly was already making his way back to one of the ward tents. Puzzled, she returned to her bed and unwrapped the gift from its covering of brown paper.

It was a Siamese cat glove-puppet, skillfully crafted and destined for a professional puppeteer rather than a child. She touched the lifelike beige fur, the pink plush nose, and the marbled, blue button eyes, then put her hand inside and wriggled the paws. With a frown, she realized that there was something tucked up inside the head of the puppet. She drew it out with her other hand.

A small card bore unsteady handwriting:

"Dear Sister, I asked one of the orderlies to buy you something from me so that you won't forget me. Puss is to keep you company and bring you luck. I hope you don't mind. When I get back home I will write to you, just to let you know that I am being brave, as you told me to be. Yours very truly, Frank Stephens. P.S. You wanted to know how old I am but I would never tell you. Keep it to yourself then: I am fifteen."

Clare brought the glove-puppet level with her face and squeezed her hand slightly, making the head bow and the paws meet together.

Fifteen, she thought in horror, he's fifteen. A baby, a mite. Furiously, she wiped away the tears that fell in great drops onto her skirt.

Through the opening in the tent she could see the convoy of ambulances setting off to go farther north, the gears grinding above a flurry of shouted good-byes. She slid the puppet off her hand and pushed it gently into her kit bag, then watched the vehicles jolt down the road that led through the hospital compound, past the virtually empty convalescent camp. As they turned in the direction of the town, the sun shone on their battered roofs and bonnets, making the drab army-green vehicles gleam like tarnished medals.

She traveled in the second convoy of motor ambulances from Rouen, passing through Amiens at midnight. Coming down the hill into the city, her eyes rested on the spire and flying buttresses of the cathedral. In the brilliant moonlight it looked like the backbone of some pre-historic animal. The river shone below as the ambulance lurched over a bridge.

She fell asleep and dreamed of strange, unhappy things, sleeping until morning, when they came upon the approach to Albert. The town sat on a hilltop, its brown, shell-pocked streets and pounded cathedral enclosed by sweeps of countryside. Immediately visible was the leaning effigy of the Virgin and Child, dislodged from its upright position on the basilica the year before by a German gun. The statue hung at a precarious angle face downward, remaining steadfast regard-less of the gradual destruction of the cathedral below.

The ambulance rattled around a bend then began the descent and subsequent steep climb into the center of Albert. Clare gazed in fascina-tion at the golden figure suspended above the modest market square, aware of the powerful local myth that if the Virgin fell the war would end in a German victory. She had given it no more credence than the rumor that the Russian army had passed through England one night with the snow still on their boots, and was unsurprised when she saw the steel hawsers supporting the lustrous statue and keeping it in place.

From Albert, they traveled northwest to Hébuterne, nearing the trenches. Ribbons of chalk dust drifted in the sun. The grass verges were mottled with it, like gunpowder. Then after the sinister dust, beauty: rolls and folds of green and yellow, corn and plow. The chalk downs and soft meadows of Picardy reminded her of England, even though she knew that beyond the high, unspoiled ground lay the tur-bulent dark of the battlefields. The ambulance rattled through wooded villages, a knot of houses on a tree-circled ridge. For an instant the road was elevated, with the ground falling away on either side, and she caught a heart-stopping glimpse of men moving like ants on a vast, unexpected heap before the road dipped again.

They traveled onward to where the road leveled out through flat, gilded fields. Broken wagons and upturned farm carts littered the roadside, the horses still shackled to the wooden shafts, bodies swollen in death. A mile away to the east, on the lip of a slight valley, was the once quiet, pleasant village of Gommecourt, its redbrick houses and farms surrounded by the woodland of Gommecourt Park. The English lines were located on the plateau in front of the trees and Gommecourt Park itself formed the enemy salient.

They reached the outskirts of Hébuterne, nine miles from Albert, situated at the northernmost tip of the Front Line. A bank of tall trees came into view, bordered by orchards and fields, with the twisted, medieval church spire at its center. As they entered the village itself, she saw that for all its ruinous appearance, Hébuterne had in recent times enjoyed a period of prosperity; what was left of its buildings and houses revealed a comfortable standard of prewar living and the distinctive church tower gave the place an enduring, patrician air. Now it was a plague village, deserted, its damaged buildings silent, its fields empty, its lanes overgrown. The citizens of the village had left, abandoning the place to its terrible destiny.

The road curved up to the red church where the field-dressing station was established. The ambulances stopped alongside and as she climbed out, Clare saw that the main part of the building had been badly shelled. The stained-glass windows and several walls had been lost in a blast that had brought the roof crashing in on the nave. The central, smaller octagonal dome was intact and acted as the hub of maneuvers from which the existing medical staff emerged.

Frances Quint was waiting at the unbroken base of what remained of the church tower. She had been detailed to meet them, and she gave them a cursory introduction to their surroundings, ending with the lanes that ran through the orchards. Clare still felt awkward with her, despite having apologized for her rudeness when they worked together at Loos; although Frances had been gracious in accepting, Clare regretted her earlier discourtesy, particularly because she had been unable to explain it.

Now Frances shaded her eyes with one hand, taking no particular notice of Clare as she pointed toward the lanes: "They use those as communication trenches to the line. When we first came here, we dug a whole new system of trenches. The French effort wasn't up to much. If this clump of trees wasn't here, and that rise, you'd be able to see straight across to Gommecourt Park. On one side is the village of Gommecourt and on the other, the village of Fonquevillers. Our boys call it 'Funky Villas.' There's a shallow valley out there, between the British and German trenches: that's No Man's Land."

Clare looked up at the blue, unclouded sky through the rafters and then at the nave. At the far end of the church the walls had been preserved to roof height. Sandbags enclosed the small altar. Hanging above it was a tall wooden crucifix. At the foot of the crucifix was a quotation, oddly, from Heraclitus, behind cracked glass: "We must know that war is common to all and strife is justice, and that all things come into being and pass away through strife."

She retrieved her kit bag from the ambulance and followed Frances down into the crypt.

The preliminary bombardment began on the morning of June 24. In the fields beyond the village, vast clouds of dust and chalk threw banners across the sky. At the roadside opposite the church, Clare saw piles of toffee-apple mortars under a sheet of tarpaulin. A few days later the ammunition disappeared, replaced by a mound of plain wooden crosses.

All week, as the guns roared and summer storms broke over the villages and hamlets of the valley of the Somme, the church swarmed with activity as final preparations were made in advance of the Big Push. Supplies were unpacked, floors swept and scrubbed, dressing trolleys and screens wheeled into place, and a fire kept going in the nave to sterilize instruments, cook rations, and dry out blankets and clothing. At the back of the church were the latrines, pits dug four feet deep. Every nurse, orderly, and stretcher bearer had to take their turn as "shit wallah," disposing of urine and excrement. The latrines stank, as did most of the land around the church, together with the creosol and chloride of lime used to lessen the risk of infection and repel the flies.

On the night of June 30, the assault battalions, loaded down with kit, ammunition, water, and supplies, moved up into the line.

The red church glowed under the blaze and flicker of the Verey lights, and the walls shook with the crackle of machine guns and indiscriminate explosions from the front line. Clare lay on her straw bed in the vault, restless like the others, listening. She could hear marching feet passing along the village street, like the scuttle of rats coming out of the rubble of the church, one vast siege of rats.

The barrage lifted with the dawn.

Six o'clock on the red church tower, and the British guns aimed at the German line from Gommecourt in the north to Maricourt in the south began to roar with an intensity that caused the entire valley to pulsate. The wide skies were engulfed in a white squall that burst apart in a black fog. And still the sun blazed high above the orchards.

Clare watched as red clods of earth flew over the trees in the direction of Gommecourt. The passion of the guns agitating the landscape stunned her. The shells shot up and up, sheathing the sky with white vapor before exploding into bloodred darkness as nearby villages were wiped from the face of the earth.

The bombardment stopped an hour later. An unearthly stillness descended over the valley. Dust began to settle on the uppermost branches of the splintered trees and on the shattered roofs around Hébuterne.

Zero hour came during that brief, ringing silence.

Thousands of British troops went over the top, climbing up the parapets, blinded by the swirling clouds of the powerful mines that had been detonated, heading straight into the crashing guns of the enemy, who were charging forward from their dugouts to obliterate every last man.

In the church in Hébuterne, Clare waited apprehensively with the rest of the medical staff. Her ears rang with the sound of the shells that were too high to be seen but which came screaming thick and fast over the trenches. The smoke from the British line of attack, intended to blind the enemy, was blown back by the scorching summer zephyr, and the Germans took advantage of it, supplementing their counterattack with hand grenades, bombs, and unrelenting fire from machine guns.

The soft furrows and folds of the countryside were driven into oblivion as shells slammed into the support trenches and rained down on Hébuterne with the ferocity of a tidal wave.

After nightfall, the wounded began pouring in through the doors of the red church. Within a few hours, Clare felt as if her training and previous experiences might never have happened, so unprepared was she for the horror of it all. The wounded came from the inundated regimental aid posts, where field dressings were applied and rudimentary attention was given to their injuries. The walking wounded entered the church on crutches, clinging to their comrades, who were themselves bandaged about the heads and limbs, their clothes glutinous with blood and matter. Others crawled in on their hands and knees, stumbling over the stretcher cases whose lacerations flowed through the canvas and onto the stone, creating a quagmire that no one was able to clear. The men without hope of survival were separated from the rest in the churchyard, classified "Moribund." Casualties suffering gas gangrene in their mortifying limbs had their wounds opened and irrigated, or were sent for immediate amputation. Most had shell-fire injuries, less clean than bullet wounds for shells broke up on impact, resulting in ghastly, multiple lacerations.

Spastic light from the guns burst through the broken windows of the church.

Clare crouched beside the wounded, cutting through clothing and puttees with heavy surgical scissors that caused blisters the size of coat buttons to form on her fingers and palms. When they burst her hands became wet and sore. She worked on all night, stemming bleeding, picking out bits of shrapnel and bullets, giving anti-tetanus injections, administering saline for shock and morphine for intolerable pain, cleaning wounds, applying dressings, strapping gallows splints to twisted limbs, fighting her own body's clamor for rest.

At daybreak she heard Sister Quint shout in a voice fractured with desperation, "God Almighty, there are medical outposts all the way back to Doullens—why can't we send some of these men on?"

Clare was sent down into the crypt, where a surgeon was working on three operating tables simultaneously, moving rapidly from one to the other. "Anesthetize—dress wounds—stitch wounds," he told her calmly while probing lesions, extracting bullets and shrapnel that had carved deep into flesh, and performing crude amputations. She stood beside him at the long tables where a succession of men writhed in torture. She held a wire cup with gauze in it over the patient's nose and mouth and tipped the anesthetic onto it carefully. She held the infected stumps of men whose legs had been blown off, pus flowing onto her hands as the solution of Eusol and peroxide was poured into the wound.

One man came in with a gaping hole in his skull; when she leaned over him, she almost fainted, seeing Ted's face, believing that it was Ted whose scalp had been blown away by the impact of a bullet. When she looked again, she saw that the resemblance to her husband was only slight, but in her weakened and exhausted state, she had imagined that it was him.

The fear that either Ted or Alex might be the next casualty brought into the vault of the red church had been slowly consuming her since the attack began. This is what love does to you, she thought, limbs quivering, this is the return on its poisonous glory. She forced herself to focus on her work.

At dusk on the second day, finding another man who could not be saved lying upon the table, the surgeon turned to a worn-out stretcher bearer and shouted, "You fucking idiot! Is it beyond your wit to bring in only those with a chance of surviving?" His rage spent itself in a series of screamed curses, each worse than the one that had preceded it.

One casualty was riddled with shrapnel and had a fractured leg. Clare had to ask another nurse to help her extract all the shards from his flesh and dress the wound. She made him as comfortable as she could. Then he asked her to remove his wristwatch.

She unfastened the leather strap and held it out to him.

Through gasping breaths, he told her, "I want you to have it sent on to my son. He's three years old and won't remember me, but as he grows up at least he'll know that I remembered him."

She turned away, wanting to give up there and then. Instead, she worked on until four o'clock in the morning, when one of the medical officers finally ordered her to take a break and eat something more substantial than a few slices of bread.

She went outside to clean herself with water she had collected in an enamel mug. She shook with exhaustion and her ears were still filled with a shrill ringing. She knew she had to eat something, but even though her stomach ached with emptiness, she couldn't bring herself to go back into the church. More than anything, she wanted to be alone.

It was a warm morning, without a breeze to stir what was left of the trees along the village lanes. The sky was already light. She crossed the street to a roofless barn and sat down on the edge of a piece of mangled farm machinery, gazing back at the main street and the movement around the church.

It amazed her to think that there were people with ordinary lives elsewhere in the world. She thought of the women of England, women with whom she had gone to school, knitting balaclavas by the fireside and praying in chapels festooned with streamers of peace, watching children who would soon be fatherless grow.

She wouldn't allow herself to think of her husband, what might be happening to him. Or the man whose handwriting filled a card decorated in silks and sent from Armentières.

A small shell exploded in the farmyard, sending a spray of earth over her feet. In the nearby fields, the battle continued like lightning. The air was obtuse with fire and dust, and the sky above the road to Gommecourt burned crimson from the remorseless guns. Star shells zipped up into the night, then quivered back on their own tails, scattering bursts of light over the trenches. She heard the measured stamp of horses' hooves along the lanes as fresh shells were conveyed to the front. The batteries concealed in the hedgerows drowned their tread in a sudden loosening of fire.

An hour passed and the firing grew less. Her ears buzzed with the unexpected calm, the endless clamor of silence.

And then, gradually, she became aware of another sound. A keening cry seemingly louder than anything she had ever heard: thousands of male voices raised on the warm morning air blowing across No Man's Land, from the obliterated village of Gommecourt to the infinite valleys around Albert. She listened, bewildered, and then, at last, she understood. It came from the battlefield, from those beyond all help, men who were drowning in the mud and sea of bodies churned up by the violence of that brilliant summer's day.

Something at the core of her being broke apart. Blindly, she stumbled forward, retching dryly into the blackened grass. As long as I live, she thought, as long as I live, I'll never be free of that sound. She wiped the bile from her mouth, gasping.

When the sun rose high over the Somme later that morning, it dragged a different sound out of the earth. It hovered over the razed orchards and unkempt lanes, filling the humid sky with a relentless, malignant drone.

She stood at the foot of the church tower, looking out over the fields where a white haze drifted. In her ears the terrible drone went on and on as out there, on the battlefield, untold legions of black flies hovered, settled, and feasted on the bodies of the wounded and the dead.

She closed her eyes and fell to her knees.

Civilization had been disassembled, there was no way back to the old way of life now, not for anyone.

21

*T*HE FIGHTING ON THE SOMME LASTED ALL SUMMER AND INTO THE autumn. One night the graves behind the red church were blown open by an exploding shell. In the chaos of the days that followed, the medical staff moved their patients and equipment to premises across the street, a farmhouse cellar. It offered more shelter but trapped the stench of the wounded within the cold brickwork. Nonetheless, when Hébuterne was hit by German gas shells the damp, ugly cellar saved lives.

The relief ambulances took away the casualties who were able to travel. They left after dusk, passing the transport limbers whose iron-rimmed wheels clattered loudly over the broken roads in Hébuterne, taking advantage of the nightly lull in fighting to get supplies up to the line. An ambulance driver told Clare that wide-scale evacuations were taking place all over the Somme, but she could see little improvement in the situation in Hébuterne.

Another difficulty arose: finding enough stretcher bearers to carry the wounded back from the trenches and regimental aid posts to the cellar. Even in the supposed quiet sectors, trench raids, shelling, and sniping meant that stretcher bearers rarely had the opportunity to rest and recuperate. In Hébuterne their number had been severely depleted due to wounding and sickness, and on a damp evening in early autumn, Sister Quint appeared in the cellar where Clare was administering morphine and asked her if she would be willing to join the stretcher bearers on their hazardous journey through the communication trenches.

"We just can't work fast enough," she said, her voice breaking with exhaustion. "No sooner do they send new soldiers out to fight than they come in wounded. We've got to get at least two more people working as stretcher bearers—would you be willing until we can arrange something else?"

For a moment, Clare hesitated. Then she nodded.

Outside, in the pitch darkness of the field, she could see only the rough lie of the land and the great opening gashes in the earth. There were casualties whose wounds left them unable to reach the regimental aid posts; hundreds of them lay out in No Man's Land, waiting for the stretcher bearers to find them. Although each night there came a point where the guns relented, allowing both sides to collect the dead and the wounded, shells continued to burst intermittently.

Clare wore a pair of soldier's boots she had found in the cellar, but the mud almost sucked them from her feet. She could hardly breathe: the smell of decomposing corpses, sinking below the surface of the ravaged earth, filled her nostrils. Helping to heave a man—or what was left of him—onto a stretcher took every ounce of strength and determination she had. Carrying him to the field dressing station was a burden made worse by the necessity of keeping the man on the stretcher as still as possible.

There were other tasks that she was called upon to do for the first time. Burying the dead was one. The corpses were taken to a nearby field, where units of the 48th (South Midland) Division who held the sector the year before had started a cemetery. Whenever assistance was needed, Clare helped to intern the corpses, having proved during her nights as a stretcher bearer that she had the strong stomach required for such work. Twice she attempted to lift a dead body that disintegrated as soon as she touched it; the corpses were those of men who had died on days of fine weather but had been left on the battlefield, their skin burned black by the sun, then rotting in the rain. Whenever possible, graves were marked with details from the soldiers' identity tags. Those who were beyond recognition and whose identity disks, made of compressed layers of cardboard, had perished with them were tipped into shell craters.

· Day after day in the cellar with the living, she cut socks from feet that were white, swollen, and dead. When it rained, the regulation puttees shrank, cutting off the circulation and causing the feet to rot. She rubbed warm olive oil into the joints and wrapped them up in whatever material could be found. She cleaned the enteric-riddled bodies of men so crazed with thirst that they had drunk from ditches and shell holes, beyond caring what might lie beneath. All this, in addition to the constant dressing and disinfecting of wounds, removing shrapnel, readying men for travel, and administering medicine.

Her mind was never at rest while her hands worked. But whenever she returned to her thin bed of straw sacking on the cellar floor, with the puppet tucked in beside her, she would take out the card dated December 1915, sent from Armentières.

The brilliant red and blue bird, its wings lifted in flight, guarded a single line of black, untidy handwriting: "In dreams my hope wanders, clothed in your skin."

At the beginning of October, sheets of rain swept across the blank expanse where the terrible debris of battle still lay. As the fighting moved to the heights above the Ancre, some distance away, ambulances carried the last patients away from the cellar in Hébuterne, and the medical staff prepared to return to the hospital back in Rouen.

Clare packed her kit bag, feeling a new weariness enter her body. She wondered if there would ever come a time when tiredness didn't drag at her limbs.

Sister Quint called to her from the dark stairwell, "Ten minutes until we leave."

Clare nodded, then felt under the frail blanket for the puppet. Her hands searched frantically, but it wasn't there. She rushed from one end of the cellar to the other, lifting abandoned objects, pulling aside tarpaulin sheets and tearing at the straw on which she had lain in her desperation to find the Siamese cat glove-puppet. It was gone.

She climbed the steps slowly, casting one final, panic-stricken glance back at the empty cellar. When she found her seat in the ambulance, she turned her head, not wanting anyone to see her crying.

She hated herself for losing the gift from Frank; during that horrifying summer it had become more precious to her than anything else she had ever owned. She felt like a child whose comfort blanket had been snatched away: bewildered, distressed, and fearful of what might happen to her without it.

The feelings didn't lessen as the convoy traveled through the devastated landscape. She was still disturbed when the ambulances reached the tents billowing on the hills above Rouen. Never previously superstitious, she tried to dispel the anxiety that gripped her as she unpacked her few belongings once more.

She went through her accumulated mail quickly: there were letters from her husband, and she tore them open, relief flooding through her as she read his words from a hospital in London where he had been sent to recover from a leg wound. He hadn't passed through her hands in that dreadful church, and she was grateful for it. He would soon return to the front, but he was alive, or as far as she could tell, he was alive. His letters were filled with ardent declarations of love that she read with guilt and despair.

Then another letter. Not from Armentières this time, but from Amiens. She recognized the chaotic black scrawl. Her rage flared after months of constraint, wanting him, and only him. She held his words tightly in her hand, ecstatic, defeated.

22

IN LOMBARDI'S LITTLE HUT, IN THE LIGHT FROM THE HURRICANE LAMP the notebook opens, a creak of paper and old leather bindings:

"I watched the beginning of the Battle of the Somme from a beetroot field.

"The night before, General Charteris himself had arrived at the house in Amiens where my colleagues and I were then based to inform us that 'The Great Endeavor' was about to begin. No one seemed to have expected Charteris; even the staff officers on the floor below us were surprised by the chief of intelligence's appearance, which was almost comical in its furtiveness. After inspecting the room where we were gathered, he told us where we should place ourselves for a decent view of the battlefield and explained that the official wires were to be at our disposal during the day to ensure that our dispatches reached London in time for the early editions. There would also be a special joint cable, prepared by all correspondents together, for the morning newspapers. We were to be given 'full facilities' for seeing what we could, and the GSO in charge of the press would keep us up to date with the latest detailed information on a daily basis.

"I listened skeptically to Charteris, unconvinced by the sudden openness. A few months before we had met Field Marshal Haig at GHQ's new headquarters near Montreuil. Haig, gray-haired and handsome, and accompanied by Charteris, had received us courteously in his château, claiming to understand our problems with censorship. He told us, 'I think I know fairly well what you gentlemen want. You want to get hold of little stories of heroism, and so forth, and to write them up in a bright way to make good reading for Mary Ann in the kitchen and the Man in the Street.'

"No one responded at first, although the atmosphere had shifted from one of cautious anticipation on our behalf to unexpressed resentment. Finally, I was the one to speak.

" 'No, that isn't what we what. That isn't it at all. With all respect, Sir, you have no right to keep the people of Britain in ignorance of what is happening to their sons and husbands and brothers. They provide you with the means to fight this war, and the very least that is owed to them is honesty, as much as that can be done without endangering the men themselves or alerting the enemy to our plans. It's their war, and it absolutely must not be conducted in secrecy. The morale of the army isn't isolated. It doesn't come from within the battalions alone but also from the knowledge that the home front is completely committed to the war and their part in it. That in turn depends upon the home front's knowledge of what is happening out here. In short, Sir, what we want to get hold of is not cheery tales and comforting myths—it's truth.'

"I saw Charteris glance nervously at Haig to gauge his reaction. Fortunately, the commander in chief took it well, and turned to Charteris to ask, 'Well, what do you think? Is there room to relax the rules somewhat?'

" 'I believe so,' said Charteris. 'I think it should be done insofar as it is possible.'

"Haig nodded thoughtfully and gave me a direct, penetrating look. 'Thank you for your honesty, Mr. Dyer. It will be discussed further.'

"The chief of intelligence's visit to the house in Amiens on

June 30 appeared to be the first indication of a change in policy. My colleagues retired optimistically that night, after a staff officer informed us that the attack would be made at 07:30 hours.

"I sat up, unable to sleep, until it was time to rise, my stomach in knots.

"As we drove out from Amiens I thought of the preliminary bombardment, which I had seen from the viewpoint we were now heading toward, and of the reports that came back from No Man's Land about the poor quality of the shells our soldiers were using. The eighteen-pounders were supposed to break up in the air, cutting through the German wire, but many exploded too soon or too late or not at all. The reports had been discredited on the grounds that there had been no substantial answering fire from the enemy, which as far as GHQ was concerned seemed to suggest that the wire had in fact been cut.

"The beetroot field was by the Albert-Bapaume road. It was beginning to grow light as Julian Quint and I made our way there accompanied by several officers. We had chosen to observe the same area, confident that it offered the best vantage point.

"Before us lay a wide crescent that stretched from Auchon-villiers, Thiepval, La Boiselle, and Fricourt to Bray. Above the lines at Bray were British kite balloons; I counted seventeen, and imagined how the landscape might look to the artillery observers in the baskets as they drifted through the clear skies.

"The intense bombardment that began in advance of the attack covered the fields in a white mist with which we were all too familiar. When it lifted momentarily I could make out the golden Virgin suspended over the town of Albert, but nothing more. The guns faded and I glanced at my wristwatch: 7:30 a.m. Howling silence. Then all at once the smoke clouds made a whooshing noise, as if something was traveling at high speed across the fields toward us. I had never experienced anything like it. And then the scream of shells and the cracking of rifle and machine-gun fire filled the air.

" 'In the very best traditions of the British Army . . . ,' Julian murmured beside me. But we couldn't see a thing.

"At ten o'clock a runner brought us a report: 'On a front twenty miles north and south of the Somme we and our French allies have advanced and taken the German first line of trenches. We are attacking vigorously Fricourt, La Boiselle, and Mametz. German prisoners are surrendering freely, and a good many have already fallen into our hands.'

"I swore at the thick fog, frustrated at our ability to hear but not see the battle that raged below. We returned to Amiens in a mood of dissatisfaction and wary expectation, unsure of what had taken place that day beyond the saturating smoke, and sent back our first reports based solely on what we had been told. But I was determined not to put my full trust in the communiqués from GHQ and ended my report: 'We cannot yet speak of victory, for it is too soon to judge the success of the opening salvos, however valiantly they were fired. This is, after all, only the beginning of the campaign, and victory—or failure—is a result, not a halfway house. What is certain is that our troops fought bravely, and they deserve every accolade that will be laid at their feet. In years to come, this day will be remembered as the hour when the British soldier was called upon to prove his worth as a warrior, and history will tell how he met that challenge with dignity, fortitude, and, above all, guts.'

"The censor passed it after drawing a blue line through the words *or failure*.

"Within forty-eight hours, it was obvious to us that the offensive was not the overwhelming triumph GHQ had expected. By translating St. Aubin's speech about the progress of the fighting into real terms, I realized that the breakthrough had not occurred, the casualties were too high, and the entire operation was sickeningly slow.

"On July 6, I toured the rear areas of the British front, talking to men who had taken part in that first day of fighting. Along with the other correspondents, I was introduced solely to those troops who had met their objectives; it irked me to be nannied by the press officers in such a way, but I was keen to interview the soldiers to build up what had until then been a very indistinct portrait of events. In my reports I concentrated on these personal accounts, preferring them to technical overviews of the fighting. I tried to be circumspect in my use of language, attempting to convey the stories as they were told to me, avoiding forays into romanticism and descriptions of battles that relied too heavily on ideas of medieval wars and jousting. I wanted to emphasize what I felt had been completely misinterpreted by the home front: that for the soldier, fighting was a confined experience about securing and holding a trench or a wood or a village rather than combat on any epic scale.

"On July 14, at half past three in the morning, I arrived at a vantage point to watch the battle for Bazentin Ridge. Again the smoke from the preliminary barrage concealed what was happening. An artillery observer filled me in on the strategies until I could picture the actual fighting through the dark smog. The offensive was rapid and successful, which turned out to be a handicap, for the generals were ill-prepared for a quick victory and sent in the cavalry too late to capitalize on it.

"In the afternoon I walked close to the front line, interviewing the walking wounded and German prisoners. One young subaltern, whose wound was being dressed at the first-aid post before he was sent on to a casualty clearing station, told me, "I don't mind having a lump of shrapnel lodged in my thigh—it means a break from the fighting, thank God." He talked about the different attitudes of the men he fought with and against, wincing as his injury was cleaned. 'What gets to me is how precarious life is here,' he said, 'how much it depends upon luck, and the temperament of those you have to fight. There's an Anglican padre at Longueval dressing station called Father Hall. Have you heard of him?'

"I shook my head.

" 'He's from Muirfield, attached to the South African Brigade. A lot of the men speak about him. He's a remarkable chap. His base is in a very unhealthy spot. There's no water there, apart from in a well in Longueval, which the Boche have got in their sights.' He paused. 'I heard that our men are so mad with thirst that they crawl down to that well even though the bloody Boche like to pick them off with their rifles. One German officer has got himself a cushy little number in a shell hole where he sits like a spider in its web, waiting with his hand on his revolver, ready to fire. He's a damn good shot, too. But do you know something? He leaves the padre alone. Never aims at him. I don't know why—they say he's not so particular, this German, and he's certainly not a God-fearing man because he shot another army chaplain, but Father Hall can go down to that well at any time of the day or night and know that he's safe. Back and forth, back and forth, collecting his pails of water. And then he goes into the trenches with cups of hot tea and even—I've heard it told—mugs of hot chocolate. And all from the well where the enemy won't shoot him.'

"I wrote all it down. I had become fascinated by the superstitions of the soldiers in the field. There was another man, a colonel with the North Staffordshires whom I interviewed at Thiepval. Initially, he was reluctant to speak to me. As we sat together sourly in his hut, I asked him whether he had a problem with me personally.

"The colonel looked at me. 'Not at all. I am merely revolted by the indifference shown to my battalion by the press. We have lost so many men in recent weeks, and yet I read nothing about our great sacrifice in your articles. I cannot imagine that there is any reason for me to talk to you when you care so little about what has happened to some of the finest men it has ever been my good fortune to know.'

"My skin prickled with humiliation.

" 'Why do you ignore us?' asked the colonel. 'Do you feel that we have failed you? That our lives are not enough?'

" 'Of course not,' I said. 'It's purely a matter of censorship. We aren't allowed to mention names or give specific details of the whereabouts of battalions, or even how many men have been killed. We have to keep things deliberately vague for fear that the enemy might be fed too much information.' I looked down at the colonel's chalk-covered boots. 'But I promise to bring enough allusions into my article about the fighting here to ensure that you are satisfied that the home front is aware of the sufferings of your men.'

"The colonel nodded, content. He began to talk about his life in the North Staffords and his experiences around Thiepval in particular. At the end of a long speech, he hesitated, and gave me a penetrating look, as if he were trying to get the true measure of me. Finally he said, 'I have no fear. I am a mystic, for all my conventional appearance. I have a strong, unshakable belief that I am immune from shell fire. It all boils down to having the power of one's own convictions, you see. While ever I can tell myself that my mind is stronger than the bullets and shells that fly toward me, I know that can get through any barrage safely. Metal is no match for man's self-belief. I truly feel that the only ammunition one needs when climbing the parapets is one's intelligence.'

"I said nothing.

" 'Do you think I am mad, young fellow?'

"I glanced up. 'As a matter of fact, I do. But I happen to think that we are all mad. There isn't one sane person involved in the war. We're mad as March hares, every last one of us. Only people who have lost their minds could live in a world such as this.'

" 'Ah.' The colonel nodded. 'I see your point. But wouldn't it be a marvelous thing if I could pass on some of my faith to my men?' His eyebrows furrowed together and he lowered his voice. 'There is something else. I know which of the men will die. Before we go into battle, I look into their eyes and there it is, writ large in the black pupils of them all. I am always right. Always.' He sat back and sighed. 'Oh, I wish to God I didn't know.' He stared up at the roof of the hut.

"I asked curiously, 'What do you see in my eyes?'

"The colonel turned back to me. He leaned forward and said, 'Fear. You're in torment. A sinner seeking an absolution that will never come.' He snorted and got to his feet, unbending like a tree in a breeze. 'If that doesn't create a breeding ground for madness, I don't know what does.' "

"Every night during the summer offensive on the Somme, I went out walking. It helped to clear my mind of the colonel's words, of the images I brought back from the fields and villages around Albert, and stopped me from waking during the early hours of the morning, when the glow of the battlefield illuminated my little room on the floor below the garret.

"We were billeted in a small mansion on the rue de l'Amiral Courbet. The house belonged to Madame de la Rochefoucault, who had another home farther out from the city. It was sparsely furnished with comfortless Empire and Louis Quinze pieces and ancestral portraits in oils congested the walls.

"At midnight, I would leave the house via the courtyard with its wrought-iron gates and head toward the river. Sometimes it rained as I crossed the canals in the Saint Leu quarter, lured by the pointed gables, steep roofs, and wooden walls of the old houses. The finest view of the city was from the cobbled east side where the tiny, black-soiled islets had been cultivated into kitchen gardens.

"One night I stood on a bridge looking down on a carpenter's yard. A gentle rain fell as flat-bottomed barges drifted along the moonlit River Somme. They reached the wooden sheds below the bridge and ropes were thrown to moor them alongside. It took me a moment to realize that the cargo was human: maimed men who screamed and flapped like wing-clipped birds as they were carried on stretchers into the yard. Then I looked over at the darkened river banks. There were figures standing there; silent, distressed women surrounded by the fertile vegetation, waiting to see if their men were among those brought in on that damp summer's night. I watched them and I shivered. There was something inordinately eerie about the scene, something more frightening than anything else I had witnessed.

"I turned away, and my thoughts went to Clare: whether she had been sent out to care for men like those brought secretly up the river, or if she was still back at base in Rouen. It was agony not to know. I thought about her tears, how they would taste on my tongue. I wondered at the tenderness of her heart, what it might be capable of, and for whom."

"In the end it was the weather that brought the Somme campaign to a close. The Germans responded by withdrawing to their new Hindenburg line, leaving a trail of destruction in their wake, and a great stillness fell over the shattered and leafless valleys of the Somme.

"Throughout that time, Amiens was a magnet for the soldier on short leave. It was no longer the capital of Picardy alone, but the principal attraction for all troops stationed in the surrounding area. They flocked to the city's hotels, restaurants, estaminets, and public gardens in search of respite from the numbing terror and grind of the trenches. The frequent air bombardments that depleted the gabled houses of Amiens's main streets did not deter them, nor did the ceaseless, forewarning boom of gunfire from Albert fifteen miles distant. Thousands of soldiers were lured into lorry-jumping to Amiens, whether they were English, Irish, Scottish, Welsh, Canadian, Australian, or New Zealanders, and they filled the streets with their shouts and laughter, and gazed longingly at the well-dressed women of the city. Only the French poilus remained oblivious to the holiday mood that prevailed in Amiens. They arrived at the station looking like unhappy vagrants in threadbare blue coats and with unshaven jaws. The Australians, in contrast, sauntered into the bars and restaurants with an aggressive confidence, their blunt humor finding plenty to amuse them as they spent their earnings prodigiously, buying drinks for anyone who cared to talk to them for a while.

"On a clear evening in August Julian and I headed out to one of the bars in the city center. A strict blackout was in place, but as we neared the popular Hôtel du Rhin a cluster of yellow, glowing dots floated in midair next to the side door of the building. The hotel was patronized by majors and staff officers of the intelligence service, most of whom we knew by sight if not by name.

"The lights came together and turned on us. A melodious French voice asked, 'Looking for a little company? A little friendship? A little love?'

" 'Sorry,' said Julian. 'Another time, perhaps.'

"The women pouted at the rejection but made no attempt to persuade either of us to change our minds; every night there were plenty of men willing to take them up on their offer.

" 'Ever been tempted?' Julian asked, when we had passed by.

" 'God, no,' I said. 'A little dose of the clap is the last thing I need.'

"We turned right onto the rue des Trois Cailloux, a busy boulevard with the railway station at one end and the Hôtel de Ville at the other. The street was an amalgamation of estaminets and shuttered shops, and crowded with soldiers moving from one congested bar or restaurant to the next. In Charlie's Bar most of the tables were occupied by serious young staff officers discussing their work. We found a space and ordered two beers.

"The sound of gunfire beyond the city filled the street. The windows vibrated.

" '*La rafale des tambours de la mort*,' I said. 'Where will it all end?'

" 'Who knows?' Julian shrugged. 'We seem to be lurching from one fuck-up to the next.'

"We remained in Charlie's all evening, watching the patrons' moods switch from gravity to resolute exuberance. The place emptied and refilled itself. A dozen Anzacs rolled in, their strident voices raised in song. The guns still boomed beyond the city, and that deathly breeze unsettled the windows and doors of the street. We talked of arbitrary, inconsequential things, and neither of us noticed how drunk the other had become.

"On the other side of the street was a *parfumier* whose windows were only half-shuttered. The delicate bottles of scent, arranged in a triptych upon a shelf draped in red velvet, glittered in the evening light. I stared at the display; the perfumes suggested a soft embrace, enticing whispers, and smooth, cool feminine limbs. The propositions of the whores on the street where I lived were spurious and repellent in comparison. I felt achingly lonely.

"Clare, I thought, oh God, Clare. Where are you? If only I could see you again. Just once . . .

"How do we fall in love? It takes years, a lifetime, to really get to know another human being. What happens is that you are drawn to aspects of that person—the color of their eyes, the curve of a smile, their kindness, their humor, the sheen on the nape of a woman's neck as she sits by a window in the sun—and then you start to seek out other things.

"I was in love and I wanted it to be the last time. I wanted this one forever.

"When the bar closed we walked unsteadily through the quiet streets, passing the sandbagged great west door of the cathedral. We reached the site of the vegetable market and stood watching elderly stallholders unloading cabbages and cauliflowers from large wagons. The dark avenue of the rue des Augustins led us back to the iron gates of our temporary home. As we crossed the courtyard, I noticed a light burning dimly in the censor's room, and knew that St. Aubin would be in there, reading *The Times* with a thoughtful scowl. I took out the heavy key and fitted it into the lock, pushing Julian in ahead. We said good night in the hall. Julian went through to the library for his habitual glass of Scotch before bed, and I went upstairs to my room.

"In the left-hand drawer of the desk under the window was a writing pad, and inside the cover was the address of the hospital where I had last known Clare to be, in Rouen.

"I tore out a page and took up my pen. There was barely any light, but somehow I managed to write.

Dear Clare,

In Cassel, between Ypres and St. Omer, there is a hotel called Le Chat Noir. It's on the rue St. Nicholas, overlooking the salient. I shall book a room for October 15, for two nights.

I will wait for you there.

With love,
Alex

X

BURNING THE LEAVES

Mont Cassel, October 1916
and Paris, Bastille Day 1917

23

"*I* RETURNED TO BELGIUM AND BORROWED A CAR, DRIVING FROM Tilques to Cassel, passing through flattened villages and ruptured fields. Rain pelted down on the windscreen and a thick mist, as though the guns of the Somme were still pounding, obscured the road ahead.

"The steep rise into Cassel was like entering another world; the eviscerated landscape of the war ceased to exist—here there were lush, overhanging trees dripping moisture and hedgerows that sprang thickly onto the road. But as I followed the twisting, potholed road into the small center of town, a chain of army vehicles, including an ambulance unit, appeared out of the mist and the cobblestoned square of the Grande Place heaved with wet, steaming horses and lorries whose tarpaulin roofs cascaded rainwater.

"I left the car at the foot of the slope leading to the church. Its tower had faded into the low-lying mist and thunder buckled in the sky as I ran through the square, clutching my father's old leather doctor's bag. I found the rue St. Nicholas, holding the bag over my head while I peered through my dripping hair for the hotel I remembered. I saw it at last: the wide front curving onto the street, the beveled windows where lamps burned on tables positioned to take advantage of the view across the rooftops to the fields of Flanders. I ran to it and pulled the chain hanging from a large brass bell set on the right-hand side of the door.

"After signing the register for two nights, I went up to the room. It was at the top of the house, at the end of a corridor, with a large iron-framed bed, framed samplers on the walls, and Chinese silk paper in sea blue. A wardrobe opposite the bed had carved panels depicting the Crusades. I wiped the condensation from the windows, but the rain and mist shrouded the view. Rivulets of water trickled from the empty window boxes of the houses on the other side of the road.

"I washed in the deep basin in the corner of the room, rubbed a towel through my hair, and sat down on the bed. I lit a cigarette, listening to the murmur of voices in the sitting room below, and the sound of the rain against the long window.

"I wondered if she would come to me, and what I would do if she did not.

"Unbearably restless, I threw on my coat and went quickly down the stairs, unlatching the main door and stepping out into the pure air. The rain had eased slightly but the mist lingered so that when I turned in the direction of the Grande Place, the houses were revealed as far as their rooftops but the fields and forests beyond remained hidden. A vague scent of cordite lingered about the streets, drifting up from the battlefields around Ypres, to the east. Mont Cassel was like an inverted volcano where the fire belched from the foot of the hill, reaching upward to the little town at its peak.

"I walked around aimlessly. Uniformed men went in and out of the shops and estaminets I remembered from my early days as a war correspondent: the Flower of the Fields, the Lost Corner, the Veritable Cuckoo. Across the square was the Hotel du Sauvage, where I had often dined in the past. Its red-painted windows were steamed up, blurring the glow within.

"I walked slowly, glancing frequently at my watch, wondering all the time if she would come to me. The afternoon light was disappearing behind an impenetrable bank of cloud.

"I stood before one of the town's oldest crooked houses, on a sharp incline. The rain had returned, pouring over the cobblestones and rushing with a clear sound toward the turreted archway of the Porte d'Aire. The sloping fields beyond the gate were concealed in the mist that curled up the hill, but beneath the dark arch stood a woman, tall and slim, looking out at that cold, creeping wall of whiteness, as still as the widows who lined the banks of the Somme in Amiens by night.

"I felt the blood accelerate through my veins. I walked toward her, empty of all things but love and fear, and when she heard my footsteps she turned and said my name, and I buried myself in the white, exposed skin of her neck. I felt her pulse leap against my mouth as I kissed the thumb-sized hollow at the base of her throat, and her hands went into the wet, dark waves of my hair, drowning us both."

"In the hotel room with the sea-blue silk wallpaper, I asked her why she hadn't responded to my card from Armentières.

" 'I wanted to forget you,' she said simply.

" 'But you couldn't.'

" 'No.'

"My emotions burned, fueling our bodies, laying them to waste.

"Afterward she leaned over me, breathing in the smell of my skin. 'I love the scent of you,' she said, closing her eyes. 'Yours is the first male body I've seen in months that isn't shattered, burned, or destroyed in some way. Wherever my hand rests there is only warmth and health. It's a miracle. Whenever I touch you, I feel amazed.'

"I ran my hands through her soft hair. 'I missed your beauty, Clare. I missed you.'

"She looked up. 'Beauty is meaningless. It exists for its own sake.'

"I smiled. 'Is that you speaking?'

" 'No, Mr. Darwin. But I agree with him.'

"I touched her mouth with mine. 'There is another theory: that beauty is the promise of happiness. And I am only happy when I am with you.'

"My hands went down to the graceful arc of her back, holding her against me, losing myself in her wide gaze.

"She laid her head on my shoulder, her fingers sweeping slowly over my stomach. Her whispers controlled my mind and body: 'I want you to be full of everything but empty without me. I want the world to disintegrate when I leave your arms . . .' "

"We dined in the Hotel du Sauvage that evening, in a room with a long row of windows displaying the whole of the Ypres salient like a general spreading a map. Haig was there, quiet and thoughtful, looking out at the dark mist below the balcony. The clambering sound of the rain on the roof above our table made us feel snug and warm.

"We drank too much, already light-headed at being with each other. I tried to impress her with knowledge that she found amusing, ridiculous even: 'Mont Cassel is the highest hill in Flanders. Conquerors have sought to claim it for more than two thousand years. It's where the Grand Old Duke of York marched his men.'

" 'Up to the top and down again?' Her smile was perfection incarnate; she drew the attention of every man in the room. They looked at her over their glasses of port and wine, wondering who she was and forgetting the owner's petulant young daughters, Suzanne and Blanche.

" 'Exactly. Although if you want to be pedantic, you would have to correct the rhyme. He had thirty thousand men, not ten thousand.'

" 'That *is* being pedantic.'

"Suzanne scrutinized us, bright-eyed, from behind the tall vase of scarlet roses on her desk. I had known her long enough to realize that her romantic imagination must be running wild. When I excused myself for a moment and went through to the cloakroom, she beckoned me over to her desk.

" 'You look so beautiful together, the two of you. I've been watching you . . . ' She clasped her hands and held them to her chest. 'Who is she, this woman with the expensive green dress and shoes?'

" 'Suzanne . . . ,' I began, laughing and shaking my head.

"The entrance door opened and two officers came in, their waterproofs sagging, their boots thick with mud. One called out to her.

" 'Will you play the piano, Suzanne?'

" 'Later, perhaps. What would you like to hear?'

" 'That you love me.'

"Suzanne laughed, flattered. I saw her glance at her reflection in the long mirror opposite.

" 'Do you know what your English customers call you, Suzanne?' I said, smiling.

"She shrugged, 'What should I care? As long as they come.'

" 'It's not an insult. They call you the Lady of Shalott.'

" 'Who is she? Also a great beauty?'

"I laughed, eager to return to Clare. 'The Lady of Shalott spent her days looking at her reflection in the mirror. She died for love, of course,' I added, knowing this would appeal to Suzanne's penchant for melodrama.

"Suzanne's large brown eyes darkened, became serious. She leaned across the desk until I could smell the rich, cloying perfume she wore. 'And what about your lover?' she asked in a low voice. 'Be careful with her.'

"I waited, curious, skeptical, amused.

"Suzanne whispered across the heavy, drooping heads of the roses: 'The shadows of your lover's face reveal a curse.'

"Despite the manifest absurdity of Suzanne's words, I was unable to dismiss what she had said, and a cold trickle of fear went through my veins, banishing the warmth I had felt until then."

"In the darkness of our hotel room, I forgot Suzanne's foolishness. After we made love, Clare told me of her childhood, the times when she had been happiest. Her face softened when she spoke of her father, and the bond she had with him through their mutual love of gardens.

" 'My father believed that a garden should be like a beautiful woman,' she said. 'She should not reveal all her loveliness at once. To unveil a secret is to create a sense of intimacy between the person who divulges and the one who receives. Gardens that have been left to fade and die abound in secrets, and when at last someone awakens them from their long slumber, the reward is sometimes greater than can be imagined.' Her eyes shone with the joy of remembering. 'My father had a gift for restoration: he could tell, simply by looking at a ravaged garden, where its greatest treasures lay. I loved him deeply. The other man, the one who took my father's place, had no talents at all. He was an empty vessel that would never be filled.'

" 'But your mother loved him,' I said, unable to make sense of the dichotomy.

" 'Did she? I often wonder if she did, or if she was simply afraid of being left alone. Women are, I think, because our whole lives are expected to revolve around others, and men especially. I was growing up quickly, and she and I had never been close. I felt threatened by my stepfather from the start. Not because he stood between the two of us, but because he was a male presence in the house that I couldn't explain. He had never known me as a child, he wasn't there for any of the events of my past. What did he know about the little girl I once was? I would sometimes look at him and feel puzzled to see him sitting in my father's chair. It was as if a stranger had suddenly appeared without warning, and I had come home to find him banishing the ghost of my father. While the other man was there, I could never feel my father in the house. The only place I could still picture him clearly, and hear his voice, was in the garden. The other man never went in the garden.'

"I had imagined that these conversations were the foundations on which our relationship would grow, like the flowers in her father's lost gardens. Not desire, which is too mutable without anything else to sustain it, but words. Gifts of memory and the reward of trust in another person.

"But there was desire too: I was obsessed by her cool loveliness, the small curves on her slim frame, the fresh scent of her hair, her long, elegant limbs. Her desire matched mine in a contest of passions. And yet . . . I once read that desire is its own reward. It isn't true: unreturned desire is a burden, not a gift. It eats away at you like a disease, if you let it. But the same can be said of reciprocated desire; the hunger to possess each other can destroy two people. With us, it was far worse— because of Ted.

"In the early hours of the morning, I found myself telling her that he had been to see me, months ago, in Tilques. She didn't say anything, but lay on her back rigid beside me, her face turned away.

"I told her, 'I think he knows. At least . . . I think he suspects *something*.'

"Her back stiffened. 'Don't be ridiculous, Alex, of course he doesn't.'

" 'Then why did he ask me if I would have fallen in love with you if I'd met you first?'

"She boiled with irritation at my persistence. 'I don't know! People do ask strange things of each other. Especially in wartime. Your mind gets messed up, you question everything—'

" 'Is that what this is,' I said, 'a bit of wartime confusion?'

" 'I'm not even going to answer that.' She turned and looked at me, her eyes wide with hurt and resentment. 'It is what it is. You're reading too much into everything. You have to stop it or you'll drive yourself mad.'

"I felt something close to panic rise in my chest, unstoppable and perverse. 'I think I am mad. I think I must be completely insane, lying here with Ted's wife.'

"She sat up, tense with fury. 'You *asked* me to come here. *You* asked *me.*'

" 'But you began it,' I went on, unable to prevent the words from leaving my mouth. They burned between us like a forest fire, destroying everything in their path. 'I would never have done anything. You ripped the page out, then came to see me in London—'

"She swung out her fist, hitting me on the side of the jaw.

" *'To hell with you.'*

"And she left, saying no more, brutally shaking off all my clumsy, increasingly desperate attempts to right the wrong I had committed.

"She left, prevailing on the owner of the hotel to find someone who could take her into Poperinghe, where she had already arranged transport back to Rouen that morning.

"She left, and for the first time in my life I questioned how I could go on, if she would not speak to me again.

"And after she had gone, I remained in the hotel room, my forehead pressed against the cold window pane, looking out at the street where she had vanished. Her physical violence that night was nothing to me. A bruise fades quickly on a man's face, but what she had said remained, as indelible as the written word. By now, the relationship seemed to be gathering a momentum of its own; I felt helplessly caught up in the swell of the wave that would either submerge us both, or carry us safely to land."

24

*I*N TWO HOURS IT WILL BEGIN TO GROW LIGHT ABOVE THE FIELDS OF white crosses. Lombardi does not speak; he only listens, scratching the ears of the tan-and-white terrier sitting on his lap.

Alex stares down at the green rag rug and murmurs, "In Cassel we had approached the razor edge of all relationships: How far can you go with each other? As it turned out, we had stopped just short of the precipice—that came later, the following year—but it was enough to smash through everything at that point."

He looks up and turns his head in the direction of the open door. "When she said that she loved her husband without passion, I rushed headlong into the idea that she was being honest. But was she? How could I possibly know? New lovers are quick to believe and easy to wound . . . When I mentioned a woman I had met recently on a train, Clare wanted reassurance that ours was simply a conversation between two strangers, nothing more. A conversation was all it was. I loved her, and only her."

He bends his head again. "That night, after we dined in the Hotel du Sauvage, when words burst and fell around us like star shells, she didn't give me a chance to explain. My words had gotten lost in trans- lation when they left me. I never meant to suggest that our betrayal of Ted was entirely her fault, although I know that's what she heard. I wanted to convey to her my confusion: How could we love him and yet deceive him so cruelly? Or did our love for each other negate our mercilessness toward him? And if it didn't, if we really were the 'evil' people she had once said we were, what was there then to love about each other?

"Perhaps it simply disturbed me that she had never made any expressions of guilt herself. I didn't know how she felt. We never spoke of it. But I was already beginning to think of the future, and what would happen to the three of us. The war wouldn't go on forever, and an adulterous affair is always about everyone caught in its snare, whether or not they are aware of it. 'Go to hell,' she said to me, and she got her wish. I was in hell from the moment she left, and even though we resumed our affair briefly the following year, I never again knew any private sense of calm. I was torn between my love for her and my deep friendship with her husband. One was always going to obliterate the other, and however it happened, I knew none of us would ever recover from the loss."

He turns back to the notebook, his fingers leafing through the pages slowly until he finds the ones he seeks.

"After she left, I threw myself into my work, trying to forget, as she had once tried to forget me. My colleagues had returned home to Britain late in 1916. We were all well-known names by then, and Sebastian Thorpe (whom I no longer spoke to unless it was absolutely necessary) and Jack Garland capitalized on their fame by publishing their collected dispatches in book form. Julian Quint and Andrew Harris did as I had done in 1915; they accepted offers to lecture at various institutions and private clubs around the country. But after my time with Clare in Cassel, I remained in France, at my lowest personal and professional ebb. Since the casualty lists from the Somme had begun filling page after page of *The Times,* the home front and the soldiers in the trenches had begun questioning the true worth and purpose of war correspondents. Of course, Sebastian Thorpe had reported the first day of battle as a great triumph for the British, but there were others, too, whom I didn't know personally, who had claimed victory for us.

"The issue of war correspondents and our role was frequently the topic of debate in the press and in Parliament. Sometimes I felt hated by the soldiers in the field. I despaired when I was given a copy of *The Kemmel Times,* a newspaper written by soldiers for soldiers, which asked sarcastically, 'Is the London press aware there are a few British troops on the Western front???' It was my lowest point, professionally, knowing that they despised us, and rightly so. I began to analyze my work carefully, determined to avoid high-flying sentiment and optimism. I became more judicious when it came to reporting on tank warfare, painfully aware that I had been as overexcited as my colleagues when viewing a tank in action for the first time. I decided to spend the winter months 'getting back to basics,' working on my professional inner demons and avoiding the clichés and sanguinity that had blighted our reporting from the Somme.

"In January 1917 the temperature fell below zero. The battlefields of France lay under a frosted veil and the airmen flying through the pallid skies above looked down on a snow desert, where dugouts appeared as small black crevices in a vast white hinterland.

"GHQ had set up its headquarters in Montreuil the previous year, and I went there often to research a report I was working on clandestinely. Montreuil was a picturesque, walled town on a hill. Once it had faced the sea, but the ground had been reclaimed and cultivated into arable land with small forests of trees between the hamlets. All the romantic, Arthurian terms used to describe the war found their natural habitat here, reaching a new level of the pageantry Ted had recognized. One needed a special pass to enter the place, and the sentries at the white post would admit visitors only when a military policeman had given them the nod. If I went there by car, the sentries would salute me, but they never troubled to acknowledge me if I walked.

"War viewed from the court of Montreuil was a noble pursuit. I often saw Haig, sitting posture-perfect astride his well-groomed horse, accompanied by two ADCs and an escort of Lancers with pennants flying. Elderly generals, colonels, and majors took strolls through the attractive streets after lunch, leaving the officers to play tennis elsewhere below the walls. The puffed-out chests of the old men were bright with medals from Italy, Romania, and Serbia, and all those who were part of the court of GHQ wore their red tabs, red hat bands, and red and blue armlets with pride. They were poles apart from the hard-working staff officers at corps, army, and divisional headquarters, who often went without sleep to ensure that the soldiers had their food and munitions.

"I knew from Ted that he had taken Clare to the Officers' Club at Montreuil. 'I'm going to show you how the other half live,' he'd told her, as they moved among the old men and the staff officers in the glittering dark. A band played ragtime, but Ted and Clare didn't dance once; instead they watched, with a sort of horrible fascination, as young women from the WAAC flirted with GHQ's finest. Afterward, Ted flew into a rage. He'd written to me about it. I understood it, as I had always understood him.

"Spurious words of mine because, despite everything, I fell in love with his wife.

"I didn't see Clare, didn't communicate with her. But it made no difference. My feelings hadn't changed and I couldn't let go, even then. Because there isn't anything else as challenging as love: finding it, keeping it, losing it. Sometimes I think love is the only adventure left to mankind; we've exhausted all other possibilities."

"When my colleagues returned from England, we were given a new home in Cassel, in an old monastery there; the double irony of that wasn't lost on me. My window would flare at night with the faint glow of distant shells, as it had in the hotel room where Clare and I had loved each other briefly. Paradoxically, while I was privately falling apart, my professional life was becoming easier. The army and the War Office had given in to many of our demands and relations between us had thawed. We were allowed far greater access to the battlefields than ever before and given more information about GHQ's maneuvers. But even this, too, had its price: we were weapons of propaganda.

"I didn't care anymore.

"In May 1917 I had a letter from Ted. He had been with Clare, in London, for two days in April and was euphoric in his love for her. He wrote of traveling back to Dover by train: '. . . Fields of mustard seed flashing brilliantly by. A red ball bobbing down a river, dozens of sun rays breaking through clouds. Whenever Clare sees those rays—even as a nonbeliever—she says, "Someone just found God." She is my whole existence. This must be rapture.'

"I felt murderous that night. I got violently drunk, then tore the letter up into minuscule pieces and scattered them from the walls of the monastery. I watched the little blue tatters flutter down to meet the smoke of the guns. I stood alone, shouting at nothing, drunk and despairing, on a crumbling, twelfth-century wall high above the plains of war.

"It had once, fleetingly, occurred to me that Ted might lose his mind, but I had pushed those thoughts away. Now I began to feel that I was losing mine."

25

L OMBARDI ASKS SOFTLY, IN THE BURGEONING MORNING LIGHT, "BUT the affair started up again?"

"Briefly." Alex rests his hands on the open notebook. "Ted had written to me, asking me if I could get any leave in July. This was 1917. We knew there was another big offensive coming up, and I had the idea from his letters that he was afraid he wouldn't survive this one. He didn't say as much explicitly, but that was the impression I got." He pauses. "I did notice one thing: his handwriting had changed. Before, even at school, he had used long, sloping strokes of the pen, often so oblique it was almost horizontal, but always legible. His natural elegance was reflected in his handwriting, and in his choice of words. But in recent weeks, his letters were covered in this sort of terrible scrawl that was almost as hard to decipher as my own handwriting. His language was different, too: abrupt and, occasionally, coarse."

He bends his head. "We arranged to meet at a small hotel in the center of Paris, near Sacré Coeur. When I arrived, in the middle of a blisteringly hot day, I saw Ted and Clare standing by the entrance, waiting for me. She wore a thin, blue print dress. She hung back like a shy little girl, but I could tell from the way that she stood, ankles crossed and arms held behind her back, that she was angry, whether with me still, or the situation, I didn't know. Actually, they reminded me again of brother and sister standing there; the same fragile, ethereal quality. It affected me deeply, seeing them together. Suddenly a thought shot into my mind: What if Ted had found out about the affair, and this was a trick, enabling him to confront us at the same time?"

He swallows, remembering. "Then Ted came toward me, smiling, and I knew we were still safe."

He returns to the notebook again, using it as he has since beginning to tell Lombardi his story: as a prompt and a buttress—and to avoid looking into Lombardi's keen eyes.

"The singing echoed around the theater in Paris:

Take me back to dear old Blighty
Put me on the train to London town
Take me over there
Drop me anywhere
Birmingham, Leeds or Manchester
I don't care . . .

"It was the evening of Bastille Day. Defenders of Verdun marched down the Champs-Élysées, red, white, and blue banners snapping in the summer breeze. The Americans had entered the war and General Pershing had given the order for his troops to recognize July 14 as a national holiday, a mark of honor to their French allies and a thank-you for their own jubilant reception. Every Parisian café with a piano plunked out "Yankee Doodle Dandy," every play contained hastily inserted lines about the bravery of the American soldier.

"Streamers issued from the stage, covering us, the audience, in bright, twirling paper bunting. We reached out our hands, got to our feet, stamped, clapped, and sang along with the sequinned girls and beaming boys sweating their joy and patriotism beneath the dazzling footlights.

"Ted glowed with happiness, like a child at his first real birthday party. He stood on his seat, yo-yoing the scarlet streamer he had caught, singing with all the delight of a man content in the knowledge that those who matter to him most are within touching distance, safe and visible.

"How I want to see my Best Girl
Cuddling up as close as she can be . . .

"My lungs were bursting with the hot, plush air of the theater, its velvet curtain smell. I looked at Clare. We had barely spoken to each other since meeting earlier that day. Her hands were cold when they brushed mine. Her voice had no resonance. It was a dead, empty thing.

"Tiddley-iddley-ighty, hurry me home to Blighty;
Blighty is the place for me!

"The song ended and we, the crowd, remained standing, expectation filling the humid room where the streamers still fluttered gaily. I wiped the perspiration from my temples; my head throbbed. The noise of the singing had seemed to come from somewhere above me, in a place I couldn't reach. The ecstatic faces swam away, pale moons in the planetary darkness of the stalls.

"I was so intensely aware of Clare standing beside me that I wondered why the crowd didn't turn to look at me, why Ted didn't stare at me with that expression of dawning horror I pictured when I lay awake at night. It seemed impossible that the world was in ignorance of what she and I had done, the betrayal that stood between the three of us with all the presence of a fourth, malignant being.

"The opening bars of the last song spilled from the piano. Ted jumped down from his seat and put his arm around Clare, reaching out to grasp my shoulder, too. The act brought me into physical contact with his wife, my face resting against her soft, moth-like hair, so well remembered, so well loved.

"Nights are growing lonely, days are very long,
I'm a-growing weary, only listening for your song;
Old remembrances are thronging through my memory,
Thronging till it seems the world is full of dreams,
Just to call you back to me.

"It was the song I had played in my apartment, in London, after we met in Trafalgar Square. After she came to my lecture in Gower Street.

"Her fingers found mine. She drew my hand to her side. I felt the silk of her dress where it touched her hipbone. The outline of it, the jutting angular wave beneath the skimming fabric, sent a rush of passion through my blood.

"Clare knew it. Her answer was there, in the grip of her fingers over mine."

"Afterward, we left the theater and crossed the Pont Neuf to the Ile de la Cité. The moonlit streets were thick with revelers, and we had to wind our way through them. We found a café in the grand style, close to Notre Dame. I glanced up at the gargoyles as we passed under the gothic splendor of the cathedral; their arched forms stared back in grim guardianship.

"The crowded café was one Ted remembered. Under a sparkling canopy of chandeliers, it served unpretentious food and had a good wine list. I thought back to the last meal the three of us had shared, in Lampedusa's two years ago, and how I had been almost nauseous with longing for Clare. Now I knew what it was to make love to her, just as Ted did. I watched the two of them talking together; Clare a little less animatedly than her husband, and I wondered if she kissed and touched him in the same way as she had kissed and touched me, if her lips had whispered across his skin, as they had mine. What did she do, when he made love to her? How did she hold her head, her body, her limbs? Did she arch her neck at the moment passion spent itself, as she did with me? Or did she lie there, as I secretly hoped, in his grasp but thinking of me?

"I was seized by a terrible jealousy as we sat around that small polished table. All my earlier misgivings and guilt were driven away as I observed them both. The wine that I had drunk fired my resentment of him and my suspicions of her. For the first time in my life, I wanted to hurt the people I loved most, and it was an appalling feeling. I lit a cigarette with trembling hands, resolving to purge myself of all the bitter, bloody emotions surging through me.

"As I felt my nerves begin to calm, I concentrated on what Ted was telling us about his experiences last summer, after he had been injured during the fighting on the Somme. He sat with his elbows on the wooden table, hunched slightly, his chin in his hands. His eyes were very blue as he recounted how the Blighty wound in his left leg had earned him a seat on the train that left Vequement.

" 'I felt a bit of an impostor, to be perfectly honest. There were so many men whose injuries were far worse than mine. When I was carried on board the hospital ship at Le Havre, where they'd labeled me "Boat Sitting," I offered to work as a voluntary orderly. They gave me the task of ticking off the wounded as they arrived. The ship was full of casualties: even the sisters' and doctors' quarters had been requisitioned for stretcher cases. I stayed on deck for most of the crossing because the weather was so beautiful, watching the gulls wheel above us, feeling the spray coming off the ship as it cleaved through the sea.'

"He paused, then went on, 'We were the first casualties of the Somme to reach England. We docked at Dover and they took us to the railway station and put us on a long gray train with a red cross painted on it. It took us straight into London, to Charing Cross, which was queerly silent and empty. I'd never seen it like that and I panicked, thinking that London must have been heavily bombed. Then one of the soldiers in my compartment explained that the public were being kept away from us. There were only stretcher bearers and VADs waiting beside a dozen ambulances. A nurse offered me a cigarette as she showed me which vehicle to board. I took it gratefully, then realized I had nothing to light it with, and turned back to tell her. She wasn't there—she and a small crowd of nurses were trying to save a man who had gone into convulsions. But there was nothing they could do.'

"Ted paused again, his face tense. 'As I stepped up into the ambulance, I caught a glimpse of the crowd standing outside the station behind a cordon. I stared at them: they moved like rats, crawling over one another to see who had come back—and in what condition.'

"His head jerked in small movements. Clare had seen it too; she lay her hands on his arm and whispered something into his ear, her mouth against his cheek. It seemed to pacify him. He sipped his wine and finished his story.

" 'I was in the hospital for three weeks, then discharged.' He looked at Clare. 'It was so strange, going back to our flat without you. It gave me a peculiar feeling to walk around the rooms alone—it was almost as if I'd died and gone back there a ghost, haunting the place where I was happiest in life.' He gave that same bright, brittle smile I remembered from his visit in Tilques. 'I made myself a cup of tea and took it onto the balcony. I sat on the wooden bench there, in the sun, looking out across the rooftops to the river. It was so tranquil, so still. When I was a child I never understood how it was possible that the sun I could see from my bedroom window in Tyringham was the same sun that rose over Cairo and Calcutta. Now it seemed even more unlikely—the knowledge that this sun would set over the fields of the Somme later that day.'

"Clare rested her head on his shoulder. She didn't look at me, but Ted did, smiling. 'I thought of you and Clare,' he said.

"My heart turned over. Oh God, I thought, he does know. He's been biding his time, waiting for the right moment to blow the whole thing apart.

"But his smile was genuine. 'I tried to picture what the two of you might be doing—Clare in her uniform at the hospital in Rouen, applying dressings, and you, Alex, standing on a road somewhere near Albert, talking to German prisoners of war.' He looked down at his wife. 'I thought about your calmness, Clare, your impenetrable calm. And Alex with his frown and his unruly dark hair. I missed the two of you so much.'

"I bowed my head, not wanting to look at him again. Jealousy was replaced by the most stultifying remorse I had ever known.

" 'I'd been back at the front only two days when Previtt was killed.' Ted's voice was low, barely audible above the thrum of conversation in the café. 'I told you about him, do you remember? He was there when I injured my ankle, a couple of years ago. We were drinking tea as the sun broke over the palisades. We'd shared a joke—I can't think what it was—and I was walking away from him when the shell hit.'

"I glanced up; Ted was staring across the room. When he spoke, it was as if he were talking to another ghost, the spirit of the boy who had died: 'Do you know what happens when a shell lands directly on a soldier? He disappears. There isn't a trace of him left.' His head jerked again, compulsively. 'I don't want to die like that, in Picardy, at sunrise. In hell.'

"I put my head in my hands, hopeless, lost. Clare murmured something to him, and he nodded, then cleared his throat. 'Sorry. *Sorry.* I don't mean to be so bloody *grim.* Let's have another drink, shall we, and forget all this?'

"I doubted whether more alcohol was good for him, but it was what he wanted. I began to talk about my work, jabbering pure gibberish— anything to try to lighten Ted's mood. I must have succeeded, for he laughed when I imitated Sebastian Thorpe's aggravating voice.

"And then Ted remembered something. He leaned toward me, his eyes clear and untroubled again: 'I say, Alex, I meant to tell you. While I was in London I bumped into Katherine. She's working at the War Office now, did you know?'

"I saw a flicker of apprehension pass across Clare's face. 'Who's Katherine?' she asked.

"Ted grinned. 'An ex-girlfriend of Alex. The word *vivacious* might have been invented for her. She was always the most tremendous fun.'

" 'Was she?' I said, leaning back in my chair. 'I don't really remember.'

"Ted laughed, 'Oh, come *on,* Alex! The two of you had a *fantastic* time together.'

" 'Then why isn't he still with her?' asked Clare, addressing her question to Ted.

" 'Because he fell for someone else. A friend of Katherine's, wasn't it?'

" 'Something like that,' I said, taking out my cigarettes. Clare sat stiffly, staring at me.

" '*Anyway,* despite your somewhat cavalier behavior, Katherine doesn't bear you any ill will. She asked me to say hello to you. So: hello from Katherine.' Ted raised his glass, smiling.

" 'When did you last see her?' asked Clare, still with her eyes fixed on mine.

" 'Ages ago.' I didn't want to be drawn any further on the subject of Katherine or my former relationship with her.

"Ted finished his glass of wine. 'You know, I never told you this, Alex, but I was always quite sweet on Katherine myself.' He gave Clare a brilliant smile. 'Nothing for you to worry about, darling, it was all a very long time ago.'

"He turned to me. 'I actually thought that I was in love with her.' He shook his head, amused. 'She came to see me one afternoon. This was while the two of you were still together. She didn't say anything untoward, but it was pretty obvious that she liked me.' He laughed. 'I was quite shocked by it, to be honest.'

"I looked at him. I could see Clare, watching both of us; she held herself very still. 'You weren't tempted, then?' I said, keeping my voice light.

"Ted shook his head. 'No, of course not. She was lovely, and I was very flattered, but your friendship meant far more to me.' He frowned slightly, seeming perplexed by the question. 'I wouldn't do anything to hurt you, Alex. You know me better than that.'

"Then he scraped back his chair, excusing himself, and walked in his easy, graceful manner through the café that hummed with talk and laughter, leaving Clare and I sitting across from each other, not speaking, but absorbing the guilt that had risen like a flame to engulf us."

26

"THE FOLLOWING AFTERNOON, I STOOD IN THE HOTEL ROOM, AT THE window, watching Clare and her husband hail a taxi in the street below. I saw a cab pull up, and the two of them climb in, her hand in his, his arm going around her as the door closed and the vehicle moved off, joining the streams of traffic abandoning Paris after the great party, returning to war.

"I sat down, my elbows on the windowsill, the sunlight warming my skin. In the louche streets of Montmartre, soldiers lingered on the terraces, postponing the moment when they, too, must head back to the railway stations. I lit a cigarette and stared at the white, ovoid dome of the basilica of Sacré Coeur, watching people going in and out of its bronze doors. The light slanted across the steps leading up to the building. I wondered how many of the visitors were tourists, how many were lapsed Catholics like me, and if they entered the place seeking succour, and whether they came out feeling strengthened or alienated by the experience.

"I got abruptly to my feet and began collecting the few items of mine strewn around the narrow, humid room: the volume of Flecker's poetry, a book of Callot's engravings, my lighter, and the theater program from the night before. In a welter of desperation I threw them all into my leather bag, then glanced across at the door separating my room from the one Clare and Ted had shared. I felt my pulse slowing, knowing what must have taken place behind the white-painted door with its ornate brass handle and lock.

"I had to leave before she returned. I had to think. To work matters through in my mind, before I lost my grip on sanity. To think of a way forward.

"The door opened.

"She stared at me, her eyes wide with anguish.

" 'What are you doing?' she said. 'What are you *doing*?'

"She walked across the room and picked up the book of Callot's engravings, throwing it at the bed. It hit the wall and fell to the floor, losing its dust jacket.

"She stood before me, her face white with anger.

" 'You thought you could leave me, didn't you?' she said. 'But you can't. You *can't* leave me. I am going to leave you.' She fought her tears. 'And I want this loss to leave a hunger inside you, an appetite that drives you to consume everything but cannot save you from starving.'

"Her breath caught in her throat. She collapsed onto the bed in a storm of weeping.

"I looked down at her, at the perfectly coiled hair, the expensive blue dress and the silver jewelry glinting at her throat and ears. At the face she showed to the rest of the world. I thought of how I had damaged her, as she had damaged me: I saw the fists curled against the small breasts, the long legs drawn up beneath her, the tears falling onto the sheet, spreading a dark stain.

"My resolve cracked like a plate. I sank onto the bed beside her, pulling her around to me, finding her mouth with mine, feverishly."

" 'We have to tell him about us.'

" 'No.'

" 'We *must*. We love each other, Clare. We can have a future together. If you say that it's what you want, I will hold you to it. There will be no return to the old life for either of us. I won't let you step back into something that you don't believe in. If you love me still, then we will build another life together.'

" 'No. There's nothing so humiliating as a marriage that's failed. Perhaps I just don't love you enough to put myself through that.'

"We went around in circles like this for hours; I wanted to talk, but whatever I said seemed only to make things worse. In the end her temper snapped and she sat up in bed, banging her fists down on the sheets.

" 'Why do men always do this?' she asked angrily, 'Why do they say, "Let's talk" and then only listen? What about you, Alex? Where is your heart? Where is its voice?'

"But I'd told her that we should confess to Ted. She wouldn't even contemplate it. Now, in the gradations of darkness caused by the evening shadows across the curtains, I searched her eyes, trying to find the truth.

" 'I think you want to be with me, Clare. I think you're simply afraid of taking that step.'

" 'It isn't that. It's what it will do to Ted. You saw him; I don't even know whether he was fit to go back—this would destroy him. I'm not willing to take the risk.'

" 'You're lying. You're giving up what you want to save him.'

" 'It isn't like that; you're just too vain to believe me.'

" 'Look at me, Clare.'

"She turned toward me, her eyes filled with fire. 'No, Alex. You listen to me, for God's sake. When we argued in Cassel, something changed between the two of us. I realized that Ted was more important to you than I could ever hope to be, and that you would always blame me for coming between you both. When I left you that morning, I vowed never to come to you again like this. I'd made up my mind. But last night, when we were in the theater, all my feelings for you came back. I couldn't help myself.' Her eyes darkened. 'Yet whatever I feel for you, it isn't enough. It isn't enough to ruin Ted's life. Don't ask me to do that, Alex, because I won't.'

" 'But you didn't want me to leave you earlier. You stopped me—'

" 'I was upset, worried. I thought you were being mean.'

" 'Mean?'

" 'Trying to score points.'

" 'No. For God's sake, no. But I can't go on deceiving him.'

" 'You're not the only one suffering. Don't you think I feel terrible too? He's *my* husband. It was awful when he left. His misplaced trust in us. Oh God, what have we become?' She put her hands up to her face, distraught.

"I said, 'We've become lovers, Clare, and I want us to be together. But not like this.'

" 'Then we must finish it, here.'

" 'But you're only going back to him because you think it is the right thing to do. Don't sacrifice your happiness for his. You're afraid—'

" 'Stop saying that, Alex,' she cried, pulling herself up and wrapping her arms around her knees. 'I'm not afraid of anything, except hurting Ted. You can see how he is. How many more times do I have to say it? We've done something terrible, and if you keep trying to convince me that it was right, then I shall only end up hating you for it. I won't leave my husband. This was . . . an error of judgment.'

"I couldn't believe that she meant what she said, but I was powerless to prove otherwise. And she had already retreated from me. When we went out for dinner, her face was closed, her eyes flickering away, gazing at nothing, unable to meet my eyes. When we danced together she held herself away from me and stared over my shoulder at the other couples swirling around the floor. We walked back to the hotel together, hardly speaking.

"In our room, I tore at the delicate fabric of her dress while she clung to me, trying to break through the barrier she had thrown up between us. My lips moved insistently across her skin.

" 'Don't leave me Clare don't leave me don't ever leave me don't leave.'

"I went on whispering the words into her long hair, as if by repeating it I could make it happen. But her decision and resolve were there, immovable, in the reticence of her touch, in the tears that washed over my arms when I held her."

"In the morning we stood together outside the hotel, the sunlight sifting through the leaves of the trees in the quiet street.

"She had asked me not to accompany her to the station. I handed her the small red valise with her married name on it, fighting the impulse to seize her, to not let go. When she looked at me there was a void behind her eyes. She seemed awkward in her beauty now, embarrassed by it. The willowy limbs that protruded from her dress were as gauche as a young girl's.

" 'Well. Good-bye then, Alex.'

"I clenched my hands to my sides. I knew I could not touch her, that the time when such things were permissible had passed.

" 'I love you,' I said, my voice hoarse. 'You can't change that. Nothing can. This isn't what I wanted to happen.'

"There was a burst of song from the street behind us. Two young officers and their companions—laughing, dark-haired French girls—stumbled over the cobblestones in high spirits.

" 'There's nothing I can do about it. You mustn't think about me. You must forget. Tell yourself . . . ' She hesitated, on the verge of saying something consequential. She changed her mind: 'Tell yourself it never happened.'

" 'But I know it did.' I was quiet, determined. 'And I can't forget. I don't want to forget.'

" 'That's up to you.' She shrugged dismissively, an impatient gesture, and I marveled that she had ever belonged to me. 'As long as you keep it to yourself, I don't suppose it matters.'

"I looked at her, aghast. She seemed to have shut me out, completely, packed away our affair like an item of unwanted clothing.

" 'Why are you being like this?' I asked, angry, desperate. 'Agree to end it, by all means. But this atrocious coldness—why are you being so bloody unfeeling about it?'

"Her eyes regarded me calmly. 'Because I can be. Because I am.'

"I looked away from her, down. There was a shard of green glass between the cobblestones. I edged it out with the toe of my shoe, then covered it with my foot. I could see other pieces glinting in the bright, hard light. Someone had broken a bottle there.

" 'Alex.' Her voice was sharp. When I glanced up, I saw that her face had a hard look that I instinctively hated, not because it made her unattractive, but because I knew that she was scared. I didn't want her to be afraid of anything, particularly not me.

" 'It's all right,' I said, lifelessly. 'I won't tell him.'

"Her relief was palpable. 'Thank you.'

"I stared at her, knowing that she was wondering how she should leave, whether to simply walk away or to embrace me. Finally she stood on tiptoe, crinkling the leather of her shoes, and kissed me clumsily, half on the cheekbone and half on my earlobe. She looked at me, one hand going out to touch me, then retreating.

" 'Be safe, Alex.'

"She turned quickly and walked away. I could read nothing from her movements, and a minute later the curve of the road stole her from me, ending my searing speculation.

"A sudden impulse caused me to spring forward and run after her.

"I reached the corner, but before I caught sight of her again, I stopped and fell back against the wall, all courage seeping away. I felt drained, empty, spent of all thought or emotion.

"In that curious state of weightlessness I turned and went back into the hotel, to tell the concierge that I, too, was leaving."

"It is getting light. Isn't it?"

Lombardi nods. "Yes, it is getting light. Soon you'll hear the lorries passing again, the other laborers going to excavate." He pauses, looking at the writer. The dawn breaking across the fields is another morning to him, long ago. "Tell me what happened. To you, and to her."

Alex leans back and gazes up at the roof of the hut, watching the day begin its slow crawl. "She had lost her trust in me. When we argued in Cassel, Clare thought my friendship with her husband meant more to me than my affair with her; it didn't. But there was nothing I could say to alter that, afterward. And I think we were both appalled by what we had done. The velocity at which we fell in love was staggering to both of us. We didn't trust it, didn't trust ourselves, or each other. And then this overwhelming desire to protect Ted, which we both had. I still thought it would be best if we brought the affair out into the open; I had the foolish idea that because he loved us both, he would somehow be better equipped to deal with it. I suppose I thought he would understand, loving us, how we fell in love with each other. I thought he would come to terms with it." He puts his hands up to his skull. "Perhaps the war had affected me more than I realized. As much, in a sense, as it had affected him, although I was always at one remove from it. I don't know. I don't know what I was thinking."

"But the affair was over. It ended in Paris."

"Yes. Well, insofar as we were no longer lovers, I actually wanted to be with her more afterward. I suppose that's normal, isn't it? Wanting what you can't have? My work suffered as a result. The last words I could be proud of came from the reporting at Messines Ridge in June 1917. The end of my affair with Clare pitched me into a chasm of desolation and remorse. I had lost her, and underlying the pain of all that was my guilt about Ted." He shakes his head, slowly, from side to side. "You can't outrun guilt. You may as well try to race a leopard; in the end it will win, tearing you apart in the process. My friendship with Ted was now corrupted by deception of the worst possible kind. How could I go on pretending to him? Even though my relationship with his wife was over, the friendship he and I had was no longer worth anything unless I told him the truth. I became obsessed with it, driven by the desire to tell him everything."

"And then?" Lombardi asks quietly.

Alex glances down at the notebook, lying open on his knee, then raises his head. His face is terrible in the strange light of early morning. "Do you remember that explosive they used in the mines at Passchendaele—ammonal? It was a mixture of ammonium nitrate and aluminium and it caused the most spectacular, cataclysmic detonations."

He takes a deep breath. "Well, you could say that I made a decision that would blow all our lives apart like ammonal."

XI

A SOUL GOES OUT IN THE SUNSET FLARE

Poperinghe, July 1917 and
Passchendaele, November 1917

27

"IN ADVANCE OF THE NEW OFFENSIVE I WAS SENT TO POPERINGHE BY a newspaper editor who wanted a series of articles on life in the town they called 'the eighth wonder of the world' and 'the last stop before hell.'

"Poperinghe was close to Ypres, and although it was occasionally the victim of shelling and bombing it never came under the same relentless assault. But throughout the narrow, uneven streets of the town there were still reminders of the dangers: on the town hall a sign warned whether the wind blowing in was 'SAFE' or 'DANGEROUS' because of recent gas attacks in the salient, and a notice in the barber's shop read: 'We do not cut hair when the Germans are shelling.'

"Every soldier knew Poperinghe; there was a permanent garrison and vast camps outside the town. Soldiers visited Pop while on leave, or upon their return, and there were scores of men who came just 'for a day out.' It had more entertainment to offer than Amiens, from the scores of estaminets and restaurants, to the cinemas and impromptu cabarets and theater shows. One café served the finest fish and chips outside Britain and the most convivial atmosphere of any restaurant could be found at La Poupeé, known to every officer as Ginger's on account of the youngest, vivacious, red-haired daughter of the woman who owned the place. While in London food was rationed, here it was plentiful, with enough liquor to sink a ship. Later I heard that more champagne corks were popped during the war at Ginger's than anywhere else in Belgium and France. Soldiers from every corner of the British Empire came to sample Poperinghe's delights.

"When I arrived there in mid-July 1917, two days after returning from Paris, the town was swarming with life. On the hottest days, when lorries and limbers rumbled along the roads, and soldiers sat in the thronging streets with their faces streaming sweat, drinking cool beer, it resembled a sort of miniature Cairo. The Germans concentrated their Gotha bombs on Poperinghe's railway station with deadly accuracy that summer too, and vast clouds of dust and smoke would rise above the tapering alleyways and dilapidated buildings.

"My base in Poperinghe was Talbot House. From the street it was an elegant, wedding-cake frill of a building, but anyone who entered its doors was immediately enfolded in the glowing warmth of this, the most popular 'soldiers' club' on the Western front. It was run by a chaplain called Philip Clayton who had been nicknamed Tubby, or Boniface after the innkeeper in *The Beaux Stratagem*. There are rumors that his rotund, spectacled form was the inspiration for Chesterton's 'Father Brown' stories; the two men knew each other well. Tubby Clayton was intelligent, kind, and humoros. His attitude to guests was summed up by two signs that hung in the house. The first read: 'ABANDON RANK ALL YE WHO ENTER HERE,' and the second, above the entrance: 'TO PESSIMISTS: WAY OUT.' There were notices everywhere in the house; another invited guests to 'COME UPSTAIRS AND RISK MEETING THE CHAPLAIN.'

"Accommodation consisted of stretchers with blankets in the bedrooms, but it was the attic of the building that gave Talbot House its heart. The upper floor had been transformed into a chapel of jewel-like beauty and Tubby always told his guests that the foundations of the house were in the loft, where a carpenter's bench served as an altar. Thousands of soldiers received the sacrament there before going into the trenches. Other forms of comfort were offered elsewhere in the house: soldiers hung about the library, relaxed in the cinema in the cellar showing Charlie Chaplin films, drowsed in the conservatory, and made their own tea in the canteen. In the evenings, the old hop store next to the garden was transformed into a concert hall.

"It was in the garden where I spent my afternoons, writing, on the veranda of the thatched summerhouse. Soldiers lounged in the conservatory, reading and drinking tea, sat with newspapers and played whist on the brilliantly green sloping lawn, or lay in hammocks under the shady trees. Tubby called them his 'khaki basking lizards.' It was a place of great peace; the white birds in the dovecote seemed to epitomize its sanctuary from the war.

"One hot afternoon Tubby came to me while I was writing. He carried two cups of tea and a paper bag full of plums. 'Do you mind if I join you?' he asked.

"We had spoken often before, on my other visits to Talbot House, but during my stay this time I had sensed him watching me. Fearing a sermon, I reminded him that I don't believe in God.

" 'That's quite all right,' Tubby said benignly, 'as long as He believes in you.'

"We talked about how he and his brother, who had been killed at Hooge in 1915, set up Talbot House. He told me about some of the men who had found refuge there. One of his many gifts was a good memory for faces and names; I asked him whether he had ever met Lieutenant Edward Eden.

"Tubby thought for a moment, his kindly face crinkling. Then his small eyes brightened: '*Ted,* you mean? Yes, I remember him very well. He was here last year, in the spring. He had some personal demons, as we all do, and was trying to work through them. He adored his wife and he spoke with deep affection of his best friend. That would be you, I suppose?'

"I couldn't speak. I stared at the lovely garden, at the soldiers lying in the sun. Two of them were playing chess, deep in concentration, the board laid on one of the winding paths. I could imagine Ted here, standing under the trees and talking to the chaplain, as one fine man to another.

'Tubby gently took my cup of tea and set it on the floor, then turned to me. 'You don't have to tell me what it is that troubles you, but the old adage of a problem shared does have some truth in it, or so I've found.'

"I told him everything. It poured out, unstoppably. Finally, I confided in him the guilt that was too heavy for me to bear, and my desperation to confess the affair to Ted. I asked Tubby what he thought I should do.

"He looked at me with such compassion that I almost broke down. 'I can't tell you what to do. That would be very wrong. Only you can make that decision. In the church, of course, we talk about repentance. But repentance has two sides to it: regret for the wrong we have done but also fear of what might happen to us because of it. The first must take precedence over the latter if we are to be truly sorry for our mistakes. Otherwise a confession, or an apology, can become self-serving.'

" 'I can see that,' I said slowly, hunching forward, my hands between my knees. 'But now I'm not sure if I've got the balance right.'

" 'Think of it this way,' said Tubby, his spectacles glinting in the sunlight. 'Repentance means that you have changed your mind about something. Now, art historians are taught, during their early studies, to detect the *pentamenti* in the works of a painter. That is, those brush strokes, alterations, and painting over the old subject that reveals how an artwork evolved, and therefore, its creator's intentions.' He paused. 'What I am saying is that perhaps you could look for the *pentamenti* in what you have done to understand it. Then, possibly, you will be in a position to correct the balance and to explain yourself more clearly, if you do decide to tell your friend everything. A confession, like an apology, has to come from the heart, not the head, from sorrow, not from fear.'

"I listened to him, watching the shadows moving around the foot of the great trees when the breeze stirred their leaves. A sudden hopelessness seeped through me. 'I feel like killing myself,' I said, shutting my eyes tightly. 'I don't want to get old, carrying this around with me forever.'

"Tubby was quiet for a moment. He scratched his white hair. Then he said, 'I once read a very judicious book. It was by an Italian nobleman, Luigi Cornaro, and written in the sixteenth century. The title was *Discorsi della vita sobria* and he wrote about the secret to a long and happy life. It was simple, according to Cornaro: eat less but healthily. The book made him famous. Tintoretto painted his portrait and he spent his last years in a palazzo, adding more material to his book. He told his readers that 'old age was a thing to be welcomed, a time of wisdom when passions have been burned away.' The most wonderful sentence in the whole book was: 'I did not know that the world could be so beautiful until I was old.'

"Those words unlocked something in my head; I heard its click. The hopelessness washed away. I saw the two soldiers fold up their chess board and pocket the pieces and go indoors. Another soldier came out and stood on the path where they had been, to smoke a cigarette. He lifted his face up to the sunlight, smiling.

"I turned to thank the chaplain, but he had gone.

I sat in the summerhouse for another hour. I felt calm; I had made my choice.

'A time of wisdom when passions have been burnt away.'"

"I sent Clare a telegram, telling her I would visit her on July eigh-teenth. I drove to Rouen and arrived in the late afternoon. We met at the Eglise St.-Maclou, a grandiose Gothic church; the sun lay golden and cold against the stone. Rouen had not been touched by the sum-mer temperatures. A few senior officers wandered about the streets; the town served as the cavalry base depot.

"I arrived before she did, and walked around the quadrangle out-side the church, trying to still my nerves at the prospect of seeing her again, and planning what I might say. I looked idly at the timbers of the buildings. There was no solace to be had here; the wood was carved with a macabre sequence of gravediggers' implements, coffins, hour-glasses, bones, and skulls. I walked away, through the ossuary where plague victims lay buried, and took shelter in the great porch.

"She came hurrying down the street, arms crossed over her chest, in uniform, head bent against the wind. I went to meet her, and she looked up as I reached her, with the impassive, indecipherable gaze that meant she was prepared to stand her ground, whatever it was I had come to tell her. I leaned down to kiss her, but she stepped away. I felt my own walls starting to rise.

"'Where shall we go?' I asked quietly, steeling my shoulders against the wind that tore through the empty square with a low cry.

"'The café, over there. I can't be seen with you.'

"'Because of Ted?'

"She gave me an impatient look. 'Because of Matron; we're forbid-den to meet men on our free afternoons.'

"We walked to the Gros Horloge. The café Clare had pointed out showed a flush of light in its window, though the doors were closed.

"I tried the long handle; the door opened and a waitress approached us immediately, steering us to the back of the wine-scented room. 'Sisters don't like windows,' she said with a knowing smile.

"There was no one else there. A green cloth with tasseled edges covered the table. Papier-mâché poppies bowed from a glass vase next to an uncorked bottle of wine. The waitress brought our order of tea, vegetable soup, and warm bread, then retreated discreetly to the other side of the room, polishing cutlery and setting it out on a deep tray.

" 'How long do you have?' I asked, tearing the bread and offering Clare half.

"She dropped it onto a side plate. 'An hour.'

"I examined the label on the bottle of claret next to the flowers as I began to eat. Everything I had intended to say had gone from my mind; I felt as though I were standing in a void, having lost all power of communication.

" 'Alex.'

"I looked up.

" 'We can't go back to how things were,' she said. 'I've made my decision and nothing you can say will alter that.'

"I frowned at her, stung by the unnecessary rejection. 'That's not why I'm here, Clare.' I tried to see beyond the cool gray gaze, the inexpressive mask, but it was hopeless.

"With an effort, I said, 'I'm going to tell him about us.'

"The façade vanished. She pushed the food away, shaking her head, her eyes intense with anxiety. 'I've told you *no*. We've ended our relationship; why tell him about something that's no longer relevant?'

" 'Our affair was irrelevant?'

" 'Don't twist my words. You know what I mean.'

"I stared at her. 'I don't like living a lie.'

" 'Is that the only reason?'

" 'What do you mean?'

" 'This is about you, not about Ted or me. Isn't it?'

" 'No, it's not . . . but I can't live with it, that much is true. But that's not why I want to tell him.' I hesitated, wondering if I could explain it as succinctly as Tubby Clayton had; how it was important to get the balance of repentance right. I tried to find the words, but they wouldn't come. Instead I told her, 'Ted is my oldest, dearest friend.

Perhaps my only real friend. At the moment our friendship is contaminated by a lie. He has a right to know—'

" 'No,' she said. 'No.' She sat back, twisting her napkin into a small blue ball.

"I grew irritated. 'Clare, I've known Ted much longer than you. I think in time he will find it within him to forgive us both, then we can all get on with our lives—'

"She shook her head again, slowly. Her voice was tinged with incredulity. 'You're a madman. You don't understand anything, do you?'

" 'What is there to understand?'

" 'Has Ted written to you lately—before we were in Paris?'

" 'Only a short letter, asking if I could get leave then. Why?'

"She looked down at the balled napkin, a slight frown on her face, as if she were surprised to find it there. Then she raised her eyes to me again, and said in a low voice, 'Ted's ill. You saw him, in Paris at the café where we went after the theater. Those movements of his, the bright smiles and then the distraction; they're all signs—'

" 'Of what?'

" 'He's *disturbed,* Alex. Terribly disturbed.' She drew in her breath, spreading out her fingers on the edge of the table. 'Sometimes he can conceal it. He's obviously able to cover up enough to fool the authorities, but I think he's shell-shocked.'

" 'Do you really believe that?' I said. 'I don't. Of course he's traumatized by what he's seen, but isn't everyone? A man who truly has shell shock can't hide it.'

" 'Yes, he can,' she said, suddenly forceful. 'I've seen men do it. If they have a purpose, if they feel that they want to go on fighting, they'll stave it off as long as possible. And then one day, they snap.'

" 'Ted hasn't snapped.'

" 'No, but he's finding it hard . . . to keep going. Sometimes, when I get his letters I can hardly read his writing—it's all over the place. He writes things that make no sense.' Her eyes filled with tears.

" 'What sort of things?'

" 'I don't know . . . as if he's writing in his sleep, dreaming. And then, sometimes, I get a more articulate letter and he apologizes for his last lines.' She looked down at the table, swallowing hard. 'I'm frightened for him. He tells me that the life he and I will have after the war is the only thing that sustains him. If you take that away—'

"I clicked my tongue against the roof of my mouth in frustration. I didn't believe anything she had told me and I couldn't understand why she wanted to persist with the lie we had begun. 'The life you and he will have after the war? Do you think he would still want that if he knew what had happened between the two of us?'

" 'I don't know. Probably not. But that's what he clings to, Alex. If you take that away, he won't have anything left.'

"She reached out to grip my hand; her fingers were like ice. Her short nails broke into the skin on my palms. '*Please,* Alex. I'm so afraid for him. When the war is over, then we can talk about this again. I agree that we should tell him, it isn't that I want to go on living a lie either, but not now. Not while he's facing death every day. Please *don't* tell him. Not now.'

"I extracted my hand, rubbing the small scrapings of skin. 'He loves us, Clare. He deserves to know the truth.'

" 'I know that, but not *now.*' Her voice rose and the waitress glanced over at us.

" 'It's for the best,' I said.

"Why was she being so obtuse? I fumed, convinced that anything would be better for Ted than to go on living in ignorance. I didn't believe he would react as she had said; I honestly thought he would feel shocked and horribly let down by us both, but that in the end, he would rather know the truth. They had been married only three years and the war had kept them apart most of the time; I had known Ted far longer, as I had pointed out to her, and felt that I understood him more than she ever could.

" She stared, seething, her skin flushed. 'You will kill him—'

" 'Clare—'

"She scraped back her chair, standing, her eyes burning, 'As if you shot a bullet through his *heart.*' "

"We said good-bye at the foot of the slope going back to the hospital compound. It had begun to rain but she refused my offer of a lift; that sort of thing was frowned upon by the hospital. I left her, wanting her again, but still angry that she couldn't see that Ted was owed the truth.

"I got back into the car, blood pounding in my ears, incensed that I hadn't been able to convince her. I drove at reckless speed, her nail marks on my hands, the pressed crescents of broken skin. When I arrived at the monastery in Cassel where we were billeted, I shut myself in my room and thought about everything that Clare had said. But I also thought about the past two years, our affair, and what it meant to be a betrayer. Guilt is its own punishment, I realized. I needed to confess.

"The day after my meeting with Clare in Rouen, I telegrammed Ted, asking to meet him. I thought that if I could see him, judge his state of mind for myself, *then* I would know what to do. The letter he sent back was perfectly lucid. There were no wild ramblings or incoherent sentences. He wrote that he couldn't possibly arrange leave so soon after our time in Paris. There was a new offensive beginning, as he and I were both aware, although he couldn't mention that in his reply.

"But it was his letter, his cloudless words, that made me doubt Clare more than ever. I *had* seen his suffering that summer, but I held fast to what I had told Clare: that there wasn't a man fighting who didn't have moments when their nerves caved in. The doubt grew until I began to suspect that she was exaggerating Ted's frail mental state because she regretted our affair. She had abandoned me and she was now making excuses to prevent her husband from finding out what had happened. I still loved her, even then, but it destroyed me to imagine that this was what she was doing.

"The day after receiving Ted's letter, I wrote to him, telling him the truth about Clare and me, about the affair and our ghastly duplicity. I asked him to forgive both of us, and to understand. And I waited.

"A fortnight passed. I heard nothing from him, nor from Clare to say that he had been in touch with her after reading my letter. I wrote to him again. This time my own letter came back to me, with Ted's handwriting heavily underlined on the envelope, *'No longer at this address.'* I was stunned, panic-stricken, and wrote another letter immediately, trying to explain my actions. He didn't reply. I wrote to Clare then, telling her what I had done, but she was either working elsewhere or chose not to respond. I spiraled into despair, drinking too much in the evenings, angry that I couldn't get away to speak to

Ted or Clare, and in my mind had endless imaginary conversations with them in which they always eventually came around to my position.

"In reality, though, there was nothing I could do. We were out of time; the new offensive had begun."

28

THE SUN HAS RISEN, BUT WITHOUT ITS SPREADING WARMTH, DUE TO the earliness of the hour. The fields lie sallow, a cold breath of pallid amber.

Lombardi looks at the writer, wondering if he will break under the weight of the words he has yet to speak, the buried wounds. In his hands, the man holds the leather-bound notebook, staring down at the thick pages covered in a black scrawl. He does not move. Lombardi thinks of a phrase he has heard often during his work in Belgium: *blatt-still*. It is a German word, spoken by the German relatives who come to the cemeteries, and it means 'still as a leaf.'

Lombardi reaches out and lays his fingers over the open papers. His guest looks up, startled, as if he has forgotten where he is.

"You must go on," says Lombardi. "Finish your story." He smiles gently and points at the untidy black script: "Read."

"The land around the southern and westerly points of Ypres was notoriously flat, apart from the sudden rise of Cassel. But to the north and east you had these gradual inclines, eyelash-shaped folds that formed a half-loop above the blasted spires of the town. The highest of these was Passchendaele.

"The opening bombardment started up on July twenty-second and lasted fourteen days. Haig was keen to capitalize on the successes at Messines Ridge with another battle in Flanders, but the ghosts of the Somme haunted the War Cabinet, making them nervous. Haig was determined to have his way. He stressed the importance of capturing the ports of Ostend and Zeebrugge, claiming that these were the main German U-boat ports, which turned out not to be true. But Haig had the support of Admiral Jellicoe, and that helped sway the War Cabinet.

"I watched the last stages of the opening bombardment. Our guns concentrated on the enemy's battery positions with disastrous results. Because of the clay soil and high water table, the area was prone to flooding, but the Belgians had dealt with that by creating an infrastructure of dikes and drainage channels. Our guns destroyed this vital network, creating conditions that would kill thousands of men and cause the campaign to limp on whereas Haig had foreseen it as a short, sharp shock for the enemy.

"When the offensive itself began on July thirty-first, the countryside was already a quagmire. Rain fell like stair rods. The force of the shells turned the churned-up ground into glutinous seas through which the infantry had to drag themselves and their guns and horses and the rest of their equipment. Rain pelted down for ten days without respite. Our men had held the line there for two and a half years, and most of them just didn't have the strength left to go on fighting. Newcomers were appalled when they first glimpsed the conditions. The mud and slime reached up to a man's thighs and beneath the morass lay the unknown thousands who had drowned there. On the Somme, the stretcher bearers generally knew that they had a good chance of reaching the wounded sooner or later. At Passchendaele there was no hope.

"I was observing the northern part of the line above Boesinghe, where I would spend most of the offensive. I spoke to some of the wounded. The Germans, in their concrete pillboxes and gun emplacements, were able to shelter from the conditions somewhat. On August third we heard that the campaign was to be postponed due to the weather. But two weeks later it began again. One afternoon I went back to the northern part of the line and to a field dressing station that had been established in some old farm buildings between the villages of Boesinghe and Elverdinghe.

"The casualties who had found their way to this small cluster of out-buildings had done so by a miracle of determination. There were already a huddle of graves in one corner of the farm; they belonged to men who had managed to get to the field dressing station only to die within a few hours. Storms raged across the plains, winds hurled through the badly shelled buildings where the wounded lay, and in the yard that had become a slough, a horse stumbled, up to its leg joints in mud, its entrails trailing. Sickened by its suffering, I drew my pistol and shot the animal, and then went through to the main ward in a vast barn.

"I walked among the wounded, more shaken by this sight than any other during the war. There was little the medical staff could do but try to keep the men as comfortable as possible, and dry. Those casualties without hope of survival were placed at one end of the shed, away from their comrades. Their injuries were horrifying, their agony unimaginable. The storm raged above their heads, where the roof and its thick wooden rafters shook in the gale and with the force of the guns.

"In the far corner of the barn, a nurse administering morphine crouched next to a filthy bundle of rags and blood on a stretcher on the sodden floor. As I came toward them I saw that the man had a hole as large as my hand in his abdomen. His mouth gaped in a silent scream.

"The nurse straightened up and turned to me. 'He was shot trying to save another man's life, then hit by shrapnel.'

" 'Can't you do anything more for him?' I asked.

"She shook her head. 'No. We've cleaned the wound and removed some of the shrapnel.' She paused. 'He doesn't have long.'

"The nurse leaned down again to pull the thin blanket up to the man's mud-splattered jaw. A tearing gust of wind battered the walls of the barn, causing the wounded to cry out in terror. I bent down to ask the nurse when they would be able to evacuate the place.

"At the sound of my voice, the wounded man swiveled his head and managed to focus his tormented eyes upon me.

"I looked at him, this near-corpse whose face was obscured beneath layers of blood and dirt, but whose blue gaze I knew, and felt the ground fall away beneath my feet."

$\mathcal{A}$LL AROUND THE REMAINS OF BLEUET FARM THE GUNS POUNDED. Shells ignited the sky above the burning village of Elverdinghe, dragging the red and orange flames across the darkness like billowing silks.

In the barn where the wounded lay, the wind hurtled through the roof cavities, beating on the vast wooden doors and lifting bales of wet straw from the floor. There was nothing the medical staff could do except pray that the storm would wear itself out before the whole structure splintered and caved in upon them.

Among the moribund casualties in the far corner of the barn crouched a man, his shadow falling over a fading figure on a soiled stretcher. The contorted face that looked up at him was white as a knuckle with pain beneath the film of mud.

"You *bastard*." The voice of the wounded man came hissing through a froth of blood. "I wanted to die without ever setting eyes on you again. You couldn't even give me that, could you?"

The nurse had gone, leaving Alex alone with Ted. He clutched the side of the stretcher, his knees sinking into the sludge on the ground, sucking at his clothing. His body shook with such violence that he had to fight to remain upright.

"Ted," he began distraughtly, "try to stay calm. Don't—"

The dry lips drew back from the gums in a ghastly smile. "I'm dying, dear Alex. Or haven't you realized that yet?"

"You can't die—I won't let you." Alex felt an uncontrollable terror rise within him.

"You can't help me . . ." A spray of blood spurted from the desiccated mouth.

Alex felt for his handkerchief with trembling fingers and blotted the red globules, then threw it away from him.

"Don't speak, Ted," he implored. "I should be the one who talks; I should be asking you to forgive me, to forgive us."

Dark blood seeped from the corner of the white mouth, going down to the blackened earlobe. "You won't get that from me, you bastard. Not even on my deathbed." Ted's breath rasped as he heaved out the words. "After I got your letter all I could think about was ending it all. They'll tell you that I was a hero."

A deep, ragged breath agitated the torn body. "*Don't believe them.* That I was courageous in battle. *But don't believe them.* I stood in front of bullets for a reason. Not to save, but to die."

"No," said Alex, unbelieving. "No, Ted." He moved the blond hair matted with clods of earth back from the cold, sweating brow.

"It's ironic, isn't it? We were raised on the classics, on wars . . ." Another jagged breath, the body heaving up from the soiled stretcher. "When this began, I wanted to go to Gallipoli. I thought I would find my worth, as a soldier, if I could disembark within sight of Troy." The hands jerked out from the side of the body. "Stupid, romantic schoolboy notions. Listen to the guns, Alex: *'The Trojans filled the air with clamor . . .'* We fought like them, for honor. Greek wars were short, though, weren't they? A day at a time, battles that lasted an hour. Our war is long, too long . . ." he gasped, his fingers clawing at the air as if he would hang his last breath upon it.

"Hold on, Ted. Hold on," Alex leaned over the stretcher, frantically trying to pull Ted into his arms, to fold his body into his and breathe life back into him.

An explosion in the yard twisted the vast wooden doors off their hinges, creating a sound like that of a great ship breaking up, becoming wrecked. A torrent of shells shredded the landscape around the farm.

Ted let out a cry and coiled his fists above his open stomach. "Why are you here, Alex? Are you going to bury me?"

"Is that what you want?" The vision of Ted's savaged body, the smell of cordite, the stench of iodine, and the roar of the pulsating guns filled Alex's senses with madness.

"I don't care. I used to dream about a glorious funeral, but that's not going to happen to me now, is it?" The wound in the stomach spilled a viscous pink fluid and he gasped, "Promise me you won't tell Clare you saw me like this. Don't tell her. Don't tell anyone. You don't know me. *Promise me.*"

Unable to free his mind of the horror around him, Alex surrendered. "I promise."

"I don't want anyone to know I died like this ... *in squalor.*" The words punched the air with their intensity. "I don't want to be buried in this place, but as I must, find me somewhere *away* from the guns ..."

Alex felt his eyes stinging with hot tears that ran down to his jaw and fell onto the shreds of his friend's shirt.

"Don't let them mark my grave." Another gasp, the breath rasping and tearing the throat. "Just find me a quiet spot where I can lie in peace, without meaning to you or anyone."

"No!" Alex shouted, reality breaking in on his turmoil, "I won't let you talk like that—I love you—Clare and I—we *both* love you—'

The final, razor-sharp breath came, the last demand issued as a scream: *"Then bury me with glory or none at all."*

The body slammed upward, heaving away from the floor with the force of an electrical volt. Alex felt the impact against his chest, as the gaping, spilling stomach struck him at an angle, splattering his face and clothes with bloody matter. As he drew back in horror, he saw the falling away, the last rattling rasp of life from the body as it dropped to the ground, the head splitting as it hit stone, the eyelids snapping open like a doll's.

He was dead. Shouting nonsensically, Alex crawled toward Ted until he was crouched above him. He looked into his eyes but the blue irises were numb. He put out his hand to touch the lifeless fingers, then pulled back.

In the darkness of the barn, convulsive light issuing through the fractured roof shone brightly on the white and gold wedding band.

The nurse returned. She bent down to pat Alex's shoulder where he sat cross-legged in the mud, head in his hands.

"It's a blessing, you know; his end has been quick compared to others. He could never have survived. He was a hero. A comrade of his died earlier today, but he told me about this man, and how he risked his life, time and again in these last few weeks, to save others." She looked down at the misshapen body. "He was a saint. He deserves to be remembered. Too many are forgotten." She frowned. "But I didn't get his name. He wouldn't tell me. And the other man, who came in with him, wasn't wearing his identity disk."

"He isn't either." Alex's voice was low, despite the still-raging storm.

Her frown deepened. "Oh, well. There's nothing that can be done about it." She turned to leave, then spun around. "You didn't know him, did you? You seem so affected by his death . . ."

"No." Alex kept his head hidden in his hands. "I didn't know him at all."

"Oh. I'm sorry." The nurse was about to walk away when Alex suddenly leaped up and grasped her arm. His eyes felt wild in his blood-streaked face. "He wanted me to bury him."

She stared at him, a flicker of puzzlement passing over her brow. Then she nodded. "Ask someone to help you."

She left Alex standing alone beside Ted's body. He opened his right hand. On his filthy palm, Ted's silver identity disk gleamed faintly. Alex closed his fingers over the disk he would guard like a heart.

He summoned every ounce of willpower he had to find one of the stretcher bearers and ask for assistance in carrying Ted's body to the corner of the farm where the open earth waited to receive the dead. The rain whirled on the wind and drummed down on the exposed rafters of the buildings standing black and empty nearby.

Alex remembered Ted's last words as they lowered the stretcher to the ground. There was no possibility of glory here, not in these visceral, shattered fields where the guns went on and on, endlessly throbbing their bullets into the darkness. Ted had asked that nothing mark his resting place; there was no more Alex could do for him than fulfill that promise.

"Would you leave me?" he asked the stretcher bearer when they had tipped the body into one of the empty graves. "I was with him, when he died. I'd like to fill in the—the grave, alone." His voice was guttural with pain, and the stretcher bearer, hearing it, nodded and struggled through the thunderstorm to return to the rattling barn.

In the far reaches of the landscape, shells burst in a hail of white stars. The lamps of war lit the earth as Alex covered the body with soil. When it was done, he stood beside the unmarked grave, the last in the row. It lay under a tree rent in two by lightning, both halves cleft with strange precision, the black branches reaching over the fresh mound as if to enfold it gently.

In the distance, the falling village of Elverdinghe glowed.

"Oh God, what have I done?"

Alex leaned his streaming head against the lightning tree, pounding it with his fists, screaming until his voice was swept away on the tempest, across the burning fields of Flanders.

"What have I done? What have I done?"

There was no answer.

Only the indefatigable guns, the rain, the winds, and the rain.

XII

ONE SHALL MAKE
OUR STORY SHINE

Ypres, July 17, 1920

30

*L*OMBARDI STARES AT HIS GUEST IN WONDER. "BLEUET FARM IS LESS than five miles from here. Have you ever been back?"

"No." He gets up abruptly from the chair and walks across to the door, gulping in the air. Then he turns to look at Lombardi. "There is a saying—I don't know if you are familiar with it—'We term sleep a death and yet it is waking that kills us.' Living is the cause of dying. Such a simple idea."

He turns back to the open doorway and leans against the wall to stare at the old trenches, where weeds glisten with dew. "How should we speak about death? What is there to say? Has anyone ever found words to describe grief, real grief? I don't believe they have. How it pervades every aspect of the afflicted, if that isn't too emotive a word. I felt afflicted by Ted's death. Not only the pain of his loss, but the stain it cast across my memories of him. Because his death was my responsibility."

"He could have been killed at any time," Lombardi says gently.

Alex shakes his head. "No."

"If he had forgiven you—"

"If he could have forgiven me, I would have known some measure of peace. As it was, he condemned me. I deserved it, of course." He lifts his head to the breeze. "Ever since, I have been searching, in all kinds of places, for absolution."

A flock of birds wheel up from the awry branches of the trees. They fly, as an arrow, in the direction of the ruins of Elverdinghe.

"What happened after he died?" Lombardi asks.

"I wrote to Clare when his name appeared on the 'missing' lists. Not to tell her that I had been with him when he died, but to offer sympathy, although it sounds so meaningless to say that now. It might seem cruel, what I did, not telling her what I knew, but I had promised Ted." He speaks through gritted teeth. "I had failed him in every other way, and this was the only thing I could do for him. I had to keep my word. She didn't reply to my letter. I knew that Ted must have written to her after I told him about the affair. I wrote again, and again, but she never responded."

"And then?" asks Lombardi.

Alex shrugs. "Not much to tell. I carried on working until the Armistice. But I had lost my enthusiasm for reporting. I'd lost my enthusiasm for life." He pauses. "I've always loved words. Now I saw how useless they were, offensive even, white maggots inching over dead men. No words could describe the horror of what I'd seen. I was glad, for that reason, too, when the war came to an end. My last dispatch was on Peace Day last year, when I and my colleagues stood together on the Hohenzollern Bridge in Cologne, listening to a speech by Haig. He thanked the war correspondents of all Allied countries and said we'd helped him to victory by boosting morale among the troops and on the home front. I didn't agree, but his conviviality was genuine enough. 'Gentlemen,' he told us, 'you have played the game like men!' How little he knew."

He hesitates, remembering. "Afterward, I was asked to go on a lecture tour of America with Julian Quint. We spent six months there. When I got back to London I called Clare. When she heard my voice she put down the receiver. She hated me. She *hates* me. She must. Our affair is the past. The war is the past. Why go bringing it all up again? She knows where to find me, if she wants to talk."

"But you love her," Lombardi says quietly.

"Yes. But you can't make someone love you in return, no matter how much you want it. And Ted's ghost would be between us, always."

"But what will you do now? You said you were searching for absolution."

"I am." Alex hunches his shoulders in a gesture of hopelessness. "But perhaps I'm looking for it in the wrong place. I don't know. I really don't know."

Lombardi can see that he is exhausted by the telling of his story. He watches his guest go out into the field and stand at the edge of the first line of crosses, staring down at the old trenches, overgrown now with cornflowers, the "bleuets" that give their name to the farm where Ted died, so close to the Villa Via Sacra.

They work in the field all day. Lombardi shows Alex where to dig in order to clear the ground for the plots of the new cemetery that will rise, literally, from the bones of the old. He directs Alex to uproot dead tree stumps, big and gnarled as giant's fists, and trundle them in the wheelbarrow over to the rubbish heap behind the hut, trailed by Kemmel.

In the afternoon, when they break for lunch in the open air, Alex says, "I can't believe how many flowers there are, growing among the weeds. When the soil is so poisoned, and when you think of what lies beneath . . ."

Lombardi passes him a mug of cold water. "I know. It's amazing, isn't it? White camomile and yellow charlock, cornflowers and poppies—they're the hardiest species. Actually, there's a very simple horticultural idea behind the cemeteries. When each one is complete, the plants within them represent the nationalities of the dead."

"What about this one?" asks Alex, wiping perspiration from his nose.

"Well, this one has an abundance of British soldiers, so it will probably be planted with daffodils, snowdrops, crocuses, and roses. In the Indian cemetery at Neuve Chapelle, marigolds and cypresses will be grown, and for where the Canadian dead lie, maples are being imported. That sort of thing."

Alex shakes his head. "It seems odd, though, to think that beauty could flourish here, amid so much death."

"The drainage system that was in place before the fighting at Passchendaele is being fitted below ground again. That will restore goodness to the soil." Lombardi drinks the last drop of water from his mug, and inclines his head toward the field. "Back to work?"

Alex nods, and follows him through the long grass to the trench.

In the early evening, while Lombardi prepares another simple meal, Alex sits outside on a tree stump, writing:

On Hill 60, the cold-eyed farmers search the torn ground for anything they can sell. At plowing time, women and children trail through the fields with baskets, searching for the millions of shrapnel balls lying out there. While the British delay the regeneration of the area with their insistence that Ypres is holy ground, the locals flog their history back to them: hat badges, buttons, cartridges, wooden trench signs. A Smith and Wesson revolver costs no more than a Trappist beer if you buy it from an old horse trough in a farmyard. Occasionally a scavenger who is too young, or doesn't know the place well, loses a limb to the unexploded shells that skulk beneath the surface of the soil.

Few travelers here, or at least those who write about their travels, seem to grasp the real meaning of the place. One guidebook, already published, describes West Flanders as 'nothing but a deserted sea, under whose waves corpses are sleeping.' It is more than that; the underworld seems to drag at one's senses. There is no escaping it, for the dead are everywhere. Beneath our feet, in mounds and water-filled shell craters they lie. It is a petrified place. When Vesuvius erupted over Pompeii, the sun didn't shine for three days. In Flanders, the sun shines constantly but *life* has been caught fast, like a fly in amber. I wonder if, in years to come, when this war is remembered only in the written word, tourists will come here as they once did to Mesopotamia, seeking a lost civilization.

After they have eaten, they sit together outside in the dwindling light as Kemmel patters off to explore. While the crickets sing at their most strident, Lombardi sets down his mug on the ground and turns to Alex.

"Last weekend, I was at a Commission Camp concert in Bethune."

He measures his words carefully before going on: "We were talking, before, about repatriation for the dead. The British government insists that our fallen remain here." He pauses. "Except one, or so I've heard."

"One?" Alex lights a cigarette, shaking the match to extinguish the tiny flame before throwing it to the ground.

"Apparently Brigadier General Wyatt, a director of the War Graves Commission, is in discussions with the War Office to bring back one unknown soldier to be buried in London. That soldier will represent the thousands of soldiers, known and unknown, who died."

Alex looks at Lombardi, his cigarette half-raised to his mouth. "Whose idea was this?"

"Some ex-army chaplain."

There is a brief silence. Then Alex asks, "How will they select the body?"

"I don't know," says Lombardi. He squints at the row of trees whose forms darken imperceptibly with each passing minute. "It's only a possibility anyway."

"If they do decide to go ahead with this," says Alex, speaking slowly, methodically, trying to ignore the tumult in his head, "where would the body be buried?"

Kemmel appears suddenly, having scaled the shallowest part of the trench to reach them. Lombardi pulls the dog up, cradling him on his lap. "They were talking about laying him to rest in St. Paul's Cathedral, but that idea has been shelved." He scratches behind the terrier's alert ears. "Some feel he should be buried under the cenotaph."

Alex shakes his head. His cigarette has died, but he goes on holding it between his fingers. "They can't do that. Cenotaph means empty tomb. If he was buried there then the monument would lose its significance."

Lombardi nods. In a deliberate voice, he says, "Which is why he will almost certainly be buried in Westminster Abbey."

There is a faint movement by the trench, as if the poppies on the old parapet have shed their scarlet petals as one in the darkness.

An unfamiliar feeling floods Alex. He barely recognizes it, except by memory: hope. It is three years since he last experienced hope—in all that time, his existence has been a matter of reflex, the instinct to survive without knowing why. Now he feels as if his whole body is being borne upward, as if the sun has risen again over the evening land-scape. His mind runs, precipitately, down paths he has never thought to consider.

From the distance comes the rumble of wheels on the roads far beyond the Villa Via Sacra. But this he doesn't hear, for his mind is filled with the sound of a voice speaking through blood: "Bury me with glory or none at all."

The shadows in the long grass deepen.

XIII

THE HOLY GLIMMERS OF GOOD-BYES

London, August and October 1920

$\mathcal{A}$LEX RETURNED TO LONDON IN LATE AUGUST. HE WAS A CHANGED man; ever since Daniel Lombardi had mentioned the possibility of laying an unknown soldier to rest in Westminster Abbey, Alex had thought of nothing else. In Ypres, he had talked to Brigadier General Wyatt of the Imperial War Graves Commission, asking him if any definite plans had been made.

"It's just an idea," Wyatt told him, as they walked around the ruins of the Cloth Hall, where one of the famous old stone lions of the Menin Gate sat, missing his right forepaw, "but one that I sincerely hope shall be realized. It would be a wonderful gesture. I am very much in favor, and have informed the War Office that I fully support it."

Through Wyatt, Alex gained an impression of the various departments of church, government, and palace that would be involved. He surmised that the funeral, if it occurred, would in all probability be held on Armistice Day. That left him only three months to infiltrate the corridors of power. He had to wheedle himself into a position whereby he was able to influence the final choice of battlefield and, ultimately, the selection of the body. It was a drastic, almost inconceivable scenario that he visualized, but it was precisely the outlandish nature of his ambition that gave him faith in its succeeding.

He had several contacts who might be able to help, but the problem was not so much telling them what he wanted, as *why,* which made it difficult to approach anyone for assistance. He had to think of a plausible reason to be involved, and on his first evening home in London, he realized that the simplest, most credible motive was staring him in the face. Having found the answer, he slept soundly that night, feeling that the initial obstacle had been removed from his path.

He rose early the following morning and after a hasty breakfast cycled into the city with his mind completely focused on the day ahead. His first visit was to the office of Henry Wickham Steed, *The Times* editor who had commissioned him to write about the cemeteries in France and Flanders. Alex recounted the rumor Lombardi had told him and then, as his reward for the scoop, asked for Wickham Steed's help in pulling the right strings to get him officially engaged to cover the entire process.

"You asked me to select one act of remembrance that interests me," Alex said, looking directly at the older man, who had himself worked as a foreign correspondent until his appointment as editor. "This is what I choose. But I don't want to be a bystander. I want to be on whatever committee is put together to see it through."

Wickham Steed listened, his dark, hooded eyes watching Alex's determined face. When Alex had finished speaking, Wickham Steed said, "Hmm." He stroked his short, pointed beard. "I'll make inquiries."

"Where will you start?"

"Leave that to me." Seeing Alex's worried expression, Wickham Steed relented, "I'll make a few phone calls and let you know as soon as I hear anything."

After leaving Wickham Steed's office, Alex cycled to Victoria Station and caught a train to Margate. He had learned from Brigadier General Wyatt that the ex-army chaplain who had suggested bringing back an unknown soldier was the vicar of Margate's St. John the Baptist Church. And Alex was in luck; Reverend David Railton was in the church when he arrived.

As soon as Alex had introduced himself and his reason for calling, Railton beamed. "I read about your knighthood in the papers. Congratulations. My wife keeps all the old newspapers from the war, so I almost feel as if I already know you." He placed a stack of hymn books on a table by the main doors of the church. The old building smelled of dust, carnations, and ferns. "Why don't you come to lunch? We could talk about this more fully."

They sat out in the garden to eat. Lunch was homemade veal pie and elderflower wine. Mrs. Railton joined them; it was she who had urged her husband to write to the dean of Westminster Abbey about his idea.

" 'It's now or never,' I said to him." He was going to write to Haig, but I said, 'Don't do that. Write to the dean instead; he's the chap you want.' " Mrs. Railton smiled. "Didn't I, David?"

Railton—who was in his early thirties—shook his head. The neat lawn and flowerbeds of the garden were reflected in the lenses of the small round spectacles he wore. "I *did* write to Douglas Haig when the war ended, but he never replied."

Alex looked at him in surprise. "When the war ended? This isn't a new idea of yours then, Vicar?"

"Not at all." Railton wafted his napkin at a persistent wasp. "It first occurred to me about four years ago—early 1916, I should think. I was stationed in Erkingham, near Armentières. I had buried a comrade that day and was feeling pretty miserable, to be honest. I was wandering around the billet, in the small garden there. It was quite dark, but there was a moon and the light fell on a grave that I hadn't noticed—it was our first day in that billet. A rough cross of white wood had been pushed into the ground at the head of the grave. There was thick black writing on it. I went over, and in the moonlight read 'An Unknown British Soldier.' Then in brackets underneath, 'Of the Black Watch.' "

He finished his pie and patted his mouth with the napkin. "It moved me to tears, to tell you the truth. No one was about—there were some officers in the billet playing cards, but apart from that it was very quiet and still. No guns firing or shells exploding. That made me think. And it suddenly occurred to me: Wouldn't it be very special to bring home one of the nameless dead to represent all those who were dying in the war?"

His wife nodded, filling three tumblers with water. "One of our congregation—a lovely man, isn't he, David?—lost four boys in the war. He came to visit us the other day and he said it was a great idea, an inspiration."

"It is," said Railton, frowning. "That's exactly what it was: an inspiration. It came to me, or, should I say, it was somehow *sent* to me."

Alex nodded, uncertain whether Railton was implying that God had spoken through him or not. "You were a chaplain during the war, then, Vicar?"

"Yes." His eyes brightened. "I was with the Scottish Territorials before the war, in fact. I love Scotland—I wouldn't mind living there one day. We shall see. Anyway, I was chaplain to the Northumberland Fusiliers initially, but I ended up with the 19th (Western) Division."

"And he won the Military Cross, didn't you, David?" said his wife proudly. "He helped a wounded officer and two private soldiers under enemy fire. That was in 1916 as well, wasn't it?"

"Mmm." The vicar sipped the glass of water. "I don't think I'll have any more of that wine, my dear, the sun is giving me rather a headache."

Alex leaned forward across the garden table. "What do you think will happen now that you've written to the dean?"

David Railton spread his hands in an ambivalent gesture. "Who can say? I am hopeful, however. I did think of writing to the king, but I was put off by the thought of his advisors. I was worried they might suggest burying the soldier in some open space like Trafalgar Square or Hyde Park. Then artists would get involved and who knows what weird structure they might devise for a shrine!"

Alex smiled, "You have a point."

"As far as I'm concerned, there can be only one true shrine and it should be in Westminster Abbey, the Parish Church of the Empire."

"He thought about writing to the papers, too, didn't you, David?" interrupted Mrs. Railton.

"Yes," said Railton. "But to tell the truth, I was a bit concerned that someone else might take it over and turn it into a stunt. I don't mean to offend you," he said, glancing apologetically at Alex. "But you never can tell with the press, can you? Though in your case, Sir Alex, it's clear that your interest comes from the heart."

Alex coughed, uncomfortable with the use of his new moniker. "I'm hoping to cover the matter, if it goes ahead. But I agree that too much press might be a bad thing—that's why, having heard of the idea before anyone else in the press as far as I know, I decided to put myself forward for it." He paused, "But you're right about my interest coming from the heart."

"I can tell," said Railton. "I always can. You may rest assured that if

I am consulted by the powers-that-be, I shall recommend you for the job!" He beamed at Alex, looking suddenly much younger.

Alex smiled back, his purpose achieved. He thanked the Railtons for their hospitality, promised to stay in touch, and walked back to the railway station feeling light-hearted, enjoying the sweet smell of the flowers in the little cottage gardens he passed, and the clear notes of birdsong that carried on the warm summer breeze.

Despite his success with the Railtons, there was little else Alex could do now but wait. Wickham Steed called him a week later to tell him that the idea had another source; the French government had announced that they intended to bury their own "Unknown Soldier" under the Arc de Triomphe on Armistice Day. Wickham Steed had spoken to the dean of Westminster Abbey, the Rt Reverend Herbert Ryle, who was keen to pursue the British scheme and Ryle, in turn, told him that he had contacted Lord Stamfordham, the king's private secretary, to put the proposal to His Majesty when he returned from Balmoral; Ryle had also met with Field Marshal Henry Wilson to discuss it in person.

In early October, Wickham Steed invited Alex to his office. Choosing his words carefully, he warned Alex that the king's reaction had been lukewarm: "His Majesty is inclined to think that nearly two years after the last shot was fired in the war, a funeral might be regarded as belated. The plans for Armistice Day have been made, the king has agreed to unveil the cenotaph, but he's rather nervous of the high level of grief in the country still. He feels that one false move could result in a morbid side show at the National Shrine."

Alex didn't speak. He looked at the faint, autumnal sunlight slanting in through the long windows and felt as if his life were draining away again. He had glimpsed hope and now it was being taken from him. The muscles worked in his jaw. "So that's it, is it? End of the whole thing?"

Wickham Steed shook his head. "No, not quite. It isn't that His Majesty doesn't approve of the idea; it's more that he wants it to be handled with the utmost care. Perfectly reasonable, in my book. He hasn't said no. My source—"

"Who is?"

Wickham Steed broke into a rare, almost impish smile. "I never reveal my sources, Alex. Suffice to say it's someone at the palace."

Alex shook his head, smiling despite his earlier disappointment.

"The dean is enthusiastic about the idea, as is Sir Henry, who feels that the wording is an important consideration. That is to say, instead of referring to an unknown 'soldier,' we should speak of an unknown 'warrior,' thereby covering the sailors and airmen who lost their lives." Wickham Steed paused. "The dean has also expressed a wish that if the funeral *does* go ahead, the body should be interred in the nave of Westminster Abbey."

Alex turned away. He looked out of the window at the tall buildings opposite. An omnibus trundled past. His mind throbbed with the memory of standing with Ted and their classmates at the end of the nave after visiting the abbey all those years ago, when Ted had first expressed a love of the place. His throat constricted with the force of the recollection and he fought to keep himself calm.

He turned back to Wickham Steed. "Should I contact the dean myself, or . . . ?"

"No. I think it's better to see how the Cabinet reacts to the idea."

"Then what do we do now?"

Wickham Steed pursed his lips, making the hairs on his neat mustache and beard rise like bristles on a brush. "We wait."

Another week passed. Alex couldn't concentrate on anything, but drifted about the city, the rain-swept streets and gray traffic seeming symbolic of London's postwar struggle and shabbiness. He felt unutterably despondent; the newspaper stands were stacked with front pages that curled in the damp air, the black headlines stressing the constant strikes and lack of employment for ex-servicemen. Every day, Alex saw former soldiers wandering the parks and stations, bewildered and suicidal about their place in society, since women still held many of the jobs they had appropriated during the war while their men were away at the front. Alex didn't begrudge the women their employment as others did; he had talked to some of them during the course of his work and knew that most were supporting their families after losing their husbands. But he understood the humiliation felt by men who had no work to speak of and whose injuries restricted the types of job they could perform. It angered him to see ex-soldiers being wheeled through the parks, sitting on the hard benches in their old uniforms and wheezing up phlegm from gas-riddled lungs, or standing outside cinemas selling bits of war memorabilia and matches. Where was the land fit for heroes that Lloyd George had promised? he raged. The war had cost millions of pounds . . . Alex was filled with a deep disgust that there was nothing left for the men who had won it on Britain's behalf.

In a café off Russell Square, he noticed a wretched-looking man hunched over a pot of tea. Alex approached him, asking, "Would you mind if I joined you?" The man looked up, surprised. He shrugged.

Alex sat down and, over a second pot of tea, drew him out. He had been an ex-battery commander and had won the Victoria Cross. The man shook his head after telling Alex this.

"When we came home," he said, "when we were demobilized and doffed our uniforms, we realized how much our welcome depended on the glamour of our clothes, with all that they implied." He gave a bitter laugh. "In mufti, we're no longer heroes, we're simply 'unemployed,' an unpleasant problem for the government." He let the small spoon rattle into the empty teacup.

One evening after his meeting with the man in the café, during one of his gloomy rambles, Alex found himself at the carved stone archway of Victoria Station. Once known as "The Gateway to the Continent," it had been renamed "The Gate of Good-bye" during the war years. It seemed to Alex as he stood there, watching the subdued passengers coming and going, that if he listened hard enough he could still hear the shouts of the soldiers as they left for the front, laughing and jostling by the bookstall that had been temporarily converted into a currency exchange counter, swapping their English pennies for francs. He glanced over at the canteen, imagining it once more teeming with men and their rifles. He breathed in, recalling the smell of cologne, Woodbines, and strong tea that had hung about the iron rafters. He closed his eyes as train doors slammed, thinking of the soldiers who had leaned out of the windows for a last kiss from their sweethearts. The shrieking whistle of a train as it pulled out of the station in a bank of steam reminded him of the women standing tearfully on the platform, some clutching the hands of small children who would never truly know their fathers.

He thought then of his own return to London in 1919, and his visits to the station in order to interview the few who came back intact, and those who had been released from prisoner-of-war camps. He remembered the desolate eyes of women walking up and down the platforms as the trains arrived. Up and down they walked, up and down, holding aloft photographs of their missing husbands and sons, questioning every man for news of their loved ones. A stab of anguish pierced his chest as he thought of Clare, who must have made her own efforts to find out what had happened to Ted. He swore under his breath, cursing that impulse of Ted's to keep his death and the squalor of it a secret.

As he walked away from the station, he wondered where Ted's name would appear on all the monuments and memorials to the missing that were being proposed. On a cross in the middle of Tyringham, the small Buckinghamshire village where Ted had been born? On a plaque in the great hall of their old school? Or carved upon the walls of Ypres's Menin Gate, when that was completed? How *shall* we remember the missing, he thought, how shall we show what cannot be seen? By tracing their footsteps from every shire of their birth to the vast, shattered fields where they had died? Or by another, more symbolic means—the bringing back of one of the unknown to be buried at the heart of England?

He shivered, pulling up the collar of his black coat against the chill wind, and walked home, brooding, the ghostly blur of the street lamps in the dusk lighting his path.

32

On October 17, at nine thirty in the morning, while Alex sat at home typing up his notes from his stay with Lombardi, the telephone rang. He went out into the hallway to answer it, the growl in his stomach reminding him that he had not yet eaten breakfast.

"Dyer here."

"Alex? Henry Wickham Steed. I have some news for you."

Alex's fingers tightened around the base of the telephone. "Good or bad?"

"A bit of both. There was a Cabinet meeting last week about the 'Unknown Warrior' business. Apparently, the majority were opposed to the idea, but Sir Henry talked them round. The prime minister was in favor anyway, and had spoken to the king."

"And?" Alex held his breath.

"The king has agreed. Once Lloyd George pointed out to him, very effectively so I'm told, that this one funeral could represent all the hundreds of thousands of missing men, His Majesty relented. The burial will take place in Westminster Abbey on Armistice Day."

Alex closed his eyes.

"Hello? Hello? Are you still there?"

Alex opened his eyes. "Yes, I'm here. What about me, Henry? Have you talked to anyone yet about—"

"My good fellow," Wickham Steed said patiently, "it hasn't even been announced yet. I understand that the prime minister will make a public statement in two days."

"But we must move quickly," Alex said in alarm. "Fleet Street will be on this like vultures on carrion—and there's less than a month till Armistice Day. My God, Henry—"

"Hold your horses. I'm not sure where we're going to find an opening for you." Wickham Steed cleared his throat. "The whole thing is to take place in utmost secrecy, for obvious reasons. At no point now, or in the future, can there be any possibility of the body being identi-fied. It's not surprising, therefore, that no one is keen to let journalists in on the act, even one as distinguished as you."

"But I've got to cover this story!" shouted Alex, panicking. "I've got to find a way in."

"No need to bawl at me, old boy."

Alex bit his lip; the last thing he wanted to do was antagonize Wickham Steed. "I'm terribly sorry," he said, hoping he sounded suit-ably contrite.

"Apology accepted," said his editor, dryly. "Now, I'm still chasing a couple of people up to see if we can get you in, because of course, people *do* change their minds and there is bound to be press interest, so handing over the job to one reporter would perhaps help keep a lid on things somewhat. But I must be truthful with you, it seems jolly unlikely. Hold tight for a bit, and I'll get back to you. Good-bye."

Alex replaced the receiver. He went back into the sitting room and opened the doors onto the balcony. It was a cold, clear morning. He breathed in the crisp air. The sky was cloudless.

For the first time since he was a schoolboy, his lips moved in prayer. "Holy Mary, Mother of God . . ."

Wickham Steed telephoned again the following afternoon. "Just to bring you up to date: a Memorial Service Committee has been formed to organize the burial of the unknown warrior. Lord Curzon is head of the committee."

"The foreign minister?" said Alex, frowning. "He's an odd choice. I thought he didn't agree with the two minutes' silence?"

"Very odd, I agree. But Churchill is on the committee, and the king will be represented by Sir Douglas Dawson. Now, here's the promising part," said Wickham Steed, obviously relishing his role. "A great friend of mine, Charles Smythe-Osbourne, is also on the committee. He's going to talk to them about having one journalist cover the procedure discreetly from start to finish. He can't get you on this committee, obviously, but your credentials are excellent—the knighthood opens doors, as you can imagine—and so he's going to raise the possibility of getting you on the Selection Committee." He paused. "What do you say to that?"

Alex felt giddy; he wanted to laugh and cry at once. "It's wonderful," he said, and leaned his forehead against the wall to steady himself. "Thank you, Henry."

"Save the gratitude until we know just where we stand." The telephone buzzed and crackled. "I say, are we about to be cut off? No? Good, then as I was saying—"

There was a loud click and the line went dead. Alex tried it again five minutes later, but it wasn't working. After half an hour, he decided to call on Wickham Steed in his office. The omnibus that he caught into the city center was claustrophobically busy; as soon as it neared Charing Cross he got out to walk in the light drizzle, glad to be free of the tightly packed bodies and the smell of damp clothes.

The editor's secretary showed him into the office; Wickham Steed was talking on the telephone. He gestured for Alex to make himself comfortable while he finished his conversation. Alex pretended to read that morning's edition of *The Times,* but listened covertly to Wickham Steed's replies to the person on the other end of the line. Not until the last moment did his eavesdropping reveal that the conversation was, in fact, about him.

Wickham Steed replaced the receiver. Alex looked up, hardly daring to breathe.

"Well now," said Wickham Steed. "That's a turn up for the books. It seems you aren't the only journalist who's gotten wind of all this."

Alex's heart began to beat fast. "What do you mean?"

"An ex-colleague of yours was also hoping to be chosen for the prestigious position of official writer on the subject."

Alex shook his head, bemused. "An ex-colleague? Who?"

"Chap called Sebastian Thorpe."

The newspaper Alex had been holding slipped to the floor, spilling its pages in a wide arc. He bent to retrieve them, his face flaming with anger and fear. When he straightened up and set the folded newspaper down on Wickham Steed's desk, the older man was smiling.

"I thought you wouldn't appreciate Thorpe trying to muscle in. Are you and he still in touch?"

"No," said Alex, shortly. "But actually, I'm about to write an article on that dire tale of his, the Crucified Canadian."

"Oh?"

"I'll tell you about it another time. But what about Thorpe and this story?" Alex hunched his shoulders in impatience. "Is he going to get it?"

"No."

Alex swallowed; relief flooded through him. Then his old anxiety returned. "And what about me? Am I on the Selection Committee or not?"

Wickham Steed leaned back in his chair and pressed his fingers together in a steeple. He rested his chin on his fingertips and looked at Alex.

"Oh, come on, Henry!" Every muscle in Alex's body had tensed. "Put me out of my misery, for God's sake!"

Wickham Steed gave another small smile. "Let me put it this way: I think you should cancel all your appointments for the next couple of weeks."

"Meaning?" asked Alex, his heart banging painfully against his ribs.

The older man kept smiling. A gust of wind came in through the half-open window, making the dust motes swirl in the pale sunlight. "You're going back to Flanders."

Alex stared at him, not trusting what he had been told.

Wickham Steed nodded. "You're on the Selection Committee." He held out his hand. "Congratulations, Alex. One day you'll have a truly great story to tell your grandchildren."

Alex's angular face broke into a wide smile. He shook Wickham Steed's hand, elation and relief making him light-headed.

"Thank you," he said to the man sitting across from him in the winter sunlight. "You have *no* idea just how much this means to me."

33

CLARE SAT ON A BENCH IN LEICESTER SQUARE, WAITING AS SHE DID every first Wednesday of the month for her companion to arrive. It was a beautiful autumn day, cold but bright, like a new penny. She felt happier than she had in months; yesterday Thomas Harman had worn his finished mask for the first time. She had sat with him in the Tin Noses Shop while the surgeon fitted it to his destroyed face. He insisted on having his back to her while the mask was adjusted because he wanted to see the effect it had on her when she saw him wearing it. When he turned slowly to show her the finished result, her amazed reaction was entirely sincere. The silver-plated mask had been tinted in an almost flawless imitation of Harman's flesh tones and the surgeon had spent several painstaking hours creating an exact replica of Harman's existing eye—even painting veins on the white of the oval glass disk that fit into the socket in the mask. Clare had leaned in closely, and told a delighted Harman that she honestly could not see the join where the mask met his skin.

"We've made a handsome chap out of you," said the surgeon, standing back to survey his work.

Harman gave a snort. "I never was a Don Juan."

Nonetheless, Clare knew that he was pleased with the result. He confided later that he was still nervous of other people and how the mask looked to them. He also wondered whether they would be more afraid of him, knowing he had to wear it, and fearing what lay beneath. Clare assured him that his concerns were normal, but that after he had ventured out of the hospital grounds once or twice, he would realize that there was little for him to worry about. Provided that he went on gaining confidence, within a month he would be going home to Cornwall, to the harbor town of Charlestown where his elderly mother lived.

"Everyone knows me there, anyway," he told Clare. "They all know what's happened. I shan't be bothered by anyone, though the cows might take fright when I stroll around the fields. I shall probably be responsible for a whole herd careering off the cliffs."

"Rubbish," said Clare. "Just wait until you leave the hospital. I don't think you're aware of how many men there are with injuries of one kind or another."

"No," said Harman. "I rather thought that most of us were dead."

Clare said nothing to this; she had told Harman little of her own past, despite his repeated attempts to get her to talk about herself. She walked back with him to the orangery, where he slipped out through the glass doors to have his first cigarette in the open air since his arrival at the hospital.

Now she sat in Leicester Square, reading a newspaper. There was page after page about the impending Armistice Day and the burial of an unknown warrior in Westminster Abbey. Clare had already received an invitation to the ceremony; the surgeon at Pinderfields had asked that she might be included on the guest list. She didn't want to think about it—the unknown warrior was supposed to represent the missing, which raised too many painful memories that she deliberately tried to steer clear of, and contemplating them would send her crawling up the walls with shame and anguish.

She read the other news and then turned to the back page. As usual, it was filled with advertisements for tours of the Somme and Ypres. One private travel bureau charged thirty-five pounds for a visit to Loos. Thomas Cook offered two kinds of tours: the first cost thirty-five guineas and offered "complete luxury," the second cost nine and a half guineas and proudly declared itself the most popular battlefield tour on the market. There were also advertisements placed by veterans;

one was for "Wonderful Battlefield Tours conducted personally by ex-Officers in High-Class private motor-cars." The cheapest, she saw—interested despite herself—were run by the St. Barnabas Society, who asked £3. 11s. 6d. for two nights with full board, third-class rail, and second-class boat travel. A small sign at the foot of their advertisement showing a woman laying a bouquet of flowers on a grave soothed: "These pilgrimages do not open old wounds: they set the heart at rest." Clare's stomach turned.

"Not thinking of going back to the front, are you, Sister?"

At the sound of the young man's voice, Clare looked up from her newspaper. She smiled with genuine pleasure at the sight of Frank Stephens, wheeled toward her by his elder sister.

"Hello, Frankie. Hello, Anna." Clare got up from the bench, folding her newspaper under one arm and bending down to kiss Frank on the cheek. She shook Anna's hand. "No, I'm not going back. I never will."

"Me neither," said Frank with such relief that the three of them laughed.

"It's so good of you to take Frank out every Wednesday," said Anna. "You mustn't do it if you have other commitments, Miss Eden."

"Nonsense," said Clare, "and on the contrary, it's Frankie who takes me out. If it weren't for him, I would live the life of a hermit."

"I can't think why," said Anna in her forthright manner. "You must have men lining up to take you out for the day."

Clare looked down at the ground. A few leaves scattered past her feet; one landed on Frank's wheelchair, wrapping itself around the spokes of a wheel.

"You can go now, Anna," said Frank, keen for his sister to leave them alone. "We'll meet you back here at half past four."

"Well, if you're sure . . ." Anna looked at him doubtfully. She saw the beseeching light in his eyes and relented, "Very well. I'm going to do some shopping."

"Poor father," said Frank. "His bank account will suffer today."

Anna gave him a gentle punch on the shoulder. "Don't take any of his cheek, Miss Eden."

"Of course not," said Clare, pretending to be severe.

Once Anna had left them, Clare asked, "Where would you like to go? We have half an hour before the film begins."

"Trafalgar Square?" asked Frank eagerly.

Clare hesitated. "Are you sure? It's terribly busy . . . "

"I know, that's why I like it. I'd like to sit beside the fountain and look at everything going on around me. Please, Sister."

Clare shook her head. "Only if you *stop* calling me Sister."

"Yes, Miss Eden."

"You can call me Clare," she said. "I really don't mind."

His handsome face flamed. "All right. Clare."

They walked toward the great square, Clare maneuvering Frankie's wheelchair expertly. They had to go around the square to the south, where there were no steps. They sat in the shelter of the huge bronze lions, out of the wind.

Frank closed his eyes. He could hear the traffic milling all about them; the horses stamping and shaking their reins, the omnibuses rattling on their awkward suspension. Then he heard a sound like a drum beating far off and opened his eyes in panic. He looked around for Clare; she had already put her hand in his and was leaning across to him.

"What is it, Frankie? The nightmare again?"

He nodded, unable to speak. It happened each time without warning: all at once he would hear that peculiar noise and then find himself back on the battlefield in the minutes before the gun exploded in his groin. He remembered it with frightening lucidity; he had been trying to lift an injured German into their trench, but the other man with him wouldn't help at all.

"It's a bloody Kraut, leave him be," Palmer had said.

"It's a man," said Frank.

"Still a Kraut."

"Help me lift him over the parapet," Frank had leaned down to put his hands under the soldier's armpits.

"I will not!"

"Look," said Frank, gritting his teeth, "somewhere this man has a mother, and maybe a wife and children waiting for him. Are you going to let them lose him?"

"Kraut women," said Palmer. He spat on the ground. "Drag the fucking thing in yourself."

Palmer had left him. When Frank crouched over the injured man, he heard a pulsating sound coming across the earth toward him and a moment later, he realized he had fallen, keeling over onto the wounded German, aware of a wetness seeping up from his groin before the pain reached his brain, knocking him out.

"It isn't happening anymore, Frankie," Clare squeezed his hand gently and touched his chin. "It's over. It's all over. You don't have to be scared anymore."

Frank gulped. "Sorry, Sis—Clare." He corrected himself with a shaky laugh.

Clare smiled at him. The drums in his head grew fainter and he said fervently, "I could look into your eyes forever."

Clare laughed softly.

"I know," he said, suddenly offended. "You can't take me seriously because I'm not a real man—"

Her skin paled in anger. "Don't ever let me hear you say that again. What happened to you doesn't make you any less of a man in my eyes. You're only nineteen, that's all, and I'm not interested in"—she searched desperately for the right word—"romance."

His hand curled around hers. "I'm sorry," he said, red-faced with contrition. "I shouldn't have said it, but sometimes I just . . . I just wish . . ." his head drooped onto his chest.

"I know," Clare said fiercely. "I know." She took her hand from his and laid it on his shoulder.

"Is there someone?" he said, glancing up, his curiosity finally getting the better of his manners.

Clare looked away. The sky had lost its crispness; a few portentous clouds drifted behind the imposing buildings around the square.

"Clare?"

She turned back to him with a brittle smile. "There was someone, once, Frankie. But not now."

For a while, Frank said nothing. Then he took her hand in his again and said, "It's indestructible, you know."

"What is?"

"Love."

Clare turned her head away again. Then she got slowly to her feet and walked behind Frank's wheelchair. "We're going to be late for the film," she said brusquely, and released the brake on the wheelchair as a flock of fat pigeons settled onto the backs of Landseer's bronze lions.

XIV

ST. POL

France, November 7, 1920

34

ALEX DROVE THROUGH COUNTRYSIDE THAT WAS BEGINNING TO HEAL of its own accord, where yellow blossoms of charlock grew in abundance over concrete bunkers, and trees sprouted fresh green shoots. On the site of swept-away villages, homes had been built from salvage, roofed in corrugated iron. Dogs tethered to sheds snuffled in the long weeds, guarding the first sign of land taken back from the war: a thin crop of runner beans on stakes.

The road from St. Omer down through Belgium had been rebuilt where necessary, and Alex saw the first completed cemeteries nearby as he drove. He stopped the car near Ypres to take a closer look. He walked up to the small iron gate and along the main path, past row upon row of neat, uniform, white headstones, each bearing the regimental badge, name, rank, number, and dates of birth and death of the grave's occupant. He remembered Lombardi's telling him that the headstones were shipped over from England, and wondered how many thousands of tons of Portland stone would still be needed for the task.

He stood in front of the Cross of Sacrifice and looked at the inscription chosen from "Ecclesiasticus" by Rudyard Kipling for the Stone of Remembrance: "Their Name Liveth For Ever More." He imagined a thin line linking the cemeteries along the old Western Front, from the smallest graveyards hidden away within woods to those huge, silent cities on the plains where the most ferocious battles had been fought. Some bore the names given to them by the soldiers themselves—Owl Trench, Caterpillar Valley, Crucifix Corner—while others were named after the battalions who had buried their own men there. He imagined how that thin line would look from the air; so thick in parts that it resembled a child's scribble, for they were everywhere, these Gardens of Stone.

He climbed back into the motor car and set out on the last stage of his journey to St. Pol. In the three and a half weeks that had passed since the news that he had been accepted onto the Selection Committee, Alex had barely had time to think. Everything had moved with astonishing speed: the Selection Committee had met only three times, but there had been a great deal to arrange. Brigadier General Wyatt had suggested that four bodies should be exhumed from each of the main battle areas: the Aisne, the Somme, Ypres, and Arras. This had immediately solved Alex's difficulty in raising the issue of the selection site. He had needed only to propose that the body from Ypres should come from the region associated with the battle for Passchendaele. Once that was accepted, he had then put himself forward to accompany the group who would disinter the body from there. That was as far as he could go. Of the four bodies taken, one would then be selected and Wyatt was firm that he should undertake this duty himself, accompanied by Lieutenant Colonel Gell, one of his staff and a member of the Directorate of Graves Registration and Enquiries. Alex had to accept that the final selection was beyond his control.

Wyatt had issued instructions to Lieutenant Colonel Henry Williams for the exhumation of four bodies on November 7, 1920.

"How will the actual selections be made?" Alex had wanted to know.

Williams replied, "Pretty simply: any of the graves bearing the inscription 'Unknown British soldier' will be suitable. Confirmation is to be by British military uniform."

The adjutant-general, Sir George MacDonogh, was assigned the responsibility of overseeing arrangements for exhuming the bodies and bringing the chosen one back to England.

"I am determined to ensure that the body remains unknown," MacDonogh told the Selection Committee. "We must bear in mind *constantly* the sacredness of our mission and the mysticism that will for all time surround the burial place. I think we should destroy virtually all written communications on the matter once it is over," he said. "The press have talked of little else since the prime minister's announcement. The idea has truly captured the nation."

He glanced at Alex, "I understand that you will be covering the whole process, but I trust that I have your support in this?"

"Of course," said Alex, reddening at being singled out. "Absolutely."

An official from the War Office raised the possibility of cremation, but Wyatt dismissed the idea: "People will identify more with a body than with ashes."

In the remaining days before the selection, signals were sent and messages transmitted to all main government departments connected with the return of the Unknown Warrior. He was to be given a field marshal's funeral, with all the pomp and ceremony that entailed.

"And a nation's gratitude," Alex added, quietly.

"Yes," said Wyatt, "most definitely that."

On November 6, the choice of ship that would bear the coffin from France home to England was finalized, as was the time of arrival, and arrangements for a nineteen-gun salute at Dover Castle. A signal was sent to the captain of the HMS *Verdun* regarding departure dates and ceremonies in Boulogne and Dover.

During all the activities, Alex interviewed everyone involved, even the two undertakers, Mr. Nodes and Mr. Sourbutts, who would prepare the body in Boulogne on November 9. As Wickham Steed had predicted, his knighthood and elevation to the Selection Committee had opened doors. He had received a friendly letter from David Railton, and in his postscript, Railton had added: "You may be interested to know that the flag I used as an altar cloth during the war (which was given to me by my mother-in-law) will be used to wrap the coffin during the service in Westminster Abbey. I feel it most appropriate that my 'battle flag' should end its days like this." Alex wrote back swiftly, telling Railton he looked forward to meeting him again during the ceremony on Armistice Day.

Railton was not the only person to contact him before he left for Flanders. As Alex packed his old leather doctor's bag the evening before departure, his telephone rang. The caller was his old adversary, Sebastian Thorpe.

"Congrats on the scoop of the century," said Thorpe in his nasal whine. Alex held the receiver slightly away from his ear; even on the telephone, Thorpe's voice grated as much as ever. "I can't say I'm not disappointed to be chosen to cover the event, but I'm sure you'll make a go of it."

"Thanks," said Alex, curtly. "Was there anything else?"

"Well . . ." Thorpe let the word drag out. "Actually, I wondered whether we could meet. Not that I want to tread on your toes or anything, but I thought it would be rather fun to have a chat about old times and this new commission of yours."

"Sorry, no can do," said Alex. "I'm leaving tomorrow."

"Are you really? Yes, I suppose you'll have to get a move on." Thorpe paused. "Where are you staying? Have the army arranged—"

"I can't tell you anything. Sorry, but that's how it is."

"Oh. Oh, yes, I see. Well. Hope all goes well for you, anyway."

"Thank you." Alex replaced the receiver sharply. He wondered what Thorpe was up to—he didn't trust the man at all. Frowning, he returned to his room to finish packing.

Late in the afternoon of November 7, the four groups who were to perform the disinterment gathered at the Military Headquarters in St. Pol, near Arras in northern France. The small town itself seemed to be sleeping; as Alex left his hotel at dusk and walked through the narrow, steep streets to the building where the bodies would be brought later that night, he had a sense of a great stillness emanating from the landscape with its huddle of houses and shell-scarred roads. It was as though the residents of the town had closed their curtains and blinds and turned down the lamps out of respect for what was about to take place.

The four groups met separately for their final instructions. Each party consisted of an officer and two other ranks, except for Alex's group, which had two officers including him. In the small room where his group assembled, none of the men spoke much. They were acutely aware of the secrecy surrounding their assignment and only offered each other cigarettes, nothing more.

MacDonogh entered the room and stood squarely before them. "It is no easy task, what we ask of you," he began. "There are still thousands of bodies out there pending burial, and the area you have been assigned is somewhat in chaos. What you must do is bring back one body, recognizable only by British military uniform, from a grave marked 'Unknown British Soldier.' You are to return here as soon as you are finished. You must have no contact with any of the other groups; they do not know your whereabouts as you do not know theirs."

He paused and looked directly at Alex. "All that remains is for me to ask you *again* to bear in mind the sacredness and mysticism of this mission. Do nothing that will bring that into jeopardy." He brought up his hand in a stiff salute. "Good evening to you, gentlemen."

A field ambulance waited in the yard to transport them to Ypres sector. They climbed in, hunching against the chill air; the temperature, already low, appeared to have sunk once more. Alex sat back silently, feeling nauseous with adrenalin.

The field ambulance took him over familiar terrain in the darkness, passing through Bethune and Armentières, then up through Ploegsteert and along what remained of the Menin Road, occasionally having to find another, undamaged route. The outskirts of Ypres were quiet despite the hundreds of newly painted taverns and hotels springing up within the town to accommodate tourists. The battered ramparts were a dark mound and the gap allotted for the building of the Menin Gate memorial was virtually empty of traffic. The Grote Market was in the process of being rebuilt and a smell of creosote hung about the place. Fields were being leveled, and on the old Minneplein, a sprawling encampment of corrugated steel Nissan huts had been erected while new houses were constructed beyond the city walls.

The road led out, heading toward Poperinghe. When Alex saw the signpost he remembered with swift clarity soldiers basking like lizards in the lush gardens of Talbot House. He wondered if Tubby Clayton still lived there and what would become of the house now. Then the field ambulance swung around a corner and Alex realized they were passing the edge of the field where Lombardi had built his Villa Via Sacra.

He peered out into the darkness. The hut was gone, the trench filled in, and the cemetery was laid out neatly, with hornbeam hedges planted to mark the boundaries. Soon immaculate white headstones would replace the wooden crosses, another Garden of Stone. It could have been any one of them, along that imaginary line from the French coast to the Swiss border.

They drove along a rough road and then veered right. He recognized it immediately. With a sharp intake of breath, he turned to his companions and said, "There—the cemetery is up there, by those buildings and that tree."

Mace, the driver, the other officer in the group, swerved the field ambulance off the road and brought it to a stop within walking distance of the cemetery. They got out. While Mace and the two other ranks unfastened the tarpaulin of the ambulance, Alex was engulfed by sheer dread.

What am I thinking? he said to himself, repulsed. I can't do this. I can't go back up there and dig Ted's body from the ground. And what if we take the wrong one? What then?

Mace broke in on his thoughts, handing him a shovel. Over his shoulder, Mace carried a sack for the body they would select, and a lantern to light their work. Trying to ease the dryness that had suddenly caused his tongue to cleave to the roof of his mouth, Alex took the shovel, shifted its weight onto his good hip, and began to walk slowly toward the rows of crosses.

He hadn't seen the place for three years. Even after telling Lombardi his story, he had still been unable to face going back. Now, in the evening light, with the rain and the star shells and the mud gone, and the screaming wounded men silenced beneath the ground, it looked completely different. But beyond the rows of wooden crosses were landmarks he remembered: the barn where he had watched Ted die was miraculously still there, missing one wall, and the lightning tree, where he had rested his head and wept, stood out starkly against the muted color of the evening fields.

They walked among the graves. There were other things besides the crosses: helmets, rusty bayonets, water bottles, dud shells. The ground was dangerously uneven. His feet sank into it, up to the ankles of his boots. He looked at his companions. They were reading the metal plaques on the wooden crosses. Many of the dead were unknowns, known only to God.

He looked over at the tree, at the cross that had been placed in the earth where Ted's body lay. A terrifying, icy fear gripped his heart when he realized that it was inscribed. He walked toward it, shivering violently, feeling nauseous again, hardly drawing breath.

"An unknown British soldier."

Relief coursed through him. He straightened up, suddenly resolute. "This one. We'll take this one."

The three men turned to look at him. Mace held up the lantern.

"It's the loneliest grave in the place," Alex said. What else could he say? Not the truth—never the truth.

Mace shrugged. "One's as good as another."

They began to dig by the flickering light of the lantern, the earth giving way easily. After a while, a fragment of white bone appeared out of the darkness. Alex shook uncontrollably. None of his companions noticed; it was bitterly cold and they were all intent on their work.

An arm emerged from the saturated uniform, and then the chest and the legs. Alex stopped digging. He thought he would vomit. The other men dug gently around the head until it surfaced, white and bald as the moon above the cemetery.

"He's wearing a wedding ring," one of the servicemen pointed out.

"Take it off—check it for any inscription," Mace said. Alex turned away; he had forgotten the ring. There was silence as it was eased from the finger and inspected under the lantern light.

"No," said the man. "Nothing. It's just a wedding ring with two interlocking bands. No inscription."

"Put it back on him then, and help me with this sack."

The ring was replaced. Alex took the rough material of the sack in his hands, letting the others handle the body. He felt the weight of it against his legs.

They put the sack on a stretcher, and carried it between them, the lantern swinging from Mace's hand, across the dark fields of Bleuet Farm to the waiting ambulance. Mace climbed back in front to drive while Alex and the other men found their seats once more. No one said a word; the enormity of what they had done affected them all. Alex pressed his hands into his stomach, hoping to quell his nausea until they reached St. Pol. He dared not think of Ted's body lying there, on the floor of the ambulance, only inches from where he sat.

They drove straight down to the Military Headquarters in St. Pol as instructed, where the chaplain, George Kendal, received them.

"Can you confirm for me that you are British?" he asked them solemnly in turn. Then: "Can you confirm that the body in your possession is British and that neither the grave nor the body itself could be established by name, regiment, or any other means of identification?"

Mace nodded. "I can confirm that, Mr. Kendal."

"Then I shall ask you now to take the body from the ambulance and place it in the chapel for the selection to take place."

The other two ranks carried the body in its thick sack to the makeshift chapel that had been assembled on the grounds of the buildings. Alex shook the hands of the men who had accompanied him to Bleuet Farm and watched them depart. When they were out of earshot, and he was safely alone in the dark yard, he threw up violently, several times, and stood bent double, gasping for breath. Recovering, he returned to his own car, parked at a safe distance but still close enough for him to see the chapel. A British NCO stood at the entrance to prevent anyone unauthorized from entering.

Alex smoked one cigarette after the other, watching as the other three groups arrived and departed. At midnight, he saw Wyatt and Lieutenant Colonel Gell enter the chapel to make the final selection. The guard at the entrance was joined by two colleagues, their breath projecting whitely as they talked quietly among themselves.

Alex looked down at his hands; he had never seen them shake so horribly. He pushed the palms flat against each other and shifted position slightly in his seat. Then he unlatched the door to vomit again. He sat back, gasping, his mouth filled with the taste of tobacco and bile. He took deep breaths and tried to picture what was happening inside the chapel, how Wyatt and Gell would choose the final body from the four. He thought of the bodies lying there on their stretchers, under the Union flags, with the smell of the grave still about them in the narrow room.

He heard footsteps and jerked his head up.

Wyatt and Gell were emerging from the chapel. Alex watched, carefully, again holding his breath. He expelled the air from his lungs, craving a glass of water and some toothpaste to clear the foul taste from his mouth.

A field ambulance swung into view, its headlamps picking out the boots of the guards as it pulled up in front of the chapel. It reversed with its back doors against the chapel entrance. Three men jumped down from the vehicle. One was an army chaplain; Alex could just make out a clerical collar. The guards cleared them to go through into the small building. They emerged minutes later, carrying the first of the three unselected bodies.

This is it, Alex thought, *the moment of truth.* His stomach rolled. Then he threw his pack of cigarettes onto the back seat of the motor car and switched on the ignition.

The field ambulance rumbled over the pitted road to Albert, throwing up shards and stones. One struck the windscreen of Alex's motor car, leaving a small blister on the glass. He could see the silhouetted line of houses on the outskirts of St. Pol, and then nothing but wide fields, stretching blackly on either side of the road, knolls of gouged earth, and the dull gape of trenches running in all directions.

The field ambulance slowed. Alex turned off the engine and let the motor car edge down to a dip in the road, under a row of sycamores. He leaned forward, his forehead touching the cold windscreen. The men got out of the ambulance; the army chaplain was carrying a lantern. They dropped the three unselected bodies into a deep shell hole several yards back from the road. Alex watched them standing on the edge of the shell hole, throwing earth down to cover the corpses lightly. The chaplain came forward, and in the glow of the lantern, made the sign of the cross three times. Then the burial party returned to the field ambulance. The lights of the vehicle blinked into life; it made a sharp turn before heading back in the direction of St. Pol.

Alex waited half an hour, then he got out of the motor car.

The bodies were close to the surface of the soil. The shell hole itself was about a hundred feet deep and half as wide again and its base well hidden from the road. There were no houses nearby, no one to see what was happening. Only the starless night sky, and the soughing of the wind in the sycamores.

Alex had to know whether they had chosen the right body or not. He couldn't change the selection, but he wanted to know. A cold film of sweat broke out on his forehead and back, but the earlier nausea and trembling had gone. Clutching a torch in one hand, he skittered down the side of the yawning shell hole, twisting his ankle as he landed at its base. He got up, wincing, then braced himself for what he was about to do.

He jammed the torch in a thick root jutting out of the soil and by its light began to uncover the bodies with his hands, the black, rotting earth falling apart beneath his fingers and lodging itself in lumps under his nails. He was determined not to let his nerves get the better of him, applying himself to the task methodically, telling himself it would be finished soon, finished and done with. All he needed to do was look for the ring with its two interlocking bands of white gold.

His insides heaved as he touched scraps of decaying flesh. Clamping his teeth together to steel himself, he felt for the fingers of each corpse in the darkness, his own fingers sliding across the hands of the dead men. He searched for the white gold bands, evidence of the marriage he had torn apart. The first corpse and the second. Nothing, and again, nothing. The third, the last one. His fingers closed over the lifeless right hand.

He knew. He let the hand fall back. He knew, and it was enough. He reached for the torch, extinguished its glow, and scrambled up to the edge of the shell hole and back to civilization.

Later, he couldn't remember how he drove back to St. Pol. When he reached the small hotel where he was staying near Military Headquarters, he was desperate to go up to his room quickly, to scrub the earth from his skin and scrape out the soil from under his fingernails.

It was three o'clock in the morning, and he expected the hotel to be in darkness. Instead, as he unlocked the front door with the key the owner had lent him, he saw a light burning in the small sitting room. He moved quietly toward the staircase, but had scarcely climbed the first few steps when the door of the sitting room swung open wide.

Sebastian Thorpe appeared in the hallway, a generous glass of Scotch in his hand.

"Mission accomplished, Dyer?" Thorpe swayed drunkenly on his feet. "Well, well, what have you been up to now, I wonder?"

Slowly, Alex turned back to the hall.

35

"WHAT THE HELL ARE YOU DOING HERE, THORPE?" ALEX WENT PAST him wearily and into the sitting room. The last thing he needed was an argument with his old enemy. If Thorpe was spoiling for a fight, he wasn't going to give it to him. All he wanted was to wash and to get into bed. Tomorrow was going to be another long day.

"I say, that's not terribly friendly, is it?" Thorpe followed him into the room and fell into a chair against the fireplace. A few glowing embers remained in the grate; the room itself was still warm. Alex moved across to the fire, holding out his hands. Then he realized they were caked in soil and thrust them into his trouser pockets, hoping Thorpe hadn't noticed.

"Let me fix you a drink," said Thorpe, making no attempt to rise from the armchair.

Alex turned to him. "I don't want a drink, and I don't think you'd better have anymore either."

"Why not? I'm on my hols, you know. St. Pol is lovely at this time of year; I can't think why I never came here before." Thorpe gave a gurgling laugh.

Alex stared at him. He had never seen Thorpe drunk. It wasn't a

pleasant experience and he knew it signaled trouble. Thorpe's beady
eyes watched him from behind his tortoiseshell glasses.

"Come on, then, out with it," said Alex, longing to be alone. "What
do you want?"

"What do *I* want?" Thorpe rested his head against the high back of
the chair. "Actually, I'm more interested in what it is that *you* want."

Alex felt a tremor of anxiety. "I'm not in the mood for riddles," he
said curtly. "State your business and then get out. Or let me get to bed.
I've no time for this."

"All right," said Thorpe, suddenly looking decidedly less intoxi-
cated. "Your little game has been rumbled, Dyer. I know exactly what
you've been up to."

Alex froze. He stared back at Thorpe, who wore a gloating smile.
"What do you mean?" he said. "What little game?"

"I see you're going to make me spell it out," said Thorpe with a
theatrical sigh. He sat upright in his chair. "The Unknown Warrior—a
marvelous idea, and one that I would have *adored* to cover, but now
I see there isn't much point, is there, when he's not really unknown
after all."

Alex clenched the muscles in his jaw. He made no reply.

"You know who it is, don't you, Dyer? The Unknown Warrior
goes by the name of Edward Eden, doesn't he, old boy?"

Alex felt for the mantelpiece behind him and gripped it. The room
contracted; he felt the floor swim up to meet him. Then he heard his
own voice say, with exaggerated calm, "I haven't got the slightest idea
what you're talking about."

"Come, come, Alex."

Thorpe's use of his Christian name brought Alex back to his senses;
he had never used it before. He knew that he had to pull himself together. "You're talking rot, as usual, Thorpe." As he spoke, the room
came back into focus and he felt more alert than he had since arriving
back at the hotel. "I don't know where you've got this half-baked idea,
but it's nonsense."

Thorpe raised his eyebrows and sipped his Scotch. "Hmm," he
murmured. "Interesting reaction—not what I was expecting, but
I suppose you've got to be pretty damned unflappable to carry off
something like this."

"If you haven't got anything useful to say, I'm going to bed. Good night." His attempt to leave was blocked by Thorpe, who leaped up from his chair and pushed a clumsy hand at Alex's chest, spilling his drink on his own obtruding stomach.

"Get your hands off me," said Alex angrily.

"Yes, you'd like that, wouldn't you? To go up to your room and forget about this." Thorpe's eyes glittered dangerously. "But I'm not going to let you do that, Dyer, do you hear? I'm not going to let you."

" 'Not going to let me, not going to let me,' " Alex mimicked Thorpe's nasal bleat perfectly. "How do you plan to stop me?"

"By going to the authorities and telling them exactly what you've done."

Alex held himself very still.

Thorpe, having delivered his punch line, slumped back down into his chair.

"I know all about it, Dyer. You see, when I heard about the plan to bring back an unknown soldier from the battlefields I knew it would be the perfect end to my career as a war correspondent to cover the story. And it really would have been. So I got in touch with all the right people, but I was told that a journalist had already been engaged for the job. *You,*" he said, almost spitting out the word. "I had hoped I might be able to get you thrown off; but everyone I spoke with told me that you were positively fanatical about the job—that you'd been chasing after it since day one. And I thought to myself: Why? Why is Alexander Dyer so hell-bent on this particular commission? Of course, it's a wonderful thing—as I said, I wanted it badly myself—but still, there seemed something decidedly iffy about your zeal." Thorpe paused, twisting his glass between his fingers. "So I spoke to a few other people. That weird albino chap, for one."

Alex felt the blood drain from his face. "Lombardi wouldn't tell you a damn thing!"

"Not if he thought I was interested for the wrong reasons," Thorpe said, agreeing. "But if I told him that I was a great friend of yours—"

"Lombardi knows who you are—I told him!"

"I didn't give him my real name, you idiot." Thorpe smiled. "Anyway, I pretended to know all about your troubled past. Don't worry, Lombardi didn't give me everything, only bits and pieces. But before I

spoke to him I had a chat with Jack Garland. He's astonishingly indis-
creet with a few drinks inside him. He couldn't tell me much either,
but he said that he *had* heard from Julian Quint that your best friend
had been killed at Passchendaele and that you'd never gotten over it."

"I don't believe you—"

"Anyway, *then* I spoke to Lombardi. I didn't approach him to talk
about you—that just came naturally. By then, I knew that Edward
Eden had left behind a beautiful young widow. And that got me thinking . . ."

"How dare you," said Alex, his eyes dark with anger. He took a step
toward Thorpe. "How dare you."

Thorpe flinched. "No, old boy, how dare *you*." He glared up at
Alex. "Anyway, I said to Lombardi wasn't it a shame about poor old
Teddy Eden."

"Lombardi would never tell you . . . "

"No, not once he realized that my questions were not entirely
above board, shall we say. He got jolly angry, to tell the truth. So I decided to try another tactic. I spoke to a couple of men from Ted's old
battalion. And one of *them* told me that Ted was quite disturbed before
he died. He'd found out his wife had been having an affair, you see.
And it seems he lost the will to live."

"No," said Alex, incredulous. His head pounded. "You're lying. Ted
would never have told anyone. He wouldn't have done that!"

"Being on the receiving end of betrayal can twist a man's mind,
Dyer. Especially one who wasn't all there in the first place."

Alex turned away and stared down into the glowing coals. "What
else?" he asked hoarsely. "What else are you going to throw at me,
Thorpe?"

"Not much." Thorpe coughed. "Ted had died during the battle for
Passchendaele, but no one knew where, of course. And I found out
that you were very keen to be among the men who dug up the body
from Bleuet Farm—that it was your suggestion, in fact."

Alex closed his eyes. "This whole thing—the Unknown Warrior—
is supposed to be a closely guarded secret."

"Nothing is secret," said Thorpe decidedly. "Not if you're determined to get answers to the questions that have been plaguing you
for weeks." He sipped his Scotch. "I followed you down here. Not to
the cemetery, of course, but here, to St. Pol. I booked myself in, then

watched and waited. I saw the various groups, including yours, coming and going. And after midnight, when the final selection had been made, I saw the ambulance containing the rejected bodies leave, and your car following some way behind. So I came back here, had a nice chat with the proprietor, and helped myself to his Scotch. All in all, a very pleasant day's work, I feel."

Slowly, Alex turned. "You have no proof," he said. "This is all conjecture."

Thorpe looked irritated. "It all adds up, old boy, it all adds up."

"No, it doesn't." Alex shook his head, the fog clearing from his mind. "You can't make any of this stick."

Thorpe's face reddened. "You went to look at the other bodies, didn't you, Dyer? To see if your friend had been chosen?"

"No," Alex shook his head again. "I'm not discussing this with you."

He was about to attempt to walk away once more when Thorpe said quickly, "That's exactly what Eden's widow said when she tried to fob me off."

"You went to see Clare?" Alex stared at Thorpe in disbelief.

"Of course. Why not? She was probably glad to see a proper man after all those maimed creatures she works with—I had hoped to persuade her to have dinner with me, but she was a cold—"

Alex's fist swung out, hitting Thorpe squarely on the jaw. Thorpe's spectacles flew off, and he dropped his glass into his lap, the Scotch spreading a dark stain over his trousers.

"You filthy swine," Alex's voice was low as he bent over Thorpe. "Don't you think she's suffered enough?"

Thorpe got to his feet, wiping his trousers and feeling for his spectacles. He found them and put them on again. He rubbed his jaw. "You're going to regret that, Dyer," he said shakily. "You're going to seriously regret what you did there."

Alex looked at him. Thorpe's spectacles sat tilted on his nose and his trousers were ruined. He looked so pathetic that Alex felt all his anger and fear dissipate. There was nothing Thorpe could do; as he had said, he couldn't prove a thing.

"You may as well go home, Thorpe, because I've had enough. Perhaps you are right, perhaps everything is exactly as you have said and there is even more to it, but we both know your theory doesn't hold water." He glanced down at Thorpe's crotch. "Unlike your trousers."

Thorpe said nothing. He stood rubbing his jaw and clutching the mantelpiece with his other hand.

Quietly, Alex said, "Your theory breaks down, I'm afraid, because the final choice between the four bodies was completely arbitrary. I wasn't there at that selection. Why would I put myself through all this knowing that? It doesn't make sense, does it?"

Thorpe looked at him warily, and Alex knew he was beginning to doubt himself. While he had Thorpe's attention, he decided to call his bluff: "Strangely enough, however, *I* have something on *you*."

A frown creased Thorpe's small, lined forehead.

Alex said in a measured tone, "As chance would have it—or is it fate, it must be, I should think, in view of all this—earlier this year I attended the Canadian War Memorials Exhibition in London. It was rather interesting and I was very taken with a bronze sculpture called 'Canada's Golgotha.' " He saw Thorpe blench and he went on, "As I'm sure you know, it was based on that little story of yours concerning the Crucified Canadian. Well, the German government didn't take too kindly to the artwork. They felt it was libelous and succeeded in having it removed from display in June. I decided to conduct my own investigation into the matter, to see if I could find any evidence of the atrocity having taken place." He paused. "There had already been an inquiry by the Canadian judge advocate general's office. And what did he find? Nothing. Merely that someone had told somebody else about it."

Thorpe shook his head, his hand still cradling his jawbone. "Not true. They found one of the men I spoke to and he signed an oath after swearing on the Bible."

"But the judge didn't believe him. When they asked him again, the man admitted he had heard the story from someone else. He wasn't a first-hand witness. So I decided to follow up the lead you had given me yourself. You said that the crucified man was Harry Band of the 48th Canadian Highlanders and that the incident took place near St. Jean on April 23, 1915." Alex took a deep breath. "I looked into it. Harry Band was apparently reported missing, presumed dead, on April twenty-fourth and his body has never been found. But Band was a private in the 16th Battalion, not an officer with the 48th Highlanders. There is nothing on file about how his death occurred. GHQ have no records of the depositions you mentioned having secured either. And when I tried to trace Valentine James, whom you quoted in your article as having told you the tale originally, I found that he was in hospital and willing to go on record stating that you had twisted his words." Alex paused. "There are other inconsistencies too, but I don't feel it necessary to go into them here. I'm keeping them for the article that will appear about this in next month's *Times.*"

Thorpe stared at him. He seemed shrunken, as tired as Alex had felt upon arrival at the hotel. "If you print that article," he said unsteadily, "you will destroy my reputation."

"Yes," said Alex. "I rather suppose I shall." He watched Thorpe's Adam's apple working itself furiously up and down his throat.

"All right," said Thorpe, finally. He sounded as if he were choking. "If I say no more about *this,* then I trust that you won't publish your article about me."

Alex nodded slowly. "You've got yourself a deal, Thorpe. Now get out of here before I change my mind."

Thorpe got out. He stumbled from the room quickly, upsetting a potted plant on the small table by the door. He didn't return to pick it up. Alex heard his footsteps thumping on the stairs.

After a few minutes, Alex went up to his own room, exhausted and trembling from the tension of the whole evening. He washed thoroughly but swiftly, then stood at the window for a moment before getting into bed.

Across the yard was the makeshift chapel where the man they were calling the Unknown Warrior lay.

36

At three o'clock the following afternoon Alex walked into the courtyard of Boulogne-sur-Mer, the old château of the port of Boulogne. He waited under a sky dank with the threat of rain for the arrival of the ambulance carrying the body and its military escort. The vehicles pulled in a short while later and a group of British and Dominion soldiers stepped forward to lift the flag-draped coffin from the ambulance. With it came six barrels of soil from the Ypres salient; at the service Alex had attended that morning in the chapel in St. Pol, Wyatt had explained that the soil was being shipped in so that the soldier "may lie in the earth so many gave their lives for" after burial in Westminster Abbey.

The coffin was carried into the château's library. It was opened there, and the two undertakers took out the body, still wrapped in its sack, and lowered it into the coffin that had been brought over by sea the previous night. Alex watched the two men secure the lid with wrought-iron bands before they lay a Crusader's sword across it. As he joined the small gathering filing out of the library he glimpsed the plate of burnished metal on the lid and its inscription: "A British Warrior who fell in the Great War 1914–1918. For King and Country."

That night, Alex stayed in a small, family-run hotel in Boulogne, sleeping better than he had in St. Pol. After an early breakfast, he left his motor car in the yard and walked back to the château, standing against the courtyard wall to watch the beginning of the procession. A gentle rain fell as the pallbearers emerged to place the casket on a gun wagon pulled by six black artillery horses and driven by a French soldier. They left the courtyard preceded by a detachment of the 6th Chasseurs of Lille. Alex followed, and as the procession wound its way through the streets, people emerged to join them. When the bells of Boulogne rang out across the town at half past ten, more than a mile of mourners were solemnly trailing behind the gun-wagon.

Alex looked about him in amazement at the parade: the local fire service walked in front, followed by many disabled French ex-servicemen displaying their military medals. Then came every child in Boulogne, all the local dignitaries, and a stream of soldiers from the French infantry and cavalry. And then there was the coffin, draped in the resilient colors of the Union flag, pulled on its black wagon. Hundreds of French soldiers followed, carrying vast wreaths from the French government, army, and navy, and from the British armed forces still serving in France. They were shadowed by Marshal Foch and Lieutenant General MacDonogh, and the men of the French army.

Alex walked alongside, past the thousands lining the streets waving French and British flags. Hundreds of schoolchildren from other towns and villages stood wide-eyed, watching; they had been given a holiday in honor of an event they would never forget.

"The Last Post" sounded through the silent, teeming streets as the cortege reached the Quai Gambetta, where the HMS *Verdun* was berthed. Standing on deck were the ship's captain and crew. Here, Alex knew, French involvement with the ceremony would end; strict orders meant that only British subjects would be permitted to handle the casket from then on.

The crowd stood quietly in the rain as Lieutenant General Mac-Donogh spoke. Then it was the French leader's turn. Foch's voice quavered with emotion as he addressed the gathering: "I express the profound feelings of France for the invincible heroism of the British Army." Alex fought back his own tears as the words rang out clearly over the harbor: "I regard the body of this hero as a souvenir of the future and as a reminder to work in common to cement the victories we have gained by Eternal Union."

After MacDonogh had thanked Foch for his speech, "God Save the King" and then the "Marseillaise" swelled as eight soldiers lifted the coffin from the wagon and carried it aboard to the bier on the quarter deck. They were followed by British servicemen who had been given wreaths to place next to the coffin. As Alex arrived on deck, he watched the blue-jacketed naval guard of honor moving into position. MacDonogh faced the coffin and a nineteen-gun salute tore through the gray sky.

As the final echoes died away, the ship's engines took on a deeper note and the HMS *Verdun* slowly drew away from France.

The ship was escorted to mid-Channel by three French torpedo boats and two French aircraft. Then she was alone as she made course for England, cutting through the waves on that overcast, damp November day, her signal lights shining, to let other ships know that the Unknown Warrior was coming home.

At length the towering outlines of the six British destroyers detailed to escort the HMS *Verdun* into the harbor at Dover loomed out of the mist. Standing at the rail, shivering in the bitterly cold wind, Alex saw their Union flags and ensigns lowered to half mast, an honor normally reserved for the king or his representative. He paced the deck, trying to stave off the chill gusts that whipped up from the foaming sea, and at one o'clock was able to discern the faint outline of the Dover cliffs rearing through the wall of fog.

The HMS *Vendetta* approached, her colors lowered. Blurred by the fog, the ship's signals flashed: "Who are you?"

The tense reserve that Alex had clung to ever since his return to France disintegrated as the destroyer signaled back: "*Verdun*, and escort, with Nation's Unknown Son."

He bent his head and wept.

XV

THE WATCHERS SEE IT ALL

London, November 11, 1920

37

THE ELEVENTH HOUR APPROACHES, AND THE GUN CARRIAGE BEARING the Unknown Warrior comes to rest before George V, who stands to attention facing the cenotaph, his sons behind him. Wearing the uniform of a field marshall, the king salutes the coffin and places a wreath of red roses next to the steel helmet that lies upon Railton's flag, in which the coffin is draped. The card tucked deep within the blooms bears the king's own distinctive handwriting: "In proud memory of those warriors who died unknown in the Great War. Unknown, and yet well known, as dying and behold they lived. George R.I."

As the king steps back, the choir begins to sing "O God Our Help in Ages Past," and the sound of weeping rises from the crowd. The gathered members of Parliament, representatives from the Dominions, ex-servicemen, and widows sit in numbed silence.

"Be thou our guard while troubles last;
and our eternal home . . ."

When the last notes of the hymn fade, the archbishop of Canterbury stands up and begins to intone the Lord's Prayer.

As the words echo over the heads of the gathered crowds, the first chime of the eleventh hour tolls the length of Whitehall, drifting on the air along with the cloying scent of thousands of white chrysanthemums. The seated dignitaries and those standing clustered in small groups on the balconies, roofs, and at windows overlooking the avenue all seem to hold their breath as the king turns back to face the cenotaph. The chimes of Big Ben fade, and the monarch touches a button, releasing the vast Union flags veiling the monument. The colors flutter to the ground, exposing the stark white column.

The king lifts his cap.

The two-minute silence begins.

Across the nation, the first minute's silence is rigidly observed in honor of those who came home, the second to remember the fallen. Traffic everywhere comes to a standstill, from the main thoroughfares linking the cities, to the remote towns that dot the undulating Pennines. The London Stock Exchange and the cotton mills of Lancashire grind to a halt, and in prisons the length and breadth of Britain, inmates rise to their feet and bow their heads. In a court in Manchester, an ex-soldier is on trial, but the proceedings are paused while the accused, the witnesses, the counsel, solicitors, prison officers, and policemen all stand to attention. In the skies above Britain, pilots shut off their engines to fly their craft in silence, their passengers standing with heads bowed, and on the world's oceans, British ships stop sailing, for the silence is to be observed throughout the Empire. "The world was for the time forgotten," someone later writes, "and the dead lived again."

In London, the silence is rent by an elderly woman's scream in Whitehall, rising and falling. The king lays a second wreath of flowers at the foot of the cenotaph's northern wall and the screaming woman subsides into sobs. Commands are shouted in the damp air for the bands to fall in. The pallbearers take their positions behind the king and the six black horses walk on again, pulling the gun carriage down the avenue in the drizzle.

Behind the official mourners comes a long ribbon of people preceded by ex-servicemen in wheelchairs, the blue of their hospital garb contrasting sharply with the unvarying black. A few, such as Thomas Harman, who pushes the wheelchair of Frankie Stephens of the Black Watch, have made a great effort to attend, honoring their comrades who have not, shall not, return. Someone has already calculated that if the Empire's dead were to walk down Whitehall four abreast, it would take them three and a half days to pass the cenotaph, the empty tomb. In the eerie morning light, the possibility that the living ex-servicemen might encounter those dead soldiers marching out of the mists does not seem improbable.

At the end of the avenue, inside Westminster Abbey, members of the royal household, servicemen and servicewomen, and one thousand widows and bereaved mothers occupy the pews. The military bands bring their music to an end as the funeral procession comes into view beyond the heads of the silent crowds.

The coffin is borne to the west end of the nave past a one-hundred-strong guard of honor, most of them holders of the Victoria Cross. Their medals reflect the watery sunlight creeping in through the abbey windows. In the center of the nave the grave lies open beneath the soaring, vaulted ceiling. Wooden bars have been stretched across the hollow for the coffin to rest upon during the service, which is kept deliberately short and intense. As the words of "Lead, Kindly Light" sound out softly, the bearer party steps forward to lower the coffin into the grave.

"And with the morn those angel faces smile,
Which I have loved long since,
And lost awhile . . ."

A silver shell filled with the earth from the battlefields of Flanders is handed to the king. The coffin descends into the dark fissure as he lets the soil filter through his fingers.

The silence that follows the voices falling away is broken by the reveille and "The Last Post" sounded by trumpeters outside the abbey. A silk pall is released to cover the coffin. Afterward, the civil and military dignitaries depart and four sentries from the armed forces approach the open grave. As the last member of the congregation files out, the waiting public are allowed in. Something of their quietness and the emotion of the day communicates itself to the visiting children, who in the hush of the great church obediently lie solitary flowers alongside the bouquets and wreaths.

The queue shows no sign of shortening as afternoon turns to evening. Mourners stand eight deep in two lines along the Embankment and Whitehall. Young mothers carry sleeping children in their arms, and old men and women clad from head to foot in black edge toward the abbey. Though the doors are scheduled to close at eleven o'clock that night, the press of people is such that they remain open indefinitely.

In Whitehall after midnight a thick fog falls. The avenue is silent but for the footsteps of those slowly moving forward in the line that stretches around Trafalgar Square and back toward Covent Garden. The huge bronze lions on their plinths provide a compass point for those who wait, the elegant buildings around the square and Nelson's column having sunk into the lamplit fog. Occasionally, there is a muffled clop of horses' hooves as mounted policemen traverse the length of Whitehall, keeping to the roadside to avoid trampling over the wraithlike figures shivering in the bitterly cold air. The bare pillar of the cenotaph rises from an enclosure of banked-up wreaths, and the sweet, earthy odor of the lilies and chrysanthemums perfume the rain.

The man entering the abbey as the hour tolls has waited all evening.

His dark hair leaks water inside the upturned collar of his coat and his narrow face is white with cold. He was also among the morning's privileged congregation in the abbey. After the service he returned briefly to his flat in Chalcot Square, but felt stifled by the evidence of his solitary domesticity. He emerged an hour later to sit on the steps of the British Museum for most of the afternoon. His intention was to go home around half past four, but the streets seemed to lead him deliberately away from his own front door. Before he was fully conscious of what he was doing, he had joined the unspeaking queue in front of the church of St. Martin-in-the-Fields, edging around Trafalgar Square and past Downing Street until he saw the north door of the abbey surface through the enveloping fog.

He approaches the nave gradually, behind a shuffling ex-soldier clutching a bunch of flowers in sodden tissue that drips onto the stones below his feet. There are candles everywhere, clusters of them normally lit by the public in prayer, using the long white tapers that always remind him of a blind man's fingers probing the darkness. Lamplight comes in through the long window at the back of the nave, but it is weak, filtering to nothing where it touches the floor. There are more shadows than illumination within the church, and the glimmers of gold in the darkness have an unreality to them, as if they are no more than a few quick brushstrokes added to an artist's impression of the abbey by night.

And then the open grave.

There was no opportunity for him earlier to view it closely and now he stares at it, numbed. On every side lies flowers, towering banks of extravagant blossom amid laurel leaves. Some have fallen upon the coffin. He can see it; it looks too small to contain the body of a man.

He forces himself to remain calm by reading some of the inscriptions on the wreaths:

"In loving memory of our darling Jim Cook, who answered his country's call at the early age of thirteen years and ten months, and then laid his life down at seventeen years of age. Ever remembered by Dad and Mam, Brothers and Sisters at home and abroad . . ."

"From little Mother to her beloved son, somewhere in France. We will remember thee in the mornings and in the night season we will not forget."

He turns the words over in his mind: "In the night season we will not forget."

He finds it difficult to tear himself away from the grave. There are murmurs behind him. At last he leaves, joining the others making their way to the exit and the frigid wind of Parliament Square. The thought of the walk home depresses him, the knowledge that when he reaches the flat it will be in pitch-blackness, reeking of dust and neglect, and the sheets on his bed will be cold enough to make him wish he had troubled to prepare a fire that morning.

The arctic wind scratches at the abbey doors. He is almost outside, the spatter of rain prickling against his skin, when he sees her.

38

CLARE STANDS IN LINE, HOLDING A WREATH OF BLOODRED BERRIES
and ivory roses, the heavy, waxy heads drooping from the rain. The
collar of her coat is turned up for warmth, but she is without a hat
as always. Her shoes and skirt are dark claret, a shade deeper than her
coat. Her hair is longer than Alex remembers it.

He lurches forward, crossing the stone floor rapidly, apologizing
in whispers to the people he has to push aside to reach her. He slips
momentarily and has to grasp her arm to prevent himself from going
down.

She turns her head and her pale eyes widen, appalled.

His grip on her arm tightens.

"*Clare*. I have to talk to you."

"*Leave me alone.*" The words come at him in a hiss. She turns
quickly back to the queue, stepping forward a few paces. Her shoes
clip quietly upon the stone slabs.

"Clare, you must listen to me."

"I've got nothing to say to you."

"But I have something to say to you. Something *vitally* important."

He is aware of a low, discontented rumble among the crowd.

"I told you, leave me alone." The elegant hands gripping the wreath tremble, and the leaves rustle against each other.

"I'll wait for you outside," he persists.

"You'll have a long wait."

"It doesn't matter. There's nowhere else I have to be."

Someone taps him on the shoulder. He shrugs off the hand, and goes outside.

The air has a clear, fresh smell that he associates with being near the sea. At first he thinks it must have something to do with the absence of traffic. Then he realizes that it is Clare's scent, the perfume she wears to remind her of her childhood on the northeast coast.

He watches the doors of the abbey, waiting to see who emerges from the candlelit shadows, waiting for her.

A group comes out clinging to one another. In the center is a weeping young woman, with an older man and woman keeping her upright—the girl's parents, he supposes. And then there is Clare, trying to slip between the other visitors and the side of the abbey.

He sprints forward, across grass that splinters with frost beneath his shoes. He reaches out and grasps her by the arm.

She pulls away, throwing back her arm so that he can't touch her without it looking like an assault.

"I'll call the police if you try that again. There are plenty of them about." Her pale gray eyes are flooded with angry light.

"Then listen to me!" he shouts. His own voice startles him; after the peculiar hush and stillness of the day it seems to echo around the moonlit grounds of the abbey as stridently as if he has yelled from the top of a mountain.

It has a similar effect on Clare. After three years of refusing to see or speak to him, she finally assents. "Very well, I'll listen. But then I don't want any more to do with you. No more letters, no more phone calls, no more trying to reach me through friends. Do you understand?"

He nods. "Where shall we go? We can't stay here."

"Not after your performance. There's the Albion Café. We can talk there."

They walk together in silence down Victoria Street, avoiding eye contact. Clare stares straight ahead, into the wall of fog. Alex keeps his head down and his hands thrust in the pockets of his coat. He wants desperately to touch her.

The Albion Café is on a narrow side street. The bright light from within spreads onto the pavement in a muddy ocher pool. Alex pushes open the door and stands aside for Clare to enter. The café is L-shaped, extending toward the kitchen at the back. Brass coaching lamps are wedged between oil paintings of London landmarks on pale green walls. The tables and chairs are finished in steel. They find a place by the window, one of several empty spots.

She looks at him. "You have to order at the till. I'll have a coffee."

He picks up the menu; it is folded in two, with a vaguely yellow, sticky stain in the crease. He puts it down and walks over to the counter. There is no one there; the waitress, a plump, middle-aged woman with obviously dyed red hair, has gone through to the kitchen. He can see her talking to the cook, who leans back from a pan of sizzling bacon. There is another menu on the counter. He picks it up, needing something to do, even if it is pointless.

He cannot stop trembling; the words move up and down, infuriating him. *Self-control,* he tells himself. *For God's sake, self-control.* But he has lost her once. The thought that he might do so again forces open the unhealed wound across his heart.

Clare watches Alex as she takes off her gloves and coat and drapes them over the back of her chair. She had managed to avoid him earlier, in Whitehall, that morning. Now, close up, she sees that he looks exactly as she remembers, as she has never forgotten: like a restless hawk.

She takes out her cigarettes from the inside pocket of her coat, then realizes she has forgotten to buy matches. She looks down at her hands; they are still trembling. She touches her throat nervously. The memory of his mouth and hands on the delicate white skin there makes her clench her fingers into her palms. The pain of it, of denying all she ever felt for him—all she still feels for him underneath the pervasive anger and lasting regret—floods through her, causing her to catch her breath. That, and the shock of seeing him again, is far greater than she has imagined during those long months of silence and separation.

She straightens as he returns.

He slides into his chair and leans his elbows on the table. "Did you want anything to eat?" he asks.

"No. But do you have a light?"

He finds his lighter and flicks it on. She puts the cigarette to her lips and inhales deeply. The flame dies on the lighter and he replaces it in his pocket.

"You still smoke," he says.

"It would appear so." She glances outside; the dark street is deserted. She looks back at him.

"Are you still living in the same place?"

"Yes," she replies.

"It's a nice flat."

"Yes." She has tensed, visibly. "Here's the waitress."

The red-haired woman comes with their order: a coffee for Clare and a pot of tea and a bacon sandwich for him. The sandwich oozes grease onto the blue plate.

"That looks disgusting," Clare says, turning down the corners of her mouth.

Alex nods. "It does. I haven't eaten all day. I thought I should try to force something down but—"

"But if you do, it will come straight back up again." She finishes the sentence for him, then turns away.

He pours himself a cup of tea. The steam is so hot he feels his chin grow damp. "What are you doing now?"

"I work at a hospital in Richmond. I'm assistant to a surgeon who specializes in facial reconstruction."

"That must be harrowing."

"No more harrowing than it was dealing with the wounded in Hébuterne. The conditions are somewhat improved though."

"Yes. I can imagine." He curses his inability to find anything remotely interesting to say, or to find the nerve to tell her what she must be told.

She sips at her coffee, bending down to the china cup.

He hesitates. "It's been an emotional day. The sheer volume of people seems to have taken the organizers by surprise. What did you think of the funeral? Were you there?"

"Yes, I was." She doesn't mention having seen him. She taps her cigarette against the ashtray.

"But you came back this evening—why?"

She lifts her shoulders slightly. "I don't know. I was . . . drawn to it, I suppose."

He looks at her for a moment. "I thought the ceremony was tremendously powerful."

"I thought it was a very good example of what's wrong with this country," she replies.

He frowns at her. "Why? What do you mean?"

"We remember the dead. But we've forgotten the living."

He opens his mouth to reply, then closes it again. She is right; he agrees with her after all he has seen on his wanderings through the city that autumn. The dead are glorious, honored, and sacred as saints, but the living will never be forgiven for not dying.

He takes a deep breath. "But the Unknown Warrior. You must have found his burial moving?"

"Yes," she replies. "Of course I did."

She draws on her cigarette and looks at him.

He has never forgotten her beauty, but the strength of his feelings when she turns her cool gray gaze fully on him is overwhelming.

She breaks into his thoughts. "You'll write about it of course," she says, then pauses. "*Sir* Alex." Her eyes darken.

He can tell that she is not teasing; she is furious. "We were all offered knighthoods, Clare, all the official war correspondents. I accepted mine on behalf of Ted," he says quickly, then immediately regrets it.

She gives a high, bitter laugh. "Oh, how absolutely splendid of you. Your sense of honor does you *such* credit." Her lip curls. "What a pity it also killed my husband—and your best friend."

His throat is dry. "I didn't kill Ted," he says. "You know I didn't. Don't say that, Clare."

Her voice is low, deliberate: "You took away everything he had, Alex, damn you. You left him with nothing to live for. Without hope. You made him *want* to die. That's why he took so many risks." Her voice shakes. "He wrote to me; I still have the letter that he sent me after he received yours. You ripped him apart, and for what? When they told me he was missing, I tried every avenue I could think of to trace him. Last year I spoke to one of the men in his battalion. He told me Ted had died. He said Ted was a hero, that he had put himself in danger to save other people's lives that summer. But you and I both know what that was all about, don't we? He was trying to get *himself* killed. It wasn't the shell shock that made him walk out into No Man's Land undefended. It was *you*. You and your bloody sanctimonious confession."

"No," he says. "No, it wasn't like that. It wasn't like that at all. Clare—"

"I loved you once. It was a long time ago. Do you know I hate you so much now that I could have snatched one of the soldiers' rifles during the service today and shot you dead—*gladly*—in front of everyone?"

He bends his head. He can't breathe.

She leans forward across the table and hisses, "Why did you tell him, Alex? *Why?* That confession of yours was *never* going to benefit Ted in any way, was it? And it wasn't because you wanted me for yourself. I don't believe you ever loved me. I don't believe you loved Ted either. You just wanted to get it off your conscience, didn't you? Wanted to forget? You selfish, cold-hearted *bastard*."

The slim fingers holding the cigarette become rigid, and the filter breaks off, sending the glowing white stub rolling across the table.

Alex picks up the cigarette stub and snuffs it out in the ashtray. Then he looks at her. "There's a line that I remember from a book I once read, although I've forgotten the title: 'You know that when I hate you, it is because I love you to a point of passion that unhinges my soul.'"

"You and your bloody quotations." She shakes her head, slowly, "No. I believe that you have no heart, Alex. And that was all I ever wanted of you."

They fall silent. Clare thinks about what he has said and her own pitiless reply. She cannot take it back.

At the table next to theirs, the waitress knocks over a salt cellar as she wipes the green surface. With a curse, she bends down to pick up the shattered fragments of glass, the white pyramid of salt.

Alex steels himself. He sits back in his chair, very straight. "I said I had something to tell you. You can hate me if it makes you feel better. But I want you to know that I have tried to atone for what happened. I have tried. And I have done the one thing that I thought would make it all tolerable."

"Don't tell me you've found God." Her sarcasm is evident.

"No."

"What then?"

He places his hands on the table, interlocking his fingers, holding them taut. "Would it make things any easier—any easier at all—if you knew where Ted was buried?"

The question hangs, fizzing in the air, like the tail end of a firework.

She stares at him.

"Answer me. Would it make it any easier?"

She cannot take her eyes from his grim, determined face. "His body was never found." She speaks slowly. "It's out there with thousands of others, in the mud of Passchendaele. They never found him."

"Would it make it any easier?"

Her heart begins to flutter wildly. Her fingers curl into her palms. "Alex," she says, her voice rising, "What in God's name are you trying to tell me?"

He reaches inside his jacket and pulls out a small object. Then, with a deliberate movement, he opens his hand.

Ted's silver identity disk sits in his palm, a fiercely guarded jewel.

Alex closes his eyes. He remembers the brown, barren field stretching into nothingness. The remains of Bleuet Farm and the white crosses protruding from the soil, the sound of the wind stealing over the earth and the high wail it makes as it floats across the Flanders plains, tearing at his nerves. The sight of the body—the fragments of blackened skin and white bone—will haunt him until the end of his days. And the sound of Ted's voice, years before, demanding, "Bury me with glory or none at all." He has kept his promise, but now his loyalty is toward the living, not the dead.

He opens his eyes. Cutlery clatters in the café off Victoria Street. The spluttering steam rises from the tea urn, sending a white vapor cloud up to the discolored ceiling.

He looks into Clare's confused, frightened eyes and tells her the truth.

XVI

TIME TICKED SILENT, ON

London, November 12, 1920

39

C LARE STANDS, MOVING AWAY FROM THE TABLE WITH PAINFUL STIFF-
ness.

The red-haired waitress looks over at them, wondering if they have argued. She puts her head to one side, regarding them with interest. They are lovers, she decides, new lovers who wear attacking expressions to protect their hearts. She averts her eyes and counts the tips in the plate on the counter, singing under her breath:

> "*And the years fly on forever,*
> *'Til shadows veil their skies,*
> *But he loves to hold her little hands and look in her sea-blue*
> *eyes . . .*"

"Do you still hate me?"

She looks at him, not speaking.

"Clare, please say something. Even if you think what I did was wrong. Just . . . talk to me."

"I don't know what to say to you, Alex."

"What are you thinking? Can't you at least tell me that?"

"But I don't *know* what I am thinking." The lights in the café seem stronger suddenly; she puts up her hand to shield her eyes from their glare. Her limbs are leaden. "I don't know anything anymore."

"Clare—"

"I have to leave now."

He scrapes back his chair. "Let me walk you home at least."

"No." She shakes her head slowly. "I would prefer to be on my own."

She turns to leave and he takes a quick step toward her, putting his hand on her arm.

"If you want to talk—" he hesitates, realizing that she is in shock. "If you want to see me, for whatever reason, then . . . you know where to find me."

She looks at him again, wordlessly.

His fingers tighten their grip on her arm. "For God's sake, Clare. I still love you. I always have. *I love you.*"

There is a flicker behind her eyes, and for a moment, he thinks she is going to say something. But instead she nods and opens the door, stepping out into the dark hour of the city night.

He sits down again and presses his hands against his aching temples.

She walks through the mist, crossing the bridge without a glance at the view she loves, at the drama of the London skyline on this November evening. She breaks into a run, heading blindly toward home, barely feeling the fine rain on her face.

She puts the key in the front door, throws it open, and pushes it shut, then goes through to the darkened sitting room and releases out the scream that has threatened to suffocate her since leaving Alex.

Tears spring through the gaps in her fingers where she holds them to her face. She cannot stop crying. Her nose becomes thick with mucus, seeping out to join the salt water that runs down her cheekbones and trickles into her open mouth. She bends forward, the racking sobs causing her to gulp for air. Rasping breaths come up from her gut, flooding her throat with bitterness. She stretches out on the floor, feeling the rough weave of the rug below her face and arms and legs. Even when the weeping stops, she remains there.

Finally, she sleeps.

In the morning, she unbends from the floor and pulls her dress over her head. She throws it in the laundry basket in the kitchen and goes up to the bathroom, turning on both taps. She drips lavender oil under the running water and then turns off the taps and plunges in.

The soap runs down her arms and her legs, finding all the crevices of her body. It washes out the years of dirt, blood, and denial. It washes out the pain she has carried around with her for the last three years, the pain and the terrible, encompassing guilt that she has tried to push onto Alex, absolving herself of all blame when she acknowledges, without a doubt, that he does not deserve to shoulder it alone.

She ducks her head into the water and shakes it gently from side to side before emerging in a spray of droplets that catches the light where it slants in through the small, fogged window. Pulling at the plug, she climbs out of the bath at the same time and reaches for a thick towel, rubbing her hair and skin, then drops the towel to the ground, feeling as clean as a newborn.

She walks through to the bedroom and feels at the back of the wardrobe, where a green print dress hangs on a wooden hanger. She takes it out and lays it on the bed until she has finished putting on her underclothes and stockings, then slips it on.

For half an hour she sits in the chair by the window in the long room upstairs, feeling the sun work its warm fingers through her damp hair. She drinks a small glass of brandy to calm herself and returns to her bedroom to dab scent behind her ears and along her jutting collarbone. Then she buckles the straps on her favorite green shoes and gathers up the red-brown coat she has not worn since 1916, in Cassel. She pulls it on, lifting her shoulders as the silk lining touches her bare forearms.

In the hallway she picks up her keys and unlatches the door. She locks it behind her and steps out, into the pale November sunshine.

All the British press cover the funeral of the Unknown Warrior to some extent, but none is so thorough as the souvenir supplement that appears in *The Times* ten days later, telling the story from its inception to the day on which the tomb is sealed. The last page of the special report reads:

The pilgrimage to the grave of the Unknown Warrior continued into last weekend. Saturday brought large numbers of people from towns and cities throughout the country. Two wounded soldiers who had each lost a brother in the war had walked sixty miles to visit the tomb and lay wreaths at the cenotaph. Thousands came from Ireland, Scotland, and Wales. The abbey doors closed on Saturday night but opened again at noon on Sunday to a waiting crowd of 60,000. Entire families were there. Some people came from parishes whose residents had scraped together the money to send one person to represent them. At the foot of the grave was a small box planted with flowers from a Nottinghamshire village that had lost sixty men to the war. Before the doors closed again on Sunday night, there was a chilling scene when a woman dressed in black knelt down before the tomb and raised her child, clad in white, up above it.

All week the crowds have been unceasing. On Monday traffic went back to normal, but when buses passed the cenotaph, the drivers slowed and saluted, and passengers stood and took off their hats. Then on Thursday, November 18, the tomb was sealed. The slab of Tournai marble that now lies across it will be replaced at some point in the near future, but the present inscription on the grave reads: "A British Warrior who fell in the Great War 1914–1918 for King and Country. Greater Love Hath No Man Than This."

The writer reports that more than one and a half million people paid the pilgrimage to the grave in the first seven days. And he knows, perhaps better than anyone, the scenes that have taken place. For he has visited the abbey every morning and every evening, sitting quietly at the end of the nave. Sometimes he exchanges a few words with the pilgrims, but mostly he sits, his thin face intense beneath his dense, dark hair, watching.

On just one occasion his concentration falters and his sudden agitation causes him to rise to his feet, when a blond woman dressed in russet and green leaves a spray of lilies on the grave. She stands there for a moment, staring down at the tomb, then turns and walks away with a quick, light step.

He does not follow her. He goes on standing there in the shadows of the abbey, unseen, like a ghost.

XVII

At the Ending
of the Night

London, November 12, 1921

40

LIGHT FALLS IN A LONG PALE BLADE ACROSS THE TOMB. THE STONE HAD been laid the day before, on the third anniversary of the end of the war. There had again been a ceremony, but more subdued than the funeral twelve months earlier; the outpouring of grief has become an invisible river of tears that shall flow through the Empire until the last member of the Great War generation is dead. Then, Alex thinks, it will cease to be, and what the nation has endured will pass into history, and into myth, along with the story of the Unknown Warrior.

He stands alone in the abbey, gazing down at the black slab of Belgian marble on which a lengthy inscription is written. The words are inlaid in brass from melted-down cartridge cases found in the British lines after the Armistice:

Beneath this stone rests the body
Of a British Warrior
Unknown by name or rank
Brought from France to lie among
The most illustrious of the land
And buried here on Armistice Day

11 November 1920, in the presence of
His Majesty King George V
His Ministers of State
The Chiefs of his Forces
And a vast concourse of the nation
Thus are commemorated the many
Multitudes who during the Great
War of 1914–1918 gave the most that
Man can give. Life itself.
For God
For King and Country
For loved ones, home and Empire
For the sacred cause of justice and
The freedom of the world.
They buried him among the Kings because he
Had done good towards God and towards
His house.

The last lines, chosen by Herbert Ryle, the dean of Westminster Abbey, are based upon a text from the Bible, and each time Alex reads them, he feels his heart soar. Around the tomb lies a great many poppies, their bright paper petals underscoring the brass letters in a scarlet mass.

There are footsteps behind him; a group of elderly mourners have come to add their wreath to those already surrounding the grave. He nods at them politely, then walks toward the open doors at the end of the nave and out into the street, where his motor car is parked a short distance away.

He drives calmly through London and then along quiet roads edged with winter trees, the memory of the gleaming words upon the black marble tombstone filling him with tranquillity. The sky is cloudless, china-blue and flawless, and the evergreens whose contours are flecked in a paler green and brown barely move in the gentle breeze.

He comes to the entrance gates of the park and drives slowly along the winding carriage drive. A dog bounds after a blue ball thrown for it by a small boy; Alex hears the child shouting gleefully as the dog leaps cleanly into the air and catches the ball in mid-arc. Then he reaches the graveled area that widens out beyond another set of open gates, where large notices warn that the grounds are forbidden to the general public, and pulls into the first parking space that he sees, at the foot of a wide terrace.

He gets out, sniffing the fresh, heather-scented wind, and throws his coat over his shoulders, walking toward the main entrance. The Gothic lines of the building seem softened by the mild weather; the stones are a warm ocher in the afternoon sunlight.

He enters the well-lit hallway, where no one is about apart from a powerfully built red-haired man who descends the central staircase holding a pack of cigarettes and feeling in his jacket pocket for either his matches or a lighter. The man swears gently, then glances down and sees Alex. There is a peculiar stiffness to his face.

"Do you need a light?" Alex asks, and holds out his own lighter.

"Thanks," says the man, moving a step closer. He takes the lighter, turning it over curiously in his hand. It is engraved *A Gift from Armentières* and on one side bears two lines from a popular wartime song. "Nice lighter," he says, handing it back. He takes a drag on his cigarette.

"Do you work here?" asks Alex, pocketing it again.

"No," the red-haired man shakes his head. "I used to live here. An ex-patient, you know."

"Oh, I see."

"I've come up from Cornwall. It's my first time back in a year. I had some business in London, and thought I'd drop in."

"Right," Alex says. He hesitates. "I've come to see—"

"I know," says the man, with a strange inflection in his voice. There is a moment's silence. Then he says, "I'll take you," and leads Alex outside, along the front of the house.

They walk to another wing of the building, where the vast glass half circle of the orangery projects onto the terrace like the bow of a ship. Huge plants grow within the orangery, whose windows rise to the second floor in an unending curve. The insides of the windows are misted with water and there are flecks of green on the glass, where small leaves have fallen and stuck fast. In the center of the room, at an ornate iron table, sits a young woman in white, her blond head bent, writing.

Thomas Harman opens the door and then leaves, quietly.

Alex enters, closing the door after him.

In the glass room where the scent of warm, moist earth and lush ferns and hothouse flowers hangs, the woman raises her head.

He looks into her gray eyes, the eyes that Edward Eden once described as having the power of a lighthouse beam on a lost sailor, and he asks, "Are you working?"

"No," she says. "Only writing."

She smiles at him.

In the glass room, she smiles, and the place is flooded with light; the glorious sunlight of winter, the still, clear light of great peace.

ACKNOWLEDGMENTS

WITH THE EXCEPTION OF THOSE WELL-KNOWN FIGURES APPEARING under their own names, the characters depicted in this novel are fictional. However, because there were only a handful of official British war correspondents, in the interests of historical accuracy many of Alex's professional experiences are based upon those of Sir Philip Gibbs; I have drawn heavily on sections from his exeptional books *When It Can Be Told* (IndyPublish.com, undated) and *The War Dispatches* (Tandem Books, 1968). A number of scenes depicting specific battles and their aftermath, as well as speeches made by soldiers and generals in this book, are very closely based on accounts given in *When It Can Be Told*. Similarly, interviews by real-life nurses in Lyn MacDonald's *The Roses of No Man's Land* (Penguin, 1993) provided the basic material for those sections dealing with Clare's work in that capacity. 'The Tin Noses Shop' in this novel was inspired by the Masks for Facial Disfigurements Department at the 3rd London General Hospital; a detailed description of the painstaking surgery undertaken there can be found in Lyn MacDonald's *The Roses of No Man's Land*.

During the course of my research I found Lyn Macdonald's *1914: Days of Hope* (Penguin, 1989), *1915* (Penguin, 1997), *Somme* (Penguin, 1993), *The Roses of No Man's Land* (Penguin, 1993), and *They Called It*

Passchendaele (Penguin, 1993) invaluable. Other important sources were Martin J. Farrar's *News from the Front: War Correspondents on the Western Front 1914–1918* (Sutton Publishing, 1998), Martin Middlebrook's *The First Day on the Somme* (Penguin, 1984), Leon Wolff's *In Flanders Fields* (Penguin, 1979), John Masefield's *The Old Front Line* (Pen & Sword, 2003), John Keegan's *War and Our World* (Vintage, 2001), James Hayward's *Myths and Legends of the First World War* (Sutton Publishing, 2002), Niall Ferguson's *The Pity of War* (Penguin, 1998), Eric Taylor's *Wartime Nurse* (Robert Hale, 2001), and Wendy Holden's *Shellshock* (Channel 4 Books, 1998).

For descriptions of Flanders and France after the armistice I relied mostly upon Stephen Graham's *The Challenge of the Dead* (Cassel, 1920), now sadly out of print. Other books that also proved valuable on this subject include David W. Lloyd's *Battlefield Tourism: Pilgrimage and the Commemoration of the Great War in Britain, Australia and Canada 1919–1939* (Berg, 1998), and Rose E. B. Coombs's *Before Endeavours Fade* (Battle of Britain International Ltd., 1994).

When it came to tracing the footsteps of my characters, I used Major and Mrs. Holt's *Battlefield Guide: Ypres Salient* (Leo Cooper, 2003), *Battlefield Guide to the Somme* (Leo Cooper, 2003), and *The Western Front—North* (Leo Cooper, 2004); Anne Roze's *Fields of Memory* (Seven Dials, 2000); and Paul Reed's *Walking the Somme* and *Walking the Salient*. In Belgium—where everyone I met was unfailingly kind and helpful—the Flanders Fields Museum in Ypres was another important source. There are two particularly good bookshops in Ypres for those interested in the Great War: The Shell-Hole and The British Grenadier.

I would like to thank Jacques Ryckebosche for his lively and interesting guided tour of Talbot House in Poperinghe. Paul Chapman's *A Haven in Hell* (Leo Cooper, 2000) was my other main source of information for life in Talbot House during the Great War.

Philip Longworth's *The Unending Vigil* (Leo Cooper, 2003) was invaluable for information on the establishment of the cemeteries and monuments created by the Commonwealth War Graves Commission. The commission themselves produce a number of leaflets that were also very useful to me.

The songs featured in the text are taken from Max Arthur's *When This Bloody War Is Over: Soldiers' Songs of the First World War* (Piatkus,

2001). Other books I read during my research, and which certainly inspired some of the ideas expressed here, include A. C. Grayling's *The Meaning of Things* (Phoenix, 2001), Christopher Woodward's *In Ruins* (Vintage, 2002) and Armand Marie Leroi's *Mutants: On the Form, Varieties and Errors of the Human Body* (HarperCollins, 2003).

For information relating to the Unknown Warrior, I relied largely upon Michael Gavaghan's *The Story of the Unknown Warrior* (M & L Publications, 2003) and various contemporary newspaper reports. Because my book was originally published in Holland and Belgium in 2005 (under the title *Begraven als een Koning*—trans. *Buried as a King*), I was not able then to draw on Neil Hanson's book *The Unknown Soldier* (Doubleday, 2005); however, during the revisions of this book for its American publication, I found *The Unknown Soldier* a helpful source.

The Imperial War Museum in London kindly allowed me to view the actual footage of the Unknown Warrior's funeral from 1920 and provided material on the pilgrimages to the Western Front made by soldiers' relatives in 1919 and the 1920s. There is also a Web site called Aftermath (www.aftermathww1.com), which is a good starting point for anyone interested in what happened in the years immediately after the war.

Geoff Dyer's brilliantly evocative *The Missing of the Somme* (Phoenix Press, 2001) was the primary inspiration behind this novel; reading it focused my interest in the Great War upond its aftermath, which in turn led me to thinking about the Unknown Warrior.

Finally, for personal support and total faith in this book, I give my heartfelt thanks to the following women: Jan Michael (whose guidance and encouragement means everything to me); Jane Judd; Petra Rijkelijkhuizen; Elsa den Boer; Alison Davies; and my mother, Doreen Lee.

In *The Winter of the World,* it is left up to the reader to decide whether Edward Eden was chosen to represent all the "nameless names." In real life, of course, despite recent debates the Unknown Warrior remains—rightly—unknown.

About the author

Insights,
Interviews
& More . . .

About the book

Read on

Life at a Glance

© Sjaak Ramakers

CAROL ANN LEE was born in Yorkshire, England, in 1969, but spent her formative years in Cornwall before moving to Amsterdam in 1999. There she married and had a son. Following her divorce, she and her son returned to England, settling in her native Yorkshire in 2005. Her first book, *Roses from the Earth: The Biography of Anne Frank*, was published in 1998; it has since been translated into fifteen languages. Lee has written several other books dealing with the Holocaust, including a biography of Anne Frank's father, *The Hidden Life of Otto Frank* (Harper Perennial, 2003). *The Winter of the World* is her first novel.

Lee is now working on a second novel. Set in the present day, the novel tells the story of childhood sweethearts who meet via the Friends Reunited Web site twenty-two years after they last saw each other. It is based on a recent personal experience.

About the author

A Writing Life
A Conversation with Carol Ann Lee

When do you write?

As soon as I've taken my son to school and walked the dog, and then until I have to pick my son up in the afternoon. In the evening, when he's in bed, I generally write again for a couple of hours.

Where do you write?

At home, at an old desk I bought in Amsterdam. It has all sorts of little pigeonholes and drawers in which I keep things of sentimental value. Standing guard on top of the desk are two thumb-sized dolls that were given to Otto Frank, Anne's father, by a group of Japanese schoolchildren. The dolls were passed down to me by Buddy Elias, Anne Frank's cousin.

And why . . . why do you write?

Because there isn't anything else I would rather do. I can't *not* write; it would be unthinkable. ▶

66 Standing guard on top of [my] desk are two thumb-sized dolls that were given to Otto Frank, Anne's father, by a group of Japanese schoolchildren. 99

A Writing Life *(continued)*

Pen, computer, or a stylus and clay tablets?

Computer, mostly, though I always keep a notebook with me for ideas that might prove useful later. Sometimes I hear characters "speaking" when I am in bed or on train journeys, and it's handy to have paper to jot down things like that.

Silence or music?

I like to listen to classical music as I work. Anything with a vocal is too distracting, though I make an exception for Kate Bush. But usually it's Philip Glass, Angelo Badalamenti, or Bond, a British female string quartet.

What started you writing?

Learning how to hold a pencil! I only excelled at two subjects at school, writing and art, and I got such good marks for my essays that I thought, hang on, I could probably do something with this....

How do you start a book?

Suddenly. Once the idea for a book takes hold, I throw myself into it completely and shut out everything else until I know whether it is going to work or not. With

> **❝** Once the idea for a book takes hold, I throw myself into it completely and shut out everything else until I know whether it is going to work or not. **❞**

4

biographies, obviously a certain amount of research is necessary, but that was also true of *Winter*. It would have been impossible to write it without delving into that period in some depth. Fortunately, I love research as much as I love writing, so it isn't a hardship. Once all my notes are in place, then I begin to plot how the book will develop, and it goes on from there.

And finish?

I never feel as if a book is really finished. I always want to go back to it, particularly in the first three months or so after I've completed it. With *Winter* I didn't want to leave the characters behind and kept reading the book over and over, unwilling to say good-bye.

Do you have any writing rituals or superstitions?

No, but I have a few inspirational quotes taped to the shelves to the right of my desk. They're an odd collection, but they do their job of forcing me to get on with things when I find myself beginning to drift. What are they? "If it is not right, do not do it; if it is not true, do not say it" (Marcus Aurelius); "Success is the best form of revenge" ▶

A Writing Life *(continued)*

(Morrissey); and "Every minute is another chance to turn it all around" (Sofia in *Vanilla Sky*). I told you they were an odd bunch!

Which living writer do you most admire?

Sebastian Faulks. He seems able to write about anything and make it interesting. I like his ideas and the way he starts his books, like a camera panning across a landscape until it settles on the figures that will occupy us. Geoff Dyer is another writer I like because he always makes me think, which has to be a good thing. Pat Barker is terrific, and I also like Linda Newbery, although her books are really for children, but her writing, and the subject matter, is dark enough to attract adults, too.

What or who inspires you?

Places. Always places. I couldn't write a book about a place I've never visited. Equally, I don't see much point in going somewhere unless I think I will one day want to write about it. Cornwall inspires me more than anywhere else, though while writing *Winter* I found northern Flanders and the area of the Somme battles hugely stirring.

> I don't see much point in going somewhere unless I think I will one day want to write about it.

6

If you weren't a writer, what job would you do?

Criminal psychologist. Or I'd work in some fusty archive somewhere because I love the smell of old paper and ink.

What's your guilty reading pleasure or favorite trashy read?

I don't have any, I'm afraid. I used to buy women's magazines, but they're so dull. The equivalent would be my television viewing; I watch the soaps and *Doctor Who* religiously.

My Ten Favorite Works of Fiction

1. *The Little Prince* by Antoine de Saint-Exupéry

2. *Birdsong* by Sebastian Faulks

3. *Rebecca* by Daphne du Maurier

4. *The Mill on the Floss* by George Eliot

5. *Wuthering Heights* by Emily Brontë

6. *The Woman in White* by Wilkie Collins

7. *Jane Eyre* by Charlotte Brontë

8. *The Turn of the Screw* by Henry James

9. *The Leopard* by Giuseppe Tomasi di Lampedusa

10. *The English Patient* by Michael Ondaatje

All's Well That Ends Well

or, On Almost Writing *Bridget Jones Goes to War*

The story behind this book is a rather elliptical one. Having written nonfiction for six years, I decided I wanted to try my hand at a novel. To me, nonfiction is extended journalism, and I liked the idea of writing something far more creative. Plus, I didn't want to be labeled a biographer or a children's author, instead wanting to be able to move freely between all types of writing.

For some time, I'd had an idea in my head for a novel about four sisters on a sprawling estate in Cornwall, and what happened to them and the estate during the Great War (this was sparked by a visit to the Lost Gardens of Heligan in Cornwall, and by memories of Charlestown, the harbor village where I'd grown up). I began writing the book, and my agent sold it to a Dutch publisher on the strength of several chapters and a long outline, but about two hundred pages into the actual book, I suddenly had a feeling that all wasn't ▶

> 66 I didn't want to be labeled a biographer or a children's author, instead wanting to be able to move freely between all types of writing. 99

9

All's Well That Ends Well *(continued)*

well. I asked my agent to take a look at it, and she came back to me within a few days, saying, "It's good, but I don't think it's what you really want to write." She'd put her finger on the problem straightaway; the book was turning into *Bridget Jones Goes to War*, which was no good at all.

I despaired for a few days (particularly because a Dutch publisher had shown enough faith in the book to give me an advance for it), then tore up the whole manuscript and sat down to think things through. I focused on the elements that I knew I definitely wanted to include, which were basically the Great War, a great love, and an element of mystery. I had been reading a wonderful book called *The Missing of the Somme*, by Geoff Dyer, and remembered the passages that dealt with the funeral of the Unknown Warrior. I'd often visited the grave in Westminster Abbey without thinking too much about it, but now I became intrigued by the whole notion of the Unknown Warrior's identity. He wasn't always unknown, after all; he must have been loved by family, friends, possibly even a wife and children of his own. Further research into how the body was chosen only increased my curiosity and suddenly I began to shape a plot from the questions rattling around my head. Who was he really? What if someone present at the funeral that day did, in fact, know who he was? What if they had somehow managed to arrange for that particular body to be chosen to be laid to rest in the Abbey? But why would someone do that? Perhaps it was all to do with a debt of honor.... Seeds began to drop, and out of that came *The Winter of the World*. (The Dutch publishers, by the way, were fortunately delighted with the new novel I had written in place of the one I'd sold them originally!)

The book is written largely from Alex's viewpoint, and I found it an interesting exercise to write about a love affair from a man's perspective. I also liked the idea of his being a war correspondent because they don't seem to have received much attention in novels from that period. Yet their lives were also often in danger, and they had very specific problems of their own when it came to censorship and pushing the boundaries of what was permissible to report.

The other viewpoint is Clare's, and in many ways, her character is like mine (though I'm unwilling to elaborate on that!). Although nursing has often been a focus in Great War novels, the matter of plastic surgery has not, and I was amazed by how many medical techniques were pioneered in the late stages of the ▶

> ❝ I found it an interesting exercise to write about a love affair from a man's perspective. ❞

war—we owe so much to doctors whose names have been forgotten today but whose skills enabled badly disfigured men to live relatively normal lives again after the war.

During my research, I traveled several times through Flanders and France, visiting many of the places I write about in the book. I was astonished by how "close" the war seems in towns like Ypres and small villages such as Hébuterne. It's as if the past is somehow still the present; it's there not just in battlefield tourism but in the very stones of the buildings (those that were left standing, that is) and in the ground itself, where the shattered bodies of thousands of men remain. One afternoon, when I was last in Ypres, I heard that the daily ceremony of sounding the Last Post at the Menin Gate Memorial would be an especially important one that evening: the body of a British soldier had been uncovered in a farmer's field just outside the city ramparts. That brought the reality of the horrors home to me, as did finding out about my own grandfather's war service on the Western Front.

But the main impetus for the book came from learning about the funeral of the Unknown Warrior and what it had

66 The main impetus for the book came from learning about the funeral of the Unknown Warrior. 99

meant to so many people who were unable to visit graves of their loved ones. Thousands of men were missing, and the bringing home of one of them caused an outpouring of sorrow unlike anything Britain has ever seen, before or since. I viewed the original grainy footage of the funeral and the body being carried through London on a gun carriage that misty day in November 1920. It reminded me how many different types of love there are, as on the ancient, flickering newsreel faces of grief-stricken mourners turned to watch the cortege go by. The love of mothers, wives, sweethearts, brothers, sisters, cousins, friends, sons, and daughters.... There is a line in the book, spoken by Alex but the sentiments are mine: "Sometimes I think love is the only adventure left to mankind; we've exhausted all other possibilities." And that is the theme of *The Winter of the World*, ultimately not war or remembrance but love. In all its strange, miraculous forms.

Finally, a few words about the title. It comes from the poem "1914" by one of the finest war poets of them all, Wilfred Owen. The poem begins on an apocalyptic note, then seems to offer hope for the future before concluding that there are some for whom the seasons will not come again: ▶

> 66 Thousands of men were missing, and the bringing home of one of them caused an outpouring of sorrow unlike anything Britain has ever seen, before or since. 99

All's Well That Ends Well *(continued)*

War broke: and now the Winter of the world
With perishing great darkness closes in.
The foul tornado, centred at Berlin,
Is over all the width of Europe whirled,
Rending the sails of progress. Rent or furled
Are all Art's ensigns. Verse wails. Now begin
Famines of thought and feeling. Love's wine's thin.
The grain of human Autumn rots, down-hurled.

For after Spring had bloomed in early Greece,
And Summer blazed her glory out with Rome,
An Autumn softly fell, a harvest home,
A slow grand age, and rich with all increase.
But now, for us, wild Winter, and the need
Of sowings for new Spring, and blood for seed.

Have You Read?

THE HIDDEN LIFE OF OTTO FRANK

In this definitive new biography, Carol Ann
Lee provides the answer to one of the most
heartbreaking questions of modern times:
who betrayed Anne Frank and her family to
the Nazis? Probing this startling act of
treachery, Lee brings to light never before
documented information about Otto Frank
and the individual who would claim
responsibility—revealing a terrifying
relationship that lasted until the day Frank
died. Based upon impeccable research into
rare archives and filled with excerpts from
the secret journal Frank kept from the day
of his liberation until his return to the
Secret Annex in 1945, this landmark
biography at last brings into focus the life of
a little-understood man—whose story
illuminates some of the most harrowing
and memorable events of the last century.

"Riveting reading . . . scrupulously
    researched and ultimately haunting. . . .
    Heart-wrenching."
                                    —*Boston Herald*

"A tour de force of history and humanity."
                                    —*Reader's Digest*

Find Out More

THE GRAVE OF THE UNKNOWN WARRIOR, WESTMINSTER ABBEY

Visit the inspiration for *The Winter of the World*. The tomb of the Unknown Warrior can be found at the west end of the nave in Westminster Abbey. The burial took place on November 11, 1920; the grave contains soil from France and is covered by a slab of black Belgian marble from a quarry near Namur. The stone was laid at a special service on November 11, 1921. One month earlier, General Pershing, on behalf of the United States of America, conferred the Congressional Medal of Honor on the Unknown Warrior and this hangs in a frame on a pillar nearby. The body of the Unknown Warrior may be from any of the three services, Army, Navy or Air Force, and from any part of the British Isles, Dominions, or Colonies. He represents all those who have no other memorial.

Westminster Abbey is situated in the heart of London, next to Parliament Square, opposite the Houses of Parliament.

Visit online at www.westminster-abbey.org.